When Love Was a Story

Alicia Sasse

Contents

Prologue

y carry-on bag swung with every step I took as I had my purse on my other arm, maneuvering my way through the boarding terminal. There were many similar people showing the same expression that I held – excited and anxious at the same time.

Don't get me wrong, I really was happy and thankful that my parents gave me the go signal to leave the country and attend university in the UK. My uncle, who was a professor there, recommended it to me and after months of waiting, I finally got the letter of acceptance.

A few squeals and celebrations later, they quickly realized that it meant that had to move far away from them. It wasn't like the other kids in our neighborhood who went to colleges in other states, I was going to a whole different continent.

Although, they showed their faith in me and I'm determined not to let them down.

A flight steward gave me smile as he examined my ticket before directing me to my seat. I heaved my bag into the overhead cabin before easily slipping into my seat.

This was going to be a long flight.

Few minutes passed by and a boy also came down the aisle, placing his carry-on inside the overhead cabin directly above the lane I was sitting on. Checking his place ticket and the little sign that showed the seat number, he bent down and sat on the space next to me.

What I always disliked about flying alone was having to put up with the awkward silence or small talk with the stranger beside me for hours.

"Hello," he greeted, his voice thick with an accent. He was English for sure, but I couldn't identify which part of England he was from.

"Hi," I greeted politely, looking back down on my lap.

I saw him stick out his hand and offered me a smile, "I'm Adam, you are?"

"Sienna," I said, gently reaching out to shake his hand, "Nice to meet you."

"Like the city?" he asked, finding my mundane name interesting.

Nodding, I spoke, "The spelling is a bit different and I'm probably far from the beauty it has."

"I don't think that," he chuckled, fastening his seatbelt, "I mean, I'm going to need good seatmate for the next eleven hours."

Well, he was going to be gravely disappointed.

Soon enough, the protocols for taking off were done. The seatbelt sign, the captain's voice sounding through the speakers, a flight steward roaming around to make sure everything was alright, the safety video, and everything else.

We were in the air after a few minutes and the moment that we were given the heads up that we were free to do anything that we desired, I reached down to my huge purse. Not because I thought that carry-on bag above me wasn't going to do a good job, but because I kept my trusty laptop in there.

Pulling out the device, I turned it on and placed it on the table tray, grabbing my headphones and plugging it in. I opened the folder where all of my writings were saved in, clicking on the file that had my recent unfinished book.

"What's that?" Adam asked when he saw the screen.

I groaned because although I had nothing playing, couldn't people understand that when I put my headphones on, it meant I wanted the world to turn off?

But of course, I can't take out all of my frustrations on this poor boy, "Stories."

He looked at the device once again while chose a playlist and settled myself in, my fingers hovering over the keys.

Seconds or minutes, time passed by.

And just like what I was afraid of, the words refused to come to me. I sat there motionless as my eyes stared at the blinking cursor. No matter how much I tried, I couldn't find it in myself to write, my thoughts and ideas didn't come out.

With being one of the youngest authors under my publisher, I started producing books at the age of sixteen. This got me praised by my teachers in high school and got me dubbed as one of the talented kids in my grade. After I graduated, I took a year off from studying to concentrate on my work.

But in the end, I was left idle. The amount of unfinished books that were saved in this laptop was too high. I dread that I might have lost it – the spark of writing.

My parents noticed the slump I was in and suggested that I should go somewhere else to fuel my so-called creative juices. Although I wasn't really keen on travelling, my uncle called up my parents and told them that he will gladly take me under his wing in university.

And after such a long period of contemplation, I finally agreed.

A playful melody sounded in my ears as the song I have chosen played in the background.

This was not simply writer's block, I believe that this was more than that.

When you have failed to produce a decent piece of literature for almost a year, it was a big problem especially when your publisher, parents, and readers are counting on you.

With my mom playing as my literary agent and my editor looking at me as if I'm some baby, I needed to pick myself up as soon as possible.

But there was this roadblock that I couldn't pass through.

"Sienna?" I heard Adam call my attention and I quickly removed the headphones to turn to him, "Are you alright?"

Nodding gently, I paused the music and sighed, "Just thinking."

"Can I read that?" he questioned and I hummed, making the laptop face him. I could see his eyes running over the words, the puny amount of pages didn't take long for him to finish and I just sat there, waiting in agony.

I've been working on this book for almost a year and I've only managed to successfully complete five chapters. I've tried, I really did, but sometimes after I've written about two thousand words, I'd be left unsatisfied with the chapter and proceed to delete it.

"Looks interesting," he commented, "I'm sure it would be great when you finish it."

"I can't finish it!" I unintentionally raised my voice. He paused for a moment and I gasped, covering my mouth as I sent apologetic looks to the other passengers who got bothered by my sudden outburst, "Sorry."

Taking a deep breath, I explained gently, "I can't and I couldn't. I've tried so many times to, but I think I'm losing my passion for writing."

I crave for that joy again. How come I've forgotten what it was like to finish chapters upon chapters in one sitting. It came to the point that my mom had to literally pull me away from my laptop because I couldn't stop.

"You sound exactly like my best friend," he told me, "Although it wasn't writing, it was singing and acting."

"Let me guess, you were in Hollywood to visit him," I assumed, "Must be famous."

"Her," he corrected, "And you have no idea."

Leaning against the arm rest, I raised a brow, "Is it going to turn in those 'falling in love with my best friend' cliché?"

A fleeting expression that I couldn't identify passed his face. He looked down and shook his head, "It almost did, but I broke her heart."

"Didn't like her as much as she liked you," I concluded but once again, he rejected the idea.

"I love her actually," he stated without a hint of hesitation that I was physically taken aback, "But she's in her own big world now and she deserves someone who can follow through with it, not some guy who will leave her because he lives a whole different life."

I blinked at him for a few seconds because sitting beside me was a very rare kind of person.

What a wonderful selfless man. From that small sentence alone, I could conclude he was already miles better than me. It was easy to say that you just want the person you love to be happy, but coming from experience, it was a lot harder to actually apply.

A part of me wanted to scream hallelujah because right next to me was the boy who probably held my next book. I could make him tell me what happened, how it happened, and why after all that, he managed to smile.

Yet I had to respect that it wasn't my story to tell, it was his.

But of course, the girl also had another point of view. For her, her love for her best friend wasn't reciprocated, it was left one-sided and she had no choice but to move on.

"She's happy now," he smiled, looking genuinely glad for her, "I let her be with a good guy, someone from her world and I know she'll be well taken care of."

They say that when you give up on love, you're a coward. Not me, when one gives up on love for a reason, they're brave for finding the strength to let go. Don't let yourself be ruled over by these emotions and dive head first into it – because there's a thing called sacrifice and you will get hurt.

"So about the book..." he trailed off to change the subject. My shoulder slumped and I leaned back against my chair.

"My last book was way easier to write," I scoffed, once again glancing at the screen, "It was based on a guy that had all of me. I was an idiot back then and probably still am."

He wasn't the first ever guy who held my attention. I'm one of those ironic romance writers who has never felt the will to love at the same degree their made up characters did. First official boyfriend – that was a more appropriate title.

We played with each other's heartstrings like a crazy guitarist. An on-and-off relationship filled with senseless fights and happy make ups has never ended well, but when it finished for real, it sparked a new idea. It was printed into words and was distributed for the world to read.

Nobody knew it was real though, because the way I twisted it showed how senseless and blind one becomes when someone falls in love. You'd think it was full of roses and chocolates, but you'll realize soon enough that roses have thorns and chocolate, in its purest form, is bitter.

"Then how about this," he said, leaning over to open a new blank file, "Start again and this time, write like how you did in the past."

"Impossible," I objected, "The memories are already dead inside my head."

"Wasn't there a famous saying?" he mentioned, "When a writer falls in love with you, you will never die."

But I have never fallen in love again since that stupid day.

When I didn't move, it signaled that he still failed to motivate me. He was stubborn though, because he continued to try, "Alright, how about write life as it happens?"

"And start the chapters with dear diary?" I scoffed, crossing my arms in front of my chest, "Not my thing."

Though it was laughable, he had pure intents. And maybe, his idea wasn't really that bad.

Tilting my head to the side, I reached out and started tapping on the keys, typing down the title of a new adventure in bold letters.

Untitled.

"What?" Adam questioned.

"Temporary," I told him, "I'll think of one soon."

And maybe I'll follow his advice. Write just like I did before – do it from real life experiences. Sprinkle it with a bit of glitter and a ton sequins to make it more interesting then have it printed for the world to see.

To be honest, I haven't lived life the way I wanted to since I graduated. The world around me moved on, while I remained where I was. If you knew, you would realize that I was the opposite of remaining still. I was the type of person to run and never look back.

Maybe all this time, it wasn't a novel that my mind wanted to create.

Chapter 1

"You may now exit the plane in an orderly fashion," a flight steward's voice sounded through the speakers, "Thank you for flying with us."

"It's over!" I stretched my arms over my head, "I'm staying away from any airplanes for a while."

I waited for Adam to slip out of his seat and stand up so I could get out as well. He grabbed his bag from the overhead cabin and a man who was walking by the aisle gave him a pat on the shoulder, "I'll wait for you outside."

"Alright Uncle Robert," he nodded to the man as he checked his belongings.

"Hey thanks," I told him just as he was to walk away. He whipped his head to face me and I continued, "For talking to me and helping with the writing."

"It's okay," he smiled, adjusting his bag on his shoulder, "Thanks for keeping me entertained as well."

And just like every airplane encounter, I watched as he walked away into the sea of people. He was just a passing face, as I was to him. But hey, he gave me a little bit of encouragement so I'll give him plus points for that.

Reaching, I grabbed my carry-on bag and proceeded to walk, ready to face whatever was ahead of me. Let me tell you, I was pretty sure that it wasn't going to be all rainbows and butterflies but then again, I didn't come here to relax.

During the flight, I managed to jot down a chapter. It was a start, and that guy surely helped by striking up a conversation whenever I showed such a disgruntled face. We fell asleep almost at the same time and he was actually the one who woke me up when we were just about to land.

I passed by the usual protocols when you enter a foreign land. I got through baggage claim and lugged my heavy suitcase around as I got outside, lining up to get a taxi.

Once I got in, the driver turned to me, waiting for my instructions. Looking up from the folder on my lap that had all of the information of my destination, I spoke the name of the university.

He nodded as he adjusted his rearview mirror, driving off to the direction of the university. I scanned through the different papers that were given to me, from pictures of the school to the different rules and regulations that I had to follow.

I'll be sharing a dorm with some other girl – hopefully a nice one. From the things listed here, it seems like a decent place to go, I heard it's one of those respected uni in the country and thanks to my ever so meddling uncle, getting me in was easy.

But like they say for most schools, it's easy to get in but it's hard to stay in.

It was a rather long drive because from what I knew, the university was detached from the main town. It was literally in the midst of a forest with its own little community surrounding it. The complete opposite of what I grew up with.

When the vehicle got passed those tall gates, I gaped at the size of the place. Multiple buildings proudly stood next to each other as a bunch of other students came running around, some also just arriving here with their bags.

"We're here, miss," the driver said, unbuckling his seatbelt as he went to help me with my luggage. Opening my purse, I looked at the meter before grabbing the correct amount of money. I still have a hard time identifying the currency, but I'll get through somehow.

Getting outside with the smaller bags I brought, I gave the driver the money along with a tip. He smiled politely before getting back inside the cab and driving away. Looking down at my suitcase, I blew a stray piece of hair before dragging the heavy thing along with me.

Checking the map I had, I maneuvered my way to the large building that had the sign 1-Ladies Dormitory at the very front.

There was a total of six in-house dorms. Three for the boys and three for the girls. They weren't large, maybe three floors each at the max, but they were interconnected with each other.

Many other girls came in and out of the building, some trying to get through, other laughing as they pulled their friends. With a heavy heart, I carried my suitcase up the stairs before I wheeled it in up to the desk where a woman sat, a long line right in front of her.

Others had a sense of familiarity and for sure most of the freshmen shared my sentiments but I was so far away from home, more so than they were.

The line was quick and when I got to the very front, she gave me a smile, "Hello, I'm Kristy, your dorm mother. What room?"

"3K," I said, reading the one printed on the paper I had. She nodded as she turned around to the drawers behind her, opening one of them to retrieve a key.

She handed it to me as she signed my form, "Meal schedules are printed there and if you have any other questions, don't be afraid to ask."

Moving away so the girl behind me can also get her key, I stared at the long staircase, audibly gulping. Bending down, I slowly climbed up the steps with my suitcase, praying that I don't fall. Maybe I should have packed lighter.

I overpack all the time, but this time it was mixed with paranoia since I wanted to be prepared for whatever situation I would find myself in.

You would think with the amount of people moving in and out each they would have the mercy to put in an elevator. Then again, the gorgeous architecture was too beautiful to mess with any kind of change.

Once I reached the third floor, I was already exhausted. Trying to catch my breath, I practically crawled to my room. The door was slightly open, which made me assume that my roommate was already in there.

Knocking lightly on the door, I pushed it open. A figure had her back turned to me as she spoke with someone through her phone, fixing up her side of the room. Glancing at the opposite end, it was bare except for a bed, a side table, and a dresser.

"Yeah, got it mum," the girl sighed, "Bye."

Hanging up, she jumped up slightly when she finally noticed me standing there.

Taking a deep breath, I gave her a polite smile as I took the initiative to greet her, "Hello, I'm Sienna."

"American," she easily concluded with an excited grin, "Oh sorry, I'm Julia."

"Do I lack the accent?" I laughed as I went to my side of the room.

When she realized that we didn't have this awkward atmosphere between us, she relaxed and shook her head, "Not really, it's mostly the way you look."

Okay then.

I placed my suitcase on top of the bed and zipped it open, my clothes and other belongings practically spilled out. I had to pay extra weight for this, but my excuse is I'm staying for about four years with only a few trips home, I think it's worth it to pay that amount just to bring this.

Unbuckling the belt that held it all down, everything sprung up. I scooped out my clothes and laid them to the side as I stared at my other things at the bottom of the suitcase.

There, at the middle of everything, laid the book that had my sweat and tears. I had debated for so long whether I should take it or not, but my brother did the decision making for me and chucked it inside when my hands were full.

I stared at it with its pastel themed cover and the cursive font that printed its title along with my name at the very bottom.

This was the reason for everything that was currently happening and I wanted nothing but to bury it.

At this point, I was willing to try anything.

"What's that?" Julia asked, peeking over my shoulder as she read the text, "Sienna Clark?"

"Yeah," I replied bashfully, hopelessly trying to block her view by stacking a few more articles of clothing on it. She was quick with her hands though, because before it could totally be lost in the sea of my belongings, she managed to snatch it up.

"I think I just won the roommate roulette," she joked, stopping right at the About The Author page. It showed a younger picture of me, three years ago when I was sixteen. The hype lasted for about a year and a half, but soon, people started moving on to the next big thing.

The only reason why this got popular was because majority of the teenage girls were able to relate to it, my readership wasn't really broad but it was enough to pass the word around and got people interested.

Unfortunately, I got too elated by the simple joy of having people ask for my autograph and reading the good reviews to remember the main thing I should be doing – writing.

Have you ever felt it? The way you construct such a wonderful story in your head yet when it's time to put it into words, you just blank out. It was like your vocabulary suddenly went down the drain and I regret not taking full advantage when I was at my height. I was truly inspired back then, I could just write for hours and hours, I couldn't concentrate on my lessons because I was too busy thinking of the next scene to take down, and reality took a backseat to this imaginary world that I managed to create.

Maybe uncle was right, I needed a change of scenery. All I did for almost a year was to stare at the light gray walls in my bedroom while my laptop sat on my desk, begging for me to use it with the same reason why I bought it.

"Lost in thought," Julia hummed as she observed my blank expression, "You know, I just love looking at the way talents suddenly become lost in their thoughts."

"What?" I questioned, taking the book back when she handed it to me.

She smiled with a shrug, "They're in another world. For musicians, they could be thinking of another beat, for actors, they're imagining the world as their stage..." she started listing off, "And for writers, they just created another reality, all in their head. May it be for poetry, short stories, novels, or anything else, it's all in there."

As she finished her explanation, I blinked down at her and she stood up before heading back to her side of the room to finish up with her preparations. This university was famous for its talents, with arts being its pride. I still haven't asked what was Julia's major but all I knew was that she had a passion in her. Because I truly believe that only a person with a mind filled with its own wonder can say something like that.

A passion that diminished within me.

My hands traced over the writings on the cover, willing my mind to remember the first time I held a copy in my hands. I was so excited, that joy of finally seeing your words on print could never be matched. I felt like I did something right, this little thing made me find my place.

And so I allowed it to become my first belonging to find its own spot in my new room. I set it on one of the shelves, unconsciously smiling at the way it appeared to watch over my bed.

Who needs a dreamcatcher when I already have a dream that came true?

Alright Sienna, we can do this.

But first things first, somebody was waiting for me, "I'm heading to the campus, I need to see my professor."

"Teacher's pet right on moving week," she teased before nodding, "Come back soon, I don't want to be a loner here all day."

I laughed, "Sure."

Stuffing my phone into my pocket, I went on my way out. As far as I know, it was moving week for the students boarding in the campus. Old ones come back from their vacations and the new ones settle into their rooms. The organizations were scattered around, trying to reel in new members and it was just the start of a year of work for everyone.

Walking under the sun as I tried to maneuver through the groups of people, I squinted my eyes trying to identify the different buildings. Looking down at the picture I've saved on my phone, I stared at the old-style architecture before moving on to the next one.

When I was sure of the right building, I went through the large doors and stared at the grand staircase right in front of me, glaring at me with its wooden glory.

Making my way to the faculty room, I knocked on the door before peeking my head in. There weren't many people in there which was understandable since it was still practically their break. Clearing my throat, I spoke, "Excuse me, is Mr. Kingsley here?"

As if on cue, the person mentioned looked up from his computer, his eyes widening in surprise behind his square glasses. He slowly turned to the door to find out the source of the voice calling out his name and when he saw me there, a huge grin appeared on his face.

Pushing himself off of his office chair, he made his way to me and invited me inside, "Sienna."

"Mr. Kingsley," I greeted formally. He frowned, his back turned to his co-workers so they couldn't see this childish display. Finally cracking, I smiled before addressing him the way he wanted, "Hey Uncle Levi."

"I'm glad you made it, I was worried since there wasn't even a call that you landed safely," he said, "Got settled in yet?"

"Sort of," I answered, "Are you busy?"

He shook his head, peeking over his shoulder to check on his laptop, "Just preparing my lectures. How about grabbing some lunch together? My treat."

"Lunch alone with your student," I muttered, "Very scandalous."

He rolled his eyes before going back to his desk to pack up his belongings, "I just want to catch up with my favorite niece."

"I'm your only niece," I pointed out.

Zipping up his messenger bag, he turned to me with that goofy smile, "Exactly."

Levi Kingsley was my mom's little brother, by only a year. He was a great writer and the fact that my mom was one of the best literary agents in New York helped him big time.

Well, it also helped me but that was beside the point.

He married to this British girl whom he met through his publisher and the rest was history. They moved to England, he got offered a job as a professor in this university and she continued on with her work being an editor. I'm only going up to that part of their story since I don't want to recount the time my cousins were brought into their tale.

We ended up in one of the restaurants just a small walk away from the university. Looking around, I noticed the couple just about my age sitting a few tables away from us. They were quiet, not even one uttering a word as they ate their lunch in silence.

Uncle saw my gaze and he propped his chin on the palm of his hand with his shoulder resting on the table, "They haven't seen each other in a while. They're probably studying in the university and though they have a lot to tell, they don't open up because they're just enjoying their time together."

Gazing at him, I lifted a brow, "You know them?"

He grinned before taking a sip of his coffee, "How about you? Do you know them?"

Something I certainly didn't miss was his mind tricks. I didn't know the couple and right now, I was positive that he didn't as well.

"Come on, you know them," he urged, "Explain why they're eating in silence."

Alright, I was going to play along.

"Probably because they're fighting," I said before subtly gesturing at the girl, "She has her eyebrows scrunched up and her lips are jotted down into a pout, she's obviously displeased. The guy refuses to meet her gaze because he just keeps staring at the burger on his plate, they're on the verge of breakup yet they don't want to call it quits yet."

When I turned back at him, he had this knowing look as he crossed his arms over his chest before nodding in approval, "See? You know them."

Shaking my head, I mindlessly twirled a french fry between my fingers, "I don't, I just made it up."

"I did as well," he told me, "We made things up based on what we saw. We created a story with nothing but a single image. You haven't lost your way, Sienna, you just came across a fallen tree that blocked your way."

See? He was playing those mind tricks again.

"Meaning?"

"Meaning you just need someone or something to give you a lift so you could jump over that tree," he explained, "And I'm going to help you find that."

Crossing my arms over my chest, I shot him another question, "Why don't you just give me a lift?"

"Because I'm too old to be part of the main story," he stated, "I'm just a side character."

"Uncle, what are you implying?" I groaned, extremely confused.

"Your new story," he said, "Is just starting."

Chapter 2

"So then, I told my mom that I'm not going to stay in Bath for my whole life," Julia droned on as we found our seats in the dining hall, "I was afraid that if I didn't tell her that, I would be stuck there."

In a span of two hours, I've found out that my roommate was from Bath, she had about five siblings and she was the youngest, making her the hardest for her parents to send off. She has this dachshund whom she got as a birthday present from her older sister, the hyper dog almost did his dump on all of her class notes and she had about nine goldfishes in her whole life.

Too much information? Tell that to her, not me.

"How about you?" she questioned, showing pure curiosity, "Where do you live? Have any pets? Siblings?"

And the spotlight was suddenly on me. I nervously tucked in a stray piece of hair and attempted to tackle her multiple questions, "Well, I live in New York..."

"New York?!" she suddenly squealed, catching the attention of the girls sitting near us, "You live in the big apple?"

To be honest, I have never understood the huge hype with NYC. Sure, it was the land of so many opportunities, but after being there since birth, I was honestly used to the long traffics, rowdy noise during one in the morning, the daily rush through the subway, and just the overall rough atmosphere.

Compared to that, this place was like a paradise of peace. Living in an apartment complex at the heart of the city contributed so much to my restlessness. It was the city that never sleeps, and my neighbors took that title to heart.

Our building didn't have a no-party rule, so almost every night, someone either above, below, or anyone on my floor was throwing one.

Everything moves fast to the point that someone behind you on the sidewalk will give you an annoyed huff if you were too slow on walking for him.

"You live in New York?" a girl suddenly questioned. She must have been alerted by Julia's sudden outburst. She gave a polite smile and sat down on one of the unoccupied chairs, "I've always wanted to stay there. I mean, there's the opportunities in London, but I have always wanted to branch out my writing when I get older."

"Sienna's a published author," Julia said with pride, before I could even tell her not to say a word about it.

Now this was the point when I wanted to slap my hand on her mouth. I've had this mantra that the last piece of information I would give to an acquaintance was my job. I don't want people to befriend me just because I managed to print something to the world.

I've managed to shed down my friends list because it took some time to learn who was really there because they liked

Sienna as a person and not that they wanted to be with Sienna Clark, the author.

The girl's eyes widened, "Really? What's the name of the book?"

I have always hesitated to say the title of my book. It was a bit corny and cliché, something the fifteen year old me thought of, but before I had time to take it back due to pure embarrassment, it was too late. Well if we were being real here, majority of the authors out there are somewhat bashful when it comes to the titles of their works.

It was really something else when you say it out loud. When we write it, it sounds so perfect but the moment it's actually vocalized then I would want nothing but for the ground to swallow me whole.

But I was being stared at like I was in a police interrogation. So I said the title and when I did, her eyes widened in excitement.

"Wait, every single girl in school read that," she gaped, "That was one of my favorite books, I can't believe that you wrote that."

Was that supposed to be a compliment?

She saw my expression and she scrambled around to correct herself, "I mean, I would have never thought I would cross paths with the Sienna Clark."

Same reactions that my classmates from high school had. When I told them that I was getting published, I was met with squeals and congratulations. I was suddenly placed in this high pedestal after remaining so lowkey during my whole stay in the school. The new attention was definitely uncomfortable at first but as time passed, I started getting used to it.

But of course, there were still some rare moments.

You know what it feels like to be talked about by a bunch of your juniors while you innocently sit there in between yours friends? It's incredibly awkward.

"I'm Meg," she smiled, "I should have introduced myself first so apologies."

"Sienna," I said just for the sake of formalities, before I gestured to my roommate, "And this is Julia, we're from 3K."

"We're on the same floor," she informed gleefully, "I'm from 3B."

I was not really keen on getting too close to many people. I know the same old story, once you graduate, you might possibly never hear from each other again. Add the fact that I live in a whole different continent from them.

My only goal here was to get rid of this block, get a degree, and pack my bags then head back home where I'll live the fast life again. Mom's waiting for a book and my uncle's waiting for another amazing story. With his mind games, I don't know if I can survive being under his watch, but hey, I'm starting to get desperate.

Kristy told everyone to get our plates from the long table found on one side of the room. Before I could even stand by myself, Julia was already dragging me along as Meg followed right behind us.

I learned that Meg's roommate was actually a year ahead of us so even though they got along, she already had her own group of friends. That was basically her indirectly asking if she could join the two of us. Just from her form and tone of voice, I got that decoded easily.

And Julia quickly took the bait, "You can come with us anytime then."

Meg showed us a grin as she nodded, expecting those words. People were so easy to read, all you have to do really was look.

"Can I just eat upstairs?" I frowned, looking down on the plate.

Kristy overheard my words and she gave me a concerned look, "Why? Are you feeling poorly?"

Glancing towards the two girls that was now occupied in their own world as they walked back to the table we were previously sitting at, I released a sigh. They haven't even noticed that I was no longer following them.

Here's the thing – I'm not used to making new friends. Maybe I've gotten so familiar with the ones that I already have that I haven't actively made an effort to meet other people in a very long time. It was a bit sad but I guess baby steps were the best way to go.

Turning back to our dorm mother, I softly nodded, "My head kind of hurts."

"Perhaps that's the jetlag," she concluded, feeling up my forehead to check if I had a fever, "I'll let you eat up there, but don't let it become a habit."

"Thank you," I smiled gently before I turned and walked out of the room.

I never meant to be a social pariah but I was seriously not in the mood to catch up with whatever pacing they planned to have with that conversation. Besides, I had to keep up with the writing thing.

Before the day ended, I should have to created at least an outline or pitch so I could send it to mom to see if it had any potential.

Or you know what, I'll send it to my uncle instead. While mom might be a good literary agent, she was more biased by seeking a story that sells, not something that had essence.

Speaking of my dear mother, I haven't even called her yet. Uncle was still in the process of getting me a new phone that could work her so up until then, all she will get from me is a message on Facebook.

Placing my food on the side table, I sat on the bed and opened my laptop. I clicked my tongue at the slow internet that this dorm house provided as I stared at my email inbox, waiting for it to load.

While it did, I opened up the file that contained the first chapter and did a read through, checking if everything was alright. Something I've learned from writing while on the move, it was there was a huge chance that none of your sentences made any sense.

The amount of times my editor told me about this was too high.

Grabbing the apple that was on my plate, I took a big bite as I proofread through the chapter. Once I was satisfied with the document, I went back to the web browser and typed in my uncle's email address before attaching the file.

'Read through this please, Uncle Levi, I need some feedback. -Sienna'

Pressing send, I bit my appl againe before opening a new file to type up the second chapter.

My fingers hovered over the keys as I thought of a title. The talk about my writer's block with my uncle came into mind and I smiled, tapping down on the letters.

The Fallen Tree.

Although I did mock the idea, I took Adam's advice. Write life as it happens, like a journal of some sorts. However, mine was in a novel form. I'd just draft it out and then change whatever is needed to be improved on once I have a clear direction for the book.

Suddenly, the door clicked open to reveal Julia with Meg right behind her, "Told you she'll be here."

There goes the peace and quiet.

"We were surprised when we realized that you weren't behind us," Julia said, sitting down on her bed, "What's wrong."

"Jetlag," I lied, unblinking as I gave her my excuse.

"Oh," she nodded in understanding, "We thought about touring the university tomorrow, lessons start on Monday so it would be good if we knew our way around."

Looking back down on the screen, I found that my uncle managed to reply so quickly to my message. Opening the email, I held back a sigh of relief when I saw the words.

'Sure. Why don't you visit us tomorrow? The family wants to see you.'

Turning back at them, I plastered a disappointed expression, "I'm sorry, but my uncle who lives nearby wants to see me tomorrow."

Her shoulders slumped as she frowned, "What time is your lesson on Monday?"

"Eight," I answered and I noticed Meg light up.

"Me too," she chirped, "Let's go together, I'll wait for you."

I was scared to get too close to them. I would see them day and night, I could only imagine the tears I would shed when I have to leave. I remember when my friends back in high school left one by one for college – each would have their own farewell party. There was a week wherein we were up until morning every day, getting drunk and saying goodbye.

I was a bit assured because I knew we would all be back together for the holidays but them? I wasn't even sure if I was going to be back here after I graduate.

While again I wasn't so sure about making new friends, I was more terrified of leaving them into dust.

"Sure," I forced myself to reply.

Taking a deep breath, I saved the file and closed my laptop before placing the half eaten apple back on the plate, "Look, it had been a long day for me, I think it's better if I go to sleep."

"You're not eating your food?" Julia questioned, eyeing the whole meal that was left untouched.

Glancing towards it, I shook my head, "I'm not hungry."

That was the end of the conversation and I tucked myself into bed when they decided to head onto Meg's room since they didn't want to keep me up with their conversation. I felt completely different from my usual self and it was making me beyond uncomfortable. Maybe all I needed was a good night's sleep, my body had more than enough after flying for about twelve hours.

Well, the jetlag stint turned out to be true because I woke up at the crazy hour of three o'clock. The room was now dark and devoid of any light due to the fact that Julia closed the curtains for the both of us. Speaking of which, the said girl was still sleeping soundly on the other side of the room.

Letting out a yawn, I grabbed my laptop and opened it, trying to see if could get some work done after getting interrupted last night.

When I accessed my Facebook, I saw that my mom has replied to my message.

'Hope you're having fun there. Don't forget to keep me updated.'

My gaze fell onto the food that I didn't eat for dinner. Reaching out, I took it and started munching on the pieces of chicken as I typed up a reply.

It was cold and a little bit bland. Oh look, just like my situation right now.

'Alright. I'm going to visit Uncle Levi later.'

Trying to sleep was useless so I just kept on eating my food. Looking at the upper right corner, I tilted my head to the side when I saw the three friend requests that were waiting for my confirmation.

One of them was Julia and another was Meg, they probably sent it to me last night when I was already asleep. I accepted both of them and when I went to check who the other one was, I paused.

Adam Nicholas.

Who was this guy?

I clicked on his profile and huffed when it showed that it was on private. That left me his profile picture and cover photo as my only reference.

When I opened it, the man in the picture was smiling brightly, his eyes being covered by a huge pair of black shades with the Hollywood sign behind him.

Even though I lived in New York, there wasn't a flight for me to go straight to England at the desired time my mother wanted. So I had no choice but to fly to California first before getting a flight to here.

I stared at his picture for a quick minute before I finally realized who it was. That cheeky grin belonged to the boy I sat next to on the plane.

The mystery of how he found me on this site was something I was really curious about.

Accepting the request, it gave me full authority to scroll through his profile.

Rubbing my hands like an evil mastermind, I was ready to do the usual investigation when a chatbox popped up. Gazing down on it, I was slightly surprised to see that it was him.

Finds me in social media? Check. Chats me the second I accepted his friend request? Check.

Was this the part where I should be fearful for my life?

Adam Nicholas: Hey, thanks for accepting.

Sienna Clark: No problem. How did you find me?

Adam Nicholas: There are not that many teenage published authors under the name Sienna. Also, it was on the file you opened earlier.

Sienna Clark: I thought I was being stalked. What are you doing up at this time?

Adam Nicholas: Jetlag, which I can assume is also the cause of your wakefulness.

Sienna Clark: Correct.

I bit my lip, there wasn't really anymore I could say but I wanted to keep the conversation going. I didn't want him to just go offline, it felt oddly normal to be talking to some guy I just met during a twelve hour flight.

There were no goodbyes with him because it was just online. Everything would be purely online.

Besides, he was like that gap between the empty period when I was up in the air – leaving him for uncharted territory.

Sienna Clark: So how's it going?

Mentally cringing at the too simple question, I tried to relax as I waited for his reply. Those three dots that signaled that he was typing was like a gun being pointed towards my head.

Adam Nicholas: Good. I'm moving into my new flat tomorrow.

Finally, we had a topic!

Sienna Clark: You're moving? Why?

Adam Nicholas: Going to uni.

Sienna Clark: I'm in uni too.

Wait, did I sound too eager on that one?

Adam Nicholas: Really? I don't want to get too excited though, we might as well be living on different sides of the country.

Sienna Clark: Then it looks like we just have to make do with chatting like this.

This was so uncharacteristic of me. Here we find out that three o'clock jetlagged Sienna Clark was not someone to be trusted. When I've gotten my coffee and then look at this, I was sure that I would want to smack myself right across the face.

But the fact that we won't see each other face to face was actually giving me confidence. He won't judge me, he won't see me overthinking, he'll just be reading what I will be writing to him.

And anything that allows me to use writing over speaking is good in my book.

In writing, you can think before you jot it down. You can pick up and eraser and do over if you made a mistake, you have control of your words before you hand it to the other person. In talking, you might as well blurt out your thoughts then instantly regret right after because you can't take it back, it was already heard by others.

And that's why I prefer that medium of communication more. It was reversible and you can control how you sound like.

Chapter 3

My eyes were fixed outside as the taxi pulled out onto the side. He told me that we have reached the destination and I blinked at the apartment complex in front of me. It was just about three minutes away and maybe ten if you decided to walk.

The reason why I took a cab was because I didn't really know the area and even though Uncle Levi messaged me the address, I was afraid that I was going to get lost. I mentioned before that I was basically staying in a forest so I was terrified of losing my way.

Handing the driver an exact amount, I got outside and stared right up at the building. I would have thought that my uncle and aunt would have opted to at least have a house instead of an apartment, but now I get why they chose this.

It was near to the school and let me tell you, just from the outside view, I knew this wasn't cheap. It wasn't high-rise or anything, but the clean and modern architecture gave the impression of class and wealth.

I got inside and looked around the lobby. There wasn't much aside from a desk, the security guard, and a few employees but it was enough to keep this place running.

Uncle was already standing there, waiting for me, "You look like you didn't sleep at all last night," he chuckled as he led me to the elevator, "No need to explain though."

I smiled, holding on to my iPad as if it was some sort of safety net. As cool as my uncle was, his wife was the complete opposite. I see her every year when they come to visit and she was sweet for the most part, but you've got to admit that she was a bit intimidating.

When we reached his level, the floor was carpeted with the hallways donning various pieces of art. He fished out his keycard from his pocket and opened the door that led into his apartment, "We're here."

I didn't know what I expected in terms of size, but this definitely went beyond it. It had a balcony-like second floor where you could several doors lined up, probably leading up to the bedrooms. The first floor had this open floor scheme where the kitchen was far beyond at one side and the living room at the other.

This was surely competing with our New York apartment.

When my uncle announced our arrival, my aunt suddenly looked up from her laptop, quickly removing her glasses and placing it on top of the stack of papers next to her.

"Emma, Andy!" she yelled out the names of my cousins as she stood and approached, "It's so good to see you again, Sienna."

Two doors from the second floor opened simultaneously and there appeared their two children. Emma Kingsley was roughly about the same age as me, but she inherited her mother's fierce look instead of the Kingsley soft features that

I got from my mom's side. Although it wasn't prominent since those glaring eyes were behind her square glasses.

Andy Kingsley was two years older than me and instead of being buff and muscular, he was on the thin side. His hair up in spikes and even though he was not the most positive person, he was admittedly a good writer. Inheriting his talents from his father and being under the careful supervision of his mom, he was already on his way to making a name for himself with three books already in the market, all hitting the bestseller mark.

Did I get along with them?

Well...

"Sienna!" Emma squealed, sliding down the railing and running up to me, quickly engulfing me in a hug. I matched her enthusiasm by also wrapping my arms around her, squeezing her just as tight.

Andy was more relaxed because he stuffed his pockets into his sweatpants and slowly went down the stairs. He offered me a small smile and when Emma released me, we shared a quick embrace.

Yes, I'm quite close with them.

Before Uncle Levi decided to move everybody to England, they lived right across the hall from us. We were certainly childhood friends and even with the distance, we remained close.

"I missed you!" she declared, her voice heavy with the accent that matched her mom's, "And you're in England now, we can do almost everything together."

"She's here to study, Emma," Andy quickly butted in, bursting his sister's bubble, sitting next to Aunt Janine, "Not to be dragged into your little quirks."

She pouted towards him, "I'm just excited that Sienna's finally here."

"Everyone's excited that she's here," he pointed out before showing me a grin, "How can I not miss my lousy writer of a cousin."

"Hey!" I protested.

Although we lived miles away from each other, I cannot deny the fact that Andy and I have a small competition going on. Sad to say, he was ahead of the race. Unlike me, who suddenly stopped because the lack of inspiration, he kept on going like a mad man.

Every word just sucks you into the story, you want to peel your eyes away yet you can't, because he has already captured you. The characters he has created and the world they live in will haunt your for days or even weeks after you have completed the book.

And that's how good he is – I'll never admit it loudly though.

"Be nice, Andy," Uncle Levi reprimanded, "You of all people should know what it's like to be stuck."

He frowned before nodding, opting to follow his father's command, "Fine."

Turning to Uncle Levi, I showed him a nervous smile before mentioning my main purpose for visiting, "So about my draft..."

"Oh right," he muttered, "I had a read-through and Janine also did the same."

I turned to his wife and the said woman looked up from her work, nodding in acknowledgement at the small mention, "It was good, just a little lacking on some parts."

"Lacking?" I questioned, taking a seat after Uncle Levi offered me one, "What do you mean?"

"Emotions," he clarified, "That used to be your specialty. The way you allow your characters to be fall into a hole of their own thoughts. You can create paragraphs and paragraphs of just them having an inner monologue, but here, you focused more on their dialogues."

I groaned before dropping my head onto the table, emitting a soft thud at contact, "I need help."

"The biggest mistake a writer can do is force an idea," Andy called out after he disappeared into the kitchen side of the room, "Breathe for a second, the more you think about the fact that you can't write anything, the more you wouldn't be able to put your thoughts into words."

Aunt Janine nodded in agreement at her son's statement, "That's why editors have learned to be patient."

Her daughter didn't take this lightly though. She peeked over the magazine in her hands with a light sarcastic quip, "You and I both know that's a lie mum."

As much as I wanted to back up Emma's statement, I chose to keep my mouth shut. It was true though, editors looked and scouted for something that sells, something that they're sure would bring in the cash flowing for their bosses. Every minute the writer didn't submit a manuscript, it was another dollar deducted from their revenue.

If I wasn't so well-connected with the big people in the industry, I'm sure my work would have been cut and chopped down into something mediocre. The big and heavy stories doesn't sell as well as the short and cliché ones in my target audience, but I forced my editors to keep the essence of the story.

In the publishing world, the author will always have the short end of the stick.

"My sister and I have a deal, you know," Uncle Levi pipped in, "I told her that I can make you write a good story by the end of your stay and if you do, she has to give you full freedom with your books."

"Sometimes, I don't know if what you're doing is good or bad, Uncle," I sighed, lifting my head up before rubbing the spot I hit it on, "Thanks, I guess?"

He shrugged before approaching one of the shelves, grabbing a sketchpad and a pen before walking back to where I was sitting. He plopped both of the items on the table and gave the sketchpad a light tap, "First lesson, outline."

"School hasn't even started yet," I mumbled and he simply chuckled, walking away for me to do the chore.

Staring down at the sketchpad, I held back a scoff. This was kind of old-fashioned in my eyes, all of my outlines were typed and saved in my computer. A sketchpad was just an easy was to lose your ideas after you accidentally leave it somewhere.

I did open it, just for the sake of everything. I paused when I saw my own Uncle's handwriting on the smooth paper. The rows and columns of phrases and ideas being continually crossed out or revised along with the dozen arrows connecting one to another.

The side of the sketchpad showed that there were some pages that was torn along the way, the rough way that some words were harshly scribbled on indicated the raw frustration my uncle felt while creating a story.

When I skimmed over the words, I realized that this was the outline for his very first book.

Another fun fact, it was my uncle who made me fall in love with reading. This same story was given to me by my mother to read back in elementary. It wasn't as deep and thought provoking as the ones he was known for now, but I was instantly drawn into his world.

The world of written words, showing another perspective on life.

After years and years, I would always go back to that novel. Its spine was on its breaking point, the pages were creased and some were even torn because I wasn't good at taking care of books before, and the paper started to see some discoloration. Still, I would at least read it once or twice a year, giving me a gentle reminder of this fascination that continued on.

The edges of the sketchpad was a little torn and bent, but it showed how old and how loved it was.

"I can't use this!" I gasped, looking around for my uncle.

"He went upstairs," Andy informed, claiming the seat next to me, sipping the tea he prepared for himself, "Are you conscious about the fact that he used that?"

Nodding vigorously, I slumped on my chair, "This is valuable to him."

"Not only to him," he muttered, reaching out to flip through the pages, efficiently skipping a few other examples of my uncle's struggles. He used his finger to stop the pages from falling before opening it up completely, showing the starting page of a new set of handwriting.

My eyebrows scrunched up in confusion as I read over the words on there. Unlike Uncle Levi's outline where each page was heavily packed, this one was spaced away from each other. Turning to the next page, my curiosity grew when I saw that the plot from the last page was discarded because the one written on this was completely new.

Andy grabbed the pen and slowly scribbled by the edge of the paper, carefully spelling out his name. I then compared his writing with the one already on the sketchpad and I finally realized – this was Andy's outline.

My cousin wasn't a Pulitzer-winning author like his father yet, but he was on the bestseller lists for months with every book he released.

"He's doing the same thing he did to me when I got stuck with writer's block," he told me, "Seemed to work for me, guess it will work for you."

Rolling my eyes, I went back to concentrating on the sketchpad, "We're different people."

"Just try it," he said as he stood up with his mug, "You're the next one in line who needs to write on that since Emma doesn't want to live the author life."

"Because it's not for me!" Emma hollered from her spot on the couch, pouting slightly at the reminder she was different from her family.

Her aspiration was geared towards a different kind of artistry. Her mind was filled with images she was ready to paint or draw on any surface she can get her hands on. Her eyes were like a pair of camera lenses, perfectly capturing a view before recreating it with her wide collection of pens, pencils, and paintbrushes.

Her parents showed no disapproval for her talents though, they didn't mind one bit that when it came to literacy, their daughter was not at the same level as them. Besides, art wasn't really so bad if you have the talent for it.

"Your sister doesn't need to be a writer, Andy," Aunt Janine reminded as she stood up, "We're ordering takeaway for lunch, want anything specific, Sienna?"

"Anything's good, thank you," I smiled politely and she nodded before bringing her things upstairs. Grumbling under his breath, Andy also walked away from the room, finding his solitude somewhere else.

And that leaves me with Emma whose mood was now down in the dumps.

"Don't feel bad," I tried to comfort her from my spot, "Your brother was just a little sad that he wasn't able to share the same things he liked with you."

She shot up from her sitting position, walking to me, "That's the point. He's disappointed that I didn't want to become a writer like you guys."

"Your passion's somewhere else," I said, "And it doesn't mean that it's a bad thing."

That was the same thing for my little brother. His passion was somewhere else and of course I was little upset that I couldn't rant to him about things related to writing, but I still cheered him on.

She plopped down on the chair Andy was previously occupying, "He was actually more excited to see you than I was."

That cousin of mine who loved to rile me up? Impossible. Emma was chirpy and preppy girl who absolutely loved any kind of company so I find it hard to believe her brooding brother would be more enthusiastic about my visit.

"He was finally happy that he could talk about his work with someone else," she sighed, "Look, he's even rooting for you."

Lifting a hand, I placed it on top of her hand as a reassuring pat, "Just keep doing what you do best, no need to worry."

"For a girl who herself is completely beating herself up for her lack of motivation, you're quite good at making people feel better," she laughed as she picked up the pencil that her mother left on the table.

Flipping to the last page of Andy's work, her fingers brushed over the written words, "You wouldn't think he was such a jerk by the way her writes."

"True," I hummed.

Unlikely love stories were Andy's specialty, mixing it with the fantasy genre. When you think of his work, you would literally be in a rollercoaster of emotions because the challenges he makes his characters face, even to the point of killing them just for the sake of love.

Where does he get it? It's still an unanswered mystery.

Turning to the next page, it was a blank sheet, "This is where yours start."

In beautiful cursive, she sketched my name at the very top of the paper. Turning her head to the side, she glanced towards me before grinning, her hand expertly moving the pencil across the paper. Her strokes were precise and she never used the eraser at the other end of the pencil.

When she dropped her drawing material, she looked right back at me. I blinked at her drawing of me and to be honest, if I were my aunt and uncle, I wouldn't force Emma to do writing as well.

Because she was talented in her own department. Her drawing of me was beautiful to put it lightly, even to the way the ends of my hair slightly turned upward, she got it. It was only a small version though, no more than five inches on the paper.

"You just need to find your muse," she laughed, handing me the pen with an encouraging smile.

Chapter 4

"I give up!" I groaned, throwing my head back as I dropped the pen on the table. Every single phrase that I managed to jot down on the paper all faced the same fate – they were all crossed out.

Emma jumped a bit at my sudden outburst, causing the paintbrush on her hand to slide down on the canvass she was working on. She gasped before turning to me and I shot her an apologetic look.

Shrugging, she squeezed on some white paint onto her palette before she calmly fixed the sudden slipup I've caused.

"Take a break for now, Sienna," Uncle Levi chuckled before waving his keycard in front of me, "Come on, the delivery man's already in the lobby."

Glancing towards his daughter, she nodded before gesturing for me to follow him. With a sigh, I pushed myself up before I trailed after my uncle as he clicked the door open and held it for me.

"So any progress?" he questioned, pressing the down button when we reached the front of the elevator. My silence was enough of an answer for him so he placed a reassuring hand on my shoulder, "That's alright."

No, it wasn't. sure I shouldn't expect instant results, especially since classes haven't even started yet, but my frustration with myself was constantly growing.

We stepped inside the shaft and we slowly descended through the building, the digital screen showing the floors we passed. My foot tapped against the metal floor as I hummed a made-up tune, drumming my fingers at my side.

Uncle quickly peeked towards my direction before he laughed under his breath, shaking his head in amusement.

"What?" I questioned, stopping my movements.

"You really are like your mother," he chuckled, gesturing to my whole body, "You're restless when something doesn't go perfectly."

I was about to protest but the metal doors opened. He gave me a slight push and led me out, already spotting the delivery man with our food. Uncle waved his hand towards him, taking out his wallet from his back pocket and I followed behind.

The glass door of the building opened, causing me to quickly glance towards its direction out of habit. I went back to the task at hand and slowly, the face of the person that entered registered in my head. Doing a double take at the familiar figure, his name escaped my lips, "Adam?"

The man paused after I called him out and he looked around the lobby. His eyes finally settled on me and he blinked first before he finally recognized me as well, "Sienna!"

Even thought the only time I've seen him was during that flight, it was enough to commit his appearance into my memory. I could picture him with his tussled brunette hair and warm brown eyes right below those thick but groomed eyebrows. He wore an oversized gray jacket over his plain white shirt and a pair of jeans during the flight. A pair of headphones were wrapped around his neck yet he never used them during the whole travel, mostly because he was busy distracting me.

Just saying, if you write your life experiences, you start to remember the little things.

Now, he was in a light blue pullover and black gym shorts, his feet being protected by a pair of black and white Nike shoes, but nothing else has changed aside from his clothing. Heck, he even had a pair of headphones with him.

"I thought we were living on different sides of the country," I said, remembering his message last night, "Fancy meeting you here."

He chuckled, nodding his head, "Same here, I just moved in though."

I blinked towards him before looking around the posh lobby. When I meant posh, I really did mean don't-even-look-at-me-peasant posh – from the crystal chandelier to the fancy furniture strategically placed around. Like I said earlier, I knew that this place was expensive and I was well aware that my Uncle had the money to house his family here, but since Adam said that he moved in, then that meant...

"Your family came here with you?" I questioned, gaping up towards him.

He looked taken aback by the question but he shook his head, "No, they stayed at our home."

Then this guy was freaking loaded.

"How about you?" he asked, "You're staying here?"

"I'm just visiting my..." I told him just as I turned around to gesture towards Uncle Levi. When I did though, I found out that he was no longer standing there, "... uncle."

Adam scrunched up his eyebrows in confusion and I mentally cursed when I realized that he left me here. Releasing a sigh, I faced him again, "Never mind."

"Then how about some lunch?" he suggested, lifting up the plastic bag he brought inside, "I make a great lasagna."

Eyeing the freshly bought groceries, I frowned slightly when I remembered that my uncle had ordered lunch for all of us, "Sorry, I already have food waiting for me."

He slightly slumped his shoulders but he shrugged, "It's alright. How about I meet you on the roof garden after?"

I smiled before nodding at his offer, "I would like that."

We rode the elevator together and I was shocked when we ended up reaching for the same floor number. Turning to each other, we remained silent as the metal box lifted us through the floors, stopping right where we needed to be.

Okay, maybe that was just a good coincidence.

I half-expected him to head to the opposite hallway but when we both walked towards the right side, I held my tongue from saying anything for now.

With a few steps ahead, I stopped right in front of Uncle's brown wooden door, lifting a hand to press the bell. From the corner of my eye, I watched Adam take out his keycard and slot it in at the door handle that was right next to the one I was standing in front of.

We blinked at each other before I gaped in shock, "You and my uncle are neighbors?!"

Before he could respond, the door clicked open and out came Uncle Levi, "You're done already?"

He noticed my unresponsiveness and he peeked out his head to look at what I was staring at, a cheshire grin forming on his face. He left the door open as he rushed inside, coming right back out with a food container and thrusting it into my hands.

I barely had any time to process everything when he slammed the door in front of my face.

What the hell?!

Slowly facing Adam, it was obvious that he holding in his laughter and he finally swung his door open before gesturing at me, "So want to go in?"

Glancing towards the door, I released a sigh. I didn't really have much of a choice, did I?

Shrugging, I took a step forward but the door opened once again and out came Uncle Levi, quickly stacking my iPad and his sketchpad on top of my meal.

"Bring her back before six," he told Adam while he slowly retreated back into his apartment. I slowly turned back to him and it was obvious he was holding back his laughter.

"I sincerely apologize for what you just witnessed," I said in the most monotonous voice I could muster, a mixture of embarrassment and mocking annoyance in my voice.

He shrugged with a playful smile, "He seems nice."

"And eccentric," I murmured under my breath, following him into his apartment.

My eyes scanned around the room the second I got inside. It was identical to the one belonging to my relatives, albeit it was looked a little less lived-in. It was bare of furniture and appliances aside from the oven-stove and the fridge right by the kitchen side.

He deposited his bag on the kitchen counter, looking around the place, "Sorry, I haven't had the opportunity to start unpacking yet."

"Yeah," I muttered, carefully putting down my belongings on top of one of the boxes, "So about that lasagna?"

As if those words suddenly flipped a switch of enthusiasm, he started to dig through the several boxes poised near where he was standing in search for a baking pan and a pot. Looking through another box, he took out several utensils.

"I'm not much of a cook," he chuckled, setting the pot on top of the stove before he grabbed the store-bought sauce from his bag, "But this is one of the few things I can get right."

After he poured out all of the contents, I took the jar from him and lifted a brow, "Pre-prepared?"

"Forgive me this time," he pouted playfully, "When I've fully settled in, I'll cook you the real deal."

Setting it down on the counter, I laced my hands behind my back as I bent down to look at him, "And what makes you so sure I'm coming back?"

"I just have this feeling," he shrugged, continuing on with his work.

It was not wise to always go with your gut feeling. Although, most of my life-changing decisions resulted from me following my instincts, you still can never be sure.

But what he said did put a smile on my face.

Leaving him with his craft or whatever, I walked over to the sketchpad and flipped it open, stopping right where I left off.

From the corner of the page, there I wrote the last two chapters I've managed to jot down – Untitled and The Fallen Tree.

Looking over my shoulder, I watched as Adam assembled the lasagna onto the baking pan and I squinted my eyes a little towards him. The dark circles under his eyes were good proof of how late he stayed up and unlike me, he didn't have the convenience of having access to the gift of makeup to cover it up.

As if a lightbulb suddenly popped up over my head, I grabbed the pencil that was inserted in-between some of the pages and scribbled down another chapter title.

3:00 Chats.

Such a simplistic and corny title but it was a start.

Pulling out my phone, I went to my Messenger app and opened the conversation I had with Adam last night. Changing up a few words, I copied it down on the paper, using several arrows to point any additional information about each line.

I then drew a picture of a plate of lasagna at the corner just for a private joke before nodding in satisfaction.

"Done," Adam hummed as he took out the pan from the oven with a tea towel acting as his source of protection from the heat.

Jumping up a little, I stepped back to check my work and I was quite impressed that I managed to fill up half of the page

– well, the whole page if you consider the mess of a plan that was on the other half.

"So where are we going to eat?" I questioned, turning to him just as he finished plating up two portions.

No chairs, no carpet, no tables, no anything in his apartment aside from a few boxes so what now?

"Roof garden?" he suggested, holding the two plates in his hands.

I wasn't really in the mood to eat where perhaps some bird might suddenly drop its crap onto my food.

"Got any throw pillows?" I asked out of a whim.

He had a curious expression but he nudged his head to point at one of the boxes, "Try that one."

Opening it, I pulled out two pillows before plopping it down on the middle of the open space. Gently emptying the rest of the contents of the box, I then laid it to the side before sliding it down towards the middle of the two pillows.

Placing my hands on my pocket, I smiled up at him, "Better than some fancy chairs and tables, am I right?"

When he was silent for a while, my lips slowly curved down.

Alright, he thinks I'm weird. Maybe I shouldn't have acted on impulse after all.

Then, out of the blue, he showed me a grin, his white teeth showing as he laughed, "You're amazing, Sienna Clark."

Ever so slowly, I sunk down until I made contact with the pillow. I was left gaping while he settled down the plates onto the box.

Well, that wasn't a reaction I was prepared for.

Alright, I was going to admit, he was kind of cute. At first, I was kind of embarrassed to be so proud of putting a damn box in the middle of two pillows but when he showed me that smile, it lifted up my mood. However, I couldn't stop think about the fact that I've just met him.

I was eating with a guy that I've met only once inside his apartment.

This was completely out of my comfort zone and if anybody asked me if I predicted anything like this happening just days after I reached England, I would have flat out said no.

Grabbing the fork, I scooped in some of the pasta into my mouth in an excuse to remain silent. I suddenly became bashful in his presence and when he noticed this, he reached out and tapped on the box right next to my plate in order to grab my attention, "Did you suddenly press the mute button in you?"

Glancing up to him, I shook my head as I wracked my brain for an excuse, "Just thinking that this is pretty good for something that was practically store-bought."

Alright, that was a pretty good reasoning.

"I told you that I'll make the real deal for you when I've got everything out," he reminded, somewhat a childish whine after, "So how's the writing?"

Okay, now we had a topic I could work with.

"I was off to a bad start but now I think that I'm going towards the right direction," I told him, remembering the new title I came up with.

"Is that so?" he replied, settling his elbow on the box, "And what made you say that?"

What made me say that? There was this boy right across from me that was making me experience all these new things. Give me some novelty, a few pieces of jokes, and an emotional rollercoaster and I would whip you up a wonderful story.

Using the same words he used on me earlier, I muttered, "I just have this feeling."

Chapter 5

After we finished the lasagna Adam cooked up, we ended up just talking about anything that we could think of. I opened the food pack that my uncle gave me and it revealed to be some cuts of vegetables and a hummus dip. I guess he figured out that his neighbor was already willing to treat me to lunch since what he gave me couldn't really be counted as a meal.

So now here I was in this guy's living room actually talking about his failed love story with his best friend.

Hey, if the writing thing doesn't turn out well, maybe I could go study to become a counselor instead. It seemed like everybody around me has some sort of problem they need help figuring out.

And that includes me.

"Then she actually confessed to me," he groaned, grabbing one of the carrot sticks before dipping it into the hummus, "I feel like I was about to faint when that happened."

I hummed in understanding, nibbling onto my own bit of vegetable, "So what did you do after?"

"I told her I love her as a sister," he replied, his expression showing that he clearly didn't meant it, "But it was better that way."

Perhaps not, because in my perspective, she liked him and he liked her. She was brave enough to spit it out and I could only imagine her pain when she found out that all this time, she was so deep into the friendzone.

I mean, sisterzone.

He did not only break one heart, but he broke two. He thought what he did was best for everyone and even went as far as pushing her to another man's direction. There was a problem though, he seemed to have forgotten about his own feelings.

In the end, the selfless side of the triangle ended up with no one.

"Let me get this straight, you loved this girl, she loved you, but you wanted her to be with someone else," I clarified and he nodded, "To tell you the truth, that was a little foolish of you."

"The guy she's with can take care of her," he muttered, "He can easily battle it out with her temper."

"Feisty," I pointed out, "Sounds like someone I won't get along with easily."

Although my friends were far from docile, they were all kind and considered people around them. They may be a little bit adventurous but I could never picture myself with somebody who was a walking timebomb.

Of course, my own best friend was an exception, but that was a story for another day.

He shook his head before taking a bite of the carrot stick, "You'll like her, everybody does."

Well, she better have the charisma if she was as famous as Adam said. What I gathered up from him was that she was the one who paid for most of the apartment so now I got a clearer idea on how he was able to move in on his own.

People like those are highly selective so I may like her but we could never be a hundred percent sure that she would feel the same.

"I don't even have a tv yet," he huffed once a wave of silence fell upon us. He figured that none of us wanted to move forward with this topic so he opted to change it, "I still have yet to go furniture shopping."

"Might I remind you that school starts on Monday so you don't have much time," I spoke, using the throw pillow to cushion my head instead of my bottom as I laid down on the hardwood floor.

"So how about going with me tomorrow then?" he suggested, peering over our make-shift table, "We can go into town and besides, I need some of your opinion because I'm horrible when it comes to these things."

"You sure are comfortable asking a girl you haven't even known for more than forty-eight hours," I pointed out, letting a light chuckle escape my lips.

"I'm not the one who entered someone's apartment after haven't knowing him for more than forty-eight hours," he retorted.

Using the box to push me up, I shot him a sheepish look, "Good point."

"So can I have your number?" he asked, lifting up his phone and I drew in a deep breath, shaking my head.

His hand dropped and was accompanied by a deep frown, I quickly stepped in to clarify, "I don't have a phone yet, you can contact me through messenger though."

Nodding in understanding, he reached down before I could hear a tearing sound. I then found out that he took a small piece of cardboard from the box, his gaze then zooming in on my sketchpad. Pointing towards it, he asked me the silent question if he could borrow it.

Getting the message, I handed it and he took the pen that was inserted there. Uncapping it, he scribbled down his number on the small piece of cardboard before sliding it across to my side of the box. Placing the pen back inside the sketchpad, he also gave it back.

"I'll see you tomorrow then," he gave me a smile before he got back up on his feet, "Now let's go, I need to bring you back to your uncle."

Oh right, I got kicked out of there.

Hugging my iPad and sketchpad close to my chest, I stood up and followed him out of the door. A few steps later and we found ourselves in front of Uncle Levi's apartment, him lifting a finger to press the bell for me. While we waited, I turned to him with a laugh, "Thanks for letting me stay and allowing me to taste your almost-homemade lasagna."

"And thank you for sharing your vegetable-hummus combination with me," he shot back, sharing my amusement at the way things turned out. Honestly, I thought that I would never speak to him again when we got off that airplane. Not only was he able to find me through the internet, but he ended up living right beside my uncle.

So universe, what else are you planning to throw at me? Please give me a bit of early warning because I wasn't anywhere near resilient.

While we were in the middle of saying goodbye, the door swung open and we instinctively took a step away from each other as we looked at the entrance, glancing at the stoic Andy, his gaze traveling from me to the tall stranger.

"Oh right, Adam, this is Andy," I introduced, "My cousin."

Not being phased with the dry expression my dear relative was showing, Adam flashed him a courteous smile and he reached out a hand for him to shake, "It's a pleasure to meet you."

Andy didn't respond and I rolled my eyes at his hostility. When I first met him when we were kids, it took some time for him to warm up to me, his own family, so I could understand the indifference he was currently showing the unknown boy in front of him.

And whenever there was the quiet Andy, right behind him was a preppy Emma. His sister popped out from the inside and when she saw Adam, a grin spread on her face as she zoomed past her brother to shake the hand that was supposed to be for him, "Hello there."

"And this is Emma," I added, catching myself off-guard with the enthusiasm she displayed, "Andy's sister."

Adam's politeness didn't falter a bit, although I did see that he was trying to subtly pry his hand away when Emma refused to let it go.

"Alright kids, that's enough," Uncle Levi came out before waving his keycard in front of us, "I need to take Sienna back to the university."

"You're staying in the dormitory?" Adam questioned and I hummed in confirmation, "Which one?"

"1-Ladies," I told him as uncle continued to push his children back into the apartment, Emma yelling goodbye at us while she was at it. Closing the wooden door and he gestured for us to go, taking the lead so I could say one more farewell to Adam, "Well, I'll see you."

He walked with us until he reached his door and he waved goodbye at me, "See you."

Uncle escorted me into the elevator and once it was just the two of us, he gave me that suspicious look, "So looks like you finally got someone to get rid of that tree."

"He was just someone I met on the plane," I snorted, turning to the other side so he wouldn't see the blush that started to appear at his accusation.

I knew for a fact that Adam and I were just acquaintances but at the mere implication of something more was enough to make me red.

Maybe one of the things that made emotions easy for me to write was because they easily twisted in me. I wasn't like Andy who always kept what he was feeling at bay nor was I Emma who liked to outright speak her thoughts. I was Sienna, a girl who loved the idea of emotions and feelings swirling through the air, clashing or dancing with the others'. No need to hold back or no need to say it out loud.

"But I'm glad to see you're making friends already," he said as we stepped out of the elevator when we got to the ground floor. He waved at the receptionist when we passed him before we got out of the building and into the cold outside.

The sun was still up in the sky as we started to walk towards the university. I made sure that I memorized every turn we did so that I would no longer need to pay an unnecessary amount just for a taxi.

"I guess you know your way from here," he muttered once we reached the front of the tall gates.

Glancing towards the inside, I nodded at him. When he was just about to turn to leave, I held out a hand to stop him, "Sketchpad."

"Keep it," he told me, jamming his hands into his pockets, "Give it back when you returned to our world."

"Our world?"

"Of putting together words amazingly sewn together to create a story," he explained, "See you on Monday, Sienna."

Letting his words sink in, my eyes trained down to the ground and it stayed that way as I directed myself towards the dormitory. Climbing up the short steps, I pushed one of the double doors to get in, observing that everyone in the foyer was heading to the dining hall.

When I saw Meg and Julia, I lifted a hand to give them a weak wave to get their attention and they eagerly signaled me to come near them.

"So how's your visit to your relatives?" Julia asked, taking out the lollipop from her mouth.

I was still shaken because of uncle's words. I mean, I knew that I drifted away from writing, but the way he said it made it sound like I left, or rather pushed myself away, from it. And what made that realization heavier than ever was that because nobody actually said it to my face before.

The most they would ask was when will I make another book, but Uncle Levi was the very first person who pointed it out straight to my face how I fell out with writing.

And that such a huge slap on my face.

"Sienna?" Julia called out, making me lose my train of thoughts. Her face was visibly concerned so I plastered a smile.

"Great," I replied with a forced happy tone, "It was so nice to see them again."

Walking into the dining hall, the girls were already getting their food from the table and I trailed behind Meg and Julia as we all lined up for ours. Today it was a plate of mashed potatoes, some cut fish fillet, and a side of steamed vegetables. From here, I could already tell the vegetables were terribly undercooked, but I'm willing to give the fish and the mash a try.

Maybe those were store-bought as well and they're claiming that they made it, just like some other guy I know.

"By the way, Sienna, can you give me some tips on getting published?" Meg suddenly piped in after we sat down on our table, "I've written this story and I was wondering if you can guide me through."

I was not the one to tell her about hard word and perseverance was one of the best ways to reach your goal because even I didn't do that – my connections made the process easier for me compared to the struggling authors, stuck in a routine of trying and then getting rejected.

"How about I give you my mom's e-mail address," I offered, "She's a literary agent."

She was nice enough but she was strict with the authors she represent. Before she even goes near to offering a publisher your work, she'll tear it apart piece by piece. The only reason why I didn't go through that torture was because I was her daughter, she was monitoring my progress all throughout.

"Thank you," she grinned before she turned to Julia as they once again fell into a deep conversation about her boyfriend from back home. I droned out their voices and focused on finishing my meal. This time, I actually stayed with them and whenever they turned their attention to me to ask or add anything to their current topic, I shot them a short but precise answer.

Classes haven't even started yet and I was already in a funk.

Before getting into bed, I took a quick shower. Meg went back into her room and I plopped down onto the mattress, relishing the soft cushion it provided.

Don't get me wrong, it was fun and all to sit in Adam's empty apartment but this was a lot comfier than that throw pillow.

"Want to go shopping some time during the weekend?" Julia suggested, closing the curtains before crawling into her bed.

She gave me a look that clearly stated that if I didn't say yes, she would throw a fit. I already ran away from her and Meg last night during dinner and I turned down her suggestion to tour around the university today so I think I wasn't going to push it, "Sure."

Closing my beside lamp, I buried myself under the sheets, my head sinking into the soft pillow. Maybe because I ploughed through the day with very little sleep, my body was more than willing to give in to a goodnight's rest.

The moment I closed my eyes, I was knocked out.

It was quite peaceful though, until I was freaking woken up by Julia violently shaking my body, "Sienna, wake up!"

"What?" I questioned weakly, my eyelids heavy for it still wanted more sleep.

She forcefully pulled away my duvet and I instinctively curled up into a ball at the sudden drop in temperature. She groaned before she grabbed my arm, still urging me to get up, "Somebody's waiting for you!"

"Hm?" I asked, sitting up as I rubbed my eyes.

"Some pretty good looking guy is waiting for you downstairs," she informed and I gave her a quizzical look, but when she ran to the door, I opted to follow so it would shut her up.

When I got out of our room, I was surprised by the amount of girls that were waiting for me as well. My eyebrows scrunched up in confusion while I allowed my slipper-clad feet to drag on the wooden floor. Ever so slowly, I went down the stairs and I could still feel a huge amount of attention following my every move.

When I finally reached the first floor, my eyes bulged out of their sockets when I saw Adam there, swaying uncomfortably due to the numerous number of girls ogling at the sight of him. He was still halfway out of the door but it was enough for anyone inside to see him and for him to have an amazing view of every single girl.

I wanted to chastise those shameless enough who were openly gawking while only clad in their sleepwear, but I don't really have much of a right since I was still in my tank top and cotton shorts.

Holding Julia's shoulder, I whispered, "What time is it?"

"About eight," she replied, her gaze still on Adam.

Scratching my head, I tried to wrack my brain if he ever said something about picking me up at this time in the morning. I knew that we were going furniture shopping but I never expected that he would actually go here to fetch me – I thought that I was heading to the apartment complex to meet with him.

He still hasn't noticed me since he was too busy trying to avoid any kind of eye contact. Turning around, my eyes searched hopelessly at the girls behind me as I mouthed, "Jacket or whatever."

One of them who had a fluffy robe on shrugged it off before handing it to me, "Here.

I shot her an appreciative smile as I put the garment on, hugging it close before I approached the only male species in this whole building, "Adam."

When he heard my voice, his posture relaxed as he watched me walk over to him, "Oh finally!"

"Can you wait for a moment?" I asked before I gestured to my current state, "I just need to dress up."

Even though he nodded and told me to go ahead, I could see the hesitation to let me leave. The way his eyes traveled to the mass amount of girls just gave a new kind of anxiousness in his system. It was simple, he didn't want to be left alone with this tidal of female hormones.

I was going to regret this but she was the closest thing I have to a friend here, "Julia?"

She was by my side in an instant and she placed on a smile while she drawled on, "Yes?"

"This is my roommate, Julia," I told him, "And this Adam, a friend of mine."

She nodded at the new piece of information, her eyes twinkling with excitement, "Pleasure."

"Can you just keep him company while I change?" I requested and I already knew the answer. Turning around, I rushed to take off the robe and hand it back to its owner before I rapidly climbed up the stairs to the third floor and into my room.

Meg knocked in my room as I was in the middle of pulling a dress over my head, "Who's the guy?"

"A friend," I answered, bending down to look for my flats, "We're just going out for a bit."

"Going out?" she repeated as she followed me when I grabbed my coat before heading out of the room, "You never told us you had a boyfriend."

"Because I don't," I corrected, shuffling down the stairs, "Like I said, he's a friend."

To be honest, we met about two days ago but that sounded so sketchy if I actually said that out loud.

In fact, this whole thing was weird. Was I really craving something out of the norm so much?

When I got back onto the first floor, Julia had already managed to repeat the same amount of information that she had told me on the first day, dumping it all on the poor Adam, "And then my ninth goldfish was already gone when I got home."

Ah, the goldfish story.

"Sorry, sorry," I apologized, putting on my coat while I approached them. Julia snapped her head towards my direction and a frown showed on her lips as she took a step away from Adam, clearly disappointed that her time with him was done. Showing her an appreciative smile, I then pointed at the door, "Shall we then?"

When I closed the door behind us, we heard multiple squeals coming from the inside. Pausing, we glanced over our shoulder before walking away from that estrogen-filled building. Living in there was like a sorority – although the occupants were varying in personalities, we were still all females and thus, any form of the opposite sex entering there would be received with a kind of excitement. Especially with the freshmen, I don't believe there was a higher year who was still that enthusiastic.

Adam finally released a sigh of relief when we were far enough, making me shoot another apology, "I really am sorry, I had no idea you were picking me up."

Gazing down at me, he shook his head and he waved off my apology, "No, it was better than letting you guess if we're actually going or not."

Well he was right, the air around us was more or less teasing when he asked me. I should really get a phone.

"So where's our first stop?" I questioned, trying to go back to our original purpose, "Any furniture shop you have in mind?"

He grinned mischievously as he took out his phone, "That's not the only thing we're going to do."

My eyebrows raised and I gave him a question expression, "Meaning?"

"Let's just enjoy ourselves for the day," he said, "Maybe you'll find a bit of inspiration on the way."

Chapter 6

"So what's your story?" Adam questioned as we got out of the taxi. Stepping onto the sidewalk, I marveled at the town that I was currently in. Geography had never been one of my strong suits so I wasn't even sure where we were, but even though it was buzzling with people, it was still relatively peaceful.

Our university was, as you say, was kind of known for its love of the arts. From journalism to majoring in theatre, they are willing to help you explore your talents. Coming from that, it was no surprise that the people in the main city started constructing their buildings and houses to reflect the famed school.

The shops were differing in colors, all distinct from the others. Each one had their own personality and while standing on the spot where Adam told the driver to drop us off at, I figured out we were smack in the middle of the shopping lanes.

"What?" I asked absentmindedly as I stared at one of the shop's windows. Pink, that was the single way that I could describe it. It looked like it was set up for a tea party with the two chairs colored with a baby pink hue and the table in-between was covered with a white cloth. Tea cups, saucers, tea pot, and fake snacks were on top.

If someone would give me that, I would have walked out on them. Sure, I could portray the girly act at times, but if you do something as frilly as that, I would smack you.

"I told you mine about my best friend," he said me, taking the lead, "What's yours?"

Which story did he want? About the single relationship that I managed to tell to the world? Or my lack of creativity that was haunting me? I damned myself the moment I proposed the idea of writing a book to my mother and now I was paying the consequences.

Being an author was an odd kind of fame. People know your name, but not your face. You'll hear them talking about you but they wouldn't know you were standing right there – only a select few were easily caught in the middle of a sea of people.

But me? The picture at the back of the book I wrote barely resembled me at all and the way my thought processed inside my head has definitely changed.

Love is and never will be as easy as roses and chocolates. Making the guy notice you will not be as simple as smiling at him. Asking a girl out could be more nerve-wracking than you could ever imagine.

All those is what I've learned by twisting my love story. I tried to give it some flair, sugarcoating almost everything. Halfway through, I realized that it was no longer true to word.

Because the breakup I experienced was not a throat-screeching, vase throwing, or hair pulling ending. Instead, it was a mutual agreement to go on our separate ways because I've noticed that there were other things that we had to figure out as individuals.

So I scrapped the whole thing and rewrote.

We were still friendly after it all – he congratulated me with the book when it first got published without a single idea that it was about him.

I wrote him a forty chaptered love letter and he didn't even know.

In the middle of the happy cheers my friends gave and the annoying demands for free copies, I figured out that this was how they now see me. Not as the girl who sat there, laughing along with the silliest jokes or not minding one bit if we would just lay in one of our houses, eating ice cream or something. What they saw was that young teen author, they distanced themselves as if one book in the market was going to change the way I treated them.

So I plucked out the friends who weren't afraid to throw me a teasing insult or to call me up in the middle of the night, expecting me to get frustrated with them and they'll just laugh my words off. They were the ones that I wanted to stay with.

Instead of answering him, I shot him an inquiry, "Is there a bookstore nearby?"

He guided me to a Waterstones shop and I pushed those glass doors to enter. Looking around, I searched for the young adults section with him trailing off behind me. This was a major bookstore, they surely have a copy.

And true to my suspicions, it sat there on one of the dark colored shelves, squished in-between two other books from the same publisher. Bending down, I took a copy before handing it to him, my heart hammering in my chest with both pride and nervousness.

I was always conflicted on what to feel with that book. My parents told me that I should be proud of myself for most people my age couldn't even come close to what I have achieved, but at the same time, it brought me this anxiety that others would think that it was corny, it was childish, it wasn't interesting enough.

They do say, your worst critic is yourself.

"Sienna Clark," Adam read out the name printed on the cover.

Jotting down a finger onto it, I said, "That's my story."

With a little added drama here and there, but essentially, that was it.

"Heartbreak?" he questioned teasingly and I rolled my eyes as we made our way to the counter.

"One of the biggest source of inspiration out there," I shrugged, "Besides, I revealed no names and such, but only he would get most of those words."

He gave the cashier his credit card while she scanned the book, "So what was his reaction?"

"He never read it," was my reply and Adam's eyes widened in surprise.

I was ready for a confrontation, ready for him to demand answers why I wrote those things that were privately ours. It never happened and even though he gave me a little pat on the back, I've soon come to realize that he didn't read it.

He was never the one to crazily look for books – he was the playful sort of guy. Also a flirt, a big damn flirt but when we were together, he was loyal. But he was still a boy who wanted to go off without someone tying him down so much. I never demanded, that was something I was cautious about, but he needed to grow up a little more.

And I admitted back then that I did as well.

I loved him and I was assured that he loved me, but people just grow apart. I was constantly worrying and at the same time, I didn't want to be the insecure girlfriend.

The question still hung in the air: Will he ever read it? Will he ever find out how much I've been pulled by him?

"Well, I for one thinks he's an absolute tool," Adam grinned in a way to comfort me, retrieving the plastic bag and credit card from the cashier. Wounding his arm around my shoulder, I jolted up as he guided us out of the store.

"Nah, you'll like him," I said, repeating the same words he told me, "Everybody does."

And everybody certainly did.

"Sometimes I'll scream onto my pillow like a love struck middle school girl at the thought of him," I shook my head, "And other times, I want to knee him where the sun doesn't shine for being so damn ignorant."

"Charming," he chuckled, steering me towards one of the furniture shops. Before we entered, that was when he finally let me go and my shoulders slumped at the loss of contact.

The store was huge to say the least. On the first floor, couches, living chairs, beds, and whatnot were all lined up as various other shoppers sat on them to test them out.

"She demanded a white couch," Adam muttered and he took out his phone, handing me the plastic bag of the book while he searched along, "And she wants at least a queen sized bed, two bedside drawers, and she would not accept a tv less than thirty-eight inches for the living room and sixteen inches for her bedroom."

"She?" I repeated, falling into step beside him, trying to keep up with his fast pacing, "Your mom?"

He glanced down for a quick moment before shaking his head, returning his attention back onto the phone screen, "My best friend, she owns half of the flat."

At first when he mentioned that his best friend paid for most of the apartment, I thought it was a just a sweet gift because I was sure celebrities like her didn't mind splurging this much on presents.

Alright, alright, call me prude or childish or whatever, but if a guy and a girl share that apartment, wouldn't you think be suspicious of something? He mentioned that she has a boyfriend so why didn't the guy say anything about this?

No matter how platonic they may appear now, we can't deny the fact that Adam liked her and the girl also used to like him back; something was bound to happen.

What was this guy's situation right now?

My eyes focusing again on his face and I saw him moving his mouth as he told me something. Snapping myself out of this trance, I heard the last of his sentence, "...good enough?"

I then turned to the bed he was pointing at before nodding, deeming it sufficient. He gestured to the saleswoman and they began to talk. He probably asked for help with the others as she was now leading us through the floors, showing us different furniture and appliances.

Who was Adam's best friend? How famous was she? A-List or just some youtube star?

What big of a chance did he miss when he rejected her feelings? Why was he so willing to put himself through the torture of being under the same roof as her when she was clearly somebody else's?

"I brought you along to help me," Adam called out, his tone light and joking, "I can't pick which sofa I should get."

"Who is she?" I unintentionally murmured and he was taken off-guard at the sudden question. Scrunching his eyebrows in confusion, he clearly showed that he didn't understand what I was trying to say, "What's your best friend's name?"

He excused us from the employee and he grabbed my shoulders, bringing us away from most of the people, "What are you going on about, Sienna?"

"Are you really going to risk yourself of falling in love again by living with her?" I fired, "Or are you just trying to turn a blind eye over this?"

Finally catching on, he released me and sighed, "It's not like that and besides, I stayed with her over the summer so it's not like it's the first time."

"And she ended up telling you her feelings," I reminded, "What if you slip up this time?"

"I won't!" his tone became louder as if he was denying it to himself more than he was denying it to me. He can lie all he wanted but I could see right through him.

He still loves her.

"Then at least tell me who she is!" I demanded, my voice matching his. He opened his mouth but when I saw the flicker of hesitation, I knew that he wouldn't say. It may be for her protection or because it might just tick me off more when I find out but I wasn't going to tolerate it.

Biting my lip, I ducked my head before I started to walk away from him. He called my name but it only made me increase my speed, dashing out of the store. Count on me to argue with somebody I just became friends with over something petty as this.

I was annoyed at him because he wouldn't admit it. The heart likes to play a game – a game that will screw up your entire life. No matter how much it wants you to think that everything was alright, you know deep inside that it wasn't.

In truth, I was just letting out my frustrations on him. He had every right not tell me and who was I to scold him? The thing was, I saw myself in him – incredibly stupid not to let go of my feelings even if I was the one to cut it all off.

My gaze then saw the small café in front of me and when I caught a whiff of the food one of the passerby was eating, it was then I remembered than I haven't taken any breakfast yet. Looking behind me back into the store, I sighed as I slowly made my way to the café.

All I ordered was a pastry and a cup of coffee, choosing to sit by the window so when the time that Adam leaves the shop, he would be able to spot me easily. Reaching into the plastic bag of his purchase, I pulled out the book it contained.

Flipping through the pages, I skimmed the lines. I didn't even recognize my own words anymore, I haven't touched, read, or even scanned through the inside of it for about a year now. So when my eyes managed to read out one sentence, I used a finger to stop the paper of the previous pages from falling onto it.

And when she told him to go, there was nothing she felt but pure regret. If given a second chance, she will surely never allow him to leave her side. She knew it was for his own food and yet, one word from him was enough to have her running back. Her heart knew that he was the home that she will always yearn for.

That, I believe, was the same kind of love that Adam was feeling. He allowed her to be with another man for her own sake but he knew that his heart belonged to her and I was afraid that, like what I wrote here, just one word from her and he'll be coming back into the pit hole known as his affection over her.

I know because that was what I felt.

Going to the very first chapter, my expression softened at the introduction my sixteen year old me has written.

She didn't really pay him mind at first but they got along splendidly. He wasn't much of a looker when they met, his dark hair was always flat on his head because he refused to wax or gel it up, he wore these silver pair of round glasses, and he was never seen without his lumpy jackets. She and her friends actually teased him that he looked like Harry Potter but he never really got annoyed for he knew that it was only some friendly banter.

Harry Potter – that was the most accurate way to describe him. I remembered when the girl next to me whispered that he looked like the boy who lived, I couldn't stop laughing and I ended up calling him that. That was freshman year and I could still remember his childlike features as if it was just yesterday.

The first time they spoke properly was when both of them were coincidentally absent for the day. Apparently, someone told him that she was gone the same day as he and he turned on the chatbox – that was the start of it all. His profile picture, at the time, was an anime character and it was still the start of the year, she couldn't remember his face. But the next day when their eyes met, she knew it was him.

When someone suddenly pulled out the chair that was across the table, I snapped my head up and stared at Adam. Without another word, he plopped down a magazine right next to the coffee cup before sitting down.

Closing the book, I then gingerly picked up the magazine and stared at the cover. There posed a gorgeous blonde girl, her blue eyes staring at you with her red lips formed into the brightest smile. Even though it was just a picture, you were held captivated by her beautiful features – from her sharp nose to those perfectly white teeth.

I knew her in an instant, she was Heart Valentine. The name sounded ridiculous but that was what made people remember her, aside from her talent of course, and she was described as Hollywood's Princess for not only ruling the music scene but for also dominating the box office.

"That's her," he pointed out quietly my eyes widened.

Flipping the glossy pages, I stopped where the article for her was written. At the bottom right of the page was a picture of the girl herself along with another familiar face in the industry – Axel Brooks, Hollywood's Prince.

I heard that they started dating recently after months of speculation. It rooted when she was pictured with him pulling her into a bridal shop and they all dismissed it as an escape from the paparazzi. Before that, there was a rumor that she was going out with a non-celebrity boy but she denied it by saying that he was just a friend that she treated like a brother.

And then it clicked.

"You were the boy she was photographed with," I gasped, blinking up at him and with the soft nod he showed, it confirmed my assumption. Finally getting it, I tapped my nails on the table before muttering, "I'm sorry."

The corners of his mouth threatened to pull his lips up into a smile. Instead of responding to my apology, he leaned back on his chair and asked me the very first thing he did when we got out of that taxi, "So what's your story?"

"Which one?"

"Why not all?" he said, "You wrote it down, you're writing it down, and you're going to write it down anyways."

Chapter 7

We entered Adam's apartment, lugging the takeout bag that we bought on the way back. After a successful day of shopping, we managed to get almost everything that we needed. We were able to carry the small ones on our own but the big appliances and furniture will be delivered sometime this weekend.

He asked if I could go on and help him with that but I had to turn him down since I know Julia was ready to explode on me if I canceled on her one more time. I did promise to visit throughout the week in-between and after my classes to give him a hand.

"You want to talk to her?" he suddenly asked as I was unpacking our food. Giving him a questioning look, he lifted his phone and waved it at my face, "I have to give her a report on where I spent a good portion of her money."

I already knew what he was talking about. The famous best friend, the cause of our first row, and the girl he was madly in love with.

And I was a hundred percent sure the more I get involved with this guy right across from me, that list would go on longer.

He didn't give me much time to respond because he already dialed her up and placed the call on speaker, putting it down on the box between us while it slowly rung while waiting for the recipient to pick up. Peering over the screen, I tilted my head at the words Sophia Valentine. I was not a huge fanatic or anything so I didn't know much but I was going to assume that Sophia was her real name.

"Adam?" came out her smooth voice. It was sweet and silky at the same time, a tone that you wouldn't mind listening to for hours and hours – no wonder she was winning multiple awards and was becoming one of the best-selling artist of this generation. Even though she was only talking, it was already melodious, just imagine when she sings, "Just in time, we just finished with the meeting."

"Done shopping, Soph," he said, using his nickname to her, "I'm going to send you the pictures later."

"Perfect," was her reply and I noticed the slight British accent slipping in there, "I hope you followed my instructions to a T."

Gazing up at Adam, I couldn't help but notice the way he had this soft smile on his face. Even though he wasn't talking to her face to face, he still adored every aspect of her. His eyes were closed and his chin was on the palm of his hand as his elbow rested on the box, "Of course, and I used some of the money mum and dad gave me."

The picture of a boy perfectly in love.

"I told you that I can pay for it," she groaned, complaining that her best friend actually paid with his own cash instead of hers. Well, that was a different reaction, usually people would snap if they used their dough on something that wasn't theirs.

But I guess if you were paid millions, you wouldn't really mind.

"But you already did the down payment, the monthly rent, internet, cable, and heating installment, not to mention a good half of the furniture," he defended, "At least let me buy my own things."

When his eyes opened and he saw me there, he jolted up as if he suddenly remembered that there was another member in this party. Please, ignore me because there was this immediate fascination within me just watching you interact with her like that. I've cooped myself up for a long ass time that I actually forgot that moments like these really do happen in real life.

And it's as mesmerizing as I remember, just like when I was in that situation.

He scrambled around as he told this to the girl listening intently through the line, "By the way, someone here wants to talk to you."

Now it was my turn to be taken aback. Shaking my head, I kept my lips sealed. With his hands, he urged me to speak but I kept rejecting the idea, pushing the phone farther from me. Giving me a stern look, he pushed the phone back towards my side of box, mouthing incoherent words.

"Hello?" Heart asked after she noticed the bouts of silence.

In a panic, I finally opened my mouth, "H-hi."

It was as if a switch was turned in her, the high spirited tone she was using on Adam changed in a second. From natural honey, her voice was now fine sugar – obviously a display of fake enthusiasm, "Oh hey!"

She has completely dropped her accent, opting to use this valley girl tone. In an instant, I now remember why I was so enchanted by her voice when she spoke to Adam, it was because it was different from the usual one I heard. Interviews and such, she was using this tone, this fake pretense.

And in the presence of her best friend, the pretense fell off.

I wasn't able to say anything else and Adam finally saw my discomfort so he sighed, "That was Sienna, Soph. By the way, you're on speaker."

"Sienna?" she repeated, probably wracking up her brain for the name, "The girl you brought in yesterday? I'm glad to know she didn't die because of the food you gave."

My eyes widened at the information – this man actually told this rich A-list celebrity of how I subtly made fun of his bare apartment, of how I laughed at him for serving me something practically store-bought, and my not-so-brilliant idea of using a box as a table and throw pillows as chairs.

And we were still doing the last one right now.

Great, I've probably lost all of my chances on getting on her good graces before I even talked to her.

"Hey, I'm a pretty good cook," he protested, though the grin on his face signaled that he was far from it and quite agreed with her.

"Tell that to my kitchen," I heard her laugh and ever so slowly, the sugary tone she was using came dwindling down, "And don't forget about that time about the eggs with my mom."

Adam chuckled lightheartedly at the memory, "I was trying to distract Aunt May while you talked to Axel!"

Aunt May? So he was that close to her mother and apparently, he also met the famous boyfriend before.

"I'm right here, you know!" we heard a faint male voice from the other line and we can both say that she also had us on speaker because there was no possible way for him to hear us. There was some shuffling from the other line and when he spoke again, it was much clearer and louder, "Anything new happening there?"

"He has a new friend," Heart filled in for him, "Her name's Sienna."

He hummed for a moment before his tone became mischievous and he let out a small laugh, "Been there for a total of three days and he has a girl already."

Once again, the mere implication was enough to turn me into a flustered mess. Casting my eyes downward towards my lap, I twiddled my thumbs as I fought back a blush. I hoped that Adam would keep his concentration on the phone so he wouldn't be able to see how affected I was by Axel Brooks' statement.

He, on the other hand, found nothing wrong with the joke and managed to shoot him a retort, "Yeah, I'm planning to leave a whole flower shop in her room."

Glancing up, he was trying so hard to keep his amusement at bay but for me, it only made me think of about his words. I could just imagine him filling up my dorm with a bunch of flowers and just like before, it made stomach do somersaults.

"Don't act so innocent, Adam, you were on it," Heart told him off, her voice turning back into the honey tone, now genuine and happy with her words, "I still can't believe that you were conspiring behind my back."

Oh so it was an inside joke.

"But hey, you ended up saying yes to me anyways," we heard Axel say affectionately to his girlfriend. Surprisingly, I thought Adam would show a look of hurt or jealousy, but he didn't. He only nodded as if the two could see him while the smile still didn't leave his face.

And this is when the testament where 'If you're happy, I'm happy' comes to life.

In that moment, I realized that these two celebrities' relationship was as true. Contrary to the many theories and gossips circulating the internet, it wasn't just a publicity stunt. I admit, I also had doubts when I first heard about it because he announced that he was doing a movie and also touring with her. Of course, with the sudden burst of mutual projects, you would think that it was being done for promotion.

But now, it verified right in front of me that what they have was real. Along with that, I learned that Axel once filled up Heart's room with flowers to the brim – perhaps with Adam's help – and I couldn't help but in awe at the phone, as if my sudden admiration would be transpired to them.

Okay I admit it, I was a complete sap when it came to these things.

These three experienced something that I was afraid I couldn't comprehend. At first, I thought that it was a stupid move from Adam to let her go and I was more than ready to support him if he ever decided to chase her back. Now though, I could see the genuine happiness he was feeling for the couple and I knew that he was never going to get in-between them. Add to that, I was sure the flower thing wasn't the first and only gesture Axel did with the help of Adam.

While I was here, I felt like I was intruding on something – something so precious, so private, and a rollercoaster of feelings.

This was perhaps the most candid I would ever witness these two celebrities.

"I think I need to be heading back," I finally spoke up, "Julia is expecting me before dinner."

It was a lie but he wouldn't let me leave without any reason.

His eyes shot back to me, a solid reminder that I was still there. I should be hurt that he forgot me but this was a noble experience no one out of their inner circle will be able to see. That was enough, I don't want to hear anything more for it was theirs to keep.

"I'm going to walk Sienna back to the school," Adam told the pair, "I'll talk to you again later."

Heart and Axel said their own goodbye and Adam ended the call. He flashed me a smile with a nod, pushing himself off of the floor.

Although I protested against it, he was adamant on escorting me back to the university. I would love to remind him of the fact that if he even took a step near my dormitory, the girls would go fawning over him like he was the last drop of water in the middle of a desert.

"You're learning an awful lot about me and I could barely get a piece of information from you," he pointed out as we were halfway there.

"You got the book," I reminded, my shoes scraping on the ground, "Read it."

"That's like touching the surface," he said, stuffing his hands in his pockets, "And you said it yourself, it's just based on your life story, not really the narration of it."

Sighing, I slowed down my pace as I tried to think of a way to give him one simple message for him to find out everything, "Just know that I truly loved him."

Deeply, terribly, catastrophically. I loved him so much to the point of no return, it was weird to think that I was only a high school sweetheart to him but for me, he was that piece of my life that I wouldn't mind looking back over and over again.

"You're mature, Adam," I spoke, finally falling into step next to him, "Even though your beloved is with someone else, you're still happy for her. Me? I'm cursing him and myself because of what we went through."

"I wouldn't call it maturity," he muttered just as we finally reached the gates, "Besides, like you said, you have your own story."

I thought that he would stop there like what my uncle did yesterday but surprisingly, he kept on walking by my side until we reached my dorm. There were a few girls hanging around outside and when they caught a glimpse of us, they paused on what they were doing to stare.

At some point during the year, I do hope that people would finally get used to us having visitors. I know it was still unlikely since the school year yet to begin but you may never know what entails for the future.

"So see you?" I questioned because there was no way in heck was I going to allow him to enter again.

He smiled before nodding, "See you."

The moment I got inside, Julia pulled me by the arm before anyone else could interrogate me and she called out a large dibs, claiming that she had roommate privileges in asking the questions.

"So how did it go?" she asked, leading me up the staircase, "I can't believe you managed to snatch a boy so quickly."

Shaking my head, I corrected her assumption immediately, "He's just a friend who asked me to help him pick out furniture for his new apartment."

And perhaps we also had a small scuffle plus I talked to his incredibly famous best friend and her boyfriend.

"Hold on, he lives alone?" she squealed just when we reached our room, "You just got the ultimate jackpot!"

Technically, he did, but when Heart finally decides to visit the flat, that was going to be another story. Far as I was aware though, she was off gallivanting on tour.

"So our girl is back," Meg grinned, inviting herself inside, "You've got to introduce him to me, you two could double date with my boyfriend and I."

"We're just friends!" I exclaimed, causing both of them to laugh at my expense. This caused me to pout childishly because none of them were taking me seriously.

Julia threw me one of her pillows, "Just banter."

I threw it back to her with huff, "Whatever. At least I got myself familiar with the town."

"Perfect for tomorrow," she clapped before starting a conversation about the items she planned on getting.

As she did that, I reached over to my drawer to take out Uncle Levi's sketchpad. Grabbing a pen, I started scribbling today's happenings – from the moment Adam entered the dormitory to the way he walked me back.

Then, I took my laptop and opened the last file that I wrote so I could start a new chapter. The last place I left off was about the chat Adam and I had so I allowed my fingers to tap on the keys, typing out a new title for the latest chapter.

Muse.

Not even minding the time as I started going into work mode, I failed to hear Julia and Meg say that it was time for dinner. They were both staring at me curiously and I pouted slightly, saving the file before placing my laptop under my pillow before following them outside.

The dinner was just like yesterday's. They were stuck in their own world and I would only insert a comment or two when they called my attention. They seemed satisfied with this arrangement since I wasn't really hindering them from their talkative gossip.

Again, my outgoingness was quickly fading.

That night, Julia quickly fell fast asleep but I didn't end up giving into slumber so quickly. Instead, I was fueled by the small peek I managed to get with the Adam's copy of my book and I ended up taking mine off of the shelf.

Ignoring Julia's light snores, I opened my bedside lamp as I flipped the pages, my eyes running through the words I read.

They ended up being in the same circle of friends. Joining the whole group as they ate by the field, he would always give her his watch for safekeeping before he would run around with the other boys – playing as if they were still children.

She would always put on his watch, right on below hers since it big enough to slide down midway to her elbow. It became a routine and she would always try to hide the fact that she gets jealous whenever the watch wasn't in her possession during lunch time. He didn't know, but she was glaring at their friend who acquired the watch before her on one afternoon.

Leaning against the headboard, I remembered it so vividly. We were all in the same class and we managed to claim one of the outside tables by the field. The boys would eat so fast so they could start playing soon and everybody thought it was childish but nobody stopped them.

Because their youth was theirs to enjoy.

He had this silver watch that he was afraid to damage during these games and so, he would always hand it to me without another word. I understood immediately what I had to do and so, I would snap it on my wrist but it always fell down because his arm was definitely larger than mine.

There was one time that he didn't hand it to me and I didn't even notice. Only when our friend mentioned that she was wearing it did I feel the first sparks of jealousy.

One time, his best friend caught her staring at him and she quickly averted her gaze right after. Her cheeks started to heat up as she tried to deny it with every bone in her body that she liked him.

But no matter how hard she tried to shake that idea, she knew that it was lie. She liked him so much that it hurts. It wasn't because of how deep her heart sunk, but it was because of how much it ached when she saw him with another girl.

The problem with him was that he was always off with some other female company. He wasn't a player, but he was a flirt. He has never gone beyond friendly banter with anybody and she thought that maybe that's why she fell for him and perhaps, she was nothing but another one of the victims of his extreme kindness.

Closing the book, I groaned as I rubbed my temples. The memories came rushing back into me and my heart started beating rapidly. Even though I've declared that I've moved on several times, I knew that I was just fooling myself.

Turning to my side, my iPad sat there on the side table, charging up for the next day. Taking a deep breath, I grabbed it as I opened the twitter app, cursing myself for being too weak and too caught up.

You'll just get hurt, you know it.

I went instantly to his account and the first tweet that I saw hit me like a ton of bricks and I could only pinch myself on the arm to stop myself from doing something too brash, 'It only took one smile to make me fall in love with you again.'

So who was it?

Scrolling down even more, I couldn't stop myself from punishing myself even more, 'I've waited so long for that moment but when it came, I can't even approach her.'

A good week or so since it was posted and I slid down to fall onto my pillow. I haven't seen him for months so I'm sure it wasn't me. Biting my lip, I tried to shake away these thoughts but it was futile – I had to accept that there was another girl.

Quickly locking the device, I set it back down on the table before opening the book again. I didn't bother on picking up where I left off so I flipped it open to a random page in a desperate need to get his words out of my head.

Perhaps what he would never know was that she loved him – more than he could ever imagine. She loved him when she heard rumors and stood by his side, staying as his friend. She loved him even when they weren't that close anymore – gazing at him from afar.

With the tears prickling in my eyes, I slammed the book down next to my iPad as I hugged my blankets tighter, closing my eyes.

I loved him, more than he could ever imagine.

Chapter 8

"Too much?" Julia asked as she stepped out of her dressing room, making me peek out from mine. I blinked up at her and nodded instantly because saying that she looked like she was ready to dance on a pole in that dress was putting it lightly. With that, she groaned before strolling back in, "I just want to make a good impression."

Good impression is being polite or spunky on the first day, not wearing a low-cut dress.

Glancing at the mirror, I blinked at my reflection as I spun around, trying to formulate a judgement on the outfit. Unlike my roommate, I didn't need something flashy nor do I have the demand to create a grand entrance so I didn't really know what I was going for.

"Alright," I heard her again, making me slide open my curtain to reveal her in a more appropriate piece of clothing. Nodding at this, a grin broke onto her face before she turned back to the dressing room she was occupying.

Shrugging, I changed back into my own clothes before gathering everything that I tried on in a pile in my arms. Heck with it, I was going to buy all of these because my shopping itch was back again. I lived in New York with friends who were as fortunate as me so we really did adore buying things.

When I placed everything on the counter, my roommate glanced from behind my shoulder and gaped at the number of clothing that I was about to pay for. She looked down on the two blouse, one pair of pants, and a single dress that was currently hanging on her arm before her cheeks started to turn pink.

"I just liked a lot of things from this store," I defended when I stepped to the side after doing the transaction, "Whatever you're thinking, it's not it."

I knew it was going to fruitless, in her little mind she was thinking of me as someone from a wealthy background. In truth, I wasn't and I vowed to never consider myself as one, that was a huge lesson that I've heard from my father. No matter what you hear, what you consider yourself will be the truth.

Though sometimes that lesson backfires but I still consider it good most of the time.

"I'm so sad that Meg wasn't able to come with us today," Julia frowned when she realized what I was trying to do, "Something about not being able to miss a chat with her boyfriend."

Fortunately, she steered the subject away from the topic I knew she was dying to open up. Was I going to deny if she accuses me of the damn word? Of course not, that would be straight lying and I know she would never buy that.

Because even I know living in the heart of New York City was not cheap, especially with the size of our apartment. I believe with both of my parents' salaries, it was very plausible that a life of comfort was easily attainable. Let's also add that aside from my parents, I was also earning my own from the sales of my book.

My little brother will soon follow, though he was more of an Emma than a me. Not in the sense that he was amazing with painting or drawing, but give him a camera and the pictures he produces were award winning.

My god, he was amazing and I was quite jealous. The only worry he has is that our mother wasn't supportive of his passion as she was with me. She was forcing him to either choose a more 'useful' career such as being a doctor or lawyer, like our father, or submit himself to the art of writing.

I don't know how he does it, but he rebels. One would think that with that word, you would picture as someone with heavy eyeliner and has a closet full of black, but he was a complete hipster – with the glasses and oversized knitted sweaters.

I really wish our mother would stop, because if she could only see his talent. He has that eye, a perspective that some-how, I could not see what he does most of the time. We could be walking by a tree and he would stop me just so he could take out his camera and snap a picture. I was confused how such a nonsense thing could capture his interest but when he showed me his shot, I understood.

The way the sunlight just poke through the leaves, the action of the greens being gently pulled out by the wind, the curves of the branches as they bowed out in different directions – parallel, never touching, yet they created such a harmony.

That was what he saw and I only figured out its beauty when I looked at it from his point of view.

"Sienna," she called out, "Why did you choose to be a writer?"

"What?" I halted when the question left her lips.

"You were lost in thought again," she explained, tugging my hand to a near bench where we could take a break, "I admire you for what you achieved, but what made you sit down and write?"

A famous quote by Anaïs Nin was one of the greatest triggers. She said, 'We write to taste life twice, in the moment and in retrospect.'

When you feel something so lovingly blissful or heartbreakingly painful, your mind demands you to remember it, to tell you to stamp it on and let yourself carry it for a lifetime. Writing was like that stamp, once you place it into words, what you felt in that moment, may it be a second or several months, it lets you relive it. You tripped? Carefully craft your words to describe how much your knee throbbed and how the red blood slowly tainted your skin. You fell in love? Recall how eminently speechless you were yet your heart was beating so loudly in your chest.

And at the end of it all, you have to look back on it and reevaluate what you just did when it happened. Give your retrospect to that situation, press pause and revel in your emotions. Writing is such a wonderful thing, it's creating a dance with words, the rhythm that only you can slow and speed up.

Taking a deep breath, I lifted my gaze to stare into her waiting look, "Because it gives life to what could be a dull moment, it's a projection of the wildest imaginations, and it releases whatever tension you have in your brain."

I write because it lifts my heart in the corniest ways.

Her expression softened at this, "I wish I could love it the way you did."

"The reason why I fell so deeply with it is due the fact that I also experienced its pain," I said, "The pressure of succumbing to the demands of the publishing business, it made me more attached to it than ever. It gave me the urge to protect it, to hold it in while it's still untainted."

"So what did he do?" she asked, "The guy from your story, I mean."

"That one was all me," I replied with a shrug, "I ended it because I thought it was best for the both of us."

You want to know how caught up I was? I wrote him a letter – a forty-chapter letter filled with everything. From the day we met to our last dance during prom when I apologized for basically stopping myself from fighting for us.

And maybe because of him I wanted a happily ever after for everyone. Then again, that ending was something miscon-strued by the various sugarcoated fairytales.

"I want to be in a relationship again, Julia," I admitted with a sigh, "But I want to fall so hard that the person would make me forget how much of an ideal guy my ex-boyfriend was. I want someone who would replace his image whenever somebody asks me who's the perfect man for me."

"What about that Adam?" she poked my side, causing me to jolt up.

Absolutely not, "I'll pass and besides, he's in love with someone else."

Someone who used to love him as every bit as he does. He basically escorted himself to his own heartbreak.

"I believe that you're far prettier than whoever that girl is," she gave me a small encouraging pat on the shoulder, "I'm sure she's no Heart Valentine."

Now would you look at the irony.

"Speaking of the Hollywood's Princess," I coughed to change the topic once again, "Have you seen her in person?"

"You're the one living on the same country as her," she pointed out, "But I went to one of her concerts along with my friends."

"She any good as the tabloids say?"

And then she grinned, her affectionately crooked canines coming into view, "She was better."

With the way her eyes twinkled with excitement, I knew I had an answer for a question I didn't even know I was asking, "Her voice is amazing, I could never imagine hearing some-one who could reach the high notes she sings and the way she could make the pitch of her voice change is spectacular. Not only that, she's a class A beauty."

Adam, I don't even want to figure out the heartbreak you openly led yourself to. He could have had the perfect girlfriend by now, someone who would give him her attention while being a gorgeous being.

The more I found out about her, the more I wanted to scream at him for wasting such an opportunity.

Though if I did that, I had to criticize myself as well. I already had the best guy in the world and yet, I let him go.

"Idiot," I unintentionally murmured to myself. Julia snapped her head towards my direction and I shrugged lightly, silently gesturing to her that it was nothing.

You know, I allowed my prejudice to reign over when it came to her. When I stood up and grabbed my shopping bags again, I gave her a soft smile. Maybe now, I might actually look forward to coming back to my dorm instead of locking myself up.

"I know you're uncomfortable with me and Meg," she mentioned, taking a step forward so she could stop my walk, "But even so, I have this hunch that we will get along."

"And what makes you think that?" I raised a brow.

"Because you can't possibly write like that and not be a good person," she smiled softly, "You wrote from your heart, so impossibly pure and I could feel the love and pain that you did just by reading your work."

After that, she shifted her body so she was back at my side before looping our arms together and practically skipping on her way, dragging me along. My grip on her tightened and that was when I realized that it could be a start of an amazing friendship.

Because she saw the good in something bitter and like her perspective of me, there was no way that someone like that could not be a good person.

That evening, after dinner and everything, we were all tucked into our beds because tomorrow was already the first day of classes. Julia was sleeping peacefully from the other side of the room while I was busy scrolling through my phone, trying to find it in me to find sleep.

I paused when I saw a picture uploaded by my roommate herself. It was in one of the stores earlier, multiple shopping bags in our arms and we posed playfully in front of a dressing room mirror.

With a huge smile on my face, I saved the picture and locked the device, placing it on my bedside table. We've decided to let the window remain open with the curtains closed, it resulted with the cloth flapping about with the wind but its striking sound coupled with the whistling whisper of the breeze, it was the perfect symphony to lull me into slumber.

The next thing I knew, Meg was shaking my body in order to wake me up. Rubbing my eyes, I saw a clearer view of her enthusiastic features, "Come on, let's go down and get breakfast before our first lesson."

I sat up and looked around the room, I could hear the birds chirping loudly from outside. Julia was still fast asleep since her class didn't start for another two hours. Meg told me to get ready and said that she would be waiting for me downstairs.

Normally, I would have taken a shower first but it was a communal bathroom and judging from the amount of ladies rushing in and out with their wet hair and clad in only their bathrobes and towels, I was guessing that there was an extremely minimal chance that I could squeeze myself in there and be ready on time.

So with a promise to myself that I'll head back right after my class, I changed out of my pajamas and tied my messy hair into a bun. I made sure my side of the room was tidy so my roommate wouldn't get a heart attack at the sight of it when she wakes up before I promptly descended down the stairs towards the dining hall.

Meg waved her arms furiously from one of the tables and I gestured back as I grabbed myself a piece of toast and a ladleful of soup. We had a good thirty minutes left and the walk wasn't that long so I considered this an opportunity to take my time, "So you and Julia had fun yesterday?"

I looked up from my meal and nodded briefly, "Yeah, and how was your chat with your boyfriend?"

It was in that moment did I realize that this was the first-time Meg and I've been alone without Julia. She was the tying force between us three, she was the one who kept up with Meg's useless chatters while mystically inserting me into the conversation with ease.

"Perfect," she grinned, nibbling on her toast, "This is the first time we've tried doing long-distance so I don't want a lack of communication to be the reason for us to break up."

Well, at least she was on the right track. For me, there were two elements of a relationship – trust and that cutesy feeling you get in your chest, as sickening as it sounded. What brings them together is communication, it was the foundation that removes any kind of doubt and misconception that ultimately leads to ugly fights and a horrible break up.

And it holds off any assumption that you create.

"Are you in a relationship?" she suddenly questioned and I didn't know it was possible for someone to choke while sipping on soup, but I did and I started to lose myself to a coughing fit. A concerned look graced her face and I waved it off while gulping a half of my glass of water as I told her to explain herself further, "How about that boy who visited you the other day?"

"Adam," I informed shortly after I've managed to regain my breath, "And there's no way, I'm still trying to get over my last one."

She blinked at me twice before her eyes widened as if a lightbulb appeared right on top of her head, "Is it the guy from your book?"

Shutting my eyelids and taking a deep breath, I felt like I was transported back to the cafeteria in my old high school. The chatter among the girls also residing in this dormitory faded into the noise of rowdy teenagers all competing for their voice to rise above the others.

Two tables away from where I sat, he was there with his goofy smile and crooked glasses. When he stood up and seemingly made his way towards us, he plopped down on the space next to me but his focus was on my other friend.

But he grabbed my attention and when I teasingly tugged on the sleeve of his jacket to tell him that I wanted to be included in the conversation, he chuckled and made a dis-gruntled face as a joke. We shared a laugh, me with my short hair that stuck all over the place and him with that lopsided grin.

Our laughter blended in with the rest of our group and it was as if we made that small corner of the cafeteria our own kingdom.

It may have already been a few months into freshman year but it was just the start to the four-year ride that we were about to enter.

"Sienna?" she called out and I snapped out of my thoughts, my mouth hanging open to find the words. She glanced towards her wristwatch before she released a sigh, "It's best for us to start walking towards the building, don't you think?"

"Yes," my gaze then went to my unfinished breakfast, "And that's my answer to both of your questions."

Chapter 9

Wꟷe all sat in the lecture hall, Meg constantly fidgeting in her seat with an impressive lineup of pens and pencils in front of her. I glanced towards my laptop and a ripped piece of paper that I asked from one of her notebooks before shrugging.

I wasn't concerned much and the number one reason why was the person who suddenly strolled into the room, calling the attention of every student, "Good morning everybody."

Meg shook my arm in order to turn my focus towards the front nd I resisted the urge to laugh when I watched my own uncle write his name on the whiteboard, "I'm Mr. Levi Kingsley and I'll be in charge of this class for the term."

"Can you believe we have a first-class author as our professor?" she barely contained a squeal, her gaze fixated on the man that I couldn't take seriously as he droned on in front. It was weird, when I was three, he was covered in mud because he spent all afternoon playing with me, my brother, and our cousins but he still danced around in our living room, much to mom's chagrin. When I was seven, he came for the holidays and busted through the door in a Santa Clause costume, complete with the itchy beard and a pillow stuffed under his shirt to imitate a bulging belly. When I was twelve, he stood in the kitchen with us and attempted to make brownies, which ultimately led to all of us spilling flour everywhere.

Those were the little things that eluded the public's attention since he brought up such a serious image. He may be a professor to the university, he may be a best-selling author to the world, but to me, he was still the same Uncle Levi who knows how to be childish and fun while being an excellent mentor.

"So as you expect, you'll be writing throughout this class," he crossed his arms over his chest, his eyes consciously making an effort not to meet mine, "And at the end of the term, you're going to pass a short story made by yourself as your last project. It's worth thirty percent of your grade so I suggest not to submit anything out of dillydallying."

Meg nodded vigorously, jotting it all down on her notebook. I proceeded to open the small draft of the story I was currently writing before I felt a small frown conquer my face. Yes, I might be on track with my book now, but this class will force me to create a new one.

I wonder how I will be able to go through with my classes. Mom did say that it was an opportunity for a change of scenery, but I guess studying was something I was anticipating but was never really prepared myself for.

The gap year I took was enough to put me off out of the concept of staying late at night with a textbook or investing my heart and soul for projects that wouldn't really matter in the grand scheme of things.

I opened my bag and drew out a novel, a silhouette of a man in front of a hazy yellow background was flashed as the cover and at the very below was Uncle Levi's name along with the title #1 New York Times Bestselling Author.

If you do anything without passion, it loses its meaning. Will and the right motivation are the two things that needs to work in order to produce anything near importance. Once you've acquired your initial goal, it's not the moment to stop, but rather, to find a new one.

And, my dear, if your goal is for you to be well-known then prepare for a life wherein you keep chasing for something impossible. There would always be someone who wouldn't recognize you, who would simply pass by your name without a mere sparkle in their eyes. The real goal you should be chasing is satisfaction and with the ideal thought of fame constantly running in your mind, you'll never be happy.

Time flew by quickly and after one last explanation from Uncle Levi, he dismissed the class. We gathered all of our belongings and I was prepared to go back to the dormitory since I had some free time while Meg had another class right after, "I'll see you."

I nodded and waved her goodbye, waiting for the last student to leave the lecture hall. Uncle Levi beckoned for me to go to the front and I did so, leaving my bag on my seat. He placed a sleek new phone on my palm and smiled, "Sorry it took so long."

"At least I have a phone now," I laughed, turning to go back to my seat. Before I could take a single step though, I paused my movements when I saw his book still sitting on my desk, "Uncle Levi, why did you start to write?"

Julia question rang in my head and my reply was still hanging in my mind. However, I was just one in the million others who use perfectly constructed sentences to convey their thoughts. Why does a person write? For others, it was because it was their job. For some it was a simple hobby. But for all, it was because there was a message that they needed to let out.

"Why?" he repeated, now gathering his things, "I started writing because my teacher from high school complimented a story I submitted to her."

"So you did it to be praised?"

"The glory and the fame," he corrected, "But it changed when I realized that if I were to use those two as my drive, every story that I will create would be empty, and you know why?"

I took a deep breath and quoted his own book to him, "The real goal you should be chasing is satisfaction and with the ideal thought of fame constantly running in your mind, you'll never be happy."

Recognizing his own writing, a bright grin flashed on his face, "Correct once again."

"Do you think that you made the right choice by turning writing into a career?" I continued to ask, following him out of the room after snatching my bag and laptop, "Wasn't it better to just treat is as a hobby."

"Not really," he shrugged, "I met my wife because of this and it gave me your two cousins so I guess it was the best choice."

A man found love through writing while I was doing my best to get rid of it through the same medium.

"Got it," I muttered, stopping right before we turned the corner, "I'll see you next class, Mr. Kingsley."

He shook his head with a small smile, continuing his walk towards the next hallway while I made my way towards the exit. Before I could reach far, somebody tapped me on the shoulder, causing me to jump up in shock. I spun around quickly to meet Adam's towering figure and I released a sigh of relief.

"Don't do that!" I groaned, taking a step back, "Headed for class?"

"Sorry," he grinned sheepishly, "And mine just finished, I'm about to go out and grab some breakfast, care to join me?"

Although I had breakfast, it was unfinished and I barely touched half of it so I was still fairly hungry. My next class didn't start for another hour and a half plus, I kind of enjoy his company. I agreed to his offer and we found ourselves at the same small restaurant Uncle Levi took me on my first day here.

We sat on the table where the couple that we created a fake backstory of once occupied. And just like them, we were met with silence and the only difference, it wasn't comfortable nor was it awkward. I couldn't place it, I wanted to speak in order to fill the air between us but I found no topic. We already talked about our first classes on the way here and after we've bantered about which food we were going to order, we had nothing else to say.

But I wasn't totally fidgeting in my seat.

"Somebody from my class invited me to this party they're having for the start of term," he mentioned when I was wracking my brain up for a subject, "I was wondering if you want to go?"

Finally!

"I would love to," I accepted graciously. I haven't been to a real party in quite a while and I realized that I was so detached from everybody else since most of my friends went on their way to different colleges. During the rare times that we were all gathered at the same city, we opted to have a quiet movie night or something instead of a rowdy music-filled, lousy excuse to have sex, kind of evening.

Don't get me wrong, I loved hanging out with them in any form, but I longed to have the same kind of craziness I experienced back when I was in high school.

Those moments when you would scream at the top of your lungs because the music was playing too loud, people were mingling even with those they have never talked to, and at the end, you had to sneak into home because you knew your parents were going to be livid once they found out.

"Great, I'll pick you up at eight," he told me, sipping his coffee.

My eyes lit up before I started digging through my bag and taking out my new phone from it, "I finally got one so I can give you my number. That removes the trek towards my dorm and the commotion the girls are likely to make."

"Not going to ask for mine?" he chuckled when he gave me his device.

I glanced up from tapping on his screen and shook my head, "You gave it to me already, remember?"

The scribbled number on a torn-up piece of cardboard was safely tucked inside my drawer, just waiting for it to be punched in.

He flashed me a wider grin, thankful that I didn't forget about it. We finished the rest of the meal in silence, only this time, it was more enjoyable. He insisted that he pay for my meal but I was adamant on paying for it on my own. He didn't fight with me on this one and we went onto different paths, with me heading towards my second class of the day.

Apparently, many were going to the same party because when I came back to the dorm after a long day, Julia jumped up and invited me to go. When I told her I already said to Adam that I was going with him, it was the worst decision I've made for the past twenty-four hours.

Just saying, I don't raise my standards that high because I make horrible decisions on a daily basis.

"You have a date," she hopped off of her bed and went to my side, opening my closet and quickly digging through my clothes.

"How many times do I have to say that he and I are just friends?" I groaned before lifting a brow at her antics, "And what are you doing?"

"You're just friends for now," she pointed out, grabbing a black dress, "Try this on."

"No," I huffed, taking a dress from her grasp and putting it back on the hanger, "And I don't want to look like the overexcited freshman that got invited to her first uni party."

"Then throw on a denim jacket and call it casual," she shrugged, sitting on my bed, "But I'm calling it a date."

Rolling my eyes, I closed my closet and shook my head, "It's not."

"Watch as he goes on and picks you up with flowers or something to impress you and then even if his friends call him, he would choose to stay with you," she smirked, "And then if he's really trying hard, he'll ask you to escape the party and go to a twenty-four hour food place to have your alone time together."

Sheesh, I thought I was the one who made up the stories between us.

"Very funny," I muttered sarcastically, "And it's not a date because he's completely in love with somebody else."

A tall and blonde superstar that nobody can compete with.

"If you say so," she sang as she stood up and grabbed my arm, "Let's get supper before you say some other excuse."

The week rolled around fairly quickly since most of the classes were filled with introductions. Friday came around and even though I initially refused, I went with the dress Julia suggested and paired it with a denim jacket. I waited for Adam's text that he was on his way so I could start walking so we could meet halfway.

Imagine my surprise when Julia came bounding in with a large smirk on her face, "Told you so."

"What?" I asked and she gestured for me to follow her. I took my purse and did so, trying to catch up with her fast pace as we bounded down the stairs. I was taken aback when

I saw Adam standing there at the entrance with a single flower decently wrapped in paper and plastic.

Watch as he goes on and picks you up with flowers or something to impress you.

Turning to my side, I raised my brows at the sight of Julia's victorious expression. She pinched my arm before going back upstairs, her footsteps loud and heavy.

"Passed by the market earlier and saw this," he said when he saw me approaching, "Thought that you might like it."

Alright, so it was not something to impress me or anything, it was just a flower he saw while doing grocery shopping. Julia was wrong and I need to stop my stupid brain from producing any ideas before I fall into this pit with no way of getting out.

"Thank you," I smiled gratefully, "Shall we go now?"

This was not a date, Adam was not interested in me, and there was no freaking way that Julia was right.

Right?

Chapter 10

We entered a shared house filled with students, it was like a scene right out of a movie. If you think high school parties were wild, check out a college frat ones. They were ten times crazier especially if it was the first one of the whole year.

"Adam," somebody called out, a beer in his hand with a wide grin on his face, "Glad you can make it."

"Sienna, this is Vance," he told me, swinging an arm around my shoulder, "He was the one who invited me."

I flashed him a polite smile while trying to keep my cheeks from burning hot because of the close proximity Adam suddenly placed between us, "Thanks for letting me come."

Personal space be damned.

"American," he nodded towards Adam, a silent conversation transpiring between them, "So the boys and I are having a chat upstairs, want to join?"

At one point, I sincerely hope that people would stop making such a big deal of my nationality. I get it, I don't have that accent that most girls from my country goes crazy for, but if I'm going to finish my degree here, then they better be prepared to have this somewhat foreign female walking around. And besides, I'm not the first nor will I be the last foreigner walking through these halls. I've already seen a number of students like me.

"You could go," I told him, subtly trying to pry myself out of his grasp, "I'll be alright."

He pulled me closer, even if that was possible, and rejected Vance's offer, "Thank you but I'm going with Sienna for tonight."

Then even if his friends call him, he would choose to stay with you.

Julia's words once again rung bells inside my head and the red was drained from my face along with the rest of the other colors. My pleas for her to be wrong was starting to scream louder in my mind and my body was now desperate to put a distance.

Because this was not good. If there was one thing my best friend from high school told me, it was that I fall in love too fast and take an excruciating slow time to move on.

And let me tell you, I don't want to fall for a guy pining over his childhood friend while trying to move on from a guy who I've consciously broken up with.

This is wrong, he's wrong, Julia's wrong, and I'm certainly hoping that I'm not.

To make matters worse, my said roommate and Meg walked through the door and when they saw our positions, their jaws dropped and Julia proceeded to shake Meg violently. The latter tried to break free from her grasp but the fact that their eyes were still glued onto us did not change.

Well, crap.

This was escalating to a point where I never imagined it will go to and frankly, I wanted everything to stop. Can't I just have a bottle of beer and call it a night?

"I'm going to get a drink," I attempted once again to wriggle out of his hold. He perked up and finally released me.

"I'll get one for you," he excused himself and Vance tipped his bottle as a goodbye while following Adam to talk about something. Once I was alone, the two girls found their way to my side and Julia was now suggestively wiggling her eyebrows.

"Not a word," I groaned, lifting a hand to stop whatever she was going to say.

But unfortunately, I was only able to halt Julia so Meg was quick to quip, "Not dating?"

I had no idea what was happening as well. Adam usually kept a respectable distance between, he has never touched me out of the blue like that and his aura has shifted as if he was actively trying to pull me closer.

If it was his way of making an impression to Vance, he could have just told and I would have played along with it.

Only one requirement was left in what Julia called as the 'signs of a date' and the moment that it comes, I don't know how I would handle it. Not with a straight face, that was for sure. I would just confront him about the Vance thing and hopefully, we could still have a peaceful night – well, as peaceful as a frat party could go.

"We'll just go and say hi to the guy who invited us," Julia said after I insistently denied Meg's accusation, "Talk to you later."

I nodded and watched as Adam waved to a few people while he made his way back to me. He had only been here for a total of one week and he was living off-campus, yet he still knew a good number of students. Either he met them before college or he was just really that friendly.

Either way, it was the total opposite of me. Aside from Meg and Julia, I never made a conscious effort to befriend anybody during my first week of class. Like I said, I was going to leave here anyways so might as well make less connections.

After what felt like forever, Adam finally managed to get to me, "Here you go."

"Thanks," I spoke, taking one of the two bottles from his grasp. I took a large swig of the alcoholic beverage, my mind begging me to get drunk. I just had this gut feeling that I would rather suffer a hangover tomorrow morning than to remember this night, "So how's it going with Heart?"

Touching the topic of the girl he loves will hopefully steer his thoughts away. However, I didn't get the results I desired and he shrugged in response, "Same as always."

Short and simple, not the one I expected. The way he said it even made it sound like he wanted to drop it right away.

My worries heightened and I downed the whole bottle in one go. He was taken aback by my actions and I excused myself to get another one, my desperation now at its peak.

Near the kitchen, there were a bunch of coolers along with a line of opened beer bottle. I took one, drinking it as fast as I did the last. Adam took my hand before I could reach for my third beer, his head shaking, "What are you doing?"

"Getting drunk," I answered truthfully, "It's a party, I'm supposed to be wobbling when I get out."

"I was planning on asking you out to the twenty-four hour diner near here after an hour but I think that it's best that we go now."

And then if he's really trying hard, he'll ask you to escape the party and go to a twenty-four hour food place to have your alone time together.

Well, shit.

"Can you hold that thought?" I gave him a tightlipped smile and although he appeared hesitant, he nodded and he released me. The moment he did, I grabbed another bottle and kept with the haste pace of consuming the alcohol.

I didn't consider myself a lightweight nor was I a heavyweight so I was fairly in the middle. Three bottles didn't have much effect on me but after chugging it all that fast plus my mental, I was fully submitting to it.

Three more of these and I would be tumbling on my way out. Perhaps then, he'll get away from me and realize how much of a waste of time I was.

Wow, my self-confidence was through the roof.

"Sienna," he stole the bottle I was grabbing and set it back down on the table, "Stop this."

I always tried to escape before anything affected me and in the end, I was the one who breaks my own heart. What right did I have to judge him for letting go somebody he loved when in truth, I did the same? It was a horrible cycle – I assume and when the thought has drilled itself into my mind, I find every possible way to escape it.

No matter how much I say I've changed, I know for myself that I haven't. And honestly, truth is a concept I was so afraid of. I avoid it as much as possible, morph it into my own reality because I'm scared for myself, I never take the risk. I'm not as free-spirited as Emma, I'm not as strong-headed as Andy, and I'm not as determined as my brother.

I'm that average, overthinking, weak Sienna Clark.

I write because reality is horrible, I write because I want to reconstruct events to the way I hoped it will end up in. However, I can't ignore the fact that I also create unhappy endings because I know for myself that trying to get a happily ever after is useless.

All of a sudden, he took my hand and started to pull me away. He was fast and I could barely keep up with my state but I couldn't tell him that I wanted him to slow down because the moment I opened my mouth, a sob escaped my lips and I felt the tears running down my cheeks.

I was crying and that was the reason he wanted to take me away so urgently.

We had nowhere to go except to the front of the sorority that was next door to the frat house. Thankfully, they had a park bench right in front and Adam situated me on it, bathing us in silence while he waited patiently for me to calm down.

"Sorry," I apologized, running a hand gently across my face, "Must be the alcohol mixing up my emotions."

"I don't think that's all," he told me, looking at me in the eyes. He searched for it, the same thing that got me crying – the ugly truth.

He wanted to find what was it and sadly for him, he wouldn't find it because even I didn't know what it was. There was no reason for me to tear up, but that was the thing that I was doing. And you know what hits me the most? He was also here with me.

The man I met last week and we were both here because of some silly implication that my roommate made.

What broke our trance was not the sudden crash coming from the party nearby, but the loud ringing of his phone that made him fumble around to search for the device. He looked at the screen and showed me Heart's picture with her name flashing on the screen, "Go answer it, I'm alright."

He had a look that showed that he didn't want to leave me alone but I gestured for him to go on. He excused himself and placed a distance between us and I used this opportunity to compose myself. Grabbing my purse, I dug for my compact mirror and cringed at my reflection – my nose was red and my eyes were puffy.

I tried to cover as much as I could with makeup but I could do so little with what I had. I glanced towards Adam and contemplated on telling him that it was best that we should start heading back. He was still invested on his phone call so I had second doubts.

How could he still be so close to her?

I mean, when I broke up with my ex, I asked him to still be friends. Of course, that was just to diffuse the tension during that moment. Remaining friends was indeed easier said than done.

Did I cry bucketloads? Hell yeah I did.

Did I show him how pathetically broken I was? It was a solid nope.

Standing up and dusting down my dress, I made cautious steps towards him and when I was in earshot, I accidentally heard bits of their conversation.

"Soph, stop worrying about me and I promise you'll meet Sienna," he said and I slowed down when he mentioned my name, "I tried going on a date with her like you said but we've ran into some complications."

A dozen butterflies entered my stomach and a red blush crept to my cheeks when I found out that this was in fact a date. Julia was completely right, my worrying wasn't for nothing, and I couldn't believe that this was happening.

But he still loves Heart, right? Where was the lie here?

"I only did this to stop you from pestering me," he chuckled lightheartedly, effectively making my heart sink, "I'm going to take her home and you take care over there."

So all of this was just to satisfy the Hollywood's Princess?

He outright stated that he invited me not because he wanted my company or whatnot, but because Heart told him to. I was just a pawn in this messed up game he wanted to play. And you know what? I should have been angry and threw a fit right there and then, I had every right to do so.

But I was so mortified that I couldn't do anything.

Sienna Clark, what happened to your spirit? It was becoming dull.

When he turned around, he was surprised to see me so close and I knew he was ready to fire a large apology. None of which I wanted to hear at this moment.

"I'm going back to the party and enjoy it with Julia as well as Meg," I managed to say with as much dignity as I could, "Thank you for this evening."

He reached out and tried to stop me but I snatched my hand away before he could. I shook my head and turned, walking back to the fraternity house with my bottom lip shaking so much that I had to bite it to stop.

I didn't stay true to my word because instead of looking for my roommate, I headed straight towards the kitchen and at the long lineup of beer bottles. The anger and sadness were bubbling up inside me, threatening to spill and I needed something to push it back down into my system.

I drank and drank, losing count of how many bottles I picked up and chugged down. Thankfully, Julia and Meg managed to spot me when I was on the brink of sinking down to the ground and crawling my way to find them.

I've gathered quite a crowd because there was this insane girl in the kitchen just consuming their whole stock of beers in one go.

With each girl supporting my sides, we trudged back to my dorm and when I fell into my bed, I started crying.

They were at complete loss on what to do and I couldn't remember much of what happened right after. All I knew was when I woke up, I had this throbbing headache but a glass of water was already there on my bedside table. I glanced towards Julia who was still fast asleep and I sent a silent thank you as I gulped it all down.

I checked my phone and just as I predicted, multiple messages and phone calls from Adam went through.

Oh so now you use my number when you could have called me last night before the party and allowed me to meet you halfway so this huge mess wouldn't have escalated this big.

I opened my browser and searched for his name online and multiple results came through – all pertaining to Heart Valentine.

There were so many paparazzi shots of the two of them, showing just how close they really were. If I didn't know better, I would have assumed as well that they were a couple. But I observed carefully their body language through a candid video I saw of them.

They were exiting some formal event, both were dressed up to the nines but the way they walked said a lot. They were near each other, arm in arm even, but there was a distance. If I wasn't so pissed off and being a sad blob over here, I would have laughed at the tango they were seemingly playing.

When Heart took a step towards him, he would subtly move farther away and when he would try to make a move, she was frigid.

They both liked each other here and it showed with the way they interacted but their actions screamed that they were afraid.

Screw them.

"Sienna?" I heard my roommate's voice and I looked up. She was now awake and was staring at me with a concerned look. I flashed her a small smile to reassure her, swinging my body so I could go down my bed but any sudden movements made my head spin, "Careful, I know Meg's roommate has some painkillers."

"Thanks," I groaned, clutching my poor head, "And I'm sorry for last night."

"Don't be," she soothed, standing up and walking over to me, "You can talk to me if you want."

"Maybe after breakfast," I tried to laugh but my brain felt like it was flopping around in my skull.

She was still worried, it was written all over her face, but she nodded and helped me go down. Meg brought over a bottle of painkillers when she went to our table and never have I been grateful for her meddlesome nature.

The girls tried their best to make sure my mind was preoccupied with thoughts other than the party. Which wasn't that hard to do since I could barely remember what happened.

But when my phone lit up, I was ready to reject the call because I thought that I was Adam again. When I did glance at the screen, all drained from my face when I saw who was the one actually trying to contact me.

Him.

It felt like somebody dumped a whole bucket of cold water over my head. My mind, my poor mind who went through hell and back last night, had to process what was happening.

You know what they say, when the mind goes off, the heart takes over.

And my heart craved for him.

With a shaking hand, I accepted the call and slowly brought it up to my ear, "Hello?"

My voice was thick and I felt like something was jammed in my throat. I haven't heard from him for over a year and now, I wanted to faint.

"Sienna?" he questioned as if he was unsure. Still, his voice wrapped me up in warmth, embracing me in a way I desperately wanted to be last night, "Sorry I couldn't understand anything that you said at three in the morning."

Three in the morning?!

"What?" I gaped, getting the attention of Julia and Meg.

"You did call, right?"

I dropped the phone onto the table and shot up to my feet, taking a huge step back as if the device suddenly turned into a venomous snake.

What did I do last night?

Chapter 11

"What's wrong?" Meg asked when I didn't move, "You look like you've seen a ghost."

I was afraid that I was going to turn into one.

"What time did you manage to drag me out of the party last night?" I questioned, taking calming breaths but still refusing to sit down.

"About half past ten or maybe it was eleven, why?" Julia answered and I quickly did the math inside my head. There was more or less a five-hour time difference between here and there so if I think about it now, it meant that I called him at ten.

I know for a fact that these two brought me home the minute they saw me so that meant that I called him up when I was darn busy downing those beers. Also meaning that there was not a single person who could tell me what stupidity I've told him.

The wisest thing to do here was to go call him back and apologize for whatever I blabbered about. I was wholly prepared to do it when my phone rang again and I was expecting it to be him. I took an exaggerated deep breath, mentally preparing myself. However, when I peeked at the screen, it was flashing an unknown number.

Look at this, it's only eight in the morning and nothing has been going as they expected.

I answered it, waiting for the caller to speak out with a hopeful feeling that I might recognize them from their voice. I didn't need to play 'guess who?' since the person already introduced herself the minute I said hello, "Hi, this is Heart Valentine."

My heart started racing and I was torn apart with either being scared shitless or being completely starstruck.

Because if you have Hollywood's Princess calling you directly, you should be jumping up and down speechless with excitement, but that's not the case when you're stuck in the situation wherein you're in an argument with her beloved best friend.

Even if you were mostly the victim here.

Meg and Julia were still looking at me and I quickly excused myself, practically sprinting out of the dining hall and up to my room. Heart was quiet for most of the way, waiting for me to speak and although that was polite of her, I could barely talk so she might as well hang up.

Dear universe, help me get through this.

Sensing that I've chosen to become mute for this conversation, I heard her release a heavy sigh, "I just want to apologize for what happened last night with you and Adam."

Again, she waited for my reply but I didn't provide her with one so she kept talking, "I don't know how much Adam told you about me but I love him, whether that is just as a best friend or more is up to you."

I was well aware that she loved him more than as a friend. So completely aware that I was regretting every single damn day since I got on that airplane.

"And when he told me about you, he was so excited and I assumed that he likes you," she said, "And I pushed him to make a move and him being Adam, complied just to satisfy my meddling."

And there I heard the deep-seeded affection she held for him. She was thankful that he was like that and at the same time, she wanted the very best out of him. She wanted his happiness, just as much as he wanted hers. She cares for him, she wouldn't be calling me right now if she didn't.

Now I had the answer to the excruciating question that I had for them: Why were they still close? It was because unlike my relationship with my ex, theirs was strong and withstanding and was bounded through time with trust and mutual understanding. May it be friendship or romantic love, the exchange between them was equal. They know that something like a confession of wanting more than being best friends shouldn't break off the greatest thing they shared.

Compared to them, my past relationship sounded so shallow and immature.

"I understand," I murmured, surprising us both that I actually said something.

Because Adam did it because he wanted her to smile and she did it because of the same reason towards him.

"Take care of Adam for me," her tone was almost pleading, a wish of a vow in her voice, "He's my best friend."

And she was strong to keep being somebody so close to him after he rejected her. I was jealous actually, because she didn't give up.

"Yes," quick replies were the only things that I could manage to say and with one last thank you, she dropped the call and I was left staring at my phone.

And even so I kind of promised her that, I think it would be best for me to just cut off all ties and save myself from any further harm. I never signed myself up for this, it just so happened to be that the guy who sat next to me on the plane was not some ordinary man.

I understood why they did what they did, but that did not excuse them for using me like that. I was a person too, somebody who was on the road to being the better version themselves just as they were. They had zero right to treat me like that.

You love each other? Don't do it at the expense of other people.

I grabbed my bag and pulled out Uncle Levi's sketchbook, roughly flipping it over to the pages where I wrote in. Funny enough, it had my small and short adventures with Adam in it as well my rumbling emotions when they happened.

Grabbing all the pages, I tore them all away and crumpled them into one big sphere, clutching it in my hands and taking deep breaths so I wouldn't turn into a sobbing mess once again.

"He's here, by the way," Julia knocked on the door softly and I instantly knew who she was referring to. She saw the sketchbook sitting on my lap and the torn pages clutched in my hands. Her eyebrows knitted together to show concern and I swallowed heavily while shaking my head, silently telling her not to ask.

I think she knew from the moment she saw me alone at the party, without my supposed date and drunk out of mind, that something happened between Adam and I. She was being cautious though, she didn't pry or any of that sort.

I stood from my seat on my bed and walked towards the stairs with her following me. I don't know whether he sent Heart to apologize or not but I've given up on my mission to find out.

Being fooled once was enough for me.

When I saw him there at the entrance hall, we didn't say a word to each other. We just stared with this silence and instead of starting a conversation in here where anybody could eavesdrop, I went past him and opened the door, walking out of the dormitory.

I could hear his footsteps behind me and stopped when we were at an adequate distance from everybody else.

I noticed something in his hand and he lifted it up to reveal my book, he flipped it open and read the lines that I, myself, have written, "The thing I regret the most was not fighting for something I knew that could work out if I tried a little harder. He was already there, all I had to do was to stretch my arm a little further."

Quoting your own work to yourself, now I know what Uncle Levi felt.

He closed the book and gaze right up to me, "You're already there, all I have to do is stretch my arm a little further.

"I wouldn't recommend it," I shook my head as I took another step back, "I haven't taken a shower yet and I still reek of alcohol."

The tension was so evident that my coping mechanism was to make a joke about this. Not the greatest idea but my brain was barely functioning in the first place, the hangover may have suddenly left because of the adrenaline rush earlier during my first phone call of the day, but I've barely eaten, I haven't taken any painkillers, and my body was still screaming at me to go back to bed.

"I'm sorry, Sienna," he told me, knocking himself on the head, "I did a very dumb move."

I looked at him and then I felt the crunching papers in my hand, causing my shoulders to slump in sadness. Taking a deep breath, I closed my mouth shut and approached him, taking his hand then placing the papers on top of his palm, closing his fingers around it, "Throw it or whatever, I don't care anymore."

His eyebrows scrunched up in confusion as he uncrumpled the papers and tried to smoothen it out with his hands, paying close attention to the writing so he could decipher it. When he figured it out, his eyes glanced up to show me this expression of disbelief. He scrambled around with his words, "Sienna... don't please. Be angry with me, but this is your work."

This was not some dramatic breakup, there was never an us and we never had a shot for a relationship because we didn't like each other.

I snuck my hands in-between his to feel the paper under my skin and as I closed my eyes, I ripped the pages apart, my heart tearing up with it.

"Have a good day," I showed him a tightlipped smile, walking around him and heading back to my dorm. He called my name but I ignored it, willing my legs to go faster.

So when I got back, I took a well-deserved shower and I wanted to stop Meg and Julia from their worrying looks so I plastered a grin on my face and tried to act cheery, "Hey, want to eat out for lunch then maybe let's go clubbing later tonight?"

"I know a pub nearby," Meg raised her hand but Julia shot her down by an incredulous look.

"I think we should stop with the alcohol for now."

"Fine," I groaned, grabbing my phone, "I'll sleep over at my cousin's tonight, if you don't mind."

Fortunately, Uncle Levi had already saved his, Aunt Janine's, Emma's, and Andy's numbers into the device before handing it over to me. I called up Emma and asked her if I could stay and she eagerly agreed, mentioning how it had been a while since we had a sleepover.

I packed a bag, told our dorm mother that I would be leaving, and said goodbye to the two before heading my way. The chances of me bumping into Adam were high, considering that they were neighbors, but as long as I kept an eye out,

I can stay away from any unexpected circumstances that I desperately wanted to avoid.

When I was near, I texted Emma so she could wait for me at the lobby and I was met with an embrace then we proceeded to go to their apartment.

"It's just me for a few hours," she said as we entered, closing the door behind her, "Dad is at the university, mum is at work, and Andy is off to who knows where."

I spotted her easel at the edge of the living room, a canvas perched on it. She excused herself to grab us both a drink while I walked closer to her work.

It was unfinished but it already showed what she wanted to portray. There was a bridge and a river underneath, reflecting a burst of colors blended perfectly. On top of the bridge showed the silhouette of two people, they were at different ends but if you turn back to the river, their figures were now close to each other, their hands intertwined.

"River Future," I heard her say, approaching me and handing me a glass of soda, "That's its name."

"Can I ask why?"

She smiled and grabbed a long paintbrush, using the tip to point towards the different elements of the painting, "Something is different with that river, it's colorful which will be a contrast with the sky that I'm going to paint."

For now, the top of the canvas sass just a clumsy layer of dark hues so I assume that was where she left off before she came and got me, "And these two, they don't know each other yet and they're unaware of each other's existence but this river shows that at some point, they're going to fall in love."

"You're incredible Emma," I murmured, bending in order to get a closer look, "I don't know how you do it."

"I only got an inspiration after I finished dad's book cover," she went over to the other canvases leaning against the wall and took one in her hands, flashing to me her painting of a man in the middle of an explosion of paints as if she just took a large brush and went loose. At first, you wouldn't think much, but in fact, it showed how much vibrancy Uncle Levi's story might portray, how all of those colors surround the main lead.

A fact not known to others was that Emma has designed all of her father's and brother's book covers since she learned about her passion for art. The first one she ever did was just a simple umbrella in front of a red background. It was minimalist but soon, it became louder and louder. They were a team, she worked around his words while he'll be so ambiguous that she has freedom of interpretation that would allow her own mind to express itself in the most beautiful ways.

And the results were always spectacular.

"How's is it going with your story?" she questioned, placing the canvas back against the wall, "Any progress."

"I've decided to start again," I spoke, sitting down on the couch, "Because I wasn't really feeling it."

She raised her brows, seeing right through my flimsy excuse, "What's the real reason?"

Trust Emma to see right through me. Seriously, I never get to take a break. Back home, my brother had a keen eye so he instantly knew what was wrong. Then we have her here, not even humoring me by biting into my bullshit.

"Some things are not worth writing," I sighed, twisting the glass in my hands, "Even if they tell you that it is."

Adam was the one who gave me inspiration for the new story I was writing but it turns out, he would be the one to stamp The End to an adventure that was only beginning.

"Is it that Adam you introduced me to?" she asked, knowing me all too well. There was a reason why I was so close to her, more than I was to Andy. She understood me before I could even utter a single word, "You like him?"

"No!" I responded way louder than I meant to. She slightly flinched at the strong denial that I suddenly displayed and I placed the glass on the coffee table as I cleared my throat, "I mean, I don't."

Impossible, I've only known him for two weeks tops so I couldn't. And in any event that I did like him, it would be futile because he loves someone else.

Someone who has seemingly moved on faster than he did.

Along with that, I still haven't gotten over my ex. He was the one I called when I was drunk and out of my mind, wasn't that a signal that I was still clearly into him? It wasn't just a drunk text, but an actual call and I couldn't even remember any part of the conversation plus I'm too scared to confront him.

Wait a minute.

I shot up from my seat and went to my bag, digging for my phone to check my messages. Sure enough, he was there on the very top of my list. So I did message him before or after that call.

With my hand thinking on its own, I tapped on the conversation and my shoulders slumped when there was only one message. When it showed in the preview, I thought it was the end for a long exchange of words, but in fact, it was the only word I sent.

Goodbye.

My head slowly tilted up and Emma was now staring at me, confused and worried at the same time. I opened my mouth as the realization sunk in, "I wanted to let go."

Chapter 12

My heart was thumping in my chest, my eyes staring at my phone screen while it tried to connect to the person I was trying to contact through a video call. I was all alone, Emma gave me her room when I told her what I was planning to do while she finished her painting downstairs.

The amount of times I started ringing him and then ending it right away was too high. The coward in me wants to think that he didn't call again so that was it, but a bigger part of me is yelling that I will never go forward unless I face him.

And suddenly, the screen turned black and what came after was the face I've only managed to see in pictures for the past year. His eyebrows were still bushy and over the place, his hair now up in spikes, his glasses covered his eyes that always crinkled at the corner at any expression he makes, and that melting gaze – he gained weight, not too drastic but it was noticeable, though it didn't matter.

"Justin," I said his name after I've avoided speaking it for a long time, "Hey."

He was just as awkward as I was, not even finding the right words to say. This demeanor of his was the reason I started falling, "Hi Sienna."

My name rolled off of his lips and I was suddenly transported back to the time he would gently whisper it to me before pressing a kiss on my lips. Even if we were currently miles apart, I could almost feel his skin under my fingertips and how ticklish he was even with the lightest touch.

That dance we shared on prom night, it was quiet and we barely made eye contact but when he did, I apologized. He accepted it with an apology of his own, but when I thought we finally made up, he released my hands and walked away after saying that he was going to look for his best friend. Although I didn't buy his excuse, I allowed him to leave.

On graduation, I was never able to say goodbye.

The only time we went near to talking was when I accidentally sent him a message meant for my other friend.

Alright, so maybe I meant to do it a tiny bit.

One part of my book that I couldn't reread was the chapter wherein I walked away and never looked back. I could remember how I dug my nails into my palm and asked him if we could break up, when I turned on one corner and was sure that he couldn't see me anymore, I wept like a baby.

All we shared after that were civil smiles and a hard game of seeing how long can we sit in the same room as we ignored each other.

I've heard that he was still as flirty as he was before we started dating, but he never took a step forward and got himself a girlfriend. It made me hope, thinking that he wanted to be with me again, but when he made no move, it came clear that all my thoughts were just a fantasy.

"Sorry for last night," even though I tried to sound light-hearted, my throat felt like it was sandpaper, "You know how I am with alcohol."

He doesn't because I never really drank except for a few sips here and there. I started to do it in senior year, weeks leading to our separation.

"I was surprised," he told me and I was aware how much I was surrounded by people with differing accents. Although Uncle Levi didn't talk like how everybody in this country does, his use of the slang and language were there and there was a tinge of influence coming from Aunt Janine with his manner of speech. This was home, this was the accent I grew up on, "I mean, Sienna Clark called me, I thought I was dreaming."

You and I both.

"I heard you're in England now," he brought up, "I never thought you would be leaving the country."

I never thought of it as well. I assumed back then during junior year that we would be attending the same college, it was a norm for high school sweethearts to think so. It didn't cross my mind the possibility of us splitting, resulting in me writing a book in my desperation to get him out of my head, and the lack of inspiration during my gap year.

Uncle Levi did me the biggest favor but now I was starting to doubt if everything was ever a good idea.

"Can I just ask you one question?" I muttered, my hand now gripping the sheets of Emma's bed, "What did I say to you?"

"You don't remember?" he gaped and when I stared at him unblinking, he got his answer. Telling me to wait, he put down his phone and I heard rustling from his side. My hand loosened and my fingers resorted to tapping lightly on her bedside table, thinking of the worst.

And when he came back, I didn't know how to react because he pointed the camera right towards a book – not just any book.

It was our story, "You kept telling me to buy it and read the thing."

It felt like the end of the world because yes, it wasn't that accurate since I did sprinkle some other drama in there to make it more interesting and I did change the character names but one look and he would know. Because those jokes that were so corny but made me laugh hilariously were written down there, those times when we snuck our hands together when eating with our friends was vividly described, and don't get me started with those private moments that I unabashedly wrote.

I wanted to end the call now but I willed myself to continue, "Did you read it yet?"

"If I said yes, what will you do?" he questioned, turning the camera back to his face. The answer was simple – nothing.

There was nothing that I could do and there was nothing I would do. All this time, I wanted him to read it, the fear of his criticism was just pulling me back.

When I didn't verbally convey my answer, he frowned slightly before reply almost apologetically, "Yes, I read it."

"I'm sorry," was the only thing I managed to say. It was a violation of our privacy but I'm a writer, I draw my inspiration from the life I live and this is reality – I broke my own heart.

Stupid, I know.

Now he has read my side of our story, of how much I didn't want to let go but I was too weak to do so. He now knew that I didn't fall in love with him like a smack of a speeding train, it was gradual and it was the little things that got me to do so.

"No, it's my fault for not paying attention to the signs," he sighed, running a hand through his hair, something that I chastised him for doing so many times, "But I really did love you, Sienna."

I blinked at my screen, his brown eyes piercing through me. I knew he did, he had told me so many times. Yet to hear it from him, after a couple of years, felt like a huge weight was suddenly lifted off of my shoulders and a ghost of a smile graced my lips, "And I really did love you, Justin."

And there we were, it was like we were in the middle of the field again. He grabbed my hand when I was peacefully enjoying a chat with the rest of our friends and he pulled me with him, my legs barely catching up with him. Still, I laughed along with the breeze, thinking that it was just one of his games.

We stopped when we were out of earshot and that was when he confessed, asking me out on our first date. The answer was a yes, it had always been a yes.

Because I was his before he even knew about it.

"Want to try it again?" he suggested, rendering me speech-less. The me a year ago would have jumped into this oppor-tunity without a second thought.

However, I did say goodbye. This was not the purpose of the call.

"No," I rejected, shaking my head, "And you know why."

Because it just wasn't our time.

He showed me a smile and let out a chuckle, "I really do."

"Friends?" I shrugged, "For real this time, no extreme politeness that it makes me cringe."

"Friends," he agreed, "Give me a call when you're back in New York, let's hang out like old times."

Getting cramped in the subway, running around the busy sidewalks, spending a crazy amount of money on useless things, being surrounded with tall buildings, and enjoying the most beautiful skyline during the night. Those were the things I dearly missed with my friends back at home and sad to say, I wouldn't be able to do them again until Christmas.

"Yeah," I grinned, my heart now singing with joy, "You'll be the first one to know."

We ended the call in the opposite direction of how we started it. At first, it was so uncomfortable as if the both of us wanted to scream out at each other but now, we've managed to resolve a problem that droned on for so long in a span of minutes.

When I got back downstairs after the conversation, Emma looked up from her canvas and exhaled loudly, "Got everything settled?"

"Yeah, I'll tell you about it later," I replied, "The others are not back yet?"

"No, but I think dad is..." she wasn't able to complete her sentence because a knock on the door cut her off. She furrowed her eyebrows in confusion, "Can you get that? I have paint on my hands."

I did what she requested, taking the last step of the staircase and heading towards the front door, turning the handle and swinging it open. I took an instinctive step back when I saw Adam standing there, to the complete surprise for the both of us.

"Sienna?!" he gaped and I noticed the crumpled pieces of paper in his hands, it was obvious that he did his best effort to flatten them but you could still see the creases, "I thought you were at the dormitories."

By this time, Emma had managed to wipe her hands and was now standing right behind me, "Yes?"

"I'm sorry, but can I speak to Sienna?" he asked, "Alone."

"I don't know, that's up to my cousin," Emma responded, crossing her arms in front of her chest.

Both of them glanced towards me and I bit my lip, feeling anxious under their scrutinizing gazes. When I did look up into Adam's eyes, I saw how he was almost pleading for me to say yes. His grip on the paper was tightening, I could hear it crunching under his grasp.

So I nodded in agreement, stepping outside and allowing Emma to close the door behind me. He released a sigh of relief, smoothening the paper once again with his hands before he presented them to me, "Sienna, please."

I stared at it, my clumsy handwriting and the tiny scribbles that I placed next to them. The arrows were pointing to different phrases on the page, looking like a weird form of connect the dots. They were all over the place, trying to make sense of something that shouldn't go together.

Just like the happenings of my life. They shouldn't go well together, a side of me gravitating to New York while the other is firmly determined to stay here, finish my education, and create a book worth publishing again. But they do, because at the end of it all, I'm just one person.

The side of the pages were torn where I forcefully ripped it away from the sketchbook. A part of the writing was cut off along with it and when I squinted my eyes, I saw the half of his name written there. I don't know if he read it or not, but I have to admit that he's part of my journey here.

Silently taking the papers from him, I examined it closely and shaking my head at my actions. It was so wrinkly that I was impressed at him for making an effort to make it legible again, he taped it up as precisely as he could at the place where I ripped it apart earlier.

I should really try to be more strong-willed.

"Heart called me, you know," I informed, neatly folding the papers, "Apologizing."

"She what?" he stilled, his voice filled with shock. He didn't even bother excusing himself when he pulled out his phone from his pocket and instantly calling his said best friend, "Sophia Heart Valentine, you called her?"

That was the first time I heard her full name, I'm sure avid fans know that but I didn't. I always thought that Heart was a stage name she somehow extracted from somewhere. To hear it from somebody so close to her, it felt a little more personal because to the world, she was simply Heart Valentine.

"I know that," I heard him say, his shoulders slumping, "But Soph, I said that I was going to take this matter into my own hands."

What kind of conversation did they have when I left him?

But she went on her own way in order to patch up something that may or may not have been her fault for the sake of her best friend. Even that gentle request to take care of him was filled with love on its own, "She did it for you, Adam. It was alright for her to do it, don't get mad at her."

He paused and turned to me, smiling softly as he covered the phone with his other hand, "I can never get mad at her."

And it was totally reciprocated.

But once again, don't drag me into this.

I found no words to respond to him so I remained silent while he finished his call with her, "Yes, I'm fine and we're alright now. I'll talk to you again later."

Oh we were alright now?

"She loves to meddle with other people," he told me, tucking his phone back into his pocket, "Even when it's already out of her control."

"But I think you're just trying to move forward," I spoke, eyeing my papers again, "I am as well, I talked to my ex earlier."

"Fell for him all over again?" he tried to joke and I slightly amused at the thought.

"No," I denied, scuffing my shoe against the carpeted floor of the hallway, "He asked if I wanted to get back together and I said no."

How could I fall for him again when in truth, I never stopped? And that conversation triggered what I was going to count as the real moving on. Now, I can let go of him with no trace of regret because the chance already presented itself onto me and I still rejected it.

The thought of spinning my head around the idea of him wasn't appealing. When I saw his face, I now remember why I got caught up on him and when I heard his laugh, I went back to the times of inside jokes but I had to face the fact that it was all in the past.

He was different now and so was I.

"I wanted to let go," I smiled to him even though my words were directed to myself, "How about you?"

He examined my face and ever so slowly, he nodded, "I think I am."

Let us share this crazy path together and may we find better people in the future.

"Can I steal you for a moment?" he lifted a hand and offered it to me, daring me to take it. I glanced back towards the door, knowing that Emma was probably still waiting for me. I then turned back to him, his expression now gentle and kind, showing a friendly beam.

I'm sure she wouldn't mind a few minutes.

So I placed my hand in his and he clasped it tightly in his grip. He pulled me forward, almost running towards the elevator and I laughed, staring at his broad back. The image of Justin pulling me along the field that used to be cemented in my mind was replaced by him. Just as we were near, the elevator doors opened and he sped up, my feet barely catching up.

Andy exited the shaft and before he could call my name, we passed by him to get inside. Just as the metal doors closed, I spoke, "Tell Emma I'll be back."

Again, he wasn't given any opportunity to speak because everything happened so fast. The next thing I knew, the elevator was taking up the floors, "Where are we going?"

"Remember the sky lounge I told you about when you first visited my apartment?" he said, his eyes on the screen that showed which floor we already were, "As an apology, I'm going to show you one of the finest sunsets this town has to offer."

The doors opened and we stepped out of the penthouse floor. There were still several rooms but what was extremely prominent was the wall made out of glass. Using his keycard, he scanned it on the glass door and opened it, stepping out into the strong wind of the outside.

When I looked in front of me, I was indeed met with a mesmerizing view of the sun slowly sinking down behind the mountains that were miles away but their peaks were still visible. The sky wasn't the ordinary orange and reds dancing together, but it was extraordinarily purple, blue, and pink. The clouds were like stretched out as if it was cotton, appearing almost feather-like.

I stretched my neck to stare up and saw the moon at the sky as well, going up at the same rate that the sun was going down. Adam had such peculiar timing because he didn't just bring me to a sunset, he brought me to experience twilight.

We were stuck in the middle of day and night.

"Forgiveness granted," I grinned at him before my eyes slowly trailed down to our hands that were still intertwined. A blush came across my cheeks and I was in a mental debate of whether I should pull away but when my gaze drifted back to his face and how peaceful he looked as he stared at the scene in front of him, my panic subsided.

My hand relaxed in his and I faced ahead, both literally and metaphorically.

Chapter 13

"We just talked, to be honest," I said, forking a piece of chicken into my mouth.

Emma nodded along, eating her own meal. After the sunset has finished, we were silent when we went back down, and never once did we mention that our hands were still clasped together the whole time. When we released because we had to go into the separate apartments, my hands felt cold without his but I just assumed that it was due to the fact that his body heat was no longer by my side.

Emma and Andy have already ordered food when I entered the apartment and although she didn't pry, I could see from her fleeting looks that she was curious. I sat her down when we got our meals and started telling about everything that happened with Adam, sparing the story about my ex for when we were going to fill the night with chatters before falling asleep.

Her brother sat opposite to us on the grey loveseat, also paying attention to what I was saying. He did need an explanation though for my sudden runaway move earlier when we crossed paths so I didn't mind.

"You fancy him," it wasn't a question like Emma's when she said the exact words to me, but it was a statement. I rolled my eyes, grabbing a throw pillow before chucking it towards his direction. He avoided with ease before shrugging, "Denial is the beginning of a person's road to acceptance."

"Why do people keep insisting that I like him?" I groaned, my fork stabbing my food, "I like him as a friend but what you're implying is that I have some sort of crush on him."

"Which you do," he told me, all confidence oozing in his voice, "I'll give you twenty-five quid if you never fall in love with him and a hundred if you marry somebody else sometime in the future. If you do fall in love with him and farther along, marry him, you owe me the same."

It was a huge gamble and I was thinking that the reason why he was so confident was because he already has a manageable income due to his writing. Even I don't know what the future entails, we don't know what happens and I can't possibly stop myself no matter how much I tell myself not to for the sake of money.

However, I missed the times when I was stubborn and didn't back down from a challenge.

"Deal."

Emma giggled next to me, shaking her head, "This is going to bite you both on the arse at the end."

"Not if I win," Andy smirked, finishing up his meal and standing up to go to the kitchen.

"Your brother is frustrating," I blew out, drinking my glass of water after eating the last bites of my food, "How can you live with him?"

"Let's trade siblings so you can find out," she laughed, crossing one leg over the other, "You'll take Andy and I'll take Sam."

My little brother, Sam, was the same age as Emma and even though I was fairly close with her, she and him get along better because they both claim that they were the black sheep of the family. I don't see them that way but there's definitely some kin shared between the two of them.

And speaking of the little rascal, I kind of do miss him. Mom was home often but she was constantly busy because she brings her work from the office while dad was out for the whole day and will come back just barely in time for dinner. It was usually just me and Sam; although we do argue a lot to the point it frustrated our mother on a daily basis, it was us against the world in most cases.

I remember when I rushed inside our apartment that the day when I broke up with Justin. I was a mess, to put it lightly. I sprinted into my room and continued to let out the sobs I managed to hold in on the way home. He knew instantly that there was something wrong but he never asked. Instead, he opened my bedroom door and sat next to me while I cried my eyes out. He was silent but that was the kind of comfort I needed at the time. He was also the one constantly worrying about me during my slump. I barely left the house, something I never did when I was in high school.

Uncle Levi came in with Aunt Janine trailing right behind him. They were supposed to come home a while ago but when they heard that I was coming and that we've already ordered our dinner, they gleefully decided to go out on a date night, both to the disgust of their two children.

They both made a spectacle of shuddering at the thought and that that was when my uncle left them with the magical retort, "When are you two moving out again?"

Their faces right after were hilarious to say the least; especially Andy, but he responded by saying that his move-out will just be transferring to the apartment on the other floor because he was still studying in the university.

"By the way Andy, we have a release date for your book so I suggest you start on the second one," Aunt Janine said, removing her coat and handing it to her husband in order for him to hang it. Andy walked out of the kitchen and nodded to his mother, swiping away a few stray pieces of his growing hair from his forehead.

With the thought that Uncle Levi just finished with his book – judging from the way Emma said it – and that Andy was well on his way to bringing out a new one, I had this unsettling feeling in my stomach. They were making progress while I was halfway to giving up mine hours earlier.

Uncle Levi saw the sketchpad that I haphazardly threw out of my bag earlier so that I could insert again the pages that Adam returned to me. Without an warning, he picked it up and I was prepared to jump and snatch it away but it was too late, he opened it and the pieces of torn up paper fell out.

So instead of leaping up to him, I dived down and grabbed the pages and shot him a sheepish smile. I was ready to be scolded for ruining such a precious object to him and his son but to my complete surprise, he started laughing.

I was left gaping when he closed it and placed it back down on the coffee table. Aunt Janine even let out a small giggle while helping me back up to my feet, "This must run in the family."

"It does indeed," my uncle said before a fatherly look dawned upon his features when he saw my worried expression, "Don't worry, I did that and even Andy did it. I'm going to be quite afraid if you didn't, it means that you're too sure of yourself and that you're not looking at it from a bigger perspective."

The papers were now clutched tightly against my chest, protecting them like they were my own babies. Andy snorted, shaking his head and going up to his room to get away from his slightly crazy family.

"We better go to bed as well, Sienna," Emma said with an encouraging smile, saying goodnight to her parents before dragging me up to her room, "Now tell me everything that happened during the video call."

No wonder she was so eager because most sleepovers I've been to was a competition of who can stay up the latest.

I recalled everything that happened, from my multiple failed attempts to when he revealed that he read my book, "Well, of course I was a bit shocked but let's be real, if my ex was a writer and suddenly came out with a book right after our relationship fizzled out, I would have a hunch as well," What got me grinning with happiness was when I told her that he asked if we should give our relationship another shot.

"He asked me though..." by this time, she was clutching her pillow and was prepared to let out an enthusiastic squeal, "And then I said no."

"I'm so happy for you!" she shrieked in enthusiasm, lunging forward to give me a hug but right before I was fully pulled into her embrace, she paused when my words finally registered in her head, "You said no?!"

If I wasn't too busy dwelling if my decision was sensible or not, I would have laughed at her reaction. She was baffled and maybe if I was my younger self, I would be the same. Wasn't this the one thing I've been wishing for since that day I broke up with him?

Well, I realized that it wasn't. The reason I rejected him was the same reason why I broke up with him.

Not yet, he knew that.

"I said no," I reiterated, slowly to get my point across. She pouted and allowed her eyes to wander, before settling her gaze outside the window. The stars peppered the sky, a view I need to remind myself not to take for granted because light pollution made it virtually impossible for me to see them back home.

But before there was night, twilight was there.

"I still don't get why you're so against the idea of dating Adam," she sighed, going back to her original position on the bed, "You're single, you're moving on, he's not bad looking, and I have this hunch that he likes you as well."

"As well?" I quipped with a raised brow, "And it's not that I'm against it, it's just that I feel like everybody's expecting it to happen and if it does, I want it to happen in my own terms."

Her eyes widened, her jaw slackening, "So you're open to the idea of you being in a relationship?"

My gaze went down to my hand and I remembered how it felt when it was in his grasp. I'm not going to fall into a spiel of how my fingers fit perfectly in-between his or yadda yadda, but I won't deny that my heart was racing and my face was red.

It was a mixture of being quick to be flustered and an underlying layer of knowledge that I freshly turned down Justin and he was in that slow recovery from his admiration over his best friend.

Because right now, we were in the middle of a huge puzzle piece that nobody knew what the complete picture looked like.

"Maybe," I tried to shrug nonchalantly, "But I'm not sure if I even want to fall for him in the first place."

All for the reason that we were on a delicate balance, it was as if we were dancing on an old hanging bridge that with one wrong move, the rope will break off. I've seen him do the pathetic tango with Heart and one thing's for sure, I don't want to be part of any of it.

And we have to remember, while I did say no to Justin, it didn't mean that I was ready to jump on another ship.

She eventually dropped the topic and we ended the night by getting ourselves mugs of hot chocolate and binge watching various movie before we finally fell asleep.

When we got down for breakfast, I almost fell into a crying fit when I saw the lineup of food that Aunt Janine had prepared. She claimed that she even looked for a fluffy buttermilk pancake recipe online in order to make me feel more at home. Having a steaming hot meal on my plate was certainly better than the mass-produced food served at the dorm.

"Sienna, get your laptop and the sketchbook," Andy told me when we were in the middle of eating. My knife and fork stopped midair so that I could glance at him questionably, "We're going out after this."

I exchanged a look with his sister before nodding, finishing my meal, and taking a quick shower before dressing up. Grabbing the things he wanted me to bring plus my wallet and phone, I followed him out of the apartment after saying goodbye to the rest of his family, "Can you tell me where we're going?"

"No," was his quick reply as he continued on walking, going inside the elevator then exiting the building. You know, Andy wasn't always my cup of tea but I trusted him. He understood me in a kind of level I had a hard time comprehending myself.

I thought there was going to be a cab that would be waiting for us but there was no vehicle in sight. He then continued to trudge towards the direction of the university and once again, I was confused as hell. It was doubled when he turned just as we were to go inside the gates of the school and kept on walking.

We entered a quaint café, its windows nonexistent and you would miss it if you weren't paying attention since the stores beside it had louder and larger signs. He entered through the glass door and I was intrigued by the interior.

It had some canvasses portraying different meals and cof-fee, at the very end was the counter with a remarkable neon sign showing the café's logo. What made it odder was the number of tables, there was a total of nine tables cramped in such a small space. Four of them could only seat a maximum of two and the other five was lined up by the couch stretching against the whole left wall. The space between the tables that created an aisle could only fit one person, making the trip towards the counter and out a one-way road.

There was a single person who was inside aside from us and the two employees at the counter. He had books filling up his whole table, his frappuccino pushed aside.

Andy waved at the person behind the register before he sat on one of the tables pressed against the couch and gestured for me to sit on the opposite side. Slowly lowering myself on the chair and placing my belongings down on the table, he quickly snatched the sketchbook before I could protest.

"Hey," I reached forward and gripped the edge of it, "Give it back."

He looked up and rolled his eyes, handing his wallet to me, "Go buy me a drink."

"Andy," I groaned and he had a look that demanded me to let go and do the task he asked. With an immature stomp of my foot, I pushed my chair back and went towards the counter.

The woman flashed me a warm smile but I couldn't take her that seriously with her plastic pink visor. I ordered us the same iced coffee just to get it over with, gave her the money, told her my name, and sat back down while I waited to be called.

"As far as I'm concerned, I will be twenty-five pounds richer soon," he smirked, plopping down the torn up pieces of paper that I still haven't taped back onto the book, "He's all that you write."

"Because aside from Julia, Meg, and your family, he's the only other person that I've bothered interacting with," I defended, inserting the pages back into the sketchbook, "So why did you bring me here?"

He reached into his messenger bag and took out his laptop, "I have a sequel to write and you need to make progress on your own book."

It dawned upon me that this was the café where Andy Kingsley wrote his greatest works. He almost sank into the couch as if he had been there a thousand times, one knee propped on the cushion while his other leg swayed around so I could hear his shoe hitting the floor. His concentration couldn't be disturbed even if I overdramatically waved my arms in front of him.

He proceeded to ignore everything else after he had gotten his coffee and I was grumpy to say the least. He was the one to drag me out of the apartment and now he had the audacity not to give me any of his attention.

Grumbling incoherently under my breath, I opened my laptop and checked out the last chapter I worked on. It was quite some time ago already so my memory of it was slightly hazy.

I took the papers and followed the arrows of the plot of the last chapter I've written. My eyes trailed around through the arrow I attached it to, I smiled at the small scribbly notes of the exchange that happened between me and Adam during the first time I went inside his apartment.

I could still remember the taste of that almost store-bought lasagna.

My fingers hovered over the keyboard for a while before I took a deep breath and pressed the first letter to a two-thousand worded chapter, the feeling of the keys under my fingers, my nail slightly hitting it causing a tapping sound to be produced.

I saw Andy glance discreetly from his work and a small chuckle escaped his lips accompanied by a shake of his head.

Smiling up to him, I placed my attention back onto my screen, our conversation was imbued in my brain that created a desire for me to write it down.

"And what makes you think I'm coming back."

When I said that, it was in a teasing tone since we barely knew each other then. It was a joke and I certainly had no idea what a development we would have gone through in just a week.

His reply, of course, was full of confidence and assurance that was accompanied by relaxed nonchalance that was still more trustworthy than most things conveyed in such a strong manner.

"I just have this feeling."

A feeling?

I took a pencil and I flipped the sketchbook to the first blank page. My hands moved on their own when I started drawing. I was nowhere near as talented as Emma, but I could easily draw beyond the stick figures.

So on the paper, I transferred the image etched in my brain. Of one bespectacled boy, whose hair stuck all around in places, whose brown eyes were so gentle and forgiving, whose expression were still as easily readable since the day I met him.

Of the boy who was miles away from me and the one I had to say no to because our lives were far different from the way we planned it to be.

Everybody got along with him so when Adam threw my own question towards me, that was my same reply.

Because he was the one that brought me free.

Andy glanced towards my work and his mouth suddenly pressed into a thin line. I scrunched up my eyebrows in confusion at his reaction, "What?"

"Nothing," he murmured, shaking his head and returning back to his work.

Chapter 14

S am was probably in school right now, dad was at work, so this was literally going to be a one-on-one with my mother. Who, as my uncle says, was a complete demon when she's mad but mostly because she's usually a sweetheart if her temper was completely intact.

And let's just say that when her face popped up on my screen, I only managed to smile at her, praying that she wasn't angry even if that meant that we were lying to the both us. There was no way that she was like that.

"Darling, we may be in different time zones but that doesn't mean you forget about us," she sighed, her tone slow and steady which is a lot scarier if you think about it, "And I heard from Levi that you've been working on something."

"Yeah, I'm a little slow though," I admitted, taking off my shoes so I could prop my feet on the bed, "I don't even have a title yet."

"No pressure Sienna but Levi's book is already in editing and even Andy's is ready for release," she reminded as if I didn't know already, "Your publisher was elated when you started selling and the bloggers started fawning about an author that was close to their own age but that doesn't keep you secured forever."

I bit my lip because she didn't have to point it out, I was already disappointed in myself. Does it ever enter her mind that her daughter was trying her darn hardest? Her small mentions of a book escalated to a demand and it stressed me out greater than it should have.

And even though I wanted to get irritated at her, I couldn't because even if she was my mother, she still has a job to do. She's just extremely considerate of me because I was her daughter, but if any other author under her supervision was placed in my position, she would have dropped them in an instant.

I wanted to force myself to write a new story but I couldn't. I then went here and somehow, I was able to start one.

One that doesn't involve a whole whirlwind plot wherein two people will just walk away at the end. Then again, maybe it will, I have no idea yet because this was still a work in progress.

"Send me the working draft," she told me and I gawked at her request. No, her voice wasn't making a request, it was full on telling me to do it without questions. Yes, as my agent she had every right to see it, but as my mom, do I really want her to read it?

The answer was no.

"Mom, I can't do that, I haven't finished it yet," I tried to argue.

But of course, she wasn't going to budge, "So that I could stop you if that story isn't worth finishing."

Welcome to the writing industry – if agents doesn't think it will sell, it will be trashed in an instant.

"Uncle Levi has been monitoring it so you can be assured it's going well," I once again attempted to find my way around this.

"Sienna Elizabeth Clark, you're hiding something," she concluded and she wasn't wrong there, plus she used my full name. Gosh, I hated it when she did that, "What is it?"

It wasn't that I didn't want to tell her, it was just embarrassing because I know my mother. Although I haven't placed character names, she will find out in an instant that the narrator was me and clearly, the timeline of happenings was a dead giveaway.

Then again, what was I really ashamed of?

I wasn't ashamed but I was afraid she will find out something I was just starting to realize.

"Nothing, can you please let it go just for this one time?" I gazed downwards, my hair covering my face from her view.

Thankfully, she learned to let it go. Maybe after all, her daughter was suddenly thrown into a new environment and she was still trying her hardest to survive.

"Alright, but call more often darling," she said, her speech now tender and motherly, all the business-like attitude disappearing into thin air, "We miss you."

"Me too, I miss you all," I've slowly adjusted to life here that I've almost forgotten what it felt like to have my mother screaming at me to get up from bed during the mornings, to have a small debate with Sam over breakfast or lunch, listen to dad drone on and on about work during dinner, and just be generally be surrounded by the people I grew up with.

New York is so fast paced, two weeks may be slow to people here but for me, two weeks was the total amount of time my friends and I went on a road trip through the tri-state area or the New York metropolitan area – well, most of it. The adventures we spent were timeless because we were a bunch of crazy kids who just graduated high school and was out in the great big world.

It was more of a miracle that our parents even allowed us to go.

By the time I came back, I almost forgotten what it was like before I left. And still, those pins saying 'I heart NYC' or those keychains that has the Statue of Liberty, even the postcards of the New York City skyline and dozen movies about the subway doesn't give that place justice.

Because it's different if you're a tourist there, you see its beauty and you appreciate it. When you live there, you see its flaws and how horrible the traffic is or how crowded the streets are, but it's what makes you fall in love with it. I've seen the good and the bad – the homeless sleeping on the sidewalks and the businessmen rushing around with their Bluetooth headpiece permanently stuck into their ears.

And yes, England is gorgeous and mesmerizing on its own, but I'm afraid it will never be home and I'm almost positive that my opinion will stay the same even after I study here until I get my degree.

I remember when I was younger when my family went and watched Wonderland on Broadway and there was a song explaining exactly what is home – it's where you'll never feel lonely whenever you're alone.

"I'll talk to you soon," I said just before I ended the call, leaning against the headboard of my bed. Exhaling loudly, I reached over for my phone and shot Andy a text, asking him if he can take me back to the café we went to yesterday because I'm determined to sit through this writing session with him.

When he replied a word of confirmation, I took my bag and my book for my next class before heading out. Since I was so keen with my subjects and to get it over with, I tried to be as attentive as I can be and that resulted with me ignoring my phone the whole time.

On my way back to the dorm, I sifted through the messages and smiled at the ones Adam sent.

Adam Nicholas: I'm feeling I should take you out to dinner as a re-do of last Friday.

I bit my lip, my fingers twiddling with each other while my brain tried to process it.

Sienna Clark: Oh really? When?

Thankfully, it sounded confident and witty instead of a flustered mess that I was right now. I felt like I was a giddy middle schooler getting asked out on her first date.

Adam Nicholas: This Friday. Dress fancy, Miss Clark.

I hastened my steps and practically ran into my dorm room. Julia was there on her bed, a book on her lap and a bag of chips in her hand. She looked up from her readings and blinked questionably at my disposition.

"Adam asked me out," I puffed out and she immediately flew out of her bed, her book falling into the side and thankfully, her chips staying inside the bag. She rushed to where I was standing and I showed her the message.

"Don't panic," she said although her body language didn't match her words at all.

"Don't panic?" I repeated her words, snatching her chips as if it was my saving grace, "You remember the last time we went out?"

She rolled her eyes, "That was one time."

Yeah, and that one time made me rip out my sketchbook.

"But," she drawled out with a teasing smirk, "Sienna has her first date since entering college."

Once again, when she actually said it out loud, it weighed heavier. Instead of blushing madly, I felt pale at the thought.

Please don't let me screw this up.

"Sienna, met any handsome British men yet?" one of my friends from back home joked while we were in the middle of a skype group call.

And it made me realize how much I wasted during my gap year. While I was not the only one in our group who did, the others took that opportunity to travel or to be productive with their lives. Those who went straight to college after graduation were well-adjusted and were in their second year.

Their stories made mine completely bland. Correction, it made mine completely sad.

Been in a hiatus and slump for a year then her uncle had to step and get her into a university abroad just to get her moving.

Pathetic.

"Yes," I played along, "And he asked me out."

We shared a laugh while my best friend urged me to send a picture. We all knew it was a joke so I deemed it safe to send a picture of Adam, which I ripped off from his profile. They all started to fawn over him and I simply rolled my eyes playfully.

"Mind if I steal him?" she grinned and I unconsciously gripped my sheets tight when those teasing yet flirty words went out of her lips. She clearly saw how my face fell and she laughed, "Nah, I already have a boyfriend."

An awkward laugh was the only reaction that I managed to show. She shot me a suspicious look that was paired a smirk, but before she could shoot a question, she was cut off.

"Stop making us jealous," another piped in, "I have yet to find a guy who can keep a conversation without them having to look down onto my boobs after a few minutes."

"Yeah, but you agreed to go on a one night stand with one of them," Gracie snickered while he was in the middle of painting her nails. Out of all of them, I was definitely the closest to her. Our mothers were friends during their younger days so it was only natural that she and I would be as well. We practically grew up together and you could imagine how much of a baby I acted when she left for college.

But nothing could beat off how she reacted when I broke the news that I was leaving for England. She literally missed a whole day of classes just because she wanted to be there at the airport. I told her multiple times not to but if I was considered stubborn, then she was doubled it.

"Oh fuck off."

Vulgar? Yes. Scandalous? Sometimes. Loud? Very. Fun? Always.

My laughter rarely subsided when I was with them and if you add the boys who were in our group, consider it a circus. Our group kept Justin and I civil after the break up, even if it was usually awkward, but because our friends were one big clique, we were forced to see each other often.

Naturally, I remained in-contact with the girls more than the guys.

"I miss you," I whined, hugging my pillow, "It's not the same without you all."

"Then let's have another sleepover during Thanksgiving break," she suggested and they all agreed with much enthusiasm but I didn't respond.

I wasn't going to come home because I didn't have a Thanksgiving break. The constant reminder of me being in another country was truly putting me down.

But I wasn't going to be a debby downer, that's for sure, "After that, let's go to mine for another sleepover during the holidays."

They once again squealed with excitement at this, "I've always loved your place because out of all of us, it's the one closest to Bloomingdale's."

Our shopping trips were always the best because we love to be thrifty just as much as the other person but it doesn't stop us from spending offending amounts of money on luxury items. From bags that would induce a heart attack on somebody to clothes that we will more or less wear once but will pay a working man's year worth of salary.

It was a blessing we loved to take advantage of and it wasn't like we do it all the time.

In our school, you dress to impress or you're going to get laughed at. It's cruel but once again, we were in New York City, designer clothes were being sold left and right. Almost all the students in our school were either scholars or coming from upper middle-class families. It came with the perks of private schooling.

"Sienna, are you coming down with us to eat?" Julia knocked softly on the door with Meg peeking from behind her.

"I'll just have a late dinner," I told them and they nodded, walking away.

"Who was that?"

"My roommate," I responded, "She's really nice."

"At least somebody's taking care of our Sienna over there," they smiled affectionately before adding in a very laughing manner, "Plus the hot Brit."

In the end, I wasn't able to eat and I didn't mind because we spent the whole night chatting even with the five-hour difference. We talked about the silliness of the past, the craziness of the present, and the foolishness of the future.

Those nights when I didn't spend talking them felt so lonely and I realized that they were home.

I can't wait to go back, the months leading up to December will now be a pain in the ass but I also have my own adventure to live here. In my first book, they were the backdrop to the scenes happening between me and Justin but this time, they were going to be that light at the end of the tunnel known as the plot.

To find my spirit and bring myself back home will be the end game here.

Grabbing my laptop, I typed on a working title for my book – Home.

Chapter 15

He sighed at the interruption, taking his plastic cup of iced coffee and sipping his beverage through the straw, "When I thought I was ready."

"You're as ominous as your father," I huffed, turning back to the chapter I was writing, my fingers tapping heavily on the keyboard, "And that's not a compliment."

He rolled his eyes before I heard him continue on his work. I glanced towards my notes and smiled gently when I saw the word I wrote in a bold marker, even underlining it because I thought it was so witty when I delivered it to Adam.

Sisterzone.

Is it worse than being in the friendzone? Perhaps, but then again, if you're in there then it meant that you guys trust each other more than as friends, but as family. Besides, he dug his own grave and I'm quite glad that he's moving on, even though the notes I was currently reading were written from the time when he was in love with her.

He still is but slowly shifting it into a different light.

"Sienna?" somebody questioned and I looked up, slightly twisting my body to see Vance walking from the counter, "It is you, how's it going?"

"Fantastic," I replied in a polite tone, "I didn't expect to see you here."

"That goes for the both of us," he chuckled before his gaze shifting towards Andy, his expression morphed into something inquisitive.

I perked up before making a move to introduce him, "Oh this is my cousin Andy."

Something akin to relief graced his face as he waved almost awkwardly at him while Andy responded with a nod of acknowledgement before resuming his typing. He bent down, shooting a subtle and teasing wink, "I thought that I had to tell something to Adam."

I knew right away what he was implying, effectively making me shut my mouth. His name was called up by the barista and he excused him as I turned back to Andy who was now smirking, his palm now up, "Pay up."

That stupid bet will be the end of me.

"As if," I swatted his hand away, switching windows to see if anybody has sent me a message. And rightly so, I could see a picture of Sam at the upper right corner and I smiled because this has been the first time he messaged me since I went away.

Opening the chat box, my eyes roamed on his words and I coughed to disguise the rumbling laughter that was threatening to erupt. He said that he was trying to impress this girl from his school and apparently, he heard that she was a fan of my book and he slipped out that he was my brother as well as promising a video chat between us.

Ah my baby brother is growing up.

"What are you giggling about now?" Andy asked.

"My little brother needs me now," I grinned, feeling slightly evil and kind of happy, "And I can't let him down, I'm going to see him tomorrow."

I typed back a reply that he could call me up during noon so that he was more or less out of school by then and I suggested that he take the girl out to some food while they're waiting. Let your big sister play cupid for now.

"Never thought I'll see the day that Sam will depend on you," he commented with an impressed chuckle.

"I think it's 'make Sienna feel homesick' week right now," I said, sipping my coffee, "Yesterday my mom called me saying that she misses me then my friends and I planned a sleepover, which I did mainly because they were talking about doing it during Thanksgiving and I wouldn't be home for that. I think Sam is just the last straw in the long list that makes me want to go home."

I was surprised that I wasn't booking a flight months earlier than when I needed to go. Then again, I was more rejuvenated to work harder because I knew that the people I desperately want to be with were supporting me.

"I'll be going ahead now," Vance tapped on my shoulder, walking out of the café, "See you Sienna."

As I waved him goodbye, Andy said, "So what does Sam need?"

"Just needing to impress a girl," I informed, humming happily while setting my chin on the back of my palm, grabbing a pencil to write on the sketchbook, "By the way, why don't you get a girlfriend?"

He glared at me while I continued to snicker, prompting him to reach out, take my eraser, and toss it right at me. Hitting me square on the forehead, I rolled my eyes and he laughed, going back to typing while I scribbled on the paper.

We were young adults but we still acted the same way we did when we were kids.

A few hours passed and that was when we finally decided that we should finish. We packed our bags and parted ways with me heading back to the dormitories and he to his apartment. There was a small bounce in my step because I was pleased with myself for completing another chapter so that meant that with the pace that I was going, I could have a working draft sooner than I expected.

Before I went up the stairs towards my room, Kristy our dorm mother, stopped me and spoke, "We're having a charity drive so if you have any things that you're not using anymore, you can donate them by dropping them in the box at 2-Ladies Dormitory."

"Certainly," I nodded, ascending through the steps until I was on the third floor. Stopping right at the door with the plate 3K, I pushed the door opened to see Julia on the floor surrounded by a pile of textbooks, looking already worst for wear even if it was still early in the evening, "What are you doing?"

"My professor is making us have a three-chapter test tomorrow and I waited last minute to study," she groaned, tugging on the ends of her hair, "I hate myself sometimes."

"Good luck," I smiled, opening my closet and looking through the clothes I brought with me from New York that I didn't want anymore.

Ripping off most of old t-shirts and dresses from their hangers, I started to throw them on top of my mattress so that I could organize them after. While watching me, it was Julia's turn to shoot me the same question, "And what are you doing?"

"Donations," I answered and she crawled towards her side of the room to grab something nearby her bed, "Can you give this as well? I already bought a new one."

She gave me an overnight bag and I nodded, using it to help me transport the clothes as well. I folded them neatly before I placed them inside the bag just as my phone rang. I peeked over to the screen to see Adam's name and I scrunched up my eyebrows in confusion – why was he calling me at this time?

I excused myself so Julia can continue to study in peace, walking out of the room and slightly closing the door behind me before I picked up the call, "Hello?"

"Want to go grab lunch tomorrow," his voice was rather nervous and shaky, "You mentioned that you didn't have any classes during that time."

Usually, I would have been completely alright with this, albeit a little bashful since we did have an impending dinner date, but I already promised Sam.

"I'm so sorry!" I breathed, shutting my eyes tight as if he was standing right in front of me. I heard his breath hitch and my conscience was full on yelling at me by this point, but I was sure he'd understand. I rarely get asked by my brother and the homesickness had been rumbling around me for quite some time now, "Is it alright if I choose family first for now?"

"Your uncle, aunt, or cousin?" his tone was now turning almost desperate and I was rather concerned. What had gotten him so rattled up like that? I checked my wristwatch and saw that yes, it was already a little late but there was still some sunlight outside so maybe I can visit him if it was an emergency or I can ask my uncle and his family to check on him since he does live next door.

"No, my brother," I corrected before finally questioning, "Are you alright?"

He never replied because there was a loud thud from his side of the call and I gaped at my device, ending the call immediately in order shoot Emma a text. I tried to contact Adam again but I went straight to voicemail.

Alright, something was definitely wrong.

I went back inside to take my coat so I could go out again but I halted when a call from Emma was going in, "Did you check on him?"

"Actually, the moment I went outside the flat, he saw me then exclaimed your name before rushing out," she recounted, "What's going on?"

Girl, I would love to know what as well.

"I'll find out soon enough," I sighed, packing up all the clothes I was going to donate inside Julia's bag, "Thanks."

I hung up and put on my coat, telling my roommate I was heading out. I planned to go over and drop this off first before

I go on and try to investigate what the hell was going on with Adam.

I only managed to get a few feet away from the dorm when I heard somebody fanatically calling my name and I whipped around to see the man in question sprinting towards my way, his long legs carrying him at a speed a track runner would be proud off.

Now if that wasn't peculiar enough, he reached out those wide arms and pulled me into a hug, pressing his sweaty body with mine, "I barely made it."

He was puffing for air but he still didn't release me. Needless to say, I was frozen on the spot. My mouth opened and closed, trying to shoot a question but I was too shock to even utter a single word.

What?

"Don't leave," he whispered into my ear, causing shivers to course through my body and I was definitely sure that it wasn't the wind causing it.

Now this was really bizarre.

Finally regaining his breath, he released me but placed me at arm's length, his hands resting on my shoulders while I simply guffawed at him. His gaze went down to Julia's overnight bag and shook his head, his left hand creeping down my arm until he reached my hand, holding it in his grasp, "Please don't go."

His hand was holding mine, his eyes bore holes through my body, his face troubled and clearly showed panic, and I was on the verge of fainting.

Taking a deep breath, I tried to internally calm myself first before speaking, "This is probably making sense to you but it isn't for me," I did my outmost best to ignore his hand that was gripping mine because right now, I needed to be sane. My heart was going at a speed that was far from normal and my mind was futile in its own attempts to calm my whole self down, "So please explain."

"I know you're feeling homesick and I know it's probably selfish of me but you can't go back to America," he told me as I felt his hold tightened.

Homesick, yes. But going back to America?

Nope, still confused, "Where is this coming from?"

"Vance overheard you telling your cousin that you're going home and then there's the sleepover, I think, with your friends and then that talk with your mom..." he explained, trying to run through all the information he had gotten.

Although it took me a few seconds, it finally clicked. His explanation was a complete mess but I concluded that he must be talking about me gushing to Andy about Sam's request and that Vance might have misunderstood everything, "Now you have that bag and you're probably on your way to the airport then I saw you so I kind of panicked..."

I cut him off by dropping the bag, because I knew that he wasn't letting go of my hand anytime soon, and shaking his arm, "Hey!"

This managed to catch his attention and he clamped his mouth shut. I took this as a sign that it was now my turn to speak, "I was just going to call my brother tomorrow that's why I had to cancel our lunch because if I call him any later with the time difference, it would be inconvenient. The sleepover isn't happening until the holidays and this bag is just full of donations that I was supposed to take to the other building before you tackled me."

Brain, good job. You actually managed to explain it in a calm and orderly manner.

That was the only thing that made him release, almost retracting as if I caught a nasty bug.

His hands stayed glued to his sides and from the way that his figure suddenly went stiff, he was making an obvious effort to keep them there. I bent down again to grab the bag, shaking my head at him, "Didn't you think I was at least going to say goodbye if ever I was going to leave."

And even if I wanted to, I sure as hell wouldn't be parading to the next flight out of here. I had my lessons, a ton of school work to do, and it was right in the middle of the semester.

"I panicked, I'm sorry," he let out, taking the bag and carrying it for me, "If it makes you feel any better, I'm not going to talk to Vance for a long time."

I blinked up at him before I couldn't help the small giggle to escape my lips. It was ridiculous, he was ridiculous, and everything about the past five minutes was ridiculous.

We started walking again and when I glanced towards him, his face trying to be amused yet the aftermath of such a weird thought was still present. Was I annoyed? Far from it actually. He had never looked more endearing than that very moment.

If that was what he felt when we barely knew each other, I wonder what he would think when I leave the country permanently after getting my degree. Then again, some crazy fight might happen between us in that span of time and we might be archenemies when the day that I finish college.

I didn't know which situation sounded more unappealing.

But then it was my turn to overthink because as if I was only realizing it now, it dawned upon me – I was going to permanently leave this place in a few years. Alright, maybe I would still come back as a tourist or when I visit my relatives but still, at one point I was going to get used to the lifestyle here then I was going to be thrown back to America again.

Maybe the reason why I wasn't so upset with leaving home was because I knew that at the end of it all, I was going to return. Here? The most I can go back to was a few weeks or months at most.

What about Julia? I'm sure that we would become close soon because she was literally the face I sleep and wake up to. Perhaps I might warm up to Meg so that meant that I will miss her too.

And what made me worry the most was the man walking beside me.

Theoretically, let's assume that I do fall for him like what everybody says. Let's also just say that deep down, he might like me as well. Then there's a chance that we might enter a relationship.

What happens then?

I have to stop myself before this disaster happens.

Help, there's that cowardice talking again.

"Want to grab a bite right now?" I questioned, stopping him right in front of the other dormitory so that we could drop off the donations, "Since our lunch was suddenly canceled?"

Because I really have to stop myself from being a coward. If I'm always too afraid of the consequences before I even try, is that the life that I think is worth living?

"As appealing as it sounds, I have to test tomorrow," he explained as we walked up to the box near the entrance of the building. We dropped the whole bag inside, hearing it plop over the other donations inside, "But let me walk you back."

This dormitory was ironically nearer to the entrance of the university so it made more sense for him to go towards the other direction and head to his apartment. Instead, he jammed his hands into the pockets of his hoodie and flashed me a smile, stepping down the concrete stairs while waiting for me to catch up.

I should really stop thinking of horrible situations before they happen.

Grinning in response, I approached him and wrapped my arms around one of his, feeling how thin his jacket was. I frowned slightly at the thought that in such a dreaded state, he simply grabbed the first article of clothing he could find and sprinted out.

Now how could I get upset with that?

"So what time are you picking me up on Friday?" with our distance decreasing, I found myself relaxing instead of switching to a fumbling mess. I heard him chuckle and I thought to myself, maybe this wasn't such a bad thing.

Chapter 16

"Are you sure you don't want to borrow the lingerie I bought?" Julia asked as she zipped up the back of my dress, effectively trapping me inside this piece of clothing for the rest of the night because there was no way was I getting out of it. It was extremely tight but because of its navy blue color and quarter long sleeves, it wasn't too suggestive, "I haven't worn it yet so it's still fresh."

"I'm sure," I breathed out, using her shoulder as support to step into my heels, "And I'm not going to consider it as anything, date or not."

The last time I allowed her crazy speculations get into my head, a huge mess came out of it – granted that it was Adam's fault for tricking me like that, but perhaps I wasn't innocent as well because I overthought all of it.

"Again, thank you for letting me borrow this," I said to Meg who was nodding while loudly chewing her apple. While Julia and I were in the midst of faffing around, she suddenly asked what the hell was I going to wear.

As you could guess, we ripped through my closet but we found nothing that I deemed appropriate and it wasn't like

I could borrow anything from Julia since we were clearly different sizes.

So In the end, Meg volunteered to lend me a dress. I thought that it was too small but she said that it was made that way, making sure it hugged every single one of your curves.

I tried to refuse but she was insistent that I looked good in it and she was backed up by my own roommate.

"You two are going out on dates and leaving me all alone," Meg pouted, leaning against the doorframe. Julia was asked out by a guy, that she met in the library if I might add which was a total meet cute, leaving Meg complaining that even though she was the only in an actual relationship among the three of us, she was the one who was going to have a lonely Friday night.

By this time, I was sick and tired of trying to convince them that I wasn't sure if this was an actual date or not.

If he says that it was one, I promised myself that I wasn't going to freak out. If he says that it wasn't, then I'm going to thank him for the friendly outing.

Was I hoping that it was a date? I had to admit that I was reaching more onto the 'yes' side.

He arrived just minutes before Julia's date did and instead of shocking me with flowers like the last time, it was only a small gesture of hello and an offer of his hand that he presented. Honestly, this was better because it kept my sanity intact. Although because it was like this, the arrow was now pointing towards the direction wherein it said that this wasn't a date.

My dress was covered by my coat and I actually used the whole car ride to decide whether I was daring enough to reveal it to him or not.

When he said fancy, it was really fancy to the point that they had a foyer area where you give your coats to this lady. My hands were shaking when I slowly slid it off my body and handed it to her. Afraid to look at Adam, I kept my eyes trained on my clutch while she gave us a tag and escorted us to the maître d'.

Adam said his name for the reservations and we were led to a booth that was private enough but was still seen by the rest of the people walking by, "So how'd you get us a table here?"

"Might have asked somebody to pull some strings," he admitted sheepishly, "But I think she was more excited than I was."

I raised a brow while the waiter filled up our glasses with water. He saw this and he was quick to correct himself, "This is by my own doing and decision, she did not influence this at all except for getting me the reservation."

He said it so stiffly and robotic that it was actually amusing.

Although we tried to ignore and forget about that small argument sparked by Heart's meddling, it hung in the air because it indeed happened and the only reason we were in this current situation was because he thought he had to make it up to me.

"I believe you," I smiled softly, taking the menu.

But I couldn't just forget what he made me go through.

I was expecting him to do the same, look awkwardly and discuss what we food we were getting to relieve a bit of tension, but what he did instead was take one good look at me before showing me the same smile I flashed him, "You look beautiful by the way."

Needless to say, I was back to being a flustered mess and this menu was the only thing that was stopping him from seeing the red blush on my face. Maybe now I'm going to promise myself be a little nicer to Meg as a thank you for pushing me into this outfit.

Maybe the people we don't exactly like will be the ones to make us step out of our comfort zone.

And maybe I should stop it with the philosophical gibberish.

"You've chosen what you want?" he asked and I gasped when I realized I took too much time in having an internal monologue to even flip through the menu. In order not to make such a complete fool of myself, I nodded and just told the waiter the first pasta dish that I saw, "That and a bottle of the chef's choice red wine."

As predicted, the bottle of wine came first. The waiter poured each of us a glass before setting it inside the bucket of ice next to our table. Adam raised his glass, "Here's to..."

His voice slowly died down, his eyes widening as if he realized just what he was about to say. I cleared my throat, finding this situation a bit compromising but I was determined to push through. So I simply ignored the lack of reason for the toasting and simply clinked our glasses together.

While he took a sip and his gaze fluttering around, perhaps of embarrassment or some other reason, I downed the whole glass. Thank heavens we were in a booth, can you imagine me doing that if we were seated in the middle?

But it did give me a jolt of confidence.

"May I clarify one thing so there would be no confusion on my part?" I questioned, waiting for him to nod before taking a deep breath, "Is this a date?"

Whoop, there it was.

He finally placed those brown eyes on me. It took him a while to answer, obviously hesitating. But when my shoulders slumped after not receiving a quick response, he finally replied, "And if it is?"

I may or may not hyperventilate but with the pep talk I've given myself earlier, we're leaning more on the latter so we're more or less safe right now, "I don't exactly know."

"Well, give me an opinion of this night at the end then I'll tell you if it's a date or not," he chuckled, allowing whatever nerves he had felt slowly melt away, and I had to be skeptical at that. Somehow, even if I knew he was joking, it was a free-way ticket out of embarrassment because if this doesn't go well, he'll say it wasn't a date and if it did, then he may say that it was one.

Our meals came and I found out that through my bumbling anxiousness, I managed to order lasagna which was not that bad considering that I once gotten squid ink pasta at one of my dates and although it tasted good, there was not a single kiss from that night.

I glanced towards Adam then to my food before slightly laughing, "Remember that lasagna you made me?"

"Which I still promised that I would make you one from scratch," he grinned, cutting his steak, "Visit my apartment soon, it gets a little lonely."

My posture relaxed because there wasn't a tinge of flirtation in his teasing tone and it sounded more like friendly banter than anything. What I've learned from the past is that overthinking a situation never ends well and maybe the best thing to do is just to take a deep breath and enjoy yourself.

So that was what we did – instead of him trying to be a good date or such that might make him look like a jerk or instead of me being a nervous wreck, we relaxed and just imagined ourselves like we were in his empty apartment again, using his moving boxes as our only furniture.

Because that was us. My thing with Justin included loud pizza places with old arcade machines and his thing with Heart was running away from the paparazzi while making a game out of it.

And our thing? It was undefined because we weren't dating yet and I don't know if he likes me while I'm still balancing the pros and cons of developing feelings for him.

But the process has started – it began when he brought me up to that roof deck where he showed me the twilight sky. He held my hand and didn't let go, seemingly prepared that the both of us were moving on from people we held the torch for.

He took the wine bottle and refilled our glasses, raising it once again and this time, actually completing his toast, "Here's to us."

I blinked at him for a second before the corners of my lips twitched up into a smile, "To us."

And we were lost in our own little world during that night. No tension, not forced or hidden flirting, but simply two people enjoying each other's company.

"So what do you think?" he dared to ask after we had ended our meals, he paid the bill, and got our coats back, "Good, bad, anything?"

"And if I say it was horrible?" I crossed my arms over my chest in a challenging fashion.

He smiled down and shrugged, "Then I'll still consider this as a date."

I paused halfway out of the door because of his words but he remained calm, offering me an arm. I had to stop my mouth from gaping before my gaze went upwards. He wasn't looking at me and I know for a fact that his emotions were unidentifiable as mine were.

Okay, this was going to be a slow burn.

Linking my arm with his, he escorted me out hailed out a cab to take us back to the university. But while we were on the ride, I turned to him and swallowed hard before I spoke, "Just saying, I had a really great time tonight."

"I'm glad," he smiled, the streetlights that we passed by slightly illuminating his face.

No, there was no kiss when he walked me back to the dormitories. Actually, it was more awkward than I predicted but we resorted to a simple wave of goodbye instead of a compromising hug or an uncomfortable handshake. Julia wasn't back from her date yet so I had to ask Meg to help me get out of the dress before bolting into the bathroom.

"In the most non-stalker like fashion, I watched you part outside," she said when I was back in my room, "So it wasn't a date."

"It was," I stated, grabbing an oversized shirt and a pair of cotton shorts, shrugging off the bathrobe I hastily put on, "Okay, theoretically that I might like him but at the same time, I don't want to like him right now but I'm open to the idea of liking him, yet I have no idea when I think I'm ready to like him, so what do you think I should do?"

"All I heard was like, like, liking, and like," she placed her hands on her hips, "You're talking just like me when I'm out shopping."

"Okay, all-knowing Megan," I shot sarcastically while I pulled on the shorts and inserting myself into the shirt, "What advice do you have for me."

"Get some paper and write exactly what you just told me, even just the first part," she instructed, sitting on my bed as I reached under my pillow and took out my sketchbook since it was the nearest thing I could grab. With the pen sitting on my bedside table, I did what I was told on one of the blank pages, the ink slightly bleeding into the paper.

I might like him but at the same time, I don't want to like him right now.

I passed it to her and she used the pen to cross out multiple words in the sentence then tossing it onto my lap, pressing it down with her pointer finger, "Now read it."

"I like him," I said without a second thought and then when it registered in my brain, I gasped while my jaw slightly slackened at her deceit, "Hey!"

She smirked, standing up and shooting me a wink, "I'm no psychologist but I recommend repeating that until you come in terms with yourself."

She skipped out of the room, leaving the door ajar and I groaned, looking down on the paper. My hands traced over the words as my eyebrows scrunched up with confusion, "Do I?"

I like him. I like him. I like him. I like him.

I fell backwards onto the mattress as I closed my eyes shut. I tried to picture us together, my hand clasped in his like last Tuesday, him pulling me with him like that twilight, his laughter echoing in my mind, his playful smiles and remarks, his teasing jabs and optimistic outlook, his caring gaze and pleasant sighs – all of them slowly disappeared until it was just an image of his back. The one I saw when he dragged me to the rooftop, the warmth that had engulfed me then and how I compared it to when he embraced me.

"I like him," it was a quiet whisper and yet, it felt like I just screamed it to the universe.

Oh gosh I like him.

I jolted back up and scrambled around to reach for the book that was just sitting on my bedside table. I flipped it open to the chapter I knew by heart – not because it was the most dramatic scene, but it was the beginning to a story I would never forget.

She was slowly turning into a green-eyed monster because as much as she wanted to deny it, those glares that she showed to whoever girl approached him was extremely noticeable to everybody else. She refused to acknowledge it because admitting it was like telling herself that she liked him.

Whenever he would approach her after talking to another girl in their class, she would huff and roll her eyes at him. She would ignore him, not because she was mad at him, but because she wanted him to give her the time of day. She wanted his attention and for her, the only way that could happen was being a bit of a dive.

It didn't backfire, because instead of walking away and waiting for her to cool down, he went down on his knees – much to the amusement of their friends – and begged for forgiveness for a fault he did not know of.

Yes, she forgave him. Aside from that, another happening occurred when she realized that the stabbing feeling in her chest was in fact jealousy.

She liked him.

If I learned about what I felt from him was caused by jealousy, this one bloomed by halting the denial. The acceptance of the 'what if' and honestly, I like this way better.

But now there's the question if he will ever feel the same about me and whether or not he does, will I ever tell him?

Chapter 17

Months and weeks have passed by and nothing out of the ordinary happened. Maybe I did become more conscious in his presence, but he never noticed it. No, I haven't made a move and he hasn't made a move. More importantly, I want to know if he even remotely likes me that way.

"Guess what!" Julia exclaimed, her iPad clutched in her hand when she squealed from her bed in excitement. I looked up from the paper that I was trying to finish for my class and only quirked a brow because I had no time to dillydally.

She grinned, flipping the device around to show me a poster of Heart Valentine, her perfect face smiling upon me with a bunch of dates and location at the bottom, "She just announced the dates for the European leg of her tour and she's stopping by the nearby city."

As if this was a sitcom, the pencil I was holding dropped at the same time my jaw did. Julia was completely oblivious to my less than enthusiastic reaction as she went on about all three of us should go buy tickets and such. It was only a three-hour drive so she then started to gush about what a ride it would be and all that.

Heart coming here equals Adam seeing her again in person. While I do not delusion myself by saying that they don't talk often, they do, but it's always different when you're face to face with the girl you used to love so much.

There goes my miniscule chance.

And to add to that, I have no idea where he was in the whole 'moving on' spectrum.

"Tickets go on sale soon, what do you say?" she asked, her eyes shining with hope as well as pleading me to say yes. I still don't see why they have to sell it so early when I read that the concert wasn't until next year.

Naturally, I agreed but in the end, I didn't have to because when I met with Adam, he announced with the same amount of glee during one of our breakfast dates, "Soph got us both VIP tickets plus backstage passes."

Watch the guy I like fall for his best friend all over again? No thank you.

"I promised Julia that I will go with her and Meg," it was the truth but I was using it more as an excuse.

"Then I'll ask her if we could let them come with us," he attempted again, raising his white coffee mug, "Please, I really want you to meet each other."

Nah. The last time she and I were even remotely involved, a huge fight ensued. Three's a crowd, Adam Nicholas. You, of all people, should know that.

"I'll think about it," I said, pushing my food around the plate with my fork.

Don't let the green-eyed monster go loose again because although it had been proven effective in the past, I highly doubt I want to use that tactic again. We finished breakfast, paid the bill, and we headed separate ways with me going to my next class.

As you could guess, I could barely concentrate and if that wasn't enough, the girl in front of me was watching some movie on her laptop instead of listening to our professor. I do admit the lecture was rather boring so I couldn't really blame her.

Craning my neck so I could see a better view of what she was watching, I almost chucked my textbook towards the laptop when I saw Heart on the screen. Once again, she was a vision of beauty and grace while placed in a movie depicting the Victorian Era. Her mouth pressed stiffly, almost arrogantly as she danced with a male partner, her hands doing intricate movements. What got you were her eyes, the intensity in her stare at the camera got left you breathless.

Didn't somebody mention that she had a movie coming up? One wherein she starred with Axel Brooks?

Now if that's what she can portray to a person she didn't love, I can only imagine her expression when she was acting with her boyfriend.

What more, I wonder what she looks like up close.

My self-esteem is going to get a good beating when I do see her in person. Look at those blue eyes and blonde hair, it screams vibrancy, which is a contrast to my dull brown eyes and brunette hair. Aside from that, she knows how to play with a person's heartstrings, that's a talent and skill that she's rumored to possess.

An hour and a half of sleep-inducing speeches from our professor, she finally dismissed us and I was actually about to doze off ever since I saw the credits roll from the girl's screen about fifteen minutes ago.

"I saw you watching," she turned in her seat, "Could have told me earlier so that I could scoot a little bit, you like the movie too?"

"Oh no, I was just intrigued by the actress," I said and her eyebrows shot up when I spoke and I already mentally rolled my eyes to what I knew she was thinking – lookie, we have an American in the class.

"I think Heart Valentine is super overrated, but I do like the plot," she snorted, closing her laptop and slipping it into her bag, "Plus she's a total corporate scam. I have a betting pool to see how long she and Axel Brooks lasts, I'm saying three months after their movie premieres."

I couldn't believe what I was hearing; I know that not everybody will like a celebrity but because of Adam, that girl that was just somebody I watched in movies or hear sing on the radio was humanized in my eyes. I talked to her, I heard her speak when her walls were down, there was sincerity and realness in her that some people forget when talking about stars.

And I also found out how rude the thought that she and Axel's relationship was just a publicity stunt. Just from the stories Adam told, they had their own struggles in order to become a couple and how they're completely head over heels for each other now. We may never know what happens behind the camera but one thing's for sure is that they're a hundred percent real.

It was not even an opinion, it was a fact.

"I'm pretty sure she's just as plastic as any other celebrity out there, she's obviously faking it," she ranted on while we exited the classroom, "She actually disgusting and her face is full of surgery, nobody that attractive can be natural."

She was natural because I saw the pictures she and Adam had when they were younger. She looked exactly the same except for the majority of her features have matured. If I was already down from listening to somebody talking her down, how much more does Adam deal with?

He was her best friend and although I know he's dying to protect her integrity and defend her always, he has boundaries and he can't just reveal to the world that he's Hollywood's Princess' best friend.

"I think she's beautiful," I stated firmly, stopping in the middle of the hallway, "However, your cynicism is not."

With a tightlipped smile, I headed out towards the main door of the building. When I did get a slap of fresh air, I didn't know whether I should applaud myself or give my own cheek a good smack. Honestly, which side was I on?

Just a few steps away and I knew which one. It was the side where I could see Adam smiling with genuine happiness and if it's Heart that could give him that then I'm onboard. I grabbed my phone and pressed his number, hoping that he wasn't in class.

Sometimes, I truly think that I'm an idiot when it comes to romance and relationships. So much for having a job that relies heavily on narrating what it was like to be in love.

Thankfully, he was able to pick up and the moment he said his greeting, I spoke, "It would be an honor to meet your best friend."

The day fell faster because I think with every hour and every second, I was pulling myself deeper and deeper into a hole I had no idea how far it would go. Might as well reach the end of this ditch.

That evening when I came back to the dorm, I immediately said to Julia, "How much do you want VIP tickets to Heart Valentine?"

I can't even remember if I had gotten any sleep last night because she was so jumpy and hyper. Adam said that he can promise the tickets but he doesn't know if he can pull the strings on the backstage passes.

And if that wasn't enough, the stress of my lessons was weighing me down heavily. I barely got the time to catch any rest, even the usual Monday breakfast with Adam turned into revising sessions. Both Julia and I had all the lights in our room open throughout the night because we were both studying until our heads started throbbing or when we felt our eyes burning.

We applied for different programs so it wasn't like we can quiz each other, but Meg does thankfully pop in at some days and that's when we try to study together. My book has taken a backseat, even Uncle Levi looked worse for wear during lectures and I know the reason to that was because he's been trying to juggle his newest novel along with his teaching job.

When my mother called to once again chastise me about not contacting her often enough, it took every will power in me not to scream. I was exhausted beyond belief and her scolding wasn't helping the least bit.

I slowly watched the transition of the environment around us – how nature was preparing itself for winter. Compared to when I first came here when summer was just on its way out, the temperature was dropping at a fast rate.

I'm from New York, cold weathers were not a foreign thing but still comparing it to what I grew up with, it was relatively colder here. I was thanking Julia for recommending me to buy the thicker coats during our last shopping trip.

"You do know that when I asked you to visit, I meant it as a way for the both of us to take break," Adam mentioned while he sat across from me on his floor. I glanced up from my textbook and sent him a silent apology, using a piece of scratch paper to remind me where I stopped as I capped back my highlighter.

Pulling my hair out of the bun I placed it, I ran my fingers through it while I shook it out a little bit for it to regain its shape. Since I had it in such a hairstyle for almost the whole day, I noticed that it curled up softly. I laughed when I saw my reflection of my phone and when I looked back up at Adam, I caught him staring.

I bit my lip nervously and perhaps it was both the greatest and worst idea because his gaze went from my overall face into a zoom towards my mouth.

With every moment like this, my heart was yearning more and more. I was literally hoping and praying by this point.

And of course, the moment was ruined by my phone blasting loudly in between us, causing him to snap out of his trance and for me to jolt up so quickly that my knee banged on the coffee table, "Shit!"

If that wasn't bad enough, the vibrations caused the mug to tip over, letting the coffee spill out. I scrambled around to get all of my things off of the table while Adam hurriedly stood up to get a dish towel to wipe it all off, "Answer the call, I'll take care of this."

It was my best friend asking for a video chat and a pang of jealousy hit me – they were all on their Thanksgiving break right now while I was stuck here sticking my nose into books so that I could memorize words I can barely understand.

Tapping to accept it, her face popped up and judging from her flushed skin and barely there gaze, I could conclude one thing – she was drunk, "Hey Sienna!"

Fortunately, Adam got up and went back to the kitchen so it spared me from the embarrassment of letting him hear my friends' slurred states. She spun the camera around, showing the various other people in the room she was with. I did remember that somebody from our high school friend group was hosting a small gathering.

"Is that Sienna the banana?" I heard a male voice yell from the background and my annoyance dwindled down into amusement at the sound of my old nickname. His face came into view and I waved almost sarcastically, "It is her! Justin, it's Sienna."

I could only roll my eyes; back then, they always teased me and Justin, even more than the girls and that was saying something. Somebody said to pass the phone and they sloppily did so, going as far as dropping the device. I heard a yelp, watching as the image on my screen tumbled around before it stopped and the harsh glare of the ceiling light was all I could see. Finally, it went into the safe hands of Justin who, I could say, looked trashed as well, "Look at how pretty my Sienna looks, did you do something with your hair?"

When we were dating, I would get mad at him whenever he drank alcohol because no matter how much he tried to deny it, he was a lightweight. And I tried my best to hide it but I found his actions and speech when he was under influence cute.

Even now.

"She's our Sienna too!" someone piped in and I grinned. My friends were adorable, I'll give them that; they make me feel as if I never left.

"What are you guys even doing over there?" I laughed, leaning back against the couch, "You're all shattered."

"No we're not!" he said louder than what was appropriate, "We miss you, I haven't talked to you in ages!"

I haven't talked to anyone in ages, not just him. Compared to his other friends though, our last conversation wasn't that long ago, "Have you already forgotten our chat?"

"Oh yeah!" he exclaimed, his eyes widening at the memory, "I asked you if you wanted to get back together and you rejected me."

I heard a loud crash coming from the kitchen and a cuss coming from Adam's mouth. I was ready to stand and investigate but he waved it off, saying it was just an accident.

Several coos were traded among the group and although his words should have been a stab, the way he was smiling goofily said that he had no ill will, "Come on Justin, grab a pillow and go to sleep. I'm no longer there to take care of you."

"I want you to be here," he pouted, "But the others are ready to take care of me."

I was quite afraid there wasn't a single sober body over there so I was crossing my fingers somebody had the sense to lock the front door so none of them could leave in their state, "I'm praying that you all make it alive."

"Where are you by the way?" he squinted his eyes, pulling the phone closer to his face as if it would decipher my whereabouts. All it resulted in was giving me a very large close-up of his nose.

"I'm at my friend's apartment," I informed and that was when one of the girls shoved him away. He was still the one holding the device though so I could still see the top of his head from the corner of the screen.

"Is it that hot British boy you were talking about?" she questioned and I gasped, placing a finger on my lips to hush her, stealing a glance towards Adam's way and relief coursed through me when I saw he was busy pouring coffee into a new mug.

"You never mentioned anything about that! Let's go out together when you get back and have a friendly catch up,"

Justin yelled happily. He really hasn't changed and now I'm thanking myself for having the courage to talk to him a few months ago. If not, we would still be awkward even if he was drunk.

Now we could say that we were amicable exes.

But before I could answer him with a teasing remark, a hand grabbed my phone and turned off the call. I gasped when I looked up, Adam handed me back the phone and placed down a fresh mug of coffee on the table in front of me. He was not pleased, it was written all over his face, but I was quite annoyed as well, "That was really uncalled for."

He didn't speak, only lowering himself back down onto his original spot on the floor. I shook my head and unlocked my phone again, making a move to call them back, "I rarely get to talk to them and now you canceled it, I don't know why but that was quite rude."

It was a little strange to give him a telling off, especially since we were both immature in our own ways. However, before I managed to tap on my friend's name and send another call, he finally said something, "But I didn't like that you were talking with him like that. Especially since we haven't properly seen each other in weeks."

My finger paused midway, just centimeters from the screen. The underlying bitterness in his tone was enough for my stomach to do a dramatic flip flop and my heart rate started to speed up. I didn't know what he was thinking but if he was not feeling that same way I was, then I wanted him to stop because right now, he was making me hope more than ever.

I placed my phone on the table, gently placing my hands on my lap as I cleared my throat, "Okay."

"Okay," he mimicked, softer and gentler.

Chapter 18

I stood there in front of Uncle Levi inside the faculty room, my shoe tapping nervously on the floor. He hummed while his eyes scanned my final paper, his red pen twirling in his fingers. I've had papers graded by my teachers in front of my very eyes before but there was this unsettling feeling when your own relative was the one doing it – especially if said relative was the reason you're even going to the school.

"It's good," he said, flipping back to the front page after he have reached the last one, "Not your greatest work but so far, yours is the best in your class."

"You're not saying that because I'm your niece, right?"

He chuckled before shaking his head, "I'm saying it as your professor. I did look around for your grades in your other classes and it's quite impressive, you've inherited your father's diligence."

"I'm telling mom that you said him and not her," I joked and he once again laughed.

I had a few minutes left before my last final exam started and I squeezed a little bit of time to see my uncle and asked him about my final paper. The months flew by and it was solidified when the temperature went from a chilly breeze to a full-on freezing temperature. There was one morning where we all woke up and there was a light dusting of snow covering the ground, everybody rejoicing that winter has finally come.

And you can bet that I booked my flight as soon as I got my exam schedule. Tonight, I'm going to go back to America and enjoy home. Goodbye tall bushy trees and scary old concrete building, hello cramped sidewalks and high-rise buildings.

I'm going to eat an extremely large pizza the moment I get picked up from the airport.

"Don't you have a test you need to be answering?" he quipped back, placing my paper on the stack with the others. I playfully rolled my eyes, getting my bag that I placed on his desk and giving him a mock salute, "See you on Christmas."

This was probably the last time that we were going to see each other in more or less a week. Here in front of me was the man who I always looked at as the fun uncle, the one that lets me stay up all night when left to his care. As I grew up, I started to ask tips from him on how to write. He saw my struggle, I never asked him to do anything nor did my mother, but he offered in his volition.

That playful man turned into my mentor.

From the day I arrived up until now, he has been there to look after me. Giving me the sketchbook, monitoring my work, and even letting me stay in his apartment when I wanted to escape; heck, he was even the one who was paying for my phone bill.

Well, of course that was after he had given a lengthy lecture about overseas calls.

He offered me a fresh start and it was just the first semester to many but it felt like it had such a huge impact on me. Bending forward, I wrapped my arms around him, "Thanks Uncle Levi."

This looked creepy if you think that we were the ordinary student and teacher. I didn't care but he did, so just to make things a little less compromising, he placed a fatherly hand on top of my head, "Anything for my favorite niece."

And it felt like we've come full circle again, "I'm your only niece."

"Exactly," redoing our exact conversation on my first day here, "Are you going by taxi to the airport? I can have Andy drive you there."

"I'll take you up on that offer," I accepted, slowly inching away towards the door, "Plus I have to say goodbye to Aunt Janine and Emma as well. I'll be there at maybe four or five."

Once he said goodbye, I went outside the faculty room and rushed towards the lecture hall wherein I had to take my exam. Let's just say that I've had a total of thirty minutes of sleep last night because I was up all night studying for my two finals – one I took earlier and this.

At some point in the middle of the twelve pages I had to answer, my brain was starting to doze off and the proctor was probably ready to send me to the clinic when he saw me slapping my head and pinching myself in order to wake myself up.

I managed to finish it even though I guessed half of the questions found on the last page. Inside my head, I felt like I was walking away from a bomb scene when I turned over my paper and went out of the doors of the lecture hall. Let's be honest, I probably looked like a zombie because of how exhausted I was.

When I arrived back to the dorm, Julia – who had finished her last exam yesterday – was pouting when I entered the room. My side was clean from any mess, a contrast to how it looked like for the duration of the semester, and my suitcase was waiting for me on the floor near my bed. She kept on insisting that I should wait for a few more days but I told her that I wanted nothing more but to spend precious time home.

She was not happy at all, but she clamped her mouth shut and said she understood my side of the argument. I laughed before I promised that since we will have a longer break after the second semester, I would stay for a few more days after the finals.

"Oh since the stress of uni is done for now," she started as I sat down on my bed, undoing my shoelaces, "What's the progress between you and Adam?"

My head snapped towards her direction and she merely smiled at me sheepishly. I groaned, falling back onto the mattress, my hands covering my face at the reminder of the said boy. Our meetings have been sparse because we were both extremely busy. However, that moment we shared during the last time I visited his apartment was engraved inside my head.

Something had definitely changed between us.

"If I say nothing, will you believe me?" I replied and I sincerely doubt she will. Then again, I also had something against her. If she wants to play the relationship card, then I could as well, "And when will you finally introduce your guy? You've been going on dates with him for months."

Since I managed to turn the tables on her, she pouted and looked the other way, "Fine."

"We still have a few more years to find out," I told her, returning to the topic about Adam, kicking off my shoes from my feet, "We still don't know how far it'll go yet or if it will even end up somewhere."

"But you like him, right?" she fired a question that if I was asked a few months prior, I would have denied completely. It was different now, I've come into terms to what I really feel about him and if the panging jealousy or flustered moments weren't enough, my erratic heartbeat surely was.

I hugged my knees to my chest as I nodded, "Yeah, I do."

"There you go," she grinned, "Just put in a little effort."

That was the idealistic scenario, but let's be realistic right now. Liking somebody is never enough, effort will not always bear fruit, and most of the time, you're just going to sit there with a love that is never reciprocated. It's bitter, it's heart wrenching, it tastes like salty tears, but it's the truth. Life is not like the novels we write with the happily ever after where the high school sweethearts get married years in the future and gets a child that is somehow a perfectly mix of their features.

Usually couples break up before they even reach a year together.

Again, I've had crushes and dates before Justin. The first one ended harsher than his, if that was even possible, because unlike with him, I was never able to enter a relationship with the boy. I cried when he moved away and I've never talked to him since.

My heart is still flooded with memories of the times we spent together but it wasn't treacherously painful, it slapped me more with a sense of nostalgia.

Still, I'll humor her, "You're right."

I looked at my watch and sighed, standing right back up and grabbing a comfier pair of shoes. I was just waiting for Meg to get back so I could properly say goodbye to her and Julia before I go to the apartment building. I told Adam that I would be spending an hour or so with him while I wait until it was time for me to leave.

Taking the shoes I just took off, I kneeled down next to my suitcase and unzipped it so I could place them inside. I stilled when I saw the neatly wrapped box inside along with a paper bag that had a Christmas design printed on it. I saw as Julia hummed, hiding her face behind her laptop and I smiled, looking at the cards of each present – Julia and Meg.

I guess they snuck it in when I was away.

"Don't open it yet," she requested, "I don't like it when people open presents I gave them in front of me."

I placed it back inside along with my shoes before I zipped it up and locked my luggage. Just in time, Meg came knocking at the door, her eyes as tired as mine but she tried portray an enthusiastic disposition, "Finally done."

Standing up, I went over to my bedside drawer to take the two gifts I placed there. Walking up to each girl, I handed them their presents with a smile, "Thank you for the past five months."

"Is this going to be a teary goodbye?" Meg snorted, but took the gift with a smile of her own, "I'm not going to be any part of it because I know for sure that I'm going to see you after break."

"Meg's right," Julia piped in, "I'm not saying goodbye because we'll see each other again next month."

It was different from when I said goodbye to my friends before I went here. They were bawling and we kept on embracing each other, promising that we wouldn't lose contact. They claimed that even though we've already separated before because they had to move for college, it was more devastating because I was moving to a different continent.

"I'll get your souvenirs and such," I laughed as they walked up to me and we did a small group hug, "I'll see you girls next year."

I was forever thankful that these two took me under their wing when I first arrived. Julia was always cheerful yet had a mature side to her when the situation arises. Meg was sarcastic most of the time, but she's always the one ready to let loose and remind us to do the same.

There was still a barrier between us but I was determined to tear it down.

They helped me with my luggage down the stairs and right before I went out of those doors, we shared another embrace. They waved goodbye as I slowly walked out, wheeling my suitcase with me.

I ordered a taxi, just like my first time arrive to that building. Mainly because it was none of my interest to drag this suitcase from the university to there, especially because the only thought occupying my head was a good night's sleep.

I entered the building and said hello to the man at the desk. Uncle had placed me under the lists of residences so I wouldn't need to have somebody else get me from downstairs. Besides, I've been here so many times that I knew this guy already.

Just a door before where the Kingsley's were residing, I knocked on the wood and it swung open. Adam grinned at me, his hand pressing his phone to his ear. He stood back and gestured for me to come in, him still speaking to the other person, "No, Sienna arrived."

I shot a glance before I secured my suitcase against the wall; whoever he was talking to, I was sure that he or she knows me or else Adam wouldn't have mentioned my name. Before I could subtly ask though, he pointed towards the other side of the room, "Help yourself to the snacks in the kitchen."

He sat down on the couch, releasing a long sigh as I went over the cabinets in order to retrieve some food. He continued on with his call while I grabbed the biggest bag of chips and headed to his fridge in order to get us a couple of drinks.

"She's not my girlfriend," he chuckled although it was slightly restrained. I froze for a second to look over my shoulder to see him staring at me. I quickly turned forward again, feeling my cheeks quickly heat up as I tried to balance everything in my arms. My face was tilted downwards so he wouldn't see my blush, placing everything on the coffee table in front of him, "Soph, I really appreciate it but we already talked about this."

A small pang in my chest resonated around my system and I bit my lip because I didn't know how I wanted to react. I shouldn't be jealous, it's a given that they're always going to talk because they're best friends. Besides, I have no right since it wasn't like I was his girlfriend or anything.

But I was not entirely sure what he thought of me as well.

He was silent for a while, probably sensing that there was something wrong with me. I shook my head, still not meeting his eyes, "Sorry, I'll just head on to next door while you finish that call."

Before I could turn around, he reached out forward and wrapped his strong hand around my wrist. It glued me to place. Slowly gazing down to him, my expression softened when I saw him looking at me with all the attention in the world.

Perhaps it was just an illusion because I was quickly reminded of the person he was talking to, "I know, Soph."

Soph, Soph, Soph.

I wonder when you will talk to me with as much affection as you talk to her.

Remembering the emotions he suddenly displayed when I was talking to Justin, I now understand what he felt. No matter how much I knew that it was only platonic, there was a fear that there was something much more.

I was being selfish, I knew that.

Clenching my fist, I didn't know if I should blame it with the constant throbbing of my head because of my exhaustion or because a thousand things were occupying my mind that all logical thoughts turned into a blur.

But I bent down and pressed my lips against his.

I felt his hand on me loosen and his phone drop onto the couch cushion. It didn't even last for more than a couple of seconds because my eyes widened in realization, leaping back with my hands covering my mouth and this gave me a good view of his face. He was as red as a tomato and I was sure that I was as well.

"I'm sorry!" I gasped, hastily turning around and heading for the door, grabbing my suitcase on the way. I quickly rushed to the apartment next to his, banging on the door for somebody to answer. When Andy opened it with a slightly annoyed expression, I almost dived inside, screaming at him to close the door.

"What the hell?!" I yelled, my legs giving out and my body sinking to the floor.

"I should be asking you that question," he said, approaching me and lifting me back up to my feet by pulling my arm.

"Drive me to the airport right now!" I demanded, pulling him with me towards the door. If I wait a minute more, Adam might knock here and everything would be over.

"What's going on?" he asked when I swung the door open, I only managed to take one step outside when I felt Adam grab my hand to stop me from moving. He opened his mouth, though he failed to say anything and the red on my face still hasn't subsided. Andy finally connected the dots by observing my flustered face and his sudden disability to form any coherent sentence.

He rolled his eyes, slapping my hand away to free himself from my grasp, "I don't want to be part of any lover's quarrel you two are having," and with that, he slammed the door to leave the two of us in the hallway.

With my cousin's choice of words, he unknowingly made this situation a lot more awkward than it already was. I tried to shake off his hold but he was determined not to let me go. He started to pull me back towards his apartment and my mouth was threatening to yell.

I didn't.

"Adam?" I questioned and he closed the door behind him, blocking it with his body. He released me and I instantly took a huge step back, hiding my hands behind my back.

"How rude of you, Sienna Clark,"

Remember how I was practically scarlet because of my actions? Well, when he spoke, all color was drained for my face and now I was seriously wondering if this was even alright for my health.

"Arriving only an hour before you have to leave for the airport, kissing me out of nowhere, running away, and now you look like the last place you want to be is here," he listed off and I gulped audibly, my fingers squeezing each other, "Are you going to add any more insult to the injury?"

My mouth just kept on opening and closing like I was some guppy. He was waiting for an explanation and I didn't even know what I wanted to say in the first place. I shouldn't have kissed him, I shouldn't have ran away, I shouldn't have allowed jealousy to get the better part of me.

But most of all, I shouldn't have fallen for him the way I did.

"I'm sorry," I murmured, looking down towards my feet, "Please just forget anything and let's pretend it never happened."

Apparently, that was the wrong option because instead of nodding in understanding like I predicted him to, he strode forward, making me shut my eyes close in nervousness. I felt his figure stop right in front of me and I was actually dreading the worst, "To hell that I'll forget about that."

He pulled me by the arm, clasping a hand on my waist and I felt him capture my lips with his. Like the previous one, my eyes widened in surprise and I was ready to pull away, but his strong grip on me didn't allow it.

His eyes were closed and the hand he used to pull me slowly slid down until he took my own. He interlaced our fingers together and I felt my body relax. Slowly closing my lids, I lost myself in the kiss.

It wasn't picture perfect, it wasn't swoon worthy like in the books, but this is what surprisingly satisfied my thoughts. All those confusion was flushed away by the feel of him and the more our lips moved together, the more I leaned into him.

And now I figured out what was our thing. It was the spontaneous moments in his apartment that were far from the romance books where we're supposed to have our first kiss in the middle of the field with the breeze carrying our emotions around, or where we should be having our last one just minutes before I leave the airport.

The thought that I had to go back to America was what made me pull away. He rested his forehead against mine, releasing my waist in order to cup my cheek tenderly in his palm, "Alright?"

"How rude of you, Adam Nicholas," I whispered breathlessly, "Kissing me like that and knowing well enough that it's going to make it harder for me to leave."

"Maybe that was my intention in the first place," he smiled, that same cheeky grin on the first day we met on the airplane. It lifted the seriousness of the situation, making me laugh and shake off his hold on me. I wrapped my arms around his torso and rested my head on his shoulder, "I'll miss you."

"I'll only be gone for three weeks," I reminded him, nuzzling my face onto his neck. It was crazy to think how fast we were able to remove the gap between us. For months, we've been circling each other with the idea of our feelings hanging around.

It was almost amusing when we had to go our separate ways because we heard Uncle Levi knocking on the door. Our goodbye was as normal as it could be, the heavy tension between us being ignored completely. I smiled at him when I was being pushed by Andy into the elevator and when those metal doors started to close, I tried to imprint his image into my brain.

Three weeks were going to be a lot hellish than I thought it would be.

Chapter 19

I stepped out of the apartment building, breathing onto my hands to warm them up in this freezing weather. Even when I asked Sam to come with me, he flat out refused and said that there was nothing that could make him get out of the house where it was nice and warm.

Well, fuck him for leaving me to Christmas shop all alone.

The first thing in my agenda was to buy myself a venti hot steaming coffee because for one, jetlag was still killing me and two, I desperately needed something to warm me up.

As I was waiting for the barista to call my name, somebody tapped me on the shoulder. I whipped around to see a grinning Justin, his gloved hands wrapped tightly around his drink.

"Hey!" I smiled, reaching up to give him a one arm hug, "Fancy meeting you here."

The amount of times I've seen him before in this exact store was actually amusing now that I think about it. Just a small peak of his features got me hiding behind the nearest person, praying that he wouldn't see me and now look where we are now.

You know what this was? Growth.

"When I heard from the girls that you were back, I didn't believe it because last time I remember, you were going tell me when you were going to come home," he chuckled just as I heard my name being called by the barista. After I got my drink, we walked out of the large Starbucks, mentally cursing the temperature again.

"Sorry about that, I was just busy trying to settle everything down," I laughed, walking down the line of stores, "You're Christmas shopping too?"

He nodded in response, bathing us in silence. I gladly sipped on my drink, the hot temperature instantly warming up my freezing lips. I sighed happily, a new spring in my step thanks to the beverage. It took me some time before I realized he was no longer right next to me.

I stopped on my tracks and looked over my shoulder to see him staring right at me, a soft gentle smile on his face, "It's so good to see you again, Sienna."

That adorably handsome face, I have longed to see it in person once again. To have those brown eyes hidden behind those glasses to once again meet my own gaze, "It's good to see you too," I laughed, nudging my head to signal that we should continue on, "Come on."

As we walked side by side, it felt like we never left each other in the first place. He still went on and on about a particular thing that piqued his interest and I would simply listen attentively. Because if there was one thing that Justin had, it was passion. Whether it was with his favorite type of cheese or the new series he was binge watching, he could go on and on about without having the enthusiasm leave his features for a single moment.

He was one of the catalysts for me to adore descriptions so much. I've liked it because it gave life to a simple phrase, it allows you to fully understand just how important it is to a character.

And that was Justin – he breathed life to so many things he loved. Maybe, just maybe, I was one of them.

I really did miss him.

"By the way, are you busy tonight?"

"Not really," I answered, pausing for a second to admire one of the outfits being shown on a display window, "Why?"

"The guys and I are planning to do something like good ol' time's sake," he said happily, the same spark of mischief never leaving his eyes, "How about you tell the girls to meet us by the subway at nine tonight?"

Just by the mention of the subway and the particular hour, I knew what he was thinking of. During those years before our parents were lenient enough to let us go on a road trip on our own, we used to sneak out during that time of the night and just enjoy the city that never sleeps up until sunrise, when we will tiptoe ourselves back home and pretend that nothing happened.

I was pretty sure my mother wasn't that stupid and clueless but she allowed me to do it nonetheless because from what I heard, she used to do the same thing when she was my age.

Last year and the one before that, we didn't do it for the obvious reason that our friendship group knows clearly well the friction between Justin and I, but since everything was alright now, it was time to do what our high school selves thought was the greatest act of rebellion.

With nothing but my phone and wallet in my coat pockets, I excused myself by telling my parents that I was just going to run to the convenient store at the other side of the street. They didn't mind – in fact, ever since I got home, they weren't as strict as they used to be and I attributed that to the fact that I've actually managed to survive on my own in another country.

Gracie was waiting at the lobby and after sharing a quick embrace, we hurried to the spot. I was met with a chorus of greetings as if this was some teary reunion, which it was considering I was the only one absent during their get together back in Thanksgiving.

The last of our friends arrived and we smiled at each other, "Ready?"

And we ran around through the streets of New York. Not necessarily doing anything, but just for the sake of it. We bought ice cream even in this frigid weather and laughed at the skeptical looks passersby gave us. We used our subway cards to their full advantage, hopping from station to station with each having another extraordinarily ordinary thing to do.

We leaped down from the benches of Central Park, earning glares from the police officers patrolling around. We posed in the middle of Times Square, the illuminated billboards flashing colored lights onto our faces. We jumped around in front of the many museums scattered around the city, not even minding that they were all closed.

This is what people really meant when they say to enjoy your youth. Be reckless and spontaneous, it's alright to get into a little trouble because right now, we were escaping our responsibilities.

"I'm tired," one of us plopped down on the stairs leading up to the many high rise buildings, "I remember having so much energy back then."

The boys returned from buying bottles of water from the cart vendor nearby. When Justin handed mine, his palm stayed open even after I took my drink from him. I glanced down on it then back up at him, his smile almost giving me a nostalgic sense.

"Let's run?" he dared and I heard a collection of hoots and wolf whistles coming from our friends. Not the one to ruin the fun, I grinned when I placed my hand in his and he pulled me along with him. I stared at his back as we weaved through the people walking on the sidewalk.

I didn't even know where we were running to, everything felt like a blur and I just placed my outmost trust on him. He dragged me around until we came to a complete stop in front of a building which I recognized perfectly because this was where I went to during those times when I didn't feel like coming home right away after school.

This was where he lived.

He went straight for the elevator and instead of pressing the floor to his apartment, he chose the highest one. I leaned back against the metal walls, remembering the last moment I was here, how I knew that we were leading to a break up and yet, I placed myself in a delusion.

A delusion that we were still living that whirlwind high school romance.

We got out when we reached the designated floor and we walked to the very end until we reached a flight of stairs. The climb wasn't long and the moment we saw the plastic door, he hurried up. It was locked, as it always used to be, but Justin had found a way around it. He pressed down the doorknob and twisted it as he slammed his body against the door.

It swung open and he shot me a cheeky smirk when his old technique still worked. I checked my phone for the time – 3:30am and the city shone beautifully. The sky was dark, not a single star in sight because the lights coming from the city overpowered it.

And I was in love with this view.

The wind whipped my hair around, turning my tame locks into a bird's nest and yet, in front of my ex, I didn't care. Because the first time I was here, I didn't look at the skyline but I looked at him because as cliché as it sounded, he was all that I saw.

But now, the small liking I had for the town in England where my university was located almost felt nonexistent. I was a city girl through and through so yes, the stars may wow me and the quiet tranquility might give me peace, but the thousand beams of light coming from the buildings and the rowdy noises even at this early in the morning immersed me into an emotion I could never replace. It was home – this was home.

"I knew you missed this," I heard Justin say, "You used to always beg me to take you here just so you could stare at the view so I instantly knew that I had to bring you here again."

What he may never know was that I only asked him to do that because I always enjoyed being alone here with him. No friends to give us teasing smirks, no parents hovering in the other room, no strangers judging us for innocent public displays of affection. When we were on this rooftop, all the world and time were ours.

"I do love it," I sighed contentedly, "Thank you."

The fact that I've been gone for months made me yearn for this place more and more. I can never move away, I can't even fathom the thought of permanently leaving.

Glancing towards him, I noticed that he wasn't marveling at the same sight as I was because his gaze was trained onto me. I paused for a moment before I attempted to resist the frown threatening to show.

"When you said no during that time I asked you to get back together..." he trailed off, unsure of how to continue. I bit my lip, taking a step towards him as I reached down to grab his hand because I already knew where this was going.

"Ever since we broke up, all I dreamt about was you knocking on my door and asking me to be yours again," I admitted, grasping onto it as if it was the last time I would do so. It wasn't, because whether I'd like to admit it or not, he was someone I hold very dear to my heart, "But you didn't."

"I thought you hated me."

Maybe it was better that we did go on our separate ways because I think we found ourselves to where we were supposed to be. A gathering like this was a reminder of where we came from, but it doesn't necessarily meant that this was where we belonged right now.

He wasn't my present just like I wasn't his.

Because I met a guy who showed me everything that Justin didn't. He presented the skyline and city lights while Adam gave me those pink clouds and stars. Justin made me do the craziest things and made me laugh the hardest while Adam placed me back firmly on the ground and got me back on track, shedding happiness back into my slump filled days.

I brought his hand to my lips, pressing a light kiss on his skin, "I loved you so much that I couldn't get you out of my head. It came to the point when I had to write a book about us and now that I'm saying it out loud, it sounds so stupid and ridiculous."

"You have a new man, don't you?"

Still perceptive even when he tries to hide it.

I smiled unconsciously at the thought because Adam and I weren't in a relationship but we did have our moments. Still, I considered it a yes, "Yeah."

"And he's everything that I wasn't?" he continued and I only managed to nod in response. He chuckled lightly, feeling him rest his forehead on top of my scalp, "You were and will always be my only high school sweetheart."

As flirty as he was, he admitted that I was the only stable girlfriend he had. In tune with this, he was the only boyfriend that I thought of so deeply like this. Those before him were just puppy love, only few got past the first date. But him? He used to be my everything.

"And you're mine," I whispered to his chest. We still had a long way to go, our paths were not meant to meet again just yet.

We just stayed like that for who knows how long. The loud noises coming from the streets, the breeze whipping all around, and just our breathes mingling with the air.

It was for the best that I left or else, I would have come running back to him when it wasn't time.

"Shall we head back, love?" I suggested with an obnoxious attempt for a British accent. He laughed as he released me, leading the way downstairs after he had locked the door once again. We texted our friends so that we could meet up one last time before we had to sneak back in order to beat the sunrise.

They sent suggestive winks towards our way – something the both of us shrugged off.

We headed towards our last destination, the place that started it all. Four and a half years ago, all of us entered this building with our pubescent minds and bodies, thinking we were all that for getting into high school.

The first few weeks when we didn't know each other seemed like it didn't happen because of how close we all are today. But it did, there was a time when we passed the hall without even stopping to say hello because we were unaware of each other's existence.

We all rounded up the back where it was hidden from the main streets. This wasn't the first time for us to sneak inside without anybody knowing – we used to do this all the time when we studied here. Seeing the piece of rock that was still miraculously there, we used it as a stepping stone to help us reach the very top of the fence. We jumped up, latched onto the fence, and used it as leverage to pull us up. We maneuvered our body so that we could fall down on the other side and when we turned around after that, we were met by the sight of the school field.

If we squinted our eyes, we could see the tables lining up to where we used to hang out during lunch time. And as we walked towards the middle, I stopped for a quick second on the very spot where Justin asked me out.

This place was filled of so many memories – good and bad.

Unfortunately, all of the school entrances were locked so we couldn't get into the building. Instead of breaking and entering, we sat down on our old table and although they've repainted it since then, I could picture the useless things we used to scribble on its surface.

"Hey, let's recreate this!" one requested enthusiastically, showing a photo of us back in sophomore year. My eyes instantly zoomed in to where I was – Justin's arm was wrapped around my shoulder and I was leaning happily against him even though I was laughing and facing towards my other friend.

Oh those carefree days.

The person who suggested it was the one guiding us and demanding that we do the exact same pose. Justin slung his arm on my shoulder after silently asking me for permission, then I turned towards my friends who glanced my way like she did in the original picture.

Since it was so dark out, we all had our phones down on the ground pointing towards us with their flashlights open to somehow illuminate ourselves. We used one phone on timer, balancing it dangerously on a pile of rocks that we gathered from along the field.

After tapping on capture, she raced to her position and we froze in our poses. Even though we were expecting it, we were still surprised by the bright flash that went off. The owner on the phone looked down on the photo and gave a thumb up, satisfied with our shot.

Unlike the time when we had to get in, getting out was harder since we didn't have a rock to step on. We managed to go back by placing ourselves in a series of carrying, pulling, and pushing each other.

"I'm going to post this on Instagram," she mentioned, referring to the picture we just took, "Anyone got a problem with that?"

Nobody disagreed with her since our parents didn't really follow us on that particular social media. We parted ways right after and at exactly 4:00, I carefully got inside the apartment and sneakily went inside my room where I tucked myself into bed and instantly fell asleep due to the tiredness that the day caused.

I had a good lay in and when I turned to my side when I woke up, it was already approaching noon. Like the usual me, I checked my phone first and I grinned when the notification that I was tagged on a picture on Instagram was flashed on.

Years had gone but you guys are still my favorite.

The first picture showed the original one and when I swiped across it, it was the version which we took last night. I was quite impressed that we managed to do it even though all of our brains must have been fogged up with sleep by that point.

Although I couldn't help but laugh at the comparison. The one taken during our high school years had lower quality but you could see how radiant our faces were, and anybody could even notice the stark difference between our young features back then to what we looked like now. And when I stared at the latest picture – we just looked like a mess. Given that we were running around New York City for the whole night and none of the girls bothered with the makeup, we appeared tired and fatigue, both because of the bigger stress of college and just the circumstances of when it was taken.

There was one thing that stayed – the raw enjoyment between all of us.

The bags were heavy under our eyes, our hairs were tangled messes, the fashionable outfits we wore during that spring day was replaced by heavy coats and scarves to provide us warmth from the cold winter. Mature and worn yet the spark was still as bright as it used to be.

I liked the picture and commented a heart before I threw off the covers from my body and finally dragged myself out of bed. Mom didn't say anything when I got down after I took a shower, she simply gestured to the food resting on the kitchen counter. I grabbed a plate and served myself a portion before I headed back into my room.

Like a routine, I took my phone and facetimed Adam. Ever since I got back, there wasn't a single day when I didn't have a call with him. Usually, he was the one to call first but I guess that it was my turn to do it.

His face popped on my screen and I grinned widely, excited to tell him of all the escapades that had happened last night, "Hey!"

"Hi," was his only reply and I was taken aback by his tone. More often than not, he was more or less as enthusiastic as I was during these talks but right now, his voice was implying that he wanted to end it immediately.

"Are you in the middle of something?" I questioned, grabbing my fork so I could at least start eating my first meal of the day, "I could call back if you want."

"No," he shook his head, "No, it's alright."

There was annoyance laced in his voice and I was never the one to pry, but being held in the dark and waiting patiently for information to come to me wasn't my strong suit.

"Then what's wrong?"

He was silent for a moment before he started grumbling words under his breath. I scrunched my eyebrows in confusion, even going as far as pressing the speaker against my ear in attempt to pick up what he was saying, "Can you repeat that?"

"It's nothing," he held off and I unintentionally stabbed my fork harder on my food than I planned.

I've had enough of broken communication so I wasn't going to drop this call until I get to the bottom of this.

"For god's sake, just tell me what's going on," I groaned, pushing my plate to the side, "I don't want my mood to go down after it went up so high last night."

Apparently, that was his trigger because his physically features now reflected the aggravation that was rumbling in him, "Well I'm so glad you had fun then."

His sarcastic delivery was enough to frustrate me and if he was pissed then so was I. I knew getting angry at him wasn't going to fix anything but if he was going to show me an attitude like that, I couldn't help myself.

Without any warning, I ended the call with a huff. After I've just said told myself that I wasn't going hang up until everything was resolved, I just did the exact opposite. Well, I've learned that if people just give me enough time to cool down, I would forgive them before they have even say sorry.

So that was what I was going to do.

"Sis, are you busy?" I heard Sam knock on my door. I shook my head and he held up his foldable reflector, "Can you help us?"

I glanced down on my phone then back to my brother. Without a second thought, I stood up and pocketed the device and grabbed my plate, "Sure, but let me finish my lunch first."

Apparently, that was the first time I met his crush in person. When we met up with her, she did little to stop the squeal she released. She even brought a copy of my book and gleefully asked me to sign it, much to the embarrassment of Sam.

You know what was adorable? Sam, who absolutely refused to do human portraits because he claimed that he can never capture what is really there in people's eyes, was actively making an effort to take her pictures. He was smitten and although I felt like an outsider because all I was doing was holding the reflector in a perfect angle to make sure the sun was giving him good lighting, it was as if I was watching their story.

"Turn slightly to the right," Sam instructed, bending down and holding his camera up. When she did exactly as he said, he stared at her before murmuring, "Beautiful."

When he muttered that single word, a blush tainted her cheeks and the bashful smile she showed was the work of his honest opinion. He stood up again and gestured for her to see the photos; I saw that it was his turn to become shy when she approached him so that their sides were touching, her eyes trained on the camera screen.

I carefully pulled my phone out of my pocket and directed the lens towards them, capturing those two together. I may not be as talented as my brother but I think he will appreciate this shot.

But as I stared at the device, my mood dampened. I turned my cellular data off and there was no WiFi network to connect to so even if Adam had or will attempt to contact me again, there was no possible way for me to answer.

"You alright, Sienna?" Sam questioned and I snapped myself out of my thoughts. I hastily slotted my phone back into my pocket and nodded.

"I'm just a little tired."

"If I went out and spent the whole evening around the city, I will be too," he chuckled, wearing his camera strap and allowing it to dangle around his neck, "I saw that picture you were tagged in on Instagram."

I frowned playfully as he turned to his crush, "Check it out, one of the guys there was the person she based her book on."

Her eyes widened at the new piece of information and I yelled at him, "Sam!"

He shrugged easily, but his crush wasn't that simple. She separated from him and went in front of me, "Are you two still close?"

I was taken aback by her enthusiastic expression, her lips grinning widely in anticipation for my answer. I looked up from her then my gaze settled on Sam, who was complaining under his breath because the girl was no longer paying attention to him. When I placed the two of them together in my point of view, it was hilarious.

So I started to laugh and they shared a quick glance of confusion for my sudden outburst. I shook my head, folding the reflector and placing it inside its case, "Yeah, we're close but it was awkward for a long time after we broke up."

"Have you ever wanted to get back together?" she asked another inquiry.

How come she hits bullseye the second time? She's good if you ask me, "I wrote a book about him, didn't I?"

"What made you let go?"

Now that I think about it, the first time I said goodbye to him was when I was drunk out of my mind during that party

Adam took me to. That text started to churn everything, but what was really the reason why I was prepared to move on?

Was it because of the ridiculousness that I've somehow only realized when I was under the influence of alcohol?

But even so, the more I thought about it, the more I realized why. When I used to think of the person I liked, it was his face plastered on my mind. Those cheeky grins and twinkling eyes behind his glasses – that was what I thought of.

Now, I couldn't even picture him because his image was replaced. It was replaced by the kind smiles and gentle touch of Adam. It wasn't because I forced myself to forget about him, it was more like my feelings for him was pushed away by my feelings for someone else.

Bringing my fingers to my lips, I still felt the kiss lingering there. It was nothing I dreamt about, but that was what made it perfect. He gave something new, something I never expected to want because Justin had always been my ideal guy.

And then suddenly, he wasn't.

"Sienna," Sam said.

"What?"

"You're blushing."

I really do like him.

Chapter 20

I was furious.

The green eyed monster has risen and there was nothing that could stop her. It had been two days since my last conversation with Adam when he blatantly refused to tell me what was wrong. I've cooled down since and have tried to contact him but he wouldn't answer.

Now I was staring at my laptop screen with a website of some gossip magazine being displayed, and right there was a paparazzi shot of Adam and Heart laughing along with their arms heavy with shopping bags. I understand that they might have met up because it was the holidays and they both went back to their original hometowns, but the least he could do was say it to me.

Okay, let's lower my standards by saying that the least he could have done was pick up my calls.

Heart Valentine, fueling an old flame?

It's well known that Heart Valentine recently became the other half of Hollywood's most high profile couple. However, back during summer before Valentine and her boyfriend, Axel Brooks, announced that they were dating, there was a speculation that she was in a relationship with a non-celebrity boy.

Yesterday, the same duo had been spotted in England, Hollywood's Princess' home country, acting cozy as said by those who saw them. All the while her boyfriend's reportedly back in his own hometown. Could this be the end of our favorite couple?

I knew that this could be some senseless rumor created by the media to rouse up some drama, but they really did their job well. I slammed my laptop shut, pressing my head on the surface of my desk in frustration.

Moved on, my ass.

"Sienna, they're here!" I heard my mom yell from downstairs and I jolted up. Tomorrow was Christmas Eve and I shouldn't let some lying man get on my nerves when I should be merrily celebrating with my family.

When I got down, I was engulfed in a hug by Emma, "It's so good to see you again."

"Not like we saw each other a week ago," I laughed, returning the embrace. I felt a hand on top of my head and I craned my neck to smile at Andy, "Hey."

Uncle Levi and his family were going to stay here for tonight before all us head down to my grandparents' place. It wasn't that far but since it was only grandma and grandpa living alone together, their home wasn't really spacious enough to accommodate all of us.

"Late as ever, my dear baby brother," mom snickered after all of us cousins have said hello. She had now placed on an arrogant smirk directed towards her one and only sibling, "Be a little punctual next time."

Even though Uncle Levi was younger, he was still taller than her so he was able to look down with a matching leer, "That's because I had the guts to leave our hometown, but I doubt you'll understand; always the coward and doesn't have a daring bone in her body."

You could almost hear the crows and lightning in the background as they did their usual stare down. Aunt Janine sighed heavily while dad just waved it off and offered her a cup of tea.

So while our oh-so responsible parents were out there having their usual sibling war, we headed upstairs to get their belongings situated. Emma was going to sleep in my bedroom while Andy will sleep in Sam's. I know that my darling female cousin was happy to see me, but like I mentioned before, she was closer to Sam so the moment we had her suitcase in order, she went off to catch up with my brother.

I didn't mind though so I just let them be. This was also an opportunity for me to continue on with my book, something I've been completely neglecting for the past week because honestly, I was on vacation mode.

But because I was reminded of one particular boy, I was now pissed beyond belief. When I opened my laptop once again and opened my Facebook to see his multiple attempts of messaging me, I wasn't in the most forgiving mood. When I switched back to the window of that pathetic article, my emotions were a mix.

Next time, answer my calls before I find out through the damn media why you were going AWOL on me.

Grabbing the sketchbook that I safely tucked inside one of my drawers, I took a pen and started scribbling down on it. The last place where I left off was during the day that Adam took my phone away from me when I was talking to Justin and my friends.

That was the first time I felt his jealousy, and when my hopes went up ten folds.

When the tip of my pen made contact with the paper, I stopped because I knew exactly which scene I had to recall. That exact moment when he was talking to Heart and I finally lost my senses. Till this day, I'm still wholeheartedly convinced that what I did was far from the expected, but it made me happy that I did it.

Well, that was me a week ago.

I bit my lip so hard until it bled because if I didn't, I would have started crying. I knew it from the start that his heart didn't belong to me and it appears that it never will. He had his best friend, an extremely attractive girl that he had fallen head over heels with, how can I ever compete?

He told me he liked me when he kissed me, right? Did he really or was it just the spur of the moment?

"Sienna, do you have a flash drive I can borrow?" Andy asked as he swung open my door, not even bothering to knock. Although his stance was calm and casual, his facial expression morphed into surprise when he saw me sitting on my desk, the pen almost boring a hole through the paper, with my eyes filled with tears threatening to fall down, "What happened?"

I gasped, dropping my hold of the writing device and covering my face with my hands, "Sorry, I don't have a flash drive."

"What's wrong?" I then heard Sam's voice and also identifying Emma's as well. Since I blocked my own vision, I had no idea what was happening. Although judging from the way the door clicked close and that I could still feel their presence, I was sure they remained inside.

"Adam's with Heart Valentine?" Emma gaped and I finally placed down my hands to see that her eyes were scanning the article flashed on my laptop.

"Who's Adam?" Sam questioned, his voice filled with confusion and panic, "What does he have to do with sis?"

He tried to peek over Emma's shoulder, also getting a good image of the paparazzi shot. It sent both anger and sadness throughout my system – his face was so joyful, a smile dancing beautifully on his lips and his eyes alight with happiness. Never in my time since I've known him did he display such merriment and it made me want to burst into another round of sobs. Because she offered him everything he ever wanted without even trying.

"A guy Sienna got involved with," Andy responded, sitting down on my bed, "And from the looks of it, the subject of her novel was off with another woman."

Sam attempted to connect the dots with our cousin's vague explanation, but his gaze switched from my teary face, the article, and Emma's sympathetic stare. With the gears in his head turning, he finally came with the correct conclusion, "You like him?!"

This was not a subject I wanted to talk to my little brother about.

"Completely one-sided, it looks like," I huffed, leaning against my chair, "Fuck, I'm so stupid to think that I had a chance with him."

I got played like a badly tuned violin. That moment when he said he liked me? Completely bullshit, if I say so myself. The Kingsley siblings shared a look before Andy spoke, and though it was conveyed in his usual bored manner of speaking, there was still sincerity laced within, "We're sorry too for encouraging you."

"Why is this the first time I'm hearing about this?" Sam groaned, plopping down on the spot next to Andy.

I harshly rubbed my eyes to get rid of the wetness that pooled in them. To get heartbroken was one thing, to cry about it was another.

"And to think we even shared a moment," I groaned, pushing my laptop to an angle wherein I wouldn't be able to see the screen. As the seconds ticked by, my sadness was once again replaced by anger, "Next time you think I'm falling for somebody, give me a hard smack on the head."

That managed to lift the mood a little bit, but Emma still gave me a hug as soon as I stood up. The name Adam was never brought up again and that mishap that happened inside my bedroom wasn't mentioned for the rest of the day. Dinner seemed to make me laugh because mom and Uncle Levi's feud kept on going so we had some sort of entertainment to take my mind off of everything.

I retreated to my bedroom earlier than everybody else, claiming that I wanted to get some writing in. This caused a certain amount of stares shot towards Emma and Sam, judging them once again for their choice of artistry. I felt kind of guilty that I unintentionally placed them under scrutiny once again, but they've reassured me countless times that they don't antagonize me for it.

This time, it was Adam's turn to repetitively call me without any response. He fucking deserves it after he did the exact same thing to me.

I silenced my phone and went to writing on the sketchbook. Instead of getting into great detail about the damn kiss, I just wrote the four letter word and moved on. What I did go into a tirade on was the evening when my friends and I went around the city.

I even went as far as drawing a small timeline of what happened in those hours. It was amazing, thrilling, and everything that I used to be. That was the Sienna I wanted myself to be, the girl who always got caught up in adventures with little care about the rules. The contrast between my outgoing personality here and my need for calm back in England just shows how much my environment and the people around me influence my actions.

I should have realized it before – I'm meant for the noisy and exciting city lights, not the twinkling and quiet twilight sky.

You know what? I'm going to get my damn degree without messing around. I'm going to keep my eyes on the prize so that I could permanently return to this place because I've had enough.

I've had enough with being so distant with my dormmates, I've had enough of being the only American in half of my classes and having people give sideward glances, I've had enough of pretending not to know Uncle Levi while sitting through his lectures, and most importantly, I've had enough of being caught up with a man who would only give me the time of day when his best friend wasn't around.

The only time I picked up my phone was when Julia called. Though I was happy to talk to her again, I wasn't jumping for joy at the topic she chose to talk about, "Did you know that Adam's with Heart Valentine?"

"Completely aware," I replied with bitterness dripping in my voice.

Fortunately, it didn't fly over her head, because her smile instantly dropped, "What's wrong?"

Unlike earlier when my cousins and brother interrogated me, I actually told her instead of making her do a pathetic game of 'solve the hidden message', "We kissed before I left and I've realized that I have no chance with him."

Now that I said it out loud, it sounded more pathetic than it actually was, but that didn't stop me from weeping once again. I held back earlier but now there was something about talking to roommate, who had actually fired up the thought of dating in my head, that made allow those tears to fall down.

"Fuck!" I yelled, causing her to flinch, "This is ridiculous."

"Have you talked to him yet?" she questioned and I saw her scrambling around on the screen. It wasn't like she can hug me like Emma did or even giving comforting pats on the back. For her, this was enough to cause her to slightly panic.

I shook my head, "I don't even want to hear his voice or see his face."

She saw me every single day so out of everybody, she was the one to watch firsthand how my shyness around him dissipated into constant wishing. How behind those heavy textbook and rage-inducing projects, I always find myself staring into thin air as I daydreamt about him.

"You know, I'm the last person who has the right to give advice about this because my love life hasn't been smooth sailing," she said and it cause me smile a little bit, "But I think you should talk to him, at least one last time."

I frowned because I didn't disagree with her. It's more like I was avoiding the inevitable news that the kiss was just a mistake, but I truly didn't hate him to the point that I refused to even speak to him. Besides, my last relationship broke off to pieces because the lack of communication and maybe subconsciously, I didn't want this one to be the same.

"I guess..." I trailed off and she grinned when I agreed.

"And if things go well, you better tell me about that kiss," her tone was silly and lighthearted, reminding me why I've always been open with her. She can be serious when you need her to be, but she'll always snap back to her excitable personality.

When I let out a short laugh, her victorious expression was the only thing I could see, "Yeah, I'll talk to him. Thank you, Julia."

"And by the way, it's already Christmas Eve here," she said, reminding me of the time difference, "So Merry Christmas Eve I guess."

"Merry Christmas Eve," I echoed before I said one more goodbye before hanging up.

Adam may or may not be asleep because it was nearly one in the morning over there, but I willed myself to do it. Taking a deep breath, I requested a video chat and my heart started to thump harshly in my chest when I heard the ringing.

And when his face appeared on my screen, I wanted to end it immediately because I never thought I would go this far.

"Crap," he muttered before I got the chance to say anything. Although there wasn't much to tell, all he needed was a view of my distraught expression, "Crap, this is my fault."

Well, he got that part right.

I couldn't open my mouth because I was afraid that a sob would escape my lips. His features were a mixture of concern and panic, staring right at me through his phone. Although I've managed to stop my small whimpers, the tears were still freely escaping my eyes and I no longer bothered to mask them.

See what you did to me?

This was our second argument and unlike the last one when he appeared on the door with an apology, this time we were miles apart. If we ever do get together and experience a long distance relationship, can we really survive when even a fight like this erupted from some frivolous situation?

"Sienna, whatever the rumors said, it wasn't true," he said, his tone pleading for me to believe him, "Please, please stop crying."

I did, actually. I knew he's telling the truth but the problem has escalated from something that could have been resolved easily by just simply picking up his phone.

"You wouldn't answer my calls for two days," I spoke, my voice cracking midway. This caused him more alarm and I heard the ruffling of his sheet, sitting up from his laying position on the bed, "When I didn't even know why you refused to do so, the next thing I heard any news about you was when you were with Heart and I know you guys are best friend but..."

I couldn't even manage to finish my sentence nor was it cohesive enough for me to convey what I wanted. I stopped and placed the phone down on my bed as I started to wipe my tears with my fingers, inhaling and exhaling while I heard him speak. I blocked him out, I needed to gain composure before I could talk to him again.

Grabbing the phone and pointing the front camera back to my face again, I almost screamed at the sight of my red nose and cheeks along with my swollen eyes. My current state was far from attractive and yet, I stayed firmly on the line.

"I was jealous," he admitted and before I was able to ask why, my bedroom door swung open. My mouth opened slightly when I saw Sam and Emma, but they beat me to it. She lunged forward in order to give me another hug while

Sam snatched the device from my hands. I tried to get it from him but he faced the front camera towards him.

"Never talk to my sister," from the usual passive manner of speaking, the threatening way and obvious anger was prevalent in the way he warned Adam. Without missing another beat, he hung up the phone and placed it down on my bedside table.

This made me erupt to another round of crying and when I felt his hand on the top of my head. I thought to myself – when did my baby brother grow up so much?

Sure, it wasn't the most mature way to handle things and right before I got the chance to hear his explanation, he was cut off. Still, I was an emotional mess because Sam, who I dearly tried to protect even in the middle of our petty arguments, was the one who gave me comfort.

Emma convinced me to go to bed right after I've calmed down. We laid together on my bed with the lights turned off so the whole room was dark. All I heard was her steady breathing though she wasn't asleep yet, judging from the constant turning off her body. I knew she was begging for an explanation.

But she didn't push, instead she rolled over to her side and looked at me, "You know, Sam was furious when I was talking about Adam to him."

"He had come a long way from letting his big sister fight his battles for him," I sighed, turning to her, "Though I think it's sweet."

"Would you mind telling me the whole story?"

So I said everything to her – from when Adam was obviously irritated at me a couple of days ago to when he finally picked up my call earlier. She didn't interrupt me for a single second, only nodding and shaking her head at appropriate times, "And I don't even know why I'm breaking down like this when he's not even my boyfriend."

"Because you like him," she stated for a fact. Somehow, that single line has been so consistent – it came from almost everybody's mouths and it was grand to think how my insistent denial turned into complete acceptance, not that it went to my favor anyway.

I groaned, covering my face with the blanket, "I know that and since he kissed me, I thought he felt the same."

"Hold on!" she jolted up into a sitting position, leaning out to open the bedside lamp, "He kissed you?!"

"Well, I kissed him first," I confessed when I remembered that aside from Julia, I never really talked to anybody about this.

"You two had a snog sesh and you didn't tell me," she gaped, all sleep gone from her system, "How? When?"

"Long story short, I kissed him then I ran away, he pulled me then it was his turn to make a move," I recalled, peeking from under the blanket, "Stupid, I know."

She plopped back down on the mattress with a huff, "If he hurts my cousin like that then there's no mercy coming from me."

That made the corners of my mouth twitch and when she saw me smile, a grin split on her face, "Good night, Sienna."

"Good night."

Family really is the best.

Chapter 21

G randma indulgently scooped up more food on my plate that I can manage, making me amused at her satisfied nod when there was practically a mountain on my plate. Whenever she sees me, she complains that I was never eating enough but to be honest, it was just her excuse to feed me more.

I wasn't complaining though.

I shared a look with Emma, who experienced the same treatment, and shared a silent laugh with her as our grandmother spoke, "You young ladies need to plump up, men always want a little more to grab onto."

Nothing more interesting than her giving us love advice. Then again, she'd been married with our grandfather for over fifty-five years so she must have done something right.

"No need to tell Sienna that," Uncle Levi gave a cheeky grin, causing both of his children and Sam to stare at him warningly. He was caught off guard by their judging gazes and I smiled as I forked mashed potatoes into my mouth. I didn't feel that upset anymore since these three were looking out for me.

But it was grandpa's turn to speak, clearly not getting the signals sent by his grandchildren, "You have a boyfriend now, Sienna?"

"A nice young lad, if I say so myself," Aunt Janine responded, ignoring my widening eyes.

Dad's hold on his utensils visibly tightened and the way my mother paused from slicing her roast beef made me want to stand up and leave the table. I've skillfully avoided mentioning Adam ever since I arrived – I told them about my classes, Julia, Meg, and even my old frustrating professors.

But completely nothing about the guy who spun my head around when I was in England.

"It's nothing, just some crush I had, but now it's gone," I muttered in order to diffuse the tension. It was a lie, but I had to say something to cancel out what my aunt and uncle just said. There was a silence that followed and as my grandmother placed down the bowl on the table next to me, I muttered under my breath in barely audible whisper, "Grandma, men are horrible."

She glanced towards her husband before releasing a hearty laugh, effectively lightening the mood, "Yes, they are."

After dinner, we waited for the clock to strike midnight as all of us teenagers sat down on the floor to get our presents from under the Christmas tree. I was awarded with a new laptop by my parents, a thick wooly sweater from Emma, a set of pens from Andy, an engraved necklace from my aunt and uncle, then finally, a stuffed teddy bear from my grand-parents – the same with my brother and cousins because we swear, we were still little children in their eyes.

I was pleasantly surprised when I unwrapped the box to reveal the coat that came from Sam because it was an extreme level up from the sweet cake set he got my last year. I was even happier by his reaction when he took out the camera lens I got him.

Christmas wasn't that eventful – the same old thing we did every year. Uncle Levi and his family left on the twenty-sixth to go back to England so they can spend the New Year there with Aunt Janine's side of the family.

"See you next month, Sienna," they bid and I waved them goodbye as they all went inside the yellow taxi.

On the twenty-eighth, four girls came rolling inside our apartment with overnight bags and bright faces to greet my family and I. It was time for our long awaited holiday sleepover and honestly, I needed some girl time in order to clear my mind.

We went for an all-day shopping trip at Bloomingdale's since there was an after Christmas sale. By the time we got home, we were filled with coffee and our feet were tired from walking all around. A big pile of shopping bags rested at the corner of my room while an air mattress was on the floor next to my bed.

"Hey Sienna," Gracie said as she paused her scrolling on my phone after she asked to borrow it, "Who's Adam Nicholas?"

"What?" I tore my attention away from the tv screen to turn to her.

She held up the screen, his face being flashed on as he requested a video chat. I rolled my eyes and continued on with my quest to choose a movie, "Reject it, it's just some jerk."

Even I noticed the strain in my voice and I knew they heard it as well. From the way I blatantly showed that I didn't want to talk about it and my now violent way of pressing on the remote control buttons, they've reluctantly allowed the topic to drop.

Because Adam was not a jerk, something simply went wrong down the line.

She shrugged and did what was told, continuing on with her previous task. When I thought I was going to get some peace, she piped in once again, "Tell me, why you didn't get back together with Justin?"

My finger froze on the play button and I slowly turned my around to see all of them were now staring right at me. I blinked once and then twice, as if doing so will remove the expecting gazes they have now set upon me.

But it didn't and I know they were asking an explanation why we're suddenly buddy buddy after being in an awkward position for almost a year or two. Add to that was the knowledge they've acquired about how I said no when he asked me to become a couple again. Especially because I've been whining to them ever since we broke up.

"You two were extra close during that night," she winked, tossing me back my phone, "We thought for sure that you two would be together again when you got back."

I was transported back to that rooftop and a fond smile went to my face at the memory. We may not have ended up in the way that we thought we were going to be in back in high school, but I will undoubtfully say that this was better. "Wait, is it that hot British boy that made you move on?"

"Oh forget about him!" I snapped unintentionally. It had been a constant tug of war between sobbing for him and being furious. For now, I was once again mad at the thought of his face, his smile, those beautiful brown eyes, and...

Damn him!

"Sienna..." they trailed off, nothing but concern on their features.

I frowned deeply, crawling on the bed and settling myself in-between two of them. We've miraculously squeezed all of us on my bed – something we haven't successfully done since middle school – so being sandwiched in the midst of four of my favorite people gave me a sense of comfort.

"I like him," I admitted softly, my fingernails picking on a piece lint on my pajama bottoms, "We kissed right before I left and suddenly out of nowhere, he got mad at me and now he did something that made me snap at him. Up to this point, we haven't cleared anything and now I'm sincerely dreading the time I have to go back to England."

First, I felt a pair of arms wrap around me and then suddenly another, before two others joined in. They didn't say anything, only allowing their warmth to engulf me to drag me out of this misery that have been going on and off.

Seriously, my mood had been as unstable as a fuckboy's relationship.

"So we still on for the New Year's party?" the shift in topic allowed me to calm down and I fell back onto the headboard with a sigh. I better meet some attractive guy to kiss on midnight and then never see him ever again just to take my mind off of Adam.

I heard simultaneous replies of agreement and we all decided on a film before we got settled under the multiple blankets and pillows I brought out. The popcorn was spilling all over my bed and the sound of laughter kept up until three in the morning.

I didn't consider myself as a heavy sleeper nor was a I light one. Loud noises can wake me up but soft ones don't. So when the girls started shaking me awake, I slowly cracked my eyes open and instead of being greeted by my white ceiling, I was surprised by the dozens of balloons. Slowly sitting up, they were standing at the foot of my bed with a stack of waffles with a single candle stuck on top, "Happy Birthday, Sienna!"

My sleep-induced brain took half a minute to buffer what was happening but when the thought settled down inside my mind, my grin couldn't get wider. Even when they urged me to make a wish and blow out the candle, I couldn't tear my eyes away from their gleeful faces. I closed my eyes and exhaled right by the flame, taking it out with my breath. They cheered and I got out of bed, stretching my arms over my head.

I was officially twenty.

"Thanks for the effort girls, but you didn't need to get my breakfast," I laughed, not even bothering with the fork when I took out the candle and grabbed a waffle, passing around the plate so they could get one as well, "Since we're having brunch with the boys later."

"We're really stretching it," my friend sighed, munching on her waffle and licking the whipped cream off of her finger, "But because this is the first time since graduating that we were able to meet up like this and it's even more precious because we all study far from each other."

For the past year, our friends had been considerate because Justin and I's somehow tragic break up. Although we've assured them countless times that it was alright for all of us to hang out without being awkward, they knew better than we did.

Because having an all-out war to see who can ignore the other one the best was always ongoing whenever we were stuck in the same room. The tension doubled when we were seated next to each other and judging from their uneasy glances, they were being cautious as well.

It came to the point where we had to separate the girls and the boys to relieve such a compromising disposition among everybody in the group.

We all met up at a diner near my apartment, the laughs shared between us was a quick reminder how this vacation was to end as quickly as it began. In just a few weeks' time, I would be back to England in a dorm that I'm not particularly excited about, to classes that I wanted to sleep out of, and to a game wherein I have to avoid a guy who I sincerely thought would be somebody who could potentially be my everything.

Damn me for falling too quickly. I knew I should have just kept it with 'just being friends' gist and went on with my life.

All my worries were lifted away when the waiter brought out a small slice of cake and all of my friends started to sing happy birthday. From the frown I couldn't help sporting earlier, my lips tugged into a smile.

I looked around my table and found myself satisfied with everything happening. Sure, there was no happily ever after but being a writer, it gave me the sure knowledge of what exactly differentiates a work of fiction from reality.

The bitter and painful slaps that life gives you are there to make sure you savor the sweet and precious moments.

We handed a waiter our phones so he could take a group shot of everybody. With my brightest smile, I felt the presence of the people I treasured and when I stared down at the picture that was captured, my happiness transpired perfectly.

My apartment became our destination right after and none of my family minded that we had almost ten rambunctious young adults being a wreck. Justin sat down on the couch next to me after he had finished with the card game he and the others were invested in.

"You two fighting?" he questioned and I jolted up at the thought that he had noticed. He saw my alerted look and he smiled softly, "I'm more observant than you give me credit for."

"I wish I would have fallen for you for the second time in a snap," I admitted, pulling my feet up onto the couch, "Then I wouldn't be this dramatic."

He shrugged, "Not really, besides, you told me straight on why we broke up. To be honest, I agree with you and it's not our time yet. Just live a little without worrying about me because you told me to do the same."

"Since when did that cheeky and childish boy that I loved turned into this philosophical man who knows exactly what I needed to hear," I laughed, reaching over to playfully pinch his cheeks. He rolled his eyes teasingly, lightly slapping my arm away.

We heard a camera sound and we turned to one of our friends holding up his phone, the lens pointed towards us, "Stop flirting you two and come here before we start another game without you."

Since I dedicated my whole morning and afternoon to them, I shared a small but peaceful birthday dinner with my family during the evening. Nothing too grand but it was what I wanted after such a hectic day.

They uploaded every photo that they took today and I made sure to reply to each and every one who sent me their well wishes. As I scrolled through my messages, my thumb paused and hovered on the screen when I saw one particular name that I was somehow expecting, but never actually thought would pop up.

Adam Nicholas.

It's my fault, I know. It's my fault for getting jealous over a simple picture of his arm around you shoulder. It's my fault that I wanted to give myself time to cool down, but I wasn't cautious enough about the paparazzi following Soph around. It's my fault that instead of calling you back to explain, I waited two days. It's my fault that I've royally screwed up my chances with you.

But today, I saw another photo that had gotten me all riled up in the worst ways. To see the two of you so at ease with each other – that hand on his cheek and his cheery smile – it made me realize what a terrible person I was. I always believed you when you said that your relationship with him was nothing but two reconciling exes who found friendship again, but I still got jealous.

This is what you must have felt when I'm with Soph.

So I'm sorry, Sienna, but I still want to see you happy. Happy birthday.

When I finished reading his message, I wanted to collapse because my emotions were going out of control once again. Instead of typing back a reply, I instantly started to request a video chat and the moment I saw his apologetic features on my screen, I knew for myself that I had already forgiven him.

"How rude of you, Adam Nicholas," I repeated the words from that fateful day, "So incredibly rude."

"I didn't like that you were with him," he admitted truthfully, "But I had no right to be mad at you like that."

"As touching as that message was," I said, choking halfway through my words, "Tell me the real truth."

He blinked up at me and I was waiting in anticipation whether we were thinking the same thing or not. The last line? I wanted to yell bullshit because I really wanted to know the god honest truth and if he says exactly that then I'm going to be elated.

Because as of the very moment, that was what I was feeling towards him. Yes, it was all romantic and such, but my possessive streak was extremely notorious. Although I wanted to see him happy, I would rather see him happy with me. If it was someone else, then I would give up and walk away.

I just hope he felt the same way.

He searched my face, trying get a single hint for what I was implying. He gave up defeat after a minute full of confusion and instead of fishing out the specific thing that will grant me satisfaction, he just said the what went into his head, "Will you go out with me when you get back?"

Not exactly what I wanted to hear but I think it was better.

Finally, after a week of nothing but avoiding each other, of hidden cries and angry calls, we've reached our end point. The greatest misunderstanding came from a single fact – we liked each other. Jealousy had creeped its way between us, causing a riff to something that wasn't fully sewn together. We were in such a fragile stage that something as petty as taking a picture out of context was enough to cause a fight.

But it meant that we were moving instead of being stagnant. For the future, I would be terrified if we don't get into another argument – it's part of a healthy relationship in my opinion. The dynamic between two people should never be perfect, there should always be gaps to keep on filling.

Not because it was boring, not because you wanted it to keep on being fun, but because there will always be something better than what you already have.

"Okay," I smiled, shifting the phone towards my other hand.

"And Soph was complaining non-stop about wanting to meet you," he chuckled in response, "Saying that I should stop being a sad slump."

I always was a walking time bomb when it came to relationships. I broke it off with my first date when I was in middle school because we were stupid and kids who thought the movies actually portrayed what a relationship should be. It didn't and the lack of achievement of something too impossible made me angry that he wouldn't surprise me with a dozen roses or even a romantic picnic at the park.

After that, I had several dates – some were friendly at the most, others were done because I got dragged around in double or group dates, and some just didn't work out so well.

But Justin was the first one to offer me something I came chasing back for more. He showed me sincerity and carefree fun. Instead of fancy restaurants and candlelit dinners, he brought me to those clubs for teenagers and midnight strolls around the city. It was far from the cliché roses and chocolates I've always demanded and yet, he was the one that got me laughing until my sides hurt and the one to push me out of my comfort zone.

And when we broke up, I've mellowed down myself. I was uncomfortable with how quickly my spirit died down, and although the aftershocks of such a whirlwind life allowed me to create a full on novel, I craved for it over and over again.

The slow pace that university offered me was dull compared to how fast days went by when I was in New York. When it came to light how Adam managed to make the heightened feeling of sneaking out in the middle of the night or those impulsive road trips look too weird compared to the quietness of his apartment and the careful tiptoe between friends and something more, my mindset shifted.

You gave me twilight skies and shining stars while he gave me city lights and lively nights.

Different things and were valued in different ways. But I've experienced already the latter, I want to relish what he can give me.

Chapter 22

I weaved myself around the apartment filled with people – not really to the brim, but just enough so that it would be difficult to maneuver around when everybody's stood up and walking around. Greeting a few people on my way and waving at Sam who was talking to his girl near the couch, I started to find a single space where people weren't screaming or chattering so loudly.

The apartment was owned by the family of two siblings who went to my old high school. Ever since the older of the pair turned twenty-one, they started holding a party every New Year's Eve. His little sister was somebody from my class and although we weren't in the same group, our friends were extremely close so that's why I managed to snatch an invitation consistently ever since this started when we were juniors.

The invite list got bigger and bigger each year – their parents aren't around to actually mind since they claim that their family always go on a trip every time and it was only when this party started that the brother and sister duo decided to stay in New York instead of traveling with their parents.

I found an empty bathroom and locked myself inside. Star-ing down on the time on my phone screen, I cursed myself when I realized that it was too late to greet him. Still, I called him up just to say the three words, "Happy New Year."

Hearing Adam chuckle blend in with the muffle back-ground music, I assumed that he was also in his own cele-bration. I leaned against the sink, closing my eyes as I heard his gentle repeat of my words. Never did I realize that I will actually be counting down the days until I come back to university.

It was half past eleven, only thirty minutes until we wel-come the new year while for him, it was already nearing sunrise, "Did you kiss anybody at midnight?"

"No," was his quick reply, "I stood awkwardly in the middle of the room while everybody locked lips left and right."

"Maybe I'll keep myself locked in the bathroom until then," I joked, before I heard a knock on the door, somebody telling me to hurry up, "But then again, I think someone needs this space more than I do."

His hearty laughter relaxed my whole system – something I needed since this party was rowdier than I had originally expected. The girls had been introducing me to men left and right, but I will always tried to subtly tell them I was not interested and I was back with the supposed hot British boy.

You can bet that they thought I was just making it up to get away from the guys, but I wanted to yell at them to say that it was the truth. Eventually, I've given up and allowed myself to get dragged into their games.

There was another knock and I rolled my eyes, "I'll call you again tomorrow."

"Good night, Sienna," he said before he ended the call. I unlocked the door and the moment I stepped out, a woman shoved her way inside.

I got myself a drink before finding a spot by one of the windows. The view was beautiful and you can see how the city was lit up more than usual, plus the amount of people walking around on the streets seemed to have doubled.

A figure stepped beside me and I never had to turn around to find out it was Justin, "What is it with your inclination to look out from high places?"

Smiling softly, I tore my eyes away from the view to meet his brown eyes, "Makes me feel like I have a bit of control and it constantly reminds me that to somebody else, I also appear as some figure passing by."

Without another word, he raised his cup and I did the same, chugging down our drinks in one go. When I laughed and wiped off a bit of liquid that slipped down the side of my mouth, he bent down and placed a kiss on my cheek. I instinctively leaned towards him, my hand reaching to run my fingers through his hair while he rested his forehead on my shoulder.

"Made up with him?"

"Yeah."

"Good," he whispered into my ear, "I'm happy for you, Sienna."

The genuine joy in his voice made me shiver, but his desperation didn't only equate from being such a caring friend, there was something more to it. His constant effort to make me smile plus the offer to get back together. There was one thing I suppressed inside my mind in order to save me from hoping – he hasn't been in a stable relationship since we broke up and he avoided me just as much as I avoided him.

"You read the book before I told you, didn't you?" I voiced out my suspicions, feeling him slowly straighten up his posture so I had to go back to looking up at him. He looked like a deer in the headlights and it confirmed everything, "Don't feel guilty. I brought that heartbreak to myself."

"I should have at least called you when I did," he admitted, looking down towards his feet, "But I thought that by that point, you would have already resented me."

He was the last person I could ever hate. He could do anything and I would still forgive him.

"When you called me, pissed drunk, I wanted to hit myself because why else would you do that? I thought of the worse," he said, "The Sienna I knew scolded me if I even gotten near tipsy, the disbelief I felt when you were the one who gotten herself in that situation made me realize what a jerk I really am."

The words were screaming in my head and I wanted nothing more but to hold him still and tell him that he was the exact opposite. He gave me all he had to offer and I gave him all of mine, but it was my fault why we ended up like this.

The Sienna he knew wasn't strong enough and she thought that were didn't belong with each other during that time.

So I placed my hands and held his face tenderly, "Be happy, because the Justin I knew could turn the worst situations into a wonderful memory."

He was my wonderful memory. Some moments were bad, they really were, but he managed to turn it around like always. He wasn't a jerk, he was far from it, and that was one of the reasons why it was so hard to let him go.

"Am I going to hate him?" he chuckled, attempting to lighten the mood.

I blinked at him as it took some time to realize that he was talking about Adam. A grin formed on my face at the thought and I remember using that exact tone of voice when I asked Adam about my doubts with Heart. So I used the same response he gave me, "You'll like him, everybody does."

He flashed his amusement on his face and nodded, "Happy New Year, Sienna."

I told him the same and instead of walking away, he stood silently by my side while I returned to staring out of the window. A few kilometers away, people were rushing to Times Square, excitedly waiting for the ball to drop. While in this apartment, somebody finally yelled that it was five minutes until we were greeted by another year.

Facing the room, I watched as people scrambled around to find their significant other. I leaned against the glass – something I would heavily not recommend – my gaze meeting my best friend's as she held tightly to the hand of her boyfriend. She flashed me a wink and I waved at her, staying on my spot.

I glanced to my side and saw Justin also smiling at the few people walking around. Our gazes suddenly connected and we shared a small laugh. You know, he could have just ran out and gotten himself a random girl to kiss.

And I could have just walked into one of the bathrooms and lock myself in there again.

But neither of us did that and instead, we just savored this small moment we had.

The music got louder and soon, people were yelling at the top of their lungs the countdown. And when they said the magic, "One!" many of them connected their lips – from strangers to long time couples.

I turned to Justin and pressed my lips on his cheek and he quickly snatched up my hand to kiss the back of it. I closed my eyes and sighed, tipping my empty glass as my own special way to greet the new year.

"I can't believe I managed to survive a whole year without talking or seeing you," he laughed, still not letting go of my hand.

"Then let's not repeat that," I told him, "That was too tor-turous for the both us."

May this year continue the wonderful streak that had been started.

The days flew by so quickly and the next thing I knew, I was already on the plane back to England. Unlike the first time I went there, the person sitting next to me wasn't the charming boy that reflected pure life in his eyes, but a woman in her forties who took this flight as a golden opportunity to catch up on sleep.

Aside from the usual polite smile, we didn't share any con-versation after. I proceeded to watch a few movies before allowing slumber to reign. I woke up when we only had an hour left for the flight and with that, I proceeded to write my book that I've completely neglected ever since I came home.

Going through customs was easy, getting a cab was not. The line was horrendous, but the man was more than happy when he learned that my university was in such a long distance from the airport so his fee will be pretty hefty. I had no other choice though, I didn't want to bother my relatives with a long drive.

He pulled up in front of the dorm buildings and I paid him before grabbing my things from the trunk. I smiled up to a few girls I knew who were also moving back in or just hanging around. If I remember correctly, Julia wouldn't be around until tonight and Meg will be returning tomorrow.

So there was only one thing to keep me occupied. The moment I got my belongings in order, I made my way outside and followed the familiar path to the apartment complex nearby.

I know that the right thing was to knock on my uncle's door and greet him along with my aunt and cousins, but I didn't manage to reach his apartment because I found myself knocking on the door next to it.

I was itching to see him since my birthday, the walls have crumbled down and now we were both in the know.

I like him and he likes me.

The door swung open and Adam's eyes widened he saw me standing there and I all but jumped in his arms. His hold on me was tight and he managed to lift me off of the ground while my hands gripped on his shoulders for support.

By this point, my hair have turned into a mess but when he stared at my face, he laughed with so much glee that it made my heart melt into a puddle. His grip of me tightened even when he carefully placed me back down on the ground. My hands went from his shoulders to the back of his neck, my nails lightly grazing on his nape, "I missed you."

"It was torture that half of the time you were gone, we were fighting," he sighed and it made me lean forward to rest my forehead on his chest.

That argument felt like it was ages ago when in fact, it was just a few weeks.

But the spell was broken by a loud thud from inside of his apartment. He let out an audible groan, slightly angling his body so he would face inside, making me release him, but a single arm remained wrapped around my waist.

I peeked from behind him and I had to remind myself not to gape when I saw a fuming Heart Valentine glaring at a sheepish Axel Brooks, who appeared to have expertly avoided a book hurled towards him, "I can't believe you allowed yourself to get photographed!"

"You know that it's hard to deny fans a selfie," he defended but he didn't sound apologetic at all, "Calm down, baby."

"How can I calm down when the world will find out that we're staying here?" she growled, her annoyance clearly evident in her voice.

But it wasn't their shouting match that made me stare – it was a combination of their charisma and pure ridiculousness of this situation.

Because even in the midst of fury, Heart was a vision of beauty and the lack of makeup made this experience even more worthwhile. Light freckles peppered her nose and cheeks, even when her blonde hair was threatening to fall off from the messy bun she pulled it into, and all those imperfections made her all the more real.

And Axel, whose cunning and endearing ways was something everybody loved, suddenly shed light why women plastered his face on their bedroom walls. His strong features and build screamed for your undivided attention. Somehow, there was still a boyish charm around him that drew you towards him and now that I was so close to him, I could see those deep laugh lines and the wrinkles by his eyes as he chuckled, making him more handsome as if it was possible.

Now, I was a first-hand witness to those fights Adam used to joke about. The public portrayed them as this playful and sweet couple, completely forgetting these small moments when it wasn't always rainbows and butterflies.

That was just the cherry on top in their supposed perfect relationship.

"Have I told you how hot you look when you're mad, Valentine?" he smirked and although this caused her to pause for a quick second as I saw a blush slowly crept onto her cheeks, it wasn't enough to dilute her anger.

"Stop joking for at least a second, Brooks!"

"Let's get you something warm to drink, it's still cold outside," Adam offered in order to pull me away from my gawking, placing a hand on the small of my back and ushered me towards the kitchen. Although it was rude and creepy, my eyes couldn't look away from those two.

When people say that when you see them, you can never look away, they really meant it.

The smirk gracing Axel's face fell off and he took four large steps until he was in front of his girlfriend. She didn't back away nor flinch, only standing her ground. He cupped her face in his hands and pressed his forehead against hers, "I'm sorry, okay? I assure you that no one's going to bother us."

The words he murmured wrapped in so much tenderness just melted away her resolve. A small frown went upon her pink lips, "I hope so."

He flashed her a small smile, urging her to do the same, "I love you."

And those three words was enough to let her annoyance and frustration go away. She smiled, her hand went up to cover his as she mimicked what he said, "I love you."

Now I know why Adam wanted to move on – the thing that these two have was amazing. They both have fire in their veins, wild and bright on their own, though their flames danced with each other. Her slight giggle at something he whispered into her ear made a grin spread onto his face and the way she rubbed his knuckles with her thumb made his whole stature relax.

Adam cleared his throat, finally finding it a safe time to interrupt the couple, "You're not the only ones in the room."

He handed me a cup of tea and I shot him a grateful look, wrapping my frigid hands around the blue mug. They slowly turned towards our direction and blinked when they saw me, this was the moment they first acknowledged my presence.

I felt his arm slung around my shoulders when he sensed my nervousness, giving my arm a comforting squeeze, "This is Sienna Clark. Sienna, I sincerely hope you know these two."

I nodded in acknowledgement, but the two made no other move except when Heart started to walk towards us, making Axel release her. Her gaze was scrutinizing, her icy cold blue eyes lost all the warmth she had reserved for her lover, and her face devoid of any emotion. She was regarded as Hollywood royalty and I see why, she moved with grace and dignity even when she was dressed in nothing but a pair of ripped jeans and a gray top, her soles bare of any footwear.

When she stood in front of me, she stretched out a hand, still calculating my movements, "Sophia Heart Valentine, it's a pleasure."

Her voice ran a shiver down my spine. It wasn't like when Adam had her on speaker, her tone was light and teasing back then. It wasn't cautious and pleading like when she called me when her best friend and I got into an argument. And especially not minutes prior when it was a mixture of fury and affection.

It was stern and there's a harsh bite at the end.

And all I could do was stare at her hand, observing how her slim fingers trailed to long and sharp red painted nails – nails that could possibly scratch my skin off. I couldn't will myself to shake it and I couldn't even dare to look up to meet her gaze nor did I want to glance up to her face.

"Cut it out, Soph," came Adam's reprimanding words.

"Cut what out?" she asked innocently, lowering her hand to her side so my view was replaced by my own feet.

"We talked about this," he sighed and I felt him pull me closer to his side, "Give Sienna a break."

"How else should I react to the girl who placed you in such a horrible and sad mood during the holidays?"

My head snapped up and I saw her knitted eyebrows coupled with that pout. So it really was true how fast he can make her mood change. But her reason for her animosity made my blood run cold – she hated me for the sole reason I caused displeasure to her best friend.

And I couldn't even pull myself together to explain myself.

Although it was immature of me not to reply to Adam's calls, he was the one who started it all. If only he didn't act so melodramatic over one picture of Justin and I then all this wouldn't have happened.

Okay, I was pointing fingers but it was not entirely my fault.

Yet apparently, in her eyes, Adam was the sweet angel who could do no wrong and I was the one who forsaken him.

We heard a chuckle and Axel wrapped his arms around her waist and pulled her body backwards to him. She didn't protest like I expected her to, especially when he placed a chaste kiss on the top of her golden locks, "Axel Brooks and welcome to the circus."

Again I was mute and I felt Adam's grip on me loosened until his arm was no longer draped over my shoulders. There was now some intangible tension around us and I genuinely wanted to run away. I did, but not in the turning around and rushing out type.

I placed my untouched drink onto the table and forced myself to smile, "I think I should go say hello to my relatives next door. It was really nice meeting you two," I threw the words out with as much nonchalance as I can, "I'll see you next time Adam."

Adam obviously didn't want to let me go, but he probably guessed that this was turning too uncomfortable for me. So he nodded, letting me head out the apartment and close the door behind me. When I did, I urged myself not to sink down on the floor and just stay there as if everything would be miraculously solved.

Taking a deep breath, I walked towards the next door and knocked, waiting for somebody to open it. Andy was the one to get it and I gave him a light hug before stepping inside, "I'm exhausted to say the least."

"After a twelve hour flight, it's to be expected," he quipped, "Want something warm to drink?"

"Nope," I replied faster than normal. Hell no, especially the last warm beverage I was given never got sipped because of some compromising situation.

Plopping myself down on the couch, I removed my shoes and propped my feet on top of the coffee table. I scanned around the room, my eyes falling to the stack of canvases by the corner, "Where's Emma?"

"Went out with a friend," he answered, sitting next to me with his laptop, continuing on his writing that I must have disturbed.

If it was a passage to meet you significant other's friends and family then I don't know how I should react with what happened next door. She was haughty, that was for sure, and it was true that she hasda personality – I expected it, but to stay there was suffocating.

She completely disapproved of me and to be honest, the braver part of me wanted to yell that I was not the one who should take all the blame. The fight we had was also partly Adam's fault.

But can you imagine me saying that to her? If she can throw a book towards her boyfriend, I can only imagine what she can chuck towards my direction.

With that, I fell to my side and let out a loud scream, startling Andy and making him jump up in surprise. I wasn't even near apologetic when he glared at me. I simply craned my neck to bury my face on the couch.

Chapter 23

I wholeheartedly accepted the apology Adam sent me in place of his best friend. He was not at fault, but I did prevent myself from visiting his place again, even when he asked me to. I also had an excuse ready at the tip of my tongue, saying that I was busy or I wanted to hang out at some other place.

When Julia, who came back two days ago, practically kicked the door open when I was leisurely typing on my laptop, I started guessing for the reason why her eyes were wide as saucers and her body was puffing for air.

Meg was right behind her and she placed a hand on her shoulder to pull her back, "Somebody's waiting downstairs for you."

"Adam?" I questioned because who else could elicit a reaction from my roommate aside from him.

"Yes," she replied, although it was obvious her composed disposition was just a façade, "And two other people."

It didn't take long for everything to click and I rushed past them, going down the stairs as quickly as my legs would allow me. Standing right there by the entrance was the mentioned boy, looking as handsome as ever, and the couple who got the residences of this dormitory whispering.

Heart and Axel looked like they were ready to strut the streets of London with their long coats and fashionable accessories. Her face appeared just like how I see her in the billboards and magazines, makeup hiding her imperfection and flaws while the soft pink of her lips was covered in a fierce red. Axel's mischievous glint was gone and was replaced by a lazy look that was attractive but could also send anybody running.

And Adam, as calm as he was compared to the other two, looked intimidating as well because of his height and this caused the trio to appear like a force to be reckoned with.

When he spotted me, a grin overcame his features and he coughed out to his best friend who couldn't make it any more obvious that the last place she wanted to be was here. She sighed, advancing towards me with her high heels emphasizing her tall stature.

"I'm sorry, Sienna," she let out and I had to look up at her to see her face, "How I acted was completely wrong but I'm infamous for being impulsive."

She was chewing her words and her tense state made her apology even more insincere. Axel chuckled behind her, finally removing the spell of being untouchable. She turned to him to shoot him a glare and he was unfazed by this, joining her side and then leaning down to whisper something, "Valentine and I are going out to town, how about you grace our friend over there a date?"

"What?"

"Get your coat and let's get out of here," Heart deadpanned, low enough so only I could hear her. I didn't want to do anything to upset her more so I ran back upstairs because I was just ticking off the checklist of her traits and pretty sure impatience was part of that list.

But of course, I didn't want to go outside in some silly cotton shorts and besides, Axel implied that he and Heart will leave Adam and I alone so a large part of me was hoping that we will go on a date. So I traded my shirt for a long sleeved dress and my shorts for a thick pair of black leggings. My fluffy lounge slippers were replaced by my ankle boots and I snatched my coat on the way out of the door.

With a promise to both Julia and Meg that I will explain why two A-class celebrities were looking for me when I get back, they let me off with a wave goodbye. We started to walk back towards the apartment and when it was just the four of us alone, Axel let out a groan, "Finally!"

"They were acting like they have never seen humans before," Heart rolled her eyes, linking her arms with her boyfriend, "I couldn't even say sorry properly because of them."

Wait, what?

"They're used to the spotlights but they can also reach their limits," Adam explained next to me once he saw my baffled expression, "Her apology was sincere."

I snapped my head towards his direction and he flashed me a soft smile. My confusion dropped, only to be replaced by a small blush at the sight of him. Aside from our mini reunion when he opened the door to his apartment, we were both holding back because of the blonde celebrity walking in front of us.

I felt him fumble for my hand until it was now in his grasp, resting our entwined holds between us.

Better.

"Sienna, let's talk some time," Heart looked over her shoulder to look at me, "Girl talk and don't worry, your man over there already gave me a hefty scolding for the way I acted."

Adam laughed at her words, moving forward and tugging me along with him, "Your temper always get the better of you, Soph."

"And I've been on the receiving end of Valentine's outburst," Axel quipped and although she wanted to look annoyed, her scowl was quick to melt into a smile when he ran a soothing hand on her arm.

"I'm sorry if it's rude to ask," I spoke, catching all of their attention, "But I noticed that you two always refer to each other by last names. Why?"

Then they shared a knowing glance, the smiles and laughter being traded gave me a small hint. It was an inside joke these two shared and from the way they looked at each other made a small pit of envy in my stomach. Not because I have feelings for either of them, but because they have something I only see in the movies or read in those corny romance novels.

Their relationship was far from dull, they've made a life out of posing for the camera and constantly being surrounded by people. Even though their faces showed how tired and worn they really were, there's still a bounce to their step and evident happiness in their features.

They argue – a lot – something I've picked up from Adam's tales and after witnessing it first-hand. But I was nothing but impressed of how quickly they snap back together with forgiveness already in their mouths even in the midst of a fight. That tender declaration of love coming from both of them was completely genuine, even being award winning actors, you cannot fake that.

Even if she doesn't want to show it, he can turn her into a flustered mess in an instant or how her fierce disposition quickly transform into a lovesick puppy once he holds her. And him? He was completely wrapped around her finger, never wanting to be apart.

They were one of those kinds of couples that I've always enjoyed writing about.

So that was why I was completely shocked when they answered my inquiry, "We used to hate each other."

"Despise was the term I used often," Heart giggled, leaning more onto him, "You should see us back then, we couldn't be in the same room without having a yelling match or glare-off."

"She kicked me on the first day we met," he recalled with a nostalgic sigh, "Though, in her words, I was an asshole back then."

"Still are," she smirked though it was full of playfulness, "But unfortunately, I chose to be yours."

Just imagine being in a whirlwind romance like theirs? Now I know why Adam have absolutely refused to come between them, they really were meant to be for each other. She was undeniably happy – even when they were fighting, the anger never reached her eyes. Her furrowed brows might be a cause of alarm, but one look at him and all her arguments will die in her throat.

We reached the building and I expected them to go inside with us but they just waved us goodbye as they entered the car parked in front. I turned to Adam and he smiled invitingly, tugging me along towards the elevator.

When we got inside his apartment, I almost burst out laughing when he took out the lasagna from the oven where he left to keep warm. He grinned at me sheepishly as he proudly stated, "Made from scratch."

"Only five months late," I snorted jokingly, "No big deal."

He chuckled while he grabbed two plates and started to portion it. I took the liberty of opening his fridge to get us something to drink and I lifted a brow at the wider selection of beverages. It was usually just a pitcher of water and a few cans of soda, but now it ranged from sparkling water to an expensive bottle of champagne.

I guessed that this was Heart's doing. Considering that two of the wealthiest celebrities under twenty-one were currently staying in this place, this should be no surprise to me.

"What do you want?" I questioned, peering through the shelves. When he responded that I should be the one to choose, I smiled while taking two cans of soda. Let us ignore the champagne and even the wine.

I've been here so many times, so it was weird to think that this would be the first time that I would eat on the dining table we purchased way back during our first week in the area; for no other reason aside from the fact that we usually ate our meals on the couch with the coffee table.

He brought out a scented candle and placed it in the middle, lighting it up and filling the air with a peppermint aroma, perfectly reminding me of the holidays. I mused that it must be some left over – something he hasn't managed to completely burn before he left to go home.

It was a crazy mix match but honestly, we've already tried a fancy dinner at an expensive restaurant and a rowdy night in a frat party, so something like this was already amazing in its own right. I wasn't going to say that I'd rather have this than the elaborate date with glimmering chandeliers hanging above us nor do I prefer that to simple nights in.

Sometimes I was in a mood for this and sometimes I wanted the other.

He pulled up a chair and I seriously had to check myself in order to keep my amusement at bay. His effort was extreme on this one so I wanted to show my appreciation.

I forked a little bit of lasagna into my mouth and I hummed happily at the taste. Well, I guess the hype was really worth it since this was surprisingly good, "Alright, chef, I admit this is amazing."

He grinned contentedly, eating his own meal as silence basked between us. Just a few more days until classes start again, and although the first few weeks will be quite lax, it will all come boiling down to the fact that we wouldn't see each other as much as we want to. Adding more insult to the injury, we've spent the holidays so far apart and during the majority those times, we refused to even speak to each other.

"I'm sorry," I muttered, "For being so ridiculously irrational. I should have known better than to believe some tabloid article."

"No," he shook his head, "I should apologize for being so jealous after a single picture. And at the end, I never heard the story of how much you had fun back home."

I perked up when he reminded me of that wonderful night out. Nothing, and I mean nothing, can beat the rush of being home and sneaking out at the late hours of the night. He urged me to tell him all about it and I did, because it was an excuse to reminisce it all over again.

Of the city I love wherein I fell in love for the first time.

"Then he took my hand and pulled me away," I smiled softly, finally reaching the part wherein Justin dragged me from the group. This was the first time his posture stiffened after chuckling and nodding throughout the events prior to this.

But I didn't want to be the girl to exclude it, because it was what really happened and I would be lying if I left it out, "He took me to the rooftop of his apartment building and the scene was gorgeous, just like how I remembered it."

By now I knew he wanted nothing more than to stop me. Still, he remained silent with his vice grip on his cutlery, perhaps remembering the last time he allowed envy to open his damn mouth for him. Of course, I put him out of his misery, "That's when I realized that he can never give me what you can."

"What?" he questioned, his eyebrows knitting together in that adorable way that made me smile.

"Before I even stepped on this country, I was warry of everything. Then you came, sat next to me on that plane, and relieved me of any nervousness. With him, I was always on a high of fun and energy, but you?"

I halted for a moment to take a deep breath, my eyes looking right into his brown ones, "You calmed me down when I needed to the most. You brought me back on track, especially with the writing part, and I will always be thankful for it."

He heard the sincerity in my words and his expression relaxed, smiling at me, "I want to thank you as well."

"For what?"

"Because you didn't turn away when I said that I loved Soph."

It was so crazy that when we met each other, we had our individual loves that we had such a hard time moving on from, "You're welcome."

And there it goes, the silence once again falling over us. As the sound of metal forks and knives scratching plates entered my ears, my mind went wandering.

Okay, our first date was a complete bust with me decidedly getting drunk and him just asking me out to satisfy Heart's meddling. The second one was sweet and got me admitting that I had actual feelings for him.

And this one was our third. We've finished the 'weaving through each other and testing waters' stage, so what was next?

I wasn't one of those people who wanted no titles nor was I the kind who sought out one in an instant. I just wanted to be in the know of the pacing – if he wanted to go slow then I would be a sloth and if he wanted to go fast then I was going to go on a speed that would make Lightning McQueen proud.

Kachow, you idiots.

But then again, why was I thinking like this if I had this inkling feeling that whatever we were going to have, it would just be for a small while.

When the door unexpectedly swung open, I stopped eating and my eyes widened to see Axel and Heart walking back in. We stared at them like a deer caught in the headlight.

They obviously knew they ruined something and by the triumphant grin on Axel's face, I wanted nothing more for the ground to swallow me up whole, "Now it's my turn to cockblock you!"

Heart rolled her eyes as she shrugged her coat off after closing the door behind her, "Some fans saw us and we thought we'll be let off after a few pictures, but they posted it online and suddenly the restaurant had this long cue. Not because people wanted to eat there, but apparently, they thought we were oh-so-willing to do an impromptu meet and greet."

"Bad luck for you two, but we're going to have our date here as well," Axel said as he went up to the ceramic dish of lasagna after grabbing two plates from the cupboard, "Hey Valentine, do we still have sparkling water in the fridge."

"I'm in a mood for champagne," Heart responded, "Let's pop a bottle open."

And I can only gape as these two set up their own dinner on the coffee table. Axel unapologetically stole the lighted scented candle and Heart got a couple of glasses then poured themselves a drink.

Apparently, having Adam in my life also meant that these two will come with him.

I whipped my head to shoot him an incredulous look but the complete relaxed expression he was sporting finally made me laugh.

Chapter 24

There were situations that I've pictured myself in. However, shopping and acting as if I was suddenly BFFs with Hollywood's Princess was not one of them. She acted so nonchalant as she held up a dress in front of her, assessing her reflection in the mirror.

The employees of the store did not even try to hide their excitement and she did a good job of ignoring the way their hands were basically shaking when she asked them something.

"I'm going to try this on," she smiled before grabbing another dress from her pile and tossing it towards my direction, something I fumbled around in an attempt to catch, "And you try that."

The dress reminded of the one Meg allowed me to borrow back during the restaurant date with Adam. It was tight but long sleeved, but unlike hers which was a dark navy blue, this one was a dark red that I began to doubt if I was daring enough to sport.

Aside from that, it was not hugging the right places and I was constantly tugging down on the hem because it kept on riding up on the back part

"Sienna," Heart called out and I took a deep breath, smoothening down the dress with my hands before going out. She wore almost an identical one, the only difference was that hers had an off-shoulder. Yet, while I looked like a sausage ready to burst, she looked every bit of attractive in that dress.

She twirled around, her blonde hair creating a curtain around her face, and shot me a skeptical glance, silently questioning me if she should purchase the article of clothing. I all but blushed in embarrassment when I saw the two of us side by side in the mirror.

Well, goodbye self-esteem.

"We should do a double date with the boys some time wearing these dresses," she shrugged when she realized I wasn't going to reply, "You look good in that."

"I feel like I'm being squeezed out," I huffed unintentionally, trying to flatten my boring brown hair, "I don't think I like the look of it on me."

Her eyes zeroed on me as her lips flattened down into a thin line, an unamused expression now making its way into her features. She clicked her tongue before standing right behind me, once again emphasizing the height difference between us, especially because I took the liberty of taking off my shoes when I was squeezing myself into this dress while her heels remained on her feet.

"Oh god, I looked hideous a few years back," she snorted, pushing her hair over her shoulder, "But you know one thing that's different now? I didn't even change that much, it all came to the gained confidence."

"I would have guessed the confidence will come from people admiring you from every side," I said, finally finding myself slowly getting comfortable around her.

She smirked at my words, as if she's on in her own private joke that I could never understand, "But I think also being criticized by everybody will also do its damage."

This made my lips go shut and I was already formulating a long constructed apology. I guess she's used to people like me because she already lifted a hand to stop my long train of thoughts, "I'm not offended, in fact, I detach myself from people that aren't part of the industry to the point that I forgot that your opinions are like this."

She was tired – physically and emotionally.

Physically in the sense that you can clearly see the outline of her heavy eyebags that had been desperately concealed through makeup and the way she carefully tries to masks her staggering steps even though she had clearly mastered the art of wearing heels. When she attempts to look calm and composed, you could see how her posture looks like it was ready to collapse. Add to that was her voice, it was turning husky and worn out, probably for overusing it throughout her still on-going tour.

And yet when you see her on-stage, she always appeared as if she had all the energy in the world.

Emotionally because her eyes, even so expressive on her own, had lost their twinkle. When she smiles, it was like staring at a ghost because of how empty they appear. Still, she tried to be the ball of joy in other people's lives, laughing easily and seeking enjoyment in the simplest of ways.

Adam told me how she used to be so clumsy, such a cryba-
by, and an overall lost girl who managed to bounce the walls
with happiness in the midst of it all. Then the idea made me
die a little bit inside – how much did Hollywood ruin her?

"Get rid that sympathetic face," she sighed, disappearing
into the curtain of the dressing room, "I chose this for myself
and although it had its downs, the ups made up for it."

I dashed into my own dressing room and I quickly tried to
peel off the dress from my body, loving the feel of oxygen
after I've sucked in my stomach for the horrendous amount
of time just to fit into the damn piece of clothing.

I made her upset again.

When I stepped out, she was already talking orders to the
saleslady, pointing at almost every single item she walked
past and asking for one in her size. She didn't even bother
with trying them on one by one, she went straight to the
counter and handed them her credit card.

So this was retail therapy in its extreme.

And if you think her power stops there, instead of carrying the bags, she told them to deliver it to the apartment
complex. Of course, with the obscene amount of money she
spent, I didn't think that they were in any position to deny
her.

"Heart," I coughed out when we were on our third shop
after I've unintentionally triggered her shopping spree, "Do
you want to grab a bite?"

She turned to me, more disheveled than I have ever seen
her. She slowly nodded her head after the cashier had handed her back her credit card.

I pulled her to the same café Adam and I went to when we first went furniture shopping for the sole reason that it was the nearest one we could reach and also because I've frequented this place since, it was nice to lessen the burden of overthinking where to eat or what to order.

"I'm so sorry," she apologized profusely, her head bowing in shame. Now her tone was no longer malicious, threatening, or full misplaced frustration.

And I thought I had mood swings.

"I completely forgot that this was supposed to be a trip for me to get to know you," she groaned, covering her face with her hands, "And I ended up exploding again. I really want us to get along, especially because you really mean something to Adam."

My posture relaxed when she said the last part and how can I honestly get worried when she had a best friend who was the most wonderful guy in the world? We already had a mutual ground – we both cared for Adam. As much as I wanted nothing but to plaster a smile on my face and wait for this day to be over, I couldn't do that.

Because she was trying, even if it was against her very nature to be the one to approach somebody. She was actually making a huge effort even if she basically acted hostile when we first met.

I should at least reciprocate it.

"Wait, do I have your approval?" I asked although I was weighing in if it was a sensible decision to open my mouth.

She dropped her hands and blinked at me, "I'm not his parents, although you wouldn't have any problems with his mom and dad because they're basically angels like their son. However, even if I didn't like you, Adam does and it was his decision to enter a relationship with you."

Just saying princess, we were not in a relationship yet.

And then she flashed me that award-winning smile of hers, but it did scare me because it was the one reserved for the cameras, it wasn't like her grin whenever she was with Adam or Axel. It was fake and it made my heart drop because it meant she wasn't comfortable enough with me.

She had walls, higher than mine will ever be. To tear them will be long and excruciating but something in me screamed that it will be all worth it.

There must be a reason why he used to be so smitten with her. What is it about her that got him head over heels in love?

And what must I do to get him to reach that point with me?

"He really cares for you," I said, smiling halfheartedly at the waiter after he had laid down our orders on the table. I didn't miss the way his eyes lingered on Heart though, "I'm sorry but this is going be my insecurity coming out, but in the occasion that you find out that he did love you as more than just friends, what will you do?"

Her eyes widened in surprise, probably afraid that I knew that she loved him like that. I did my best to keep my expression stoic though, hoping that she wouldn't find the truth in my face. Desperately wishing that sshe wouldn't realize how I do know and how I'm also aware of Adam's past feelings.

To throw a tantrum because he was so close and even staying in the same apartment with his best friend was ridiculously immature. Sure, the me a few years ago would have ensued a fight but who was I to complain when I also care so much for my ex?

I think trust was what was going to keep our relationship going because there would always be a third party and if not, distance would continue with its attempts to tear us apart.

"Theoretically, if that happens..." she trailed off, her gaze settling on her plate, "Then I'll say thank you."

"Thank you?" I repeated.

"Thank you," she confirmed, finally glancing up to meet my eyes, "I can't say that I love him to that degree as well anymore, because I'm in love with Axel. He's my prince charming, someone who I never realized that I needed because I was too busy being in my own bubble locked up in this grand tower. I can't replace him, I can never even fathom the thought of being with somebody else except for him and it's silly because we haven't even been dating for a year and yet, I love him like this."

You know what it was like to be completely in awe with somebody else's relationship? I only think of that when it's about fictional couples, but to be in the presence of someone who bravely announced her love and affection to somebody else with no hesitation, it blew my breath away. Not a single pause to think when she was saying her speech, it flowed so easily from her mouth that I was sure it wasn't rehearsed.

And now I was completely jealous. I wanted that surety, that lack of insecurity. She knew her relationship, she knew her partner, and she knew herself.

Me? I was barely aware what class I had for a particular day.

But then I remembered how she had to go through heart-break before she was able to claim her happiness.

Well, love really is a rollercoaster ride. And let me tell you, sometimes it wasn't going to be fun but you've already sat in the cart and started the ride. Most of the times, you have no other choice but to stay there and see how it plays out.

Have I ever looked as love struck as she currently was? Have I ever stared wistfully at thin air as if it was the person himself?

Maybe, when I was too crazy for Justin. I wanted to feel it again though, and I wanted to experience it in a more grandeur style.

"You're good for him," she finally said after I've been under her speculative gaze the whole day, "Not overly dramatic, nothing too fretful, but just enough emotions to keep him on his toes."

I had no idea if that was a compliment, if I was being completely honest.

"A few weeks from now, Axel and I will be leaving because we both have our jobs to think about," she told me, taking a long sip of her hot coffee, "Adam and I have been apart since I was fifteen, I believe, when I moved to California. Aside from the video chats and customary holiday visits, I don't see him that much. He changed without me knowing, and he'll continue to do so."

I can only imagine what these two went through. Fifteen was the time when I was finally stripping myself off of my awkward phase – I was nailing down how to do my make-up, I started buying designer clothes, I bought a lot of skin products all recommended by my dermatologist to get rid of any horrible acne, and I was slowly gaining myself a new boyfriend.

For Heart and Adam? A dynamic that went from seeing each other almost every single day turned into a separation where none of them were fully aware of at the time.

"You used to like him as more than a friend, didn't you?" I shot out, shocking both of us with my straightforwardness.

So much for keeping it a secret.

And now her face turned so pale that I was genuinely concerned if she was going to faint at that very moment. But she recovered by swallowing hard, her fingers tapping nervously on the surface of the table. I held my breath in anticipation for her answer, I already fired the gun now I was just going to see if the bullet was going to hit her or if she will skillfully dodge it.

She chose the former by clearing her throat loudly and after a taking a long sip from her glass of water, she nodded, "Correct."

To hear it from Adam was one thing, for her to admit it herself was another, "That's why I'm asking you to take care of him. He deserves the world, he may have not chosen me and it did break my heart when he told me so, but he has chosen you. I know him, he doesn't take anything less than what he think is right."

She was strong and the bond she and my boyfriend shared was as well. It endured a distance worth the Atlantic Ocean, as well as a confession that was infamous for breaking friend-ships. Still, they valued each other just the same.

That was when I finally got the signal that it might be a while before she can trust me with her true self, but I have just gotten her approval. Even if she said that I don't need it, Adam thinks the world of his best friend and I don't want to him to be disappointed because we don't get along. She's important to him and I understand that, for that reason I want her to like me.

Because I don't want to be with a man who doesn't place his friends as one of his top priorities since I know fully well that if I started dating a guy my friends doesn't like, you bet the relationship will be over in a snap.

"Thank you," I murmured, a small smile appearing on my face.

"So have you done it with him yet?" she questioned boldly, making me choke on my own spit, a deep blush heating up my cheeks. She saw my reaction and she started to laugh freely, covering her mouth with her hand, "I'm only joking."

I bit my lip in embarrassment as she continued to giggle good-naturedly at my expression.

"How about we go around a few more shops after we eat before going back to the boys?" she suggested, gingerly gliding a knife through her baked salmon, "I promise to act more rationally with buying things."

When both of us have finally loosened up, the experience was much more enjoyable. The stores already appreciates it when I come in and buy things from them, but they absolutely adore it when Heart does it.

My style is very versatile – I can go from ripped jeans and sneakers to long dresses and high heels with a quick snap so it was always a fun gamble when going out as all my purchases depended on my mood.

And I think Heart just needed someone to play dress up with because after she had a full evaluation of just how many clothes she bought – realizing that it was all too ridiculous even for her – she started to pick things for me. This got the many salesladies and salesmen fawning over the two of us, ready to give her whatever she asks whether it was the same dress in a different color or another size.

"We're back," she declared after we have managed to carry all of the shopping bags we have accumulated throughout the whole day.

Axel and Adam weren't even talking when we came in, they each took the opposite sides of the L-shaped couch as their eyes were glued to the their phones even though the TV was running in front of them. When Heart cleared her throat loudly to catch their attention again, that was the only time they looked up.

"So how was your girls' day out?" Axel questioned, standing up from the couch and getting the bags from his girlfriend's arms.

"Fantastic," she grinned, kissing him on the cheek and heading up to her bedroom with him following behind.

Releasing a happy sigh, I plopped down on the couch next to Adam and rested my head on his shoulder. Although it was a great day, at the end of it all, I was still exhausted.

"Had fun?" he questioned, wrapping an arm around my shoulders and soothingly massaging my shoulder. I hummed contentedly and I saw him smile when I glanced up to see his face, "Good."

"She has quite the energy," I laughed, kicking off my shoes and resting them on the cushion of the couch.

He chuckled lightly, now moving his hand to run his fingers through my hair, which relaxed me in the best way possible, "Maybe because she haven't been out with a girl her age for some time now."

"I did kind of feel that she was rather lonely," I muttered, "But it's alright, I like it."

"I told you that you'll like her," he pointed out, reminding me of that exchange that have felt like forever ago.

But then again, meeting him really did feel like it had been ages.

Chapter 25

"You wrote it down, you're writing it down, and you're going to write it down anyways," Uncle Levi read out loud and I merely smiled at him, trying to contain my nervousness. He glanced up towards me before nodding, sliding the iPad back to my side of the table, "Keep it up, but you're going too slow after you had such a good pacing in the beginning."

"I'm sorry," I frowned slightly, tucking the device back inside my bag, "I wasn't able to do much when I was back home and I got kind of distracted since I came back."

He glanced up and sighed, "Although I like him for being your source of inspiration, remember that I still am your uncle and my dearest brother-in-law will not appreciate it if he learned that I simply allowed his daughter to go off with a man."

Seriously? He plays the overprotective older male relative now?

"Uncle, you know Adam," I told him, reaching over to grab a fry from the middle of the table, "He's a good guy."

"I'm aware," he nodded, "And it's not like you're a child anymore. Just be careful, Sienna."

"I think I know how to protect myself," I laughed, gently slicing my chicken, "But thank you."

"You're stubborn, impulsive, and willful," he listed off and I had to scoff. Although, his tone mellowed down as he added, "With one of the brightest spirits I have ever seen and that's what I missed most about you."

Blinking up at him, I smiled warmly before continuing with my meal. While my father was passive with these kind of things, my mom trying to think of business more than the art, and Aunt Janina looking at the technical side, my writing was on the verge of being too robotic.

But uncle made sure I didn't lose sight of what it truly was – an expression. He didn't give up on me and while I think I've dulled down a lot since when I first started, he was a constant reminder that maturing does not mean being monotonous.

After we had finished eating and he paid the bill, he went off to the university. Classes were starting tomorrow and he was trying to finish his preparation for the new semester. I glanced down on my watch and headed to the dormitories – it's been a while since I got to chat with Julia and Meg without me constantly looking at the time or being dead tired.

And besides, I owed them complete compliance during an interrogation session.

Julia even went the extra mile to grab her study lamp, close all of the lights in our room, and directed the said lamp towards my direction. Meg was facepalming beside her while I only watched on with amusement at my roommate's antics.

"Alright, talk," Julia demanded in this weird accent in a way to imitate those detective shows, but if you mixed it with her native accent and her horrible attempt, it was hilarious.

Meg rolled her eyes before pushing the curtains open and turning off the damn lamp as she mimicked Julia's tone, "Alright, stop."

Thank you for having at least one sensible person between them.

Julia grumbled some things about her being a killjoy but she turned on the ceiling lights again and sat down on the bed next to me, "But in all seriousness, how did you meet Heart Valentine? I mean, I kind of already had an idea that she and Adam knew each other because of the headline last December."

"Aren't we going to talk about the thing with Adam?"

"We all knew it was going to happen so no point in that," Meg shrugged, sitting on the carpet, gesturing for Julia to throw her a pillow, "I'm more interested on Hollywood's Princess."

"She's Adam's best friend, they've known each other since they were kids."

Julia gasped, "And nothing ever happened between them?"

I had the same damn reaction. No matter how political people wanted to be, it was kind of expected that a boy and girl who had been best friends for most of their lives will eventually come together. Something did happen – he fell in love with her and she fell in love with him.

But they valued something more than their feelings, which was their friendship.

"Nothing happened," I lied because their story was definitely not mine to tell, "I knew it for a while now."

"And you never told us?" she pouted and I rolled my eyes, throwing a pillow towards her direction.

"How on earth was I going to bring it up?" I huffed, "Oh hey, you know that celebrity you've been fawning about? He's the best friend of the guy I really like."

"That would have been nice," Julia's eyes widened and from there, I knew she was completely serious. I laughed, my annoyance melting away into pure joy at her sincerity.

I smiled before opening my luggage that still remained unpacked since I came here. The most I did was pull something out to wear every now and then, but other than that, it remained untouched. Zipping it open, I grabbed the various tacky New York souvenirs and handed it to them, "Just saying, this was my first time in a gift shop back home and it's a lot more interesting than what my friends let on."

"I saw that picture on Instagram," Meg brought up, shaking the snow globe then watching as the fake snow fell on the tiny replica of The Statue of Liberty, "Who was the guy who had his arm around you?"

Laying back down on my bed, I stared up at the ceiling, "My ex, the same guy I based my book on."

Julia let out an overdramatic gasp and Meg surprisingly mimicked it. Sighing, I closed my eyes as I tried to remember that evening. That adventurous night filled with laughter and nostalgia – it was if college and life didn't smack us all in the face and instead, we were just ten high school students sneaking out at midnight.

And it reminded me why I held them so dear. They brought out a side of me that I have seemingly lost since we've graduated. The Sienna who ran freely without a care of the consequences. Now I was cautious in everything, and although it proved to be good, it didn't feel right.

My so-called relationship with Adam was a slow and steady burn. During those moments before Justin and I dated, I remember diving head first to his advances.

Even when it came to making friends, I placed a huge barrier between me and these two, but I remember literally befriending my high school group by just a couple of coincidental circumstances.

"Girls, what's your impression of me?" I dared to ask, sitting right back up. They were obviously caught off-guard by my question so I further explained, "I mean, what do you think is my personality."

"You're careful and distant," Julia answered, shocking me because that was the last thing I thought she was going to say. Actually, I was more surprised at how blunt she was, "But I understand, you're in a different country so you're taking your time to adjust."

Careful? Distant?

"But I'm not careful," I breathed out, "I'm used to running all over the place and to be honest, being idle here bores me."

"Yeah, because being piss drunk after a frat party is definitely boring," Meg scoffed.

I gave her a deadpan look before walking towards my closet and grabbing my coat, "I'm just saying, it's go to class then back here or I go to Adam's place. All I see are darn trees and although it's peaceful, one thing that coming back home made me realize was that I'm not made for this kind of life."

"It's just this place, most of the cities across the country are pretty lively."

"But that's the thing, I'm not staying in those places, I'm staying here," I muttered, "So what do you say?"

The two of them exchanged a look and then back to me, "Say to what?"

"Well, my first class starts at nine, Meg's at nine-thirty, and Julia's at eleven," I listed off, "If we leave now, we can all make it in time."

"Leave where exactly?" they shot again and I looked over my shoulder before shooting them a wink, something the new me would have never done.

"I don't know."

I have never seen two girls so afraid in their life at the mere thought of driving. But here we a\were, we got a rental car and were now on our way to drive miles and miles away from the university. We had nothing but our wallets and phones, we didn't even bother with a charger.

Since we were still in the country part, I could bring down the window and scream with joy. I was the one behind the wheel and we were going at such a fast pace, bordering the speed limit.

Meg was next to me, holding onto her seatbelt while Julia was at the back, gripping onto the headrest of Meg's chair like a vice, "What have you done to our Sienna?"

I brought her back.

To be reckless, to fear nothing.

We stopped a few times for gas, but that was it. None of us knew where this long winding road took us, but we just allowed ourselves to get lost. By this time, Meg had given up in reasoning out with me while Julia looked like she was ready to let go herself.

The night approached quickly and soon, the sky was peppered with beautiful twinkling stars and a quarter moon. I found a space at the side of the road and I pulled over, stopping right there and turning off the engine.

The two other girls were skeptical when I stepped out of the car and took a deep inhale. We were really far from any town so all we saw were roads and fields. The wind blew through my hair, messing it up more than it already was. My phone had lost all of its battery so it was nothing more than paperweight in my pocket.

"So what do you think?" I questioned, urging them to step out as well. They did a complete one-eighty before their gazes landing on me once again, waiting for an explanation, "Wasn't it thrilling? This was what my friends and I used to do back home, just keep on an adventure we never knew where or when it was going to end."

"It was completely out of our comfort zone," Julia said, smiling happily as she wrapped her coat tighter around her body, "But I don't regret coming with you."

"How come you have never shown this side of you?" Meg asked, tentatively sitting on the hood of the car.

Because even I lost that side of me. I used to always go out but due to my slump, that horrid gap year, I forgot what it felt like to feel the rush of the breeze, to expertly move through the sidewalk crowds, and to enjoy with little restraint.

I became a full-pledged writer because I realized how painful heartbreak could be. But when I remember the short entries I had in my journal before the stupid breakup, it was filled with so much emotions. Most of them were happy thoughts, and that was what I tried to write down in the first place.

To be stupid and dumb. I've been caught, I've been scolded, but that never deterred my spirit.

How weak and dependent was I to lose myself because of a guy?

"I came to England with more hesitation than hope," I admitted, "But now, it's the other way around and I could finally remember why I got hurt and why writing became my true love."

I have always jumped without looking and the conse-quences have always hit me hard.

You're stubborn, impulsive, and willful.

Looking back up, I lost myself with the sight of the stars. Light pollution had made it impossible for me to see them back home, but now I can watch them shine.

With one of the brightest spirits I have ever seen.

"I missed you," I whispered under my breath, seeing my reflection through the sideview mirror.

Welcome back, Sienna Clark. I missed that spark in you, that insecurity that you hid with laughter, those imperfec-tions you embraced with open arms, that lack of caution that got you into so many horrible situations.

But most of all, I missed it when you let yourself ride your thoughts. You have never feared them before, but that break up with Justin made you afraid because that was the one time you let your feelings reign before your rational thinking. You've became afraid of what you were feeling.

Closing my eyes, I knew that I would be cursing myself during class, but I couldn't find it within me to care the moment, "Let's go back?"

"Where are we anyway?" Julia asked, going back inside the car, "And how do we get back?"

"Who knows," I shrugged, snapping on my seatbelt, "Don't worry, we still have eight hours until my first class."

Did we make it on time? Yes, because I simply drove straight so we didn't get lost. We arrived back at the university with enough time for a quick shower before I bolted to my first class. It was a bit sad that Uncle Levi wouldn't be the first professor I see during the week, but I worked with what I have.

Of course, no sleep did take its toll on me. While the professor was droning on about introductions to the course and such, my eyelids felt so heavy. I tried to pay attention, I really did, but by the time he was saying something about the chapters we had to read, my mind was full on sleep mode.

I felt something hit me on the back of my head, causing me to jolt up in attention. Looking down, I saw a crumpled up piece of paper and I rolled my eyes – what was this? Third grade?

Glancing over my shoulder, I was slightly surprised by Vance who was sitting a few rows behind me. He caught me looking at him and sent a wink towards my way before turning his focus back to the professor.

Once the class was done, I quickly packed up my bags, took the piece of paper and chucked it towards him. He snickered at my childish retaliation and waited for me to catch up with him.

"You're the last person I imagined to see in this course," I said, "And aren't you a year higher?"

"I cross-enrolled," he explained, stopping right in front of another lecture hall, "Glad that I did, I wouldn't be able to see such a pretty face so early in the morning if I didn't."

I huffed in annoyance before he burst into chuckles, placing a friendly hand on my shoulder, "I'm only kidding, Sienna. Besides, I would never hear the end of it from Adam if I did try to flirt with you for real."

My mouth clamped shut and my cheeks burned with just the mere thought of him being slightly possessive. He was the jealous type, I've learned that through our petty arguments but there was still a thrill to it.

He saw my reaction to his words and a mischievous smirk found its way on his lips, "Wait a minute, are you two dating now?"

Well... Can I say that it wass complicated?

"We're not..." I muttered my quiet reply, "Together in that sense, if that's what you're implying."

Under his scrutinizing gaze, I felt like he could see right through me. Thankfully for now, he allowed it to pass, "Right, I want weekly updates, Sienna."

"You're saying that as if we're also about to make friendship bracelets," I couldn't help but laugh.

"No, but I've known Adam far longer than you have," he told me with an underlying tone of caution, "Don't play with his heart like a fiddle, I'll put my trust on you for now."

Really, Vance would get along with Uncle Levi and Andy, they were all so ominous, "Whatever you say."

I had one more class to go through before I could sleep so the last thing I wanted to do was to waste my energy on this guy. He saw my tired expression and fought back another smile, "I'll see you soon, Sienna."

Chapter 26

I prayed to the heavens that Julia and Meg wouldn't embarrass me. I already apologized ahead of time that I wouldn't be able to stay with them throughout the night, but I think they were ready to forgive me when I gave them the VIP tickets.

Heart just finished doing the sound rehearsals and she had an extra thirty minutes until the meet and greet so she opted to relax inside her dressing room. To be honest, hanging out with Hollywood's Prince and Princess before the latter's concert wasn't something I ever thought of happening.

Yet here we were. She was standing in front of the mirror while she switched between two different jackets, trying to see which one looked better with her outfit. Axel was in a long call with somebody who I presumed to be his manager, judging from the negotiations going through. Then there was Adam, who was happily munching on the snack the crew left inside this room.

He kept offering me some but I turned him down every time because I could barely stomach how surreal this situation was.

"Sienna, what do you think?" Heart turned to me, still holding up the two jackets.

My eyes switched between the two – one was a knitted grey that looked cozy and fashionable at the same time, the other was a red hoodie-esque that would definitely suit her image.

"Red one," I replied and she smiled happily, tossing the grey sweater on the couch and putting on the one I chose.

She examined me before crossing her arms over her chest, "What's in that little head of yours and why do you like you're about to throw up any second now?"

Adam stopped chewing and Axel momentarily paused his conversation to scoot farther away from me. I wanted to glare at him, but we all knew that I did not have the guts to do so.

This was just too weird even for me.

I felt Adam's large hand run smooth circles on my back, leaning towards me so he could take a good look of my face, "She's right, you don't look so good."

"I'm fine," I assured them, "Just a little out of it because this is the first time I get to go backstage during a concert."

"Not as exciting as you thought, right?" Heart said, clicking her tongue when she glanced down on her watch, "I need to go meet the fans, how about you come with?"

"Me?" I gasped, pointing towards myself.

She rolled her eyes and nodded, "Yes, you. Now let's go."

Axel had to stay behind because of his call, but he made sure his girlfriend parted with him after a sweet peck on her cheek. I got to meet her manager, a woman named Taylor who Adam described as one of the stuffiest yet caring people he have come to know.

We stood at the side while Heart happily hugged and posed with each of her fans. I was tempted to hide behind Adam when I saw Meg and Julia coming up in the line. Julia was about to jump all over the place and while Meg was better at keeping her giddiness at bay, you could obviously see her excitement.

"Hello," Heart greeted when they approached her. Although I was crossing my fingers, they ultimately went into a tirade of both admiration and, to my sheer embarrassment, of how they knew me, "Really? So you're the girls Sienna asked a favor for."

My face went pale when I thought there were maliciousness in her voice, especially when it was paired with her sweet smile that was perfectly practiced for the public. Adam went down to grab my hand and gave it a reassuring squeeze, smiling softly down at me.

The trust he puts on her was astounding.

"I hope you take care of her, she's someone who is very dear to a person I love," she told, earning more affection points from the two.

She posed for the camera and as they walked away, Heart sent a wink towards my direction and continued on with the line. This caused me to relax, being assured that there were no ill feelings.

I continued to quietly watch and observe the other fans. At the very end of the line, I squinted a bit to see and my eyebrows shot up at the person I saw, "Vance?"

Adam perked up at the mention of his friend and his grip on me tightened. I started worrying again but then I looked at his face and I was completely dumbfounded at what I saw.

He was laughing. Okay, so he had some reservations since we were still in the middle of the meet and greet, but he was full-on snickering behind his other hand.

Heart finished with the second to the last fan and when she saw who was to come next, the practiced smile slipped off of her face. She glared at him with all her might and placed her hands on her hips, "What the hell are you doing here?"

"Is that any way to greet an old friend?" Vance smirked and I knew her willpower was slipping away.

Heart turned to us and stomped her foot childishly, pointing an accusing finger towards Adam, "Why the hell did you bring him here?"

"I didn't, I was as shocked as you were," Adam defended himself, "But thank you for the entertainment."

"Adam!" Heart screeched, finally turning off her sweet celebrity image.

Vance reached out and hugged her from behind, almost as if he was trapping her and she was obviously struggling in his grip. Still, he wasn't budging, "Come on, I paid for a picture with Heart Valentine, the least you can do is oblige so I can get my money's worth."

"Release me, you buffoon," she protested.

"Let her go, Vance," Adam chuckled, pulling me along to where they were standing, "We don't want her angry just when she's about to perform."

Vance obliged but his teasing smirk still didn't go away, "You're still the same old you, Soph."

Soph. The only person I have heard call her by that name was Adam.

What was Vance's relationship with Heart?

She marched her way back to the backstage, probably to prepare for the concert itself, and the majority of the crew followed her. It was only us plus a few others cleaning up the room who were left.

Vance's gaze softened, his eyes glued to the celebrity's retreating figure, "She's as feisty as I remembered."

"Be careful with yourself, she has a boyfriend now," Adam warned, clapping him on the back, "And he would not be happy if he learned that you did that to his girl."

"You don't have to worry, I backed down years ago for you," he sighed, turning to face Adam only for his eyes to trail down to our joined hands, "Though that seemed to be pretty useless as well."

"Can somebody explained what's happening?" I groaned, looking at the both accusingly.

Adam released me and I unconsciously let out a sound of protest when he did. My eyes widened at my reaction and Vance obviously tried to hold in his laughter while Adam was futile in fighting the red tinting his ears.

Talk about being needy.

Clearing his throat to get rid of the tension, Adam finally addressed my confusion, "Vance used to go to school with Soph and I. He always teased Soph until it got her fuming, but we both know the reason why little boys pick on girls."

He liked her, and probably still does.

That longing look, I've seen it and have done it so many times to know what it meant. From what I picked up, he stopped trying to make advances because of his friendship with Adam. But that didn't erase the fact that he still harbored some feelings for her.

"Very funny," Vance rolled his eyes before placing his gaze back to where Heart exited, "But you're right, she's in a different world now."

She was liked by so many people, even before reaching stardom, and yet, she only had eyes for Adam. She nurtured that crush of hers for years and all it took was one rejection from him for her to stop. Would I have ever gotten the strength to do the same thing she did?

Then again, somebody was there to catch her. Axel snatched her up when Adam let her go and the result was one amazing love story that was supposed to be reserved for the romance books.

And me? I was the one to let go and I was also the one who willingly fell into Adam's arms.

Reaching out, I wrapped my arms around one of his. I leaned against him and puffed my cheeks in an immature manner when I could practically hear Vance's teasing remark that was about to leave his lips, "Not a word."

"I know," he laughed, slowly walking towards the exit, "I have to meet some people up at front, I'll see you soon."

When he was gone, I blinked up at Adam, "You mentioned before that you didn't want Heart for yourself, why didn't you give her to Vance?"

Because although Vance liked to tease people, he seemed kind and genuinely a fun guy.

"I never asked Soph to like Axel, she just did on her own volition," he explained, "If she fell in love with Vance, I wouldn't stop him, but she didn't."

I didn't have much time to dwell on it since Adam started walking us back to Heart's dressing room. By the time we got there, she was already in her first outfit with somebody fitting in her earpiece. I found out that Axel was already onstage hyping up the crowd and doing his own performance.

There was a screen near where Taylor was standing, it showed what was happening onstage. I watched in amazement as he jumped, danced, and sung flawlessly without sounding breathless. Although charming, there was something passive about his attitude and maybe that was the image people had been gushing about.

"Heart is coming up," a man walking by spoke to his walkie talkie just as the said person strutted onwards with a couple of dancers walking behind her.

Adam found his spot next to me once again and urged me to pay attention to the screen just as Axel was ending his song with a ridiculously high note, "That's how you do it."

Confident, attractive, oozing with charisma – Hollywood's Prince.

"As fun as it was being in front of you," he told the crowd, basking in their applause, "There's another person who would like your attention and I want you to cheer loudly for her."

They yelled, they clapped, they screamed her name, "May I present to you, the woman I'm proud to call mine, Heart Valentine!"

Heart walked up the stage, microphone in hand and she winked at Axel as she started singing to her first song. They had a bit of interaction onstage before he exited, getting congratulated by the members of the crew.

But I couldn't even look at him because my eyes were focused on Heart. She was captivating onstage and when I heard shuffling of movements from the guy next to me, I muttered under my breath, "This isn't what you fell for, is it?"

Because the person I was watching was not candidly finding her way through life, this person performed flawlessly. It was as if she wasn't even human, but a doll shaped to be perfect.

Although at first I didn't want to admit it, Adam was right. I did like her just like he thought that I would. Not because of her celebrity status, but because I got to see the real her – to see how ill-tempered, how emotional, and how caring she was. Once she dropped the pretense, I could the girl Adam carried the torch for.

I saw the person I thought I had to compete with to win his affections.

We were completely different.

She was controlled, she welcomed the chains with open arms while I wanted nothing more than to feel the breeze whipping through my hair because of the freedom I felt.

Turning around, I walked back to her dressing room. Adam didn't follow me, he savored the moment of watching his best friend perform. When I was about to reach for the doorknob, it suddenly flew open to reveal a fixed up Axel already out of his stage clothes.

"Not watching the show?"

I looked up at him, meeting those dark brown eyes and I couldn't read a thing from them. He was heavily guarded as well. With their lives right now, they were all keeping their walls up. I took great pride in being able to read other people, but with these two, I couldn't.

And a relationship with Adam equates hanging out with them as well.

I have to be stuck in a room with two people who would never show who they truly were because in their eyes, I was a stranger. I was an outsider who had no right to know because I met them after the fame, the beautiful glamor of stardom.

I completely understood why, they probably had people try to take advantage of them everywhere. But at the same time, I didn't like being with those who were like that.

Show me the truth.

When I started liking Adam, it was when he was stripping away all of his secrets. I got to see the real him, I stopped myself from overthinking what I was feeling.

"I just need to sit down for a while," I murmured, feeling sick to the stomach because of where I was. I should be out there with the audience, bouncing up and down in the crowd with Julia and Meg, unaware of how much these artists were faking it. I wasn't supposed to be back here, playing pretend with people who were masters of that art.

"Did he do something to you?" he asked when I weakly sank onto the loveseat. He was referring to Adam and although he had a contribution to this, he wasn't the cause of my uneasiness.

It never really settled down in my mind that even though he was just the best friend, my life would also change.

Axel released a heavy sigh and went to the mini-fridge, taking out a cold bottle of water and handing it to me, "Here, I can't leave with you like that."

"I'm fine," I lied through my teeth, "You were great out there."

He stared down at me intently before releasing another sigh, sitting on the chair right across from me, "That guy helped me get my girl so I think the least I could do is help him with his."

"I'm not his," I corrected, placing down the water bottle on the coffee table, "Not really and I'm not sure if ever."

"And why's that?"

Was I really going to open to this man?

For now, yes.

"Because this situation I'm in right now is just temporary," I told him, gesturing around the room, "I'm going to leave England after college, I'm going back home to New York to write a book, and being calm and composed is not something I am. Adam has a different pace from me, he's slower and carefully thinks of his movements before acting upon them."

"But isn't that better?" he fired back, stopping me from say-ing anything more, "If you're going too fast, you're going to crash. He could be the one to stop you from doing something dangerous."

Easy for him to say, his girlfriend was somebody like him – somebody who doesn't mind living a forced life.

"Look, that guy is a lot of things but one thing's for sure and it's that he likes you," he said, though he was biting his words because conversations like these doesn't happen often for him, "He hasn't shut up about you since we arrived so if you're going to break his heart, do it when we're already gone so I don't have to hear about it."

I gaped at his words and the harshness it conveyed, but what he did say after that calmed me down a bit, "But I don't recommend doing so because he doesn't deserve to be left like that and from what I've picked up, you like him as well. Don't you think it's a waste to stop something before it could happen?"

He left me with those words and I was alone to drown in my thoughts. Well, breaking something up before it could hurt was my schtick. I did it with Justin and the aftermath was worse than what could have happened if I didn't break up with him before we could have talked it out.

Yet if I didn't do that, I wouldn't have met Adam.

Then again, maybe it was better if I haven't met him, I wouldn't be in this predicament.

"Sienna!" Adam rushed inside the room, "I heard from Axel that you weren't feeling well."

He kneeled in front of me, cupping my face in his strong hands and taking a good look at my face.

Warm.

I closed my eyes and leaned in to his touch, my heart feeling heavier by the second, "You're missing her performance."

"I've seen her perform countless times," he told me, his thumb running across my cheek, "And right now, you're more important. Are you hurt?"

I am, by your words. They're too caring, too kind, too sweet. It makes me picture what it would be like to be with you and it's a contrast to every reason why I think we wouldn't work out.

Opening my eyes, I stared at his worried expression and I knew for myself that I was a goner, "Yes, but it's alright."

Chapter 27

"Call me more often, will you," Heart laughed as she hugged Adam tightly, "Especially since Axel's going back to America now."

Adam chuckled and placed a gentle hand on the top of her head, "I'll miss you, Soph."

They released their embrace and while Adam said his good-bye to Axel, Heart approached me with a friendly smile, "I'm glad I got to meet you, take care of him for me."

I couldn't say a word in reply so instead, I smiled back at her. They immediately left right after and I was alone with Adam once again in his apartment. Now, the uncertainty had made its presence known once again and I really thought we would be over it when he kissed me back in December.

There was a blanket of awkwardness that fell upon us. It was so uncomfortable that I felt like I was going to choke, but he realized that there was something wrong.

Though sadly, I couldn't say it out loud why I was being bothered. Even I knew it was a stupid reason.

"Sienna..." he trailed off, followed by a stiff cough. He was hesitating, probably afraid of the unknown conversation that might ensue.

We were going nowhere with this, "I need my uncle to check my progress on my book, will it be okay if I go next door?"

He let me go, knowing how the situation was. When I arrived next door, Emma was happily painting on a new canvas, Andy was nowhere to be seen, Uncle Levi was out as well, and Aunt Janine was on the dining table with stacks of manuscripts next to her laptop.

"Where's uncle?" I asked after dropping my bag on the couch and saying a quick hello to my aunt, "I want him to look over my progress."

Emma looked up from her painting, "He said that he had something to do at the university, he'll be back soon though."

Gesturing for her to continue on her work, I observed my aunt for a moment. She was busy reading over manuscript after manuscript, her pen twirling between her fingers as she made quick notes on each page. I've known her since I was born and I really admired her for being steadfast and strong, yet I couldn't understand why uncle willingly left America for her.

Taking out my laptop, I silently asked if I could sit from across her. I've always seen her as the serious aunt to Uncle Levi's playful vibe. She was easily frustrated by him but you could see that they still have that spark from when they first started going out.

From what I've heard, Andy was conceived before they got married. It wasn't a shotgun wedding to save their faces, but uncle proposed to her during the midst of the pregnancy and they got married a little bit after Andy turned one. That was when mom was pregnant with me and all of the wedding pictures showed her growing stomach underneath her lilac bridesmaid dress.

Aunt Janine had a good eye for detail and was an extremely intelligent woman. But why? I thought uncle adored his home country.

"I'm beginning to wonder why you're staring at me so intently, dear," she suddenly spoke, lifting her eyes from her the paper she was reading, "What's on your mind?"

"Why did you marry uncle?" I shot out all of a sudden. No need to beat around the bush.

Her eyebrows scrunched up at the unusual questions, but my inquiry certainly caught her daughter's attention. She dropped her paintbrush and wiped her hands on a piece of cloth before taking the seat next to mine.

She watched on with amusement as both Emma and I looked at her in anticipation – like we were little children again begging for her to read us a fairytale.

"Levi was very famous in our office, he was the newly signed author in our publisher and it was rumored among the ladies that he was quite attractive," she started, placing down the manuscript back on the pile, "Of course, I also wanted to have a glimpse of him. I was young, single, and many of my friends were already smitten."

I have seen photographs of the young Levi Kingsley and although he wasn't drop dead Adonis-type kind of handsome, he was above average looking and maybe his career as writer did boost up his charisma.

"He came in looking all serious and in a classic Levi moment, he tripped on the rubbish bin on his way in," she sighed affectionately at the memory, "The whole office went silent and maybe because I have been so stressed that whole week, but I just started laughing like it was my first time to ever see something funny. I was the only one who did and my coworkers were terrified for me."

This time, she was full-on grinning, which was contagious since Emma and I mirrored her expression, "Everything calmed down eventually and just before he left the office, he came over to me and asked me out."

"So dad asked you out because you laughed at his embarrassing moment?"

"I asked her out because nobody was that candid with me before," we heard uncle's voice answer for his wife. We turned around and he was smiling, his coat still on and the door wide open, "She talked me down during our first date, pointed out how arrogant I was, and told me straight on that she didn't want a relationship."

"Swoon worthy, mum," Emma laughed sarcastically, now looking at her father, "What did you do?"

"We had our differences but I convinced her that we can work around them," he answered, his tone full of adoration like he and his wife were back to being newlyweds, "Because that day in the office, I found somebody who was different and who made me look at myself from a different perspective. I told myself to never let her go."

I found somebody who was different and who made me look at myself from a different perspective. Now that sounded awfully familiar, didn't it?

"So you moved to England for her?" I couldn't help but ask.

"In order for a relationship you sometimes need to compromise," he told me, "I left my home country, but she said goodbye to her last name, her old hometown, and we decided to live here since I got a job offer at the university."

I knew from the start that I had to make some sacrifices, I always expected it, yet I never wanted to do it.

"I could have easily rejected him and just went on to marry a man who wouldn't have to make so many adjustments to both of our lives, but I don't regret anything," Aunt Janine smiled and I knew in an instant that this was genuine. She wasn't the type to go all mushy, unlike her daughter who was a hopeless romantic, but in that moment, she showed to us how much she loved my uncle, "Being in a relationship is a decision and I am confident to say that I made the right choice."

With those words, I jumped up to my feet. Emma flinched slightly at my fast movements but neither of her parents gave out any surprised reactions. Instead, they shared a knowing look and Uncle Levi even stepped to the side in order to let me through.

"How did you know?" I couldn't help but ask.

He chuckled, shrugging nonchalantly, "I know you more than you think. That, and you're exactly like your mother."

"Which means?"

"She took a month after your father proposed before she gave him her answer, and all I had to was to look her straight in the eye and ask her if there was any other man, would she still choose him."

If there was any other man, would I still choose him?

Whatever vigor that ignited in me died down. To my uncle's surprise, I slowly went back to my seat and resumed back to my typing as if all of his pep talk never happened.

"Wait, what happened?" he questioned out loud, his hands in the air.

I blinked up at him and sent a sad smile, "I guess you don't know me more than you think."

I did not love Adam – I liked him, I was infatuated by him, I think he was a very handsome and kind guy. But if he thinks some romantic speech like that would have me pounding on his door, then he got another thing coming.

Because I wasn't like him and Aunt Janine who went through ups and downs before finally deciding to settle down on one place, I wasn't like my parents who took almost a month after the proposal before agreeing to get married.

No, I was just a girl who was still trying to find her way through life. Against all my initial beliefs, I did not need a man for me to suddenly jump up and remember that I was who I was.

But I just needed to find myself again.

Relationships and all that jazz were always fun when did right, but I didn't want my uncle to say straight up that I was going to choose Adam out of all the men out there when we barely went to any dates.

"At least you got one thing right," Aunt Janine laughed towards her husband, "She's exactly like her mother – she knows what she wants."

And she was right in that respect.

"Now I need to go on and prepare dinner," she sighed, closing the manuscript she was reading, "Andy's bringing a girl home."

"Andy's bringing a girl home?" I repeated in disbelief and I turned to Emma for confirmation.

She nodded, also repressing her amusement, "They've been seeing each other for a while now but this is also the first time I'm going to meet her."

"We're never going to let him live this down," I giggled, closing my laptop so I could help my aunt with the cooking.

"Be nice," Uncle Levi warned playfully, "I'm sure he has enough teasing from one sister, but now he practically has two."

Emma high fived me and the both of us continued on with dinner. We were thankful for the open floor plan so the kitchen was nowhere near cramped. Though we did fight for counter space but aside from that, it was fun cooking with both of them.

We were in the middle of setting up the table when the door swung open. I was carefully carrying the dish that had the salad Emma whipped up and I almost dropped it when I saw the figure my cousin was holding hands with.

Uncle Levi blocked her view of us by being the first to greet her but that didn't erase the fact that I was shocked beyond belief. I first set down the bowl on the table because for one, I knew that Emma would freak if I dropped it.

But once I did, I screeched at the top of my lungs, "Julia?!"

Both her and Andy stilled at my loud outburst. All of the people in the room turned to me, my relatives all with questionable expression but my roommate had now paled at the sight of me.

"Sienna?"

Chapter 28

"T he guy you've been dating is my cousin?" I gaped, shoving Andy from her side.

"He's your cousin?" she quipped back with the same disbelief.

"You two know each other?" Andy fired, finding his spot between us.

Emma was full-on laughing from behind us, she didn't even bother to hide her amusement at the whole predicament. Meanwhile, the three of us just stood there, our gazes switching towards each other.

"Sienna's my roommate," she said, "Again, you two are cousins?"

Oh god no, he was cheating on you behind his back because there was no other possible reason why I was standing here inside his apartment.

Girl, of course he was my cousin.

"I'm out," I placed my hands up in mock surrender, "Bye."

She reached out and gripped my wrist, "Don't."

Girl, I'm not affected in any way that you're dating my cousin. I could care less, as long you both were happy. But like what my uncle said, Andy already has one sister teasing him. Plus, there was going to be some sort of uncomfortable tensions because of this dramatic entrance.

"You owe me a ton of explanation when you get back to the dorm," I pointed towards her, my tone light to assure her that I wasn't upset or any of that sort, "So if you'll excuse me, I'm going to tell Meg all about this so you can feel how stupid it is to be interrogated."

With a tight lipped smile and a joking salute to everybody in the room, I quickly got out. Though I only managed to take a couple of steps before I went back in. I smiled sheepishly as I quietly grabbed my coat and other belonging before heading out once again.

Gosh, I just finished dealing with all the Heart and Axel fiasco now I had to think about that.

I paused just in front of Adam's door, staring at it. It was screaming at me, telling me to go on and knock on it. Talk it out, say I wasn't sure where I want us to go – say all of the uncertainty I was feeling.

And ask for forgiveness because I can never give my all to him.

But I didn't.

I simply continued on with my steps, heading towards the elevator. Was it a good decision to do so? Probably not.

Meg wasn't there when I got back to the dorm so I opted to wait around in my room instead. I took out the sketchbook and flipped it open to a page I was very proud of.

Justin's sketch.

Why was it so easy to love him yet it was totally different from Adam?

When he asked me out, I was so ready to jump in. Maybe it was high school innocence, but I did not feel any hesitation when I said yes. I wasn't inkling for him to ask me to be his girlfriend, I was just happy when he did. There was no impatience, there was no tiptoeing, just laughter and joyful acceptance.

But Adam? I couldn't even ask him if he wanted to be in a relationship with me. Every time we take a step forward, something happens and we take five steps back.

It was tiring.

While he gave up Heart because she lived in another world, he had somehow forgotten that he did as well. He freaking lives with celebrities as if it was nothing, while I was a writer who belonged to the world of words and emotions.

And he should stay here, while I should go back to New York.

"You're making a confused face again," Meg knocked lightly on the opened door, "Where's Julia?"

"Meeting my aunt and uncle," I told her, slamming my sketchbook shut, "Apparently, the guy she was seeing was actually my cousin."

"No!" she gasped out, her eyes widening in delight at the prospect of new gossip, "It had turned rather boring here, I'm all here for new excitement."

Well, at least on her end it was boring. Truthfully, I just wanted a break.

"So how did you find out?"

"I was in their place when she waltzed inside with him," I said, "A lot of questions were fired."

She chuckled and instead of going back to her room, she plopped down on Julia's bed. She didn't say anything for a while and in the least creepy way possible, I swear, I observed her.

Meg was, as you could say, the most stable one among us three. She had decent grades, enough money to keep up with our crazy shopping trips, and a very happy relationship with her boyfriend. She wasn't as excitable as Julia nor was she as distant as I was.

But she was too grounded – there wasn't adventure in her veins. She never sought the thrill that unpredictability gave, it was very clear during the impromptu road trip. She was terrified and worried the whole way.

Boring.

Then again, that lifestyle gave her something I craved of from time to time as well. She didn't need to overthink or worry, because everything was already picture perfect.

Stability.

"Now I think I've given you sufficient time to think about whatever is on your mind," she started off with a slight smirk, "Care to share your thoughts?"

What was I going to ask her?

Then let's start with the first matter at hand, "How did you and boyfriend get together?"

That mischievous expression slipped right away, "What?"

"Was that too personal?" I slowly retracted back just in case I offended her.

She shook her head and stood up from Julia's bed, made her way to my side of the room, and sat next to me, "No, but you never asked about him before so it was a surprise."

"Well, you're in a nice and stable relationship, Julia is off to meet her guy's parents, and I'm just..." I stopped right before I could say something I wasn't even sure of.

I was just stuck.

"We started dating when we were sixteen," she said after she realized that I wasn't going to finish that sentence, "He was visiting his relatives for the summer and they just happened to be right across the street. I fancied him immediately so I started flirting and he gladly took the bait."

Look, even the start of her relationship sounded like it was from some summer teen romance book.

"We've been doing long-distance since then because he lived in another city so university wasn't really that different."

Did it help me come to a decision? Not really. I just wished I was as well-adjusted as she was.

"You can talk to me about him, you know," she murmured softly, almost tentatively. Of course, she was referring to Adam.

Julia said they noticed that I was pulling away so I guess she knew that I wasn't going to be that open to her. This was another problem, why was I holding myself back?

They've seen my outgoing side and how I was ready to let loose and yet, I couldn't even ask them about some feeble relationship problems. In fact, I've been trying to solve everything on my own.

But then again, I've always been like this. No one knew about the impending break up when I was with Justin, no one knew that I even had a crush on him before we went out, I just kept my mouth shut. I wasn't the type to blab to other people what I was feeling because those emotions were mine and mine alone to treasure.

The fact that they met Adam and teased me to him before I even started to like him was just a proof of how important it was to me that I hold it in. They were jumping to conclusions before I could think of what I wanted to feel. It was like our relationship was crowded already before I even entered it.

There were too many people just watching us that we couldn't figure it out ourselves. We had Meg and Julia, Heart and Axel, and let's not forget my uncle and his whole family.

"I just think that instead of just him and me, you know, talking things out, there are a lot of other people who wants put their nose in," I sighed, trying to say this in the least offending way possible, "I really wish it was us again, in the middle of his apartment, laughing and talking about the most nonsense things."

Before that stupid frat party, before he cut off my call with my friends, before that impulsive kiss.

Just two people with their box furniture, learning new things about one another.

"Then I don't see why you can't do that," she shrugged, shifting her position so that I would look at her directly in the eyes, "You don't need labels for everything, Sienna. If you simply enjoy his company, and probably adore him, then you just keep hanging out with. You can't keep pressuring yourself like this."

I blinked at her over and over again. What she said was so painfully simple, something that shouldn't even be pointed out.

But usually, we forget the easy route.

"You know what?" I muttered with a small smile, "I'm going grocery shopping tomorrow."

"Not the reply I expected but at least you look better," she laughed.

We waited for Julia to arrive and just like she predicted, we were there ready to interrogate her. Apparently, they met because she visited the library when it was full and there was only was seat left, which was right next to Andy. They started to talking and later on, he asked her out.

"I just couldn't find the right time to introduce him to you two," she said with a slight pout, "Though I should have then I wouldn't have made an embarrassing spectacle in front of his whole family."

"For all it's worth, that was a fantastic way to break the ice," I joked and although it would probably be a bit weird at times, at least I knew both of them would be well-taken care of.

But for now, I had to deal with my own problems.

That morning after breakfast, I immediately told the girls that I would be out for an indefinite amount of time. Meg already had a good idea why and I was sure she would fill Julia in.

Like what I said to Meg, I first went to the grocery before I headed right to Adam's place. I pressed on his doorbell and when he opened the door, he looked like he just rolled right out of bed. I lifted a brow at his disheveled state.

He stared at me for a few seconds before the situation registered in his head, "Shit."

He attempted to smoothen out his bed hair and straighten up his shirt. It was futile though because instead of looking more appropriate, he just looked panicked.

There was one thing that Meg got right – I did adore him.

"I don't mind," I laughed, leaning up to kiss him on the cheek, then I proceeded to invite myself in, "At least I'm sure that you're hungry."

After he had shaken himself from his initial shock, there was now a baffled expression on his features. I didn't blame him, I practically left him hanging yesterday.

Maybe I could go with Meg's route so that in the end, none of us gets hurt.

I smiled softly up at him, setting down the groceries on the kitchen counter, "Let's talk if you want to."

Although I pretended to be light and preppy while he was still in the room, my heart felt so heavy in my chest. It took a monstrous effort to hum a sort of happy tune, as if I really was nonchalant about the whole thing, while I was prepping the food.

Once he excused himself in order to fix his appearance, I sank to the floor. The spatula was still in my hand when I did and I have honestly never felt more pathetic.

That was a lie, I feel pathetic all of the time.

Why the hell did I say that we could talk? Just so I could tell him straight on that the idea of being his girlfriend horrified me?

I wanted to scream and maybe I should – I haven't done that in a while if I was being honest. It was so easy to be lost in your emotions here, there wasn't much to distract and the trees could only hold my interest for so long.

I know my philosophy was to be a little bit reckless from time to time but my heart could only take so much.

Reaching up, I fumbled around to turn off the stove. The last thing I wanted while I was having my own existential crisis on the floor was to have our food burning.

Dear Sienna Clark, what have you gotten yourself into?

It was as if I could see my spirit dying down once again. Everything felt so suffocating, the exact opposite of what people expected. The open air, the fresh breeze, all the damn trees, nature at its finest to inspire a university filled with student with the best imagination.

And yet, I felt more restricted than ever.

There was variation among the people I encounter, that was for sure. But I wasn't eccentric like that girl with the rainbow-colored hair sketching barefoot on the school field and I wasn't so invested in my work that I could literally block out the whole world.

I loved being in touch with my surroundings, I loved letting it carry me, so that was why I had this feeling that this place just wasn't right for me.

Yes, I could write again, but that was more of my uncle's doing than anything else. I could bring that sketchbook anywhere and I could still write, it wasn't as if I had to stay.

Now I felt like I was just staying for the sake of it. For the sake of my degree for my family, for the sake of riding through my whole university life with Julia and Meg, and most of all, just for the sake of seeing what Adam and I could be.

Did I like him just because he was the first guy to approach me and ergo, I invested all my time on him? Was it because everybody expected us to be dating? Even myself?

It was then I felt a figure sit down on the floor next to me. I didn't look because who else could it be?

"Last year, I visited my best friend and for the first time, I saw how painful and miserable she thought her life was," he started to say, prying the spatula from my hand and setting it aside, "That wasn't the Soph I knew, what I saw was someone calculative with walls surrounding her. She used to be so carefree and wore her heart on her sleeve."

I was silent, I didn't know what to reply. Add to that, I had no idea where he was going with his little speech.

"I thought that I had to pull her away, she was drowning. But then she told me straight on that she didn't want to be saved, that she'd rather stay the way she is," he then said with a somewhat forlorn expression, "Of course, I had to respect her wishes so I let it be, thinking it was better if I could look out for her from a distant."

Then ever so slowly, he turned his body to face me, "Then when I got on that plane to return home, there was this girl who sat next to me. She was sarcastic and incredibly down to earth but just from the way she talked about writing, it was obvious that there was a flame in her that already started to flicker away."

My shoulders slumped because it was as if I betrayed my one true love. That passion I once felt for writing, for seeing words dance to a beautiful story, was fading. He worded it so perfectly that it was like a huge stab on my chest.

"But as I got to know her, she wasn't the type to give up on that flame," he stated tenderly, reaching out but not exactly touching me just yet, "It's small but she protects it. She knows that it's going away but she isn't letting it and she's doing her hardest to keep it alive, it brought my spirits up because after I watched my own best friend give up in front of my very eyes, there was someone who did her best to stay afloat."

Now it was my turn to face him. For so long, I was just staring at the kitchen counter because I was scared to his expression. When I did, it took my breath away and I felt tears welling up. Because what I saw was a man who looked like he fought a war – he was tired.

It occurred to me that the whole time I was having this melodramatic dilemma, I never thought about him. I was hurting before because of my ex, but he also felt like he was being swallowed whole because of his best friend. And now, I learned that he tried to save her but she turned away from his helping hand.

Just like what I was about to stupidly do.

While I was wallowing in misery how I couldn't find my way back, all he saw was a girl who was trying. My struggles, he looked at it like it was a silver lining.

So I crawled to him until I was kneeling right in front of his figure. Placing my hands on his shoulders, I said nothing while I pressed my forehead against the top of his head. When I did, he felt like it was finally safe for him to touch me.

As he positioned his hands on my waist, he whispered softly under his breath with so much sincerity I truly thought that I was going to cry, "Stay with me, Sienna."

I finally got my answer earlier. I liked him because I needed him. While he thought I was that single ray of sunshine, he was mine as well. He radiated positivity, always cheering me on without a hint of hesitation, even during the time when we barely knew each other.

And right now, I felt like he needed me as much as I did him.

"Okay," I answered, closing my eyes.

We were exactly where we needed to be at the moment.

Chapter 29

I eyed Adam as his gaze was fixated on the book in front of him, his eyebrows scrunched up and his hand constantly reaching up to scratch the side of his head.

He never really minded whenever I show up at his door unannounced. It was so common that he once joked that he was on the verge of giving me a key. Best believe that I shot that idea down in an instant.

Going too fast there, partner.

"Are you sure that you're okay that I'm here?" I questioned, catching his attention and breaking his concentration, "I can leave so you can focus, you know."

"I'm sure that I could be alone in a cabin on top of a cliff and I still wouldn't be able to understand this lesson," he chuckled, bookmarking the page he was on with a pencil before shutting the book close, "I'm exhausted."

Glancing towards the blinking cursor on the laptop screen, I quite agreed with him. During the whole time he was studying, I was trying to keep up with my writing because the timeline gap between the sketchbook and the parts that I've actually written was growing too big.

So while he was trying to cram as many information in his head, I grinded chapter after chapter just to catch up. Even though I was the one who worried about him being distracted, I was the one completely out of focus.

Let me tell you something – he was adorable just looking completely confused in front of his book. He even had this habit of picking up his pencil, taping the eraser end on the table, and then releasing it. Instead of going back to reading, he would simply watch the pencil roll until it hit another object. He did it every few minutes or so.

"You want to go out then?" I suggested, "Let's grab a bit to eat or something."

His face lit up in the best way possible, just the prospect of being away from his apartment seemed like the most attractive idea I have thrown his way. He nodded happily, his brown eyes sparkling with excitement. I do admit that we haven't been really going out in technical terms. We just knew that we were together but dates were possibly non-existent because of how busy we both were.

"Alright, let me just finish this chapter and then let's go," he said, a new kind of motivation igniting within him as he opened his book once again.

I suppressed a laugh because even though he wanted nothing more but to escape, he was still the responsible kind.

Couldn't say the same for me.

I switched windows after I saved my document because I felt like I was going to be burned out if I kept going. I instead starting messaging my friends through our group chat, catching up with the happenings. For once, all of us were awake and actually online at the same time.

Reaching out for the glass of water Adam gave to me earlier, I chuckled along through the conversation. However, that cheerfulness was short-lived when one of them sent one particular picture.

You know Justin and I go to the same college, right?

Yeah, what happened?

So there's this girl that I know through another friend and she posted this on her story.

Right there on my screen was a photograph of Justin and his female companion all cozied up. He had her arm around her and she had face nuzzled by his neck, both of them smiling happily at the camera. There was a sticker of a heart at the upper right corner and nothing else. Both of them were obviously intoxicated, it was obvious from the faraway look in their eyes.

But that did not discount the fact that he found someone.

Well, this was interesting.

Sienna, the drama!

I leaned back and rolled my eyes, as if they were standing right in front of me. If they were expecting to solicit a violent reaction from me, then they were about to be gravely disappointed. Sure, I was surprised but I wasn't going to enter a jealous fit because of this.

I was completely secure right now.

Internally smirking, I reached for my phone and subtly pointed it towards the guy right across from me. All of his attention was still on the book and I believe that I can freaking clang a gong and he still wouldn't look up.

So I made sure he was focused and the tapped on the circle at the bottom of the screen. It made a slight shutter sound but thankfully, my suspicions were correct – he was still focused on his studying.

I sent the photo to the group chat and paused to watch the show because while they did not get a reaction from me, I certainly got one from them.

Holy shit.

Wait, are you in his house?

Damn you're smooth, Sienna.

He really is cute, I'm jealous.

Sweet, sweet victory.

"If you're going to take a picture of me, at least say so," he suddenly chuckled, glancing up from the text. There was an amused smile on his lips while I looked like I was a dear caught in the headlights.

I dropped my phone on the table and looked down bashfully, feeling my cheeks heat up in embarrassment. Still, this was Adam we were talking about, he wouldn't get upset over something like, "Come here, I'm going to show you something."

I was in no position to argue so I quickly stood up and rounded the table. Once I was in arms-length, he grinned in satisfaction and pulled me right towards him, situating me right on his lap.

He was not good for my poor heart.

I was so shocked that I couldn't even move but when he saw my face, he started laughing and embraced me tighter, resting his forehead on my shoulder, "I just need to recharge."

My mouth clamped shut but still, the nervousness was flushed away and it was replaced by a surge of affection. I gently touched his linked hands with the tips of my fingers to pry them apart. Lifting one of them, I placed a soothing kiss on his palm, fighting back a smile when he hummed contentedly.

Why would I be jealous if I had someone like him giving me all his attention?

"Come on, let's go out," I said and he shook his head, resuming his initial position with his hands firmly around my waist.

And finally, I fully grinned, leaning back and forcing his head to look up at me.

I like him, I like him so much.

I can no longer contain the giddiness that have erupted in my stomach since he pulled me to our current position. His tingling laughter erupted from his mouth at my change of demeanor and I stopped it by daringly pressing my lips against his.

And I poured everything into that kiss. It was for New Year's when the both of us had no other choice but to stand in the middle of a room filled with people locking lips for good luck, because the person we want to be with was miles away. It was the grand hello none of us managed to say because Heart Valentine thought it would be spectacular to give me that intimidating glare of hers. It was the assurance that what we currently have was perfect.

For now, I was his and he was mine.

Maybe I should stop thinking about the future for the time being.

When we pulled back, he had this literal beaming smile that was so contagious. He unraveled his linked hands and hooked one of his arms by the crook of my knees while his other one supported my upper body. He lifted me up and just circled around, causing me to squeal in utter delight.

These were the moments that you truly wanted to ingrain in your memory. It was just the innocence and good natured feel of two people foolishly falling for each other. They both knew there was world out there filled with things that was bound to be the cause of great stress but inside this apartment, to the sound of nothing, our giggles mingled with the air and it was just truly us against everything else.

It was cheesy, it was straight out of the romance books, but it was the way I wanted it to be.

He gently placed me down on the ground but I still had my arms wrapped around his neck, breathless with the residual laughter, "Now can we go? I'm starving."

"Of course," he said, kissing me once more before finally letting go, "The usual?"

"The usual," I confirmed, allowing him to lead me out.

"Oh cut the bullshit, Sienna," Gracie mercilessly cursed at me and I had to flinch at the raw frustration it resonated.

This was the rare time that it was just us video calling without the others. There was a reason why I kept her close to me – she was straight to the point and no nonsense.

Exactly what I needed since I just loved beating around the bush most of the time.

"You broke up with Justin because you said that you both wanted to grow more as people since you overheard some of his classmates saying that you were holding him back, because you couldn't balance out his recklessness since you were free-spirited as well," she recalled and I glared at her through the screen. I did not need her reminding me the specific reason after I've repressed it from my own memory, "And okay, you're still growing but now you're with another man?"

"I never said that I wasn't going to date anybody else," I huffed, thanking the heavens that Julia was out and Meg had to stay late at the library because she had a project with a partner. If they were here, they would have already hear this whole conversation, "What did you expect me to do?"

She tugged on the ends of her blonde hair, "You're fooling yourself! You like him because he's safe and convenient."

I gasped, "That's not true and you know it."

"I've known you since we were in diapers and you were trying to freaking steal my pacifier," she pointed out with a lifted brow, "You still love Justin."

If she was expecting me to put up a fight and deny everything then she was wrong, "Yeah, and so?"

I still loved Justin and what was wrong with that? I think we've both established than no matter how far we grow apart, we would still love each other. Just because I did, doesn't mean that I couldn't like anybody else or that he was not allowed to be with other girls. It was alright because while we do still immensely care for one another, we were not together anymore.

Her gaze softened, the fierceness in them gone, "You're going to get hurt, Lili."

And of course she was going to pull out my old nickname. When we were young, I had such a hard time pronouncing Sienna so my parents called me Lili instead, out of my middle name Elizabeth. Of course, it didn't stick once I actually learned to say my name but Gracie still used it as a tactic in order to put down my walls.

Please, even my family didn't use it.

But she still got me, because my heart sank when she said it out loud. I casted my gaze downwards because I couldn't even look at her face properly without tearing up even just a little, "I know."

From the start, I was prepared to be. But what else could I do? Feel sorry for myself and repel against any other kind of relationship?

Adam offered me something and I took it. I genuinely do have feelings for him so it wasn't like I was forcing myself.

"Fine," she muttered, "But at least don't hurt him."

If I left him or never even gave him a chance, he would have been so downtrodden. You heard what he said to me in his kitchen and like I said, I needed him as much he needed me.

That wasn't bad, right?

Right?

Please tell me I'm right.

"Gracie," I murmured, still not looking up, "I want to fall in love with him."

But I've always felt that there was something holding me back.

"You know that's not something you can force," she sighed, her tone filled with empathy, "But if you want to give up, I'll be on the first flight there to be a shoulder to cry on."

My gaze snapped upwards and I saw her sad smile. That was when I knew she was sincere and that was when I also knew that she didn't believe that I could actually do it.

Chapter 30

"You're a little out of it," Vance pointed out from beside me.

One of the perks, okay somehow it was more of a disadvantage, to having Vance in one of my classes was that I rarely got bored. But also, I barely got to understand anything from the professor.

"Just thinking," I murmured a reply.

He hummed before snickering, mischievousness written all over his features, "Thinking of ways to surprise him on Valentine's Day?"

If I was drinking anything, I would comically spat it out by now. I couldn't believe that I actually freaking forgot about Valentine's Day. I looked over to my laptop screen to see the date and my head started panicking more when I realized it was only a few days away.

Great, I was such a good somewhat-girlfriend that I actually forgot.

"Yeah," I played along instead of having him mock me, "Any suggestions?"

He smirked and started suggestively wiggling his eyebrows. I knew immediately what he was implying and I rolled my eyes, slapping him lightly on the arm, "You're a creep."

"But I'm sure he'd be glad if ever you decide to go my route," he chuckled teasingly, "Take my word for it, Sienna."

I told myself that he was just joking but how the hell did I end up in a lingerie store literally the next day. Julia held up a cute set and I groaned, covering my face in embarrassment, "Why am I doing this?"

Meg swung an arm around my shoulder and laughed, "Because it's his job to bring the flowers, the wine, and chocolates and it's your job to bring the other thrill."

I looked at her incredulously and she started laughing heartily because of how mortifying and corny she sounded. Really, it sounded like from a weird teen sitcom that got canceled by the second episode.

"What's his favorite color?" Julia questioned, putting the hanger back on the rack, "Or you could go innocent with white or be extra alluring with black."

"Do you even hear yourself," I huffed, breaking free from Meg's hold, "Let's get out of here, I'm not even sure if I can do this."

She and Meg shared a look, one that I knew I wasn't going to like in the end. Julia sighed dramatically, looping arms with me, "Fine, let's go find you a nice outfit then because I'm sure you're going on a date."

"Well, he hasn't asked me out yet," I frowned as she led me out of the shop, "We're days away and we talk to each other all the time and not once did he ask me out on a date."

"It's the twenty-first century, how about you be the one to ask him out?" she suggested.

She did have a point and besides, maybe he was just a little bit busy. I mean, if Vance never told me then I would have completely forgotten.

Meg appeared behind us with a mischievous grin, dropping one paper on my hand, "For you," then she gave a similar one to Julia, "And another for you."

Why did I expect this?

However, Julia was not. Her cheeks reddened so fast and she looked like she was on the verge of yelling, "This wasn't part of the plan."

"Don't look at me like that, you have a guy as well," she winked, ignoring her complaints of embarrassment.

Alright, next time I was going to need to warn Meg and Julia about doing these things in front of me. All things considered, the man that Julia was dating was my cousin and just the thought of what she was implying made me want to barf.

But nonetheless, I thanked them both for thinking of me. They reignited the romantic spirit within me so once we were finished with the shopping, I quickly headed to Adam's apartment.

Though when he opened the door for me, my heart wasn't prepared for his conversation with somebody on the phone, "Make sure the bouquet gets there on time."

If this was his way of dropping hints then I was all for it.

He invited me inside while still on the phone. I looked around and my giddiness double when I saw the box on the coffee table. It was in gold wrappings, a gorgeous red ribbon on top.

I bit my lip and happily sat on the couch, waiting for him to end his call. The shopping bags on my arms felt lighter by the second because while it was kind of out of character for me, I was bubbling with excitement just from this.

He didn't have to go all out since it wasn't that big of an occasion, but here he was putting in all the effort.

I was so tempted to peek over to the box but I held back, he was right there in front of me.

"Sorry about that," he smiled welcomingly, placing his phone back down, "Oh you went shopping."

"Yeah," I nodded, hugging the bags as I placed them on my lap, "What's all this?"

He glanced towards the box, knowing full well that that was what I was talking about. Then, a full-on grin placed itself on his face, taking the box from the coffee table and sitting down next to me.

I immediately swiped away my shopping bags onto the floor, looking at him expectantly.

Then what he said next absolutely shattered everything.

"Soph's birthday is coming up, I'm going to have this and a bouquet delivered to her dressing room since she's going to have a concert on that day," he informed with so much happiness – the same happiness I displayed minutes ago.

"Oh," I breathed out, willing myself to calm down, "When's her birthday?"

"The fifteenth," he chuckled, placing the box back down on the table, "So it's pretty close."

Named Heart Valentine and was born a day after Valentine's Day. Her parents really did her a world of favors.

"Anything planned for the day before?" I drawled out sheepishly.

He was thoughtful for a second and it took my everything not to gape at him. Either he had a huge ass surprise for me and was simply playing dumb or he really forgot and was actually dumb.

"I have a test for my first class so that's not fun," he shrugged.

Okay, I was done.

I immediately stood up and picked up all my bags, "I'm going back to the dorm."

"Already?" he shot up to follow me to the door, "You just got here."

Well, apparently I haven't been here long enough.

"I have to study," I murmured an awful excuse.

And you have to fawn over Hollywood's Princess – don't worry, we both have our priorities.

It wasn't like I was asking him to suddenly forget about her. I get it, she's a very valuable part of his life and I would never dare to replace her or even make him choose between us. All I ask is a bit of that affection directed my way.

If Valentine's Day wasn't such a big deal to him, then he should consider it one to me.

Okay, so maybe I forgot about it but in my defense, I lost track of the dates completely. He was here, clearly aware of what day it was, and he still didn't bring it up.

For fuck's sakes, I was getting whinier and whinier by the second. Even I was tired of hearing myself complain so I should just get myself out of this situation before it escalates.

"You're lying," he stated a matter-of-factly, staring at me right in the eye, "What's wrong?"

I was simply being petty, "Nothing."

"Come on," he smiled encouragingly, trying to get the shopping bags out of my hands.

Couldn't he just understand that for this one moment, I didn't want to be with him because the last thing I wanted was to get angry at him for something as trivial as this?

Since he was so bad at reading the situation, he kept on tugging on the bags while I had this steel hold on them. And of course, the one bag that had to be the casualty was the one with the lingerie. It ripped open and out came the flimsy lace.

By this point, I was too tired to embarrassed.

But him? He stared at the blasted thing like it was his first time seeing one.

I nonchalantly bent down and picked it up, stuffing it inside one of the other bags.

"What was that?" he managed to choke out, looking back up at me.

"I don't know, maybe I'm going to video call Justin later."

It was a foul move and maybe because I was getting more annoyed by the second was the reason why I said that. He, however, finally gotten rid of his shock and his face was now overtaken by a new emotion.

He suddenly bent down and picked me up by my thighs and plopped me back down on the couch, "You will do no such thing."

Oh so now you remember me as the girl you should be romanticizing. I had to roll my eyes at this – he acted all possessive but didn't even bother to think what I felt over him and Heart.

Screw him.

"Whatever," I huffed, sitting back up and flattening my hair, "Yeah you made your point. Can I go now?"

Here was the thing with Adam – he knew whenever there was something wrong but at the times, he doesn't know what that specific thing was. But still, no matter how angry he became because of what I just said, his gaze softened and kneeled down on the carpet so he was looking up at me, his hands rubbing my thighs in some sort of defeat.

"What's wrong?" unlike earlier, this was wrapped in tenderness that made my anger slowly melt.

But this very argument was what sparked all my insecurities back. He wasn't immersed in a relationship and I get it, we weren't official but hello, you have a girl right here in front of you who would love nothing more than your attention. And yet, the only thing in his mind was Heart's birthday. Shouldn't he notice that the day damn day before is literally a day celebrating love and such?

Couldn't you at least ask me out without me having to say it?

Were you so immersed with her gifts that you completely forgot? My excuse was that I lost track of the days and date so

I managed to forget that fourteen was closer than I initially thought.

But you? You acknowledged that her birthday, the fifteenth, was close and yet you can't say the same for Valentine's Day?

Oh Adam, you have your priorities and sadly, I have mine as well – my pride.

So for now, I was going to hold my fire, "Really, it's just one of those days."

And to make sure he really did believe me, I forced a smile and pressed a kiss on the top of his head, "But I do have to study so I need to go."

"Sienna..." he trailed off, still not letting go of me.

"If you're worried about what I said about Justin, don't be," I laughed, my heart aching because I had to sound light and joking, "I'm yours right now."

Are you mine though?

Actually, don't answer that question because I wasn't ready for it yet.

"Okay," he mumbled under his breath, finally releasing me.

Looks like my Valentine's date was a bowl of popcorn and some romcom. Maybe I can convince Meg to go with me to an actual cinema because the last thing I wanted was to stay cooped up in my dorm and her boyfriend was miles away so she wasn't doing anything in particular as well.

Chapter 31

I blinked at the laptop screen, watching a couple argue for the umpteenth time since the movie started. I couldn't keep track how many times I've rolled my eyes and I was sure Meg shared the same sentiments.

Although we understood that this was the least interesting movie we could watch, I think it was a given that we should watch a romantic movie with an awful plot just for kicks on this wonderful day.

Because while neither of us were actually single, we were dateless for Valentine's day.

"Still don't get why you're not out with Adam," she sighed, continuously picking up pieces of popcorn from the bowl, "I mean, it's good for me since I don't have to spend this day alone but is there anything wrong between you two?"

So finally we were having this conversation.

When I arrived the other day asking her if she would rather go to the cinema or just stay in the dorm to watch a movie, I knew she was already curious. Especially after I appeared so giddy after our shopping trip.

Although she did a fantastic job of holding off her questions, I knew she was itching to ask and admittedly, I was also on the verge of spilling everything because I just wanted to talk to somebody about it.

Meg was far more subdued compared to Julia when it came to gossip so I shouldn't really be surprised it took her this long to initiate it.

"Nothing's wrong," I murmured my reply, my eyes still on the screen as if I was still paying attention to the film, "In fact, everything's perfectly normal."

"Which is something that does not interest you," she pointed out, "So what happened?"

"I just rather be here than to spend a dinner or whatever with him worrying about his best friend's birthday," I told her, reaching forward to pause the movie so I could turn to her, "And not even a single word from him except the customary good morning text."

She was silent right after and I instantly figured out that she was holding back. Meg always had an opinion, something I was annoyed at times but more frequent than not, I was quite grateful for.

She didn't look at me, but only stared at the paused video. It was a scene wherein the horrible actress was sobbing, badly if I may add, while the actor just stared at her at this awkward stance.

I was sure Miss Hollywood's Princess would never be in a scene like that. She was perfect and that was why I thought to myself that I could never compete with her, no matter how much Adam will say that he treats us differently.

"I moved on from my ex and I don't even talk to him aside the group chats," I shook my head at the thought, "And yet he talks to her every single day but anytime I feel jealous, I'll feel guilty because he assured me so many times that he had moved on as well."

The last time I had a one-on-one conversation with Justin was on the New Year's Eve party. After that, all our talks had been with our other friends. Though I'd admit there were time wherein I was so tempted to just call him up, especially when I was having problems with Adam, but I didn't because it wouldn't be fair to all three of us.

But that was because he was my ex so of course there would be a barrier and I'd say Adam would have every right to be upset when I do so.

It was different between him and Heart though, because they've been friends their entire lives and even though they did fall for each other at some point, neither of them acted upon it and still remained in this platonic friendship.

So it stripped me off of the right to be jealous. If they lasted this long without any romantic relationships between them, I could never interfere with this solid friendship that they have built.

"This is going to be a hard pill to swallow," she muttered quietly and I knew that the long pause that followed was her contemplating her next words. Whatever it was, I was sure that I wouldn't like it, "But just because you've moved on, doesn't necessarily mean you're ready to love again or even enter a relationship."

Ding ding ding, I was right – I didn't like it.

And the main reason? She had a point.

Heck, even at the back of mind I thought about it. Not for me, but for Adam. Heart, I'm afraid, will always be his one and only.

While I was just a passing phase.

Wasn't it just convenient for the both of us? He was the first guy I was with like this ever since that horrible break up and I was the girl who still stuck with him even though he was still so close to the girl he liked before.

Scratch that, loved.

And he still loved her. Maybe not in the way before but he still held this impenetrable affection for her.

"It's okay though," I whispered, "It's not like I ever planned this would last."

"You keep talking him down for loving someone else," she spoke with a raised brow, "But even I can see that you love somebody else as well."

Just like what Gracie pointed out before. While I do like Adam, I still loved Justin. That was why I kept holding myself back, because I was going to be a hypocrite if ever I was going to get mad at him.

"I know."

Maybe she expected that I would deny everything so her eyebrows shot up in shock when I did the exact opposite.

That was the end of our conversation, a bland stop if I may say so, because somebody knocked gently on the door and poked her head inside, "Sienna, your boyfriend is downstairs."

Because of the number of times he came here for me and because I was still seen often with him, the other ladies thought that he was my boyfriend. While not entirely wrong, they weren't right as well.

"Thank you," I shot her a small smile pushing myself up to my feet, "I'll be back."

"No you won't," she quipped, a sarcastic smirk on her lips, "If I were you, go change into that lingerie first."

I frowned and I tried to shake off what she was implying, "Meg..."

She shot up and headed straight to my closet, opening a bunch of drawers until she found the right one. She threw to me the one she and Julia got for me and then started flipping through the hangers to build an appropriate outfit.

"I'm not going out with him!"

She looked over her shoulder towards me, an unamused expression being shot my way, "Then what? Say to him that you'd prefer to spend Valentine's day as a single woman instead?"

She pulled out a dress and a pair of tights, placing it on my bed, "If you're going to play this stupid game then play it well."

With those piercing words, she left the room with a hard slam on the door. The lace, so flimsy, felt heavy in my hands and her small speech just rendered me mute. It was cruel, but the truth was intertwined with it.

What kind of game was Adam and I playing?

All I knew was that this was less likely to end in something good.

I dressed up with the clothes she picked out in the end because I'd rather be prepared since I don't think she was going to be in the mood to continue that horrible movie.

Grabbing the coat hanging on my bed post, I let it dangle on my arm as I headed downstairs.

My heart sank when I saw him, a bouquet in his hands as he looked deep in thought. I paused just before I got down from the last step, willing myself to calm down. I had to be ready, I had to act normal.

With one sharp inhale, I convinced myself to approach him.

When I was a few inches away from his figure, he looked up to see me. It took him a few seconds before he actually acknowledged my presence. He flashed me a smile and presented the flowers, "You thought that I would forget?"

You did actually. Don't pretend that you've known all this time. The least you could have done if you actually knew was either talk to Julia and Meg to make sure I wasn't going out. However, Julia made no mention for me to stay in the dorm and Meg was down to do whatever, whether it was to watch a movie here or out. She never specifically told me she wanted to be in the dorm.

"Lucky you that I didn't go out," I said jokingly yet I was already entering my passive-aggressive phase. Still, I took the bouquet with a grateful smile, "So you got anything planned?"

"Do you mind walking back to the apartment?" he questioned though he already knew the answer to that.

I took his offered arm and started to make our way out. I should be glad and thankful that he actually went out of his way to do this for me, but I couldn't because this was just a blatant slap to my face that I wasn't his priority.

Adam was kind, so kind that it was hard to be upset with him.

Was it shallow to say that I wasn't going to be satisfied with just a dinner in his apartment? While I do appreciate whatever effort, it just doesn't feel anything special or different from the usual times we hang out.

As we ventured through the trees, the world so dark around us, my brain demanded me to remember this moment, my heart was telling me to be careful, and my whole system just trying to be assured. I knew how this was going to end, how it was going to be so painful that I was sure tears would be heavily involved.

In that very second, I thought to myself that I didn't want a game. I wanted genuine smiles and that floating feeling of falling in love. I didn't want to be surrounded by doubt and stopping myself from being jealous just because I think that I have no right to be. It shouldn't be like this. It should be alright for me to be envious from time to time, I shouldn't be so guilty about it.

I shouldn't be in a situation wherein I couldn't even tell him that I wanted to celebrate Valentine's day with him. Actually, he was with me now so he shouldn't even forget in lieu to his best friend's birthday. I didn't want to be with someone who treated me as an afterthought, who surely attempted to string something that seemed romantic and planned last minute.

What happened to us?

The beginning stages were so beautiful. He ran and ignited whatever spirit that was on the brink of diminishing. There were goodbye kisses just mere seconds before I had to leave for the airport, there were tight embraces after spending a whole break apart with an argument between us, there were light moment wherein it was just the two of us trying to get to know each other.

But now? I couldn't even say out loud what I really felt.

"Could I ask you something and promise me you wouldn't get mad instantly," I breathed out, gripping his arm tighter to stop him from taking another step.

He glanced down to my face to see how serious I was and he nodded, releasing me so he could stand directly in front of me. He gestured for me to go on and with my hands wringing behind my back, I asked, "Is it alright if I call Justin, I just really want to talk to him about something?"

Like how to get myself out of this situation or was I being plain unreasonable?

Of course I asked Adam first. It was out of respect for my current relationship with him. Something I wished he reciprocated whenever he gushed about Heart to me.

He placed a cold hand against my cheek, a sort of reassurance that he was nowhere near bothered with my small inquiry, "It's alright, I trust you."

Was it foul play that I was running to my ex? I just needed advice, to be honest. Julia was too optimistic to see how soured I was feeling, Gracie would probably just curse at me again and give me a lengthy lecture before she could even help me, and you know what happened between Meg and I.

Besides, it was Justin who kept checking in with me to make sure I was still happy with Adam.

I gazed up to the night sky, watching the stars as they peeked through the crossing branches of the towering trees.

It was a scene I have never been privileged to see before I came here. There was a man in front of me, his attention on me.

But that was only for tonight.

"Let's go," I said, looking back at his face.

He piqued my curiosity when instead of pressing his floor number on the elevator, he went straight to the penthouse. Through the glass windows, I could see the blanket on the ground a paper bag right on the middle.

He swiped his keycard and got us outside. Because of the elevated height, it was colder here than on the trek from the university so I hugged my coat tighter around my body. The wind whipped my hair around, causing me to curse myself for not even remembering to bring a hair tie with me.

It was either I keep my coat shut with my hands or I use them to tame my hair. Well, I already guessed that I looked ridiculous so I didn't bother with both, only crossing my arms and watching as Adam settled himself down on the blanket and patting the spot next to him.

"I thought about a candle but I think the wind wouldn't let us do that," he told me before pulling out a flashlight from the paper bag and setting it down between us before turning it on, "So I improvised."

And you know what hurts more? I find him completely adorable and he still holds my affection.

"Can we skip the food, I'm still rather full," I muttered just as he was about to reach into the bag again, "I just want to enjoy my time with you."

Because right now, I don't know what to do or how this would end.

But he nodded, pushing the flashlight slightly away and scooting closer to me. I smiled softly, resting my head on his shoulder and closing my eyes.

Hoping, wishing, and praying that this would last.

Chapter 32

Justin blinked at me through the screen and I pouted towards him, hugging my pillow tighter to my chest, "Say something!"

"While I do agree that it's nice that you're giving him the chance and being sensitive to his feelings and his friend ship..." he trailed off before his eyebrows scrunched up in concern, "But all I got from that was what he would feel, it's as if you never thought about how you've been so confused and worried the whole time."

"I think the reason why I called you was because I know for myself that I'm confused and worried," I deadpanned.

He sighed, running a hand through his brown hair, "What I mean is, you're too scared of hurting him when you, yourself, are currently hurting."

I casted my gaze downwards, back to my fuzzy purple socks as if they were my saving grace. I picked on a piece of lint because to be completely honest, I had no idea how to respond to that.

Obviously I didn't outright say to Justin that I still loved him, though I had a huge hunch that he knew that already. I went through a whole tirade though but I left out specific names, the little secret that Heart Valentine was the famed best friend wasn't something for me to blab.

"What happened to my banana?" he spoke softly, his words wrapped so tenderly, "Where's the spark in her eyes?"

She extinguished it herself.

"I miss you," I murmured, looking at his bespectacled face, "Sorry I bothered you."

He shrugged, a small smile on his lips, "I get to see and talk to you so I think this was a win in every way."

Finally, I grinned full before breaking into a laugh. Somehow, this heavy feeling flew away from my chest and I was suddenly back in front of him, like an ocean didn't separate us. For this small moment, he sat in front of me and not through the computer screen.

And that was when it settled in me that I have never loved someone as much as I did him.

He was the sparkle in my eyes, he ignited my spirit, he made me fearless.

"Thanks Justin," I said, "I'll call again soon."

He nodded, that joyful expression still there, "You better and take care of yourself, Sienna."

"I will."

When his face disappeared, I was left to stare at the blank screen. My shoulders slumped and I leaned back against my headboard, just thinking of how I should approach this.

It was really a jerkass move but Justin was right, instead of being consumed by that giddy feeling, all I could think of was worry and guilt. Adam did make me feel some sort of special way, those weren't empty kiss or cold embraces.

But it just wasn't the same.

I changed windows and opened up my manuscript. I managed to catch up with the sketchbook so it was pretty up to date with the happenings.

I scrolled up towards the first chapters and read through them, just how confused my thoughts were. Yet, Adam cleared all of that up and made me smile once again. Sadly, we couldn't find that same glimmer in our relationship.

Taking a deep breath, I scrolled towards the very last page and cracked my knuckles – this was going to be a very long night.

I just kept on writing, my fingers tapping rapidly against the keyboard, hearing it clack with every hit. My eyes switched from the black keys towards the bright screen, watching as letter by letter appeared with my movements. This rush, I've missed it so much because for once, I wasn't glancing towards a sketchbook every now and then.

All of this was still fresh in my memory. These words were being written out as I experienced them. That guilt, that sinking feeling, that uncertainty, and most of all, the heartbreak.

And perhaps the worst of it all, he wasn't mine.

Julia poked her head in a few hours later to call me down for dinner. When I murmured an incoherent reply, she sighed and knew exactly that I wasn't going anywhere. Being the amazing roommate that she was, she came back half an hour later with a mug of steaming coffee, setting it down on my bedside table.

I smiled gratefully towards her as she went to her side of the room, also investing herself with her laptop. While I was sure she was doing school works, I wasn't bothered at all that I had a quiz tomorrow and I didn't even plan to open my notes.

All I knew was that I wanted to finish this.

His face was etched in mind, his smile, his frown, his micro expressions. Those deep chuckles whenever he was amused, his lips slightly parted whenever he was studying, the way he moved his fingers over the paper, hovering but not actually touching the book. His words that were so easy to read because he laid his heart on his sleeve.

For the world to see but only a few could experience his thoughts.

I finished at five in the morning, my head throbbing but I have never felt more exhilarated. Julia was fast asleep so I had to tiptoe out with my empty mug. Before I left though, I grabbed my coat first then I headed downstairs. I made sure to wash my mug and then I shrugged on the coat, creaking the large door of the entryway open.

I was greeted by the pitch black night – well, morning. My hands instantly froze so I had to stuff them inside my pockets and whenever I exhaled, I could see the frost forming.

The only people you could see were the ones brave enough to endure the cold for a morning jog. Slowly going down the steps of the dormitory building, I took one more glance over my shoulder before I ran.

The wind slapping my skin gave me a new form of energy. I looked ridiculous since I was still in my pajamas and my slippers weren't the best footwear for running but I didn't care. I didn't care that my lungs was struggling to gather oxygen, I didn't care that my legs were starting to get sore or that my hair couldn't even be considered a bun anymore.

I just wanted to feel alive again.

Because I just knew by the end of the week, I wouldn't have the motivation to do anything.

I stopped at who knows where. The university was large with its own community and while I have taken some time to go around, I doubt I could be so familiar with it to that point that I knew every nook and cranny.

Though I didn't mind that I was lost, I actually quite enjoyed it.

Now how was I going to do this?

My eyes went down to my feet, squinting to see more clearly in the dark. My gaze landed on the bush right next to where my slippers were, the few droplets of moisture. These were the small things that Sam would absolutely freak out about. He would have whipped out his camera in two seconds flat.

Sam had a more vivid way to capture things as they happen. I, as a writer, only can do so in retrospect.

Hold on, we had a middle ground.

With my numbed hands, I reached into my pocket to take out my phone. She was going to murder me but it was worth the shot since right now, my brain couldn't think of anything else.

"Sienna, do you have any idea what time it is right now?" I heard Emma's tired voice through the line, "I hope this important."

"Your wonderful cousin is wondering if you can do a favor for her," I breathed out, continuing my way through the university, "I'll do whatever you want as an exchange since it's pretty big."

"And now my wonderful cousin is scaring me," she shot back, "What is it?"

My eyes focused up towards the sky, watching the few stars that remained bright even though it was near sunrise, "Lend me your talent."

The cashier smiled politely at me as she handed me the bag that contained my purchase. I then headed towards the next shop, which was a printing store, and asked for the work that I left there.

I looked down on it, feeling its weight in my hands. To write more than a hundred thousand words doesn't seem much of a big deal to me, but to see it in its physical form, it was really something else.

It had been almost a week since that run and for a better half of that said week, I caught a cold which I kind of predicted. I've really been pushing myself lately so I wasn't surprised but this was college, so I still had to attend my classes even though I was on the verge of dying.

Now it reduced into nothing more but a couple of sniffles so I was good.

With a slow and steady pace, I made my way towards the apartment complex. Andy opened the door for me and his eyebrows shot up at my creepy ass grin. I didn't bother with makeup today so my eyebags were out for the world to see and I do admit that my skin had been the palest it had been.

I invited myself in and I was surprised at how preppy I was acting considering the reason why I came here.

"Sienna, you didn't call that you were coming," Uncle Levi frowned when he saw me, "I would have ordered extra food."

"It's alright," I shrugged, for once, food was the last thing on my mind. I took out the thing that I got printed and shoved it into his hands, not even saying a word.

He was taken aback at the sudden present but he placed down the mug he was drinking from and flipped it over so he could see the front page.

Then he stilled.

"I know your bet with mom is after I graduate, but I think a semester and a half sufficed," I attempted to joke but I knew that he already felt that there was something wrong, "I'm going to send it to mom, but I thought that I should get your approval first since you're my mentor."

Andy made his way next to his father and tried to see what caused such a reaction. He read over the words and he too mimicked his expression, "So where's the sketchbook?"

"With me," Emma suddenly piped in, going down the stairs, "She brought it to me at six in the morning a week ago."

I grinned sheepishly and she sighed dramatically, handing me the said object, "You owe me."

I opened it and my fingers rapidly flipped through the papers, skipping the pages that contained Uncle Levi and Andy's handwritings. I stopped just where my pages started and as I went through them, I couldn't help the sense of nostalgia.

When I thought about capturing the moments so vividly as they were happening, I knew it was impossible for me to do so. Those have passed and it wasn't like I had my phone ready to take a picture at every given second.

So I asked Emma to draw them down for me. As a writer, I've learned to pay attention to the fine details and because of this, she was able to recreate them perfectly just the way I remembered it.

But she had some difficulties though and she claimed that anybody would think that she had a crush on Adam for the sheer amount of pictures that she accumulated. I told her specifically not to draw me, but to draw Adam as I saw him.

To draw how I experienced him.

That goofy charm that he showed when he sat across from me while we sat on his empty apartment floor. His pleading features when I presented him the ripped pages of the sketchbook when I got angry at him. That masked confidence during our first kiss. The way his hair flopped when he held me in the kitchen.

And the one I adored the most – that warm expression when he kneeled in front of me when I was so overwhelmed during Heart's concert.

That was when I knew I wanted him close.

"What are you planning, Sienna?" Andy asked cautiously as all three of them watched me plop down on one of their dining chairs.

"We write to taste life twice," I muttered, reciting my favorite line, "In moment and in retrospect."

I then proceeded to dump everything I purchased earlier onto the table. It was a large assortment of craft materials and needless to say, they were more confused than ever.

Whatever story I wrote on that manuscript had been tainted already and I was sure that it would be more so when it goes through editing. I hid the most precious moments because once again, those were exclusively for us to reminisce.

What was written there wasn't an explosive romance that ended up in heartbreak like my first book. No, it was a story that had every intention of making you feel light on your feet and have that sense of hunger for self-discovery.

It was the kind of story that made you want to run at dawn to random places or the kind to make you want to chase the twilight sky.

I ripped the pages that contained Emma's drawing and proceeded to start my handiwork.

"She's gone mad," Emma quipped.

"No," Uncle Levi shook his head, his hand tracing the text of my manuscript, "That's still our Sienna, but I think this time, she managed to get rid of the fallen tree."

"Oh that thing you told me when I got blocked?" Andy rolled his eyes, "I guess that Adam did help her."

Uncle nodded, "And she decided to run with the clear path."

Chapter 33

Alright, deep breath, we can do this.

When I happily declared that I was done, Emma refused blankly to let me go next door in my state. She whipped out all of her tools and started doing my hair and makeup.

"At least look like you made an effort."

"But I did make an effort," I frowned just as she clicked her tongue because she was in the middle of doing my contour.

"What I mean is your appearance," she explained. She was silent for a while as she kept on doing her work but after what felt like forever, she spoke once again, this time in quieter voice, "Because maybe it's the last time."

My lips pressed into a thin line and when I looked down on my hands, they were shaking. The high of planning finally settled down and was now replaced with this anxiety tumbling in my stomach. In Adam's perspective, I haven't been acting weird because I didn't want him to think that our last days together were bad memories.

She placed the brush on her dressing table and smiled at me from her reflection on the mirror, "Done."

"Do you think I'm doing the right thing?"

She turned to me and shrugged, "I don't know the whole story but I think the way you're doing it is a lot better than what other people has done."

"Well here goes nothing," I exhaled loudly, standing up and turning to her.

Thank god I at least put on something decent before I came here.

When we came back downstairs, Aunt Janine was finally home and unsurprisingly, reading my manuscript. Her pencil as twirling between her fingers, her eyes rapidly skimming through the words printed on the paper.

While I just planned to smoothly go out and knock on Adam's door, she had other plans. She saw me gather my handiwork and she cleared her throat, stopping whatever momentum I gathered.

"You know, we usually submit a file before actually printing it," she said, removing her reading glasses and placing it down on the table, "Though I have a pretty good idea why you didn't."

"You think it's plausible?" I shot back.

I did it because one it goes through editing, there was a hundred percent chance that some aspects would change. As a writer getting published, it was inevitable. But because I printed it out, it meant that whatever I wrote there, I wanted all of it to stay.

Okay, do the copyediting where you fix my grammar and sentence flow but every single scene should stay.

Even the top authors could rarely demand that.

"I think you know for a fact that it isn't," she replied, "But I'm sure your mother could convince your editors for you."

Oh right, my mother doesn't even know that I finished the book.

"Now you can go," she laughed to lighten my mood, taking what I did and placing it in my waiting hands, "Good luck."

"You think I'm doing the right thing?" I fired the same question I asked her daughter earlier.

The mother and daughter duo shared a quick glance and Aunt Janine flashed me a motherly smile, "You don't owe anyone a relationship, but do I think you owe him an explanation so just make sure to get your point across clearly."

I tried to reciprocate with a smile but all I managed was a forced one. With the pages clutched in my grip, I went out of their apartment and walked a few steps until I was in front of Adam's. Closing my eyes and preparing myself to drill his expression into my memory, I lifted a fist to knock on his door.

"I was about to call you," he grinned the second he opened the door, "Vance invited us to another party, a good way to start the weekend."

Everything started with a party and just when I was about to end it, another one arrived.

"Can we talk first?"

From my solemn tone, his happy disposition quickly slipped off of his features, "What's wrong?"

Us. Actually, me.

I walked past him and slowly settled myself down on his couch, keeping my face neutral but inviting at the same time.

He closed the door, still with that inquisitive look, before he made his way next to me.

"I had Emma do a little something," I said, carefully handing him my work. It was the pages torn from the sketchbook sewed together. What took me long wasn't exactly the putting it back together, but to write again on every single page.

I had Emma occupy only half of the page so I could still add my own personal touch to it.

On the very front was just two words, Dear Adam. (

He turned to the next page and froze for a moment when he saw the beauty that was Emma's drawing of him. She truly had a beautiful talent and every day I wished that she would stop feeling bad for choosing it instead of finding love in writing.

Yes, our family was so involved in the publishing world, but how can't she see how absolutely breathtaking her works are? Whether she chooses a brush or a pencil, she just lose herself and the results were mesmerizing.

But going back to this, she had managed to draw an image of him when we were in the airplane. The first time I met him, full of doubts and a hundred thoughts running through my head. I was on the verge of giving up and on that moment he sparked the conversation with me was something I would eternally be grateful.

I chose the scene where he told me he loved Heart. Back then, I didn't know who his best friend, all I knew was that all of his affections were hers and the heartbreak, still so fresh on that day, was written all over his face.

"I love her actually," he stated without a hint of hesitation, "But she's in her own big world now and she deserves someone who can follow through with it, not some guy who will leave her because he lives a whole different life."

His features looked far from peaceful, in fact, he looked defeated. I remember how he couldn't even look me in the eye when he said his confession. I mean, he was turned to me but his gaze probably on my forehead or my nose because there wasn't any eye contact. That little detail was what made the picture whole and I was amazed how Emma managed to capture it.

That excerpt was taken straight from my manuscript. I did this to all of the pages, there was a line taken straight from the book that was written in blue ink, then underneath in pink, was my message to him.

You, till this day, have no idea how much you saved me when you sat next to me on that plane. You managed to take away any nervousness and replaced it with this vigor. I have a confession, when you told me about Heart on that day – which I had no idea who she was back the – I was ready to interrogate you because I thought I found my next inspiration. But I thought to myself, that wasn't my story to tell, but it was mine to hear.

He was quiet and it was probably better since I already had a speech ready inside my head. If he did talk, it might fly out of mind so it was better that he was just silently absorbing this.

"So how's the writing?" he asked, forking another bite of lasagna into his mouth.

"I was off to a bad start but now I think that I'm going towards the right direction."

"Is that so?" he replied, settling his elbow on the box, "And what made you say that?"

Using the same words he used on me earlier, I muttered, "I just have this feeling."

Page two was taken on our first meal together. It was when we unexpectedly meet right in the lobby of this very apartment complex. He brought me into his place when it was empty aside from his moving boxes, which made into his makeshift furniture.

There was playfulness in his smile, his fork tightly in his grip while his other hand settled on top of the box. One thing I adored during that time was his curiousness, while I was trying to get to know him, he was trying to figure me out. He just knew how to get the conversation flowing, to touch the right subjects.

Something that I couldn't see from him anymore.

When I asked you if I was going to like Heart, you said yes. Of course, I was doubtful of your straight answer so I questioned you how could you know and you threw that last line towards me. Now here's another confession – all I saw was you when I threw the words back to you. Because I met you, because of everybody who I could possibly be enjoying lasagna in an empty apartment with, it was you. You were the reason why I had a feeling that everything was going towards the right the direction, and I guess I was right, just as you were about Heart.

The next one was the worst of all. It was the first time I felt betrayed – the frat party. The very thing that ignited this whole thing. While I wouldn't consider it a whirlwind romance, because trust me, this was tame compared to a lot of other people's relationships, but it wasn't smooth sailing as well.

If it never occurred, this wouldn't be happening right now.

Next was an image of pure guilt and regret. Emma accurately got it down on paper, how even the way his shoulders were tensed and his phone was still clutched in his hand midair. It burned me like someone threw boiling water towards my way.

"I only did this to stop you from pestering me," he chuckled lightheartedly towards the phone, effectively making my heart sink, "I'm going to take her home. You take care over there."

He outright stated that he invited me not because he wanted my company or whatnot, but because Heart told him to. I was just a pawn in this messed up game he wanted to play. And you know what? I should have been angry and threw a fit right there and then, I had every right to do so.

But I was so mortified that I couldn't do anything.

Unlike the first two, he actually lifted his gaze from the paper to look at me. While I did express how furious I was, what he never knew was the melancholy that spiraled within me. That was the point in time when I was the most insecure about myself.

I masked that sadness with anger. If he only knew how much it felt like he ripped out my heart and wrung it in front of my very eyes. So my next move back then was to rip out the pages that reminded me of him.

Instead of saying anything, I gestured for him to continue on reading.

This was something you probably wanted to forget. Sorry, but it's part of who we are. While it may come to a surprise to you, being angry wasn't my first thought. I don't want you to feel bad though because what bloomed after this was my favorite memory of us – the twilight sky. I chose only a limited amount of scenes because I didn't want to push Emma, but know that when you pulled me to the rooftop and all I could see the was your back tugging me along, it was when I first thought of liking you.

But this was also when I first learned that I would always play second fiddle to Heart Valentine.

The next one was what melted my heart because it was such a precious scene. At the same time, it was a bitter reminder that that was our first and last true moment of happy romance. The ones that followed always had someone poking their nose in.

Clenching my fist, I didn't know if I should blame it with the constant throbbing of my head because of my exhaustion or because a thousand things were occupying my mind that all logical thoughts turned into a blur.

But I bent down and pressed my lips against his.

Our first kiss and when I acted so impulsively that it was laughable now, but incredibly embarrassing during that time.

His expression was surely something that a surprise. The adrenaline made everything feel so vivid, how his lips parted into a gape and how his eyes were wide in shock. However, I asked Emma to make sure his eyebrows were slightly furrowed because I remember that in the midst of all that disbelief, there was confusion with it.

This doesn't need a long message except for this one: This was when I knew I was yours.

And finally, the last portrait and to be honest, if I gave Emma more time, I would have asked her for more than four but with only a week, I could only bother her for so much.

He kneeled in front of me, cupping my face in his strong hands and taking a good look at my face.

Warm.

Taken backstage of Heart's concert when I started blabbing to Axel and when I first said my hesitations out loud. But now as I looked back on it, I realized something so wrong – I should have stopped here.

Correction, we should have stopped there.

His features were plastered with concern, so many worries in his handsome face. And I was the cause of it. While it did make me weak in the knees, I couldn't even say it to him what was causing my distress. Still, even with all that, that drawing just radiated with the same warmth he wrapped me in that made me so sorry to let go.

I have one wish for you and I know it wouldn't be easy, but please hear me out at least. Don't stop caring for me as I will never for you. You give me that sense of comfort and while I would love to hold on tightly to that, we both know it isn't for the best.

He turned the page over, expecting another one but when there was none, panic started to fill his eyes because he could obviously read the tension. Plus, that last message was the least comforting one of all.

"You could have just told me that you forgot Valentine's day," I spoke, filling the air with a kind of sound after we just sat there looking at the drawings, "I already knew you did when I came here and all you could gush about was Heart's birthday."

"If this is about the fourteenth then I can..." he started but I cut him off before he could finish the sentence by raising a hand to stop him.

Please, just let me say this before I break down.

"I've been jealous of Heart for so many times and I never said a word to you because I knew which side you would take," I said sadly and he flinched because he knew it was true, "But I would never ever make you choose between us and besides, I have no right because she has been in your life for far longer than I have been."

I turned away from him, opting to look ahead because I couldn't handle his reaction.

"I know she's different and she would always have a special place in your heart, but even if you say that you've moved on, I couldn't help it," little by little, I was finally voicing these thoughts out and each word made me feel lighter, "Meg said to me, just because you've moved on, doesn't necessarily mean you're ready to love again or enter a relationship."

God, who knew that in the end, I would be quoting Meg?

"And that goes both ways," I finished.

I couldn't hold him accountable for everything. I was at fault too because I allowed myself to get swayed when I knew Gracie was right when she accused me that I still loved Justin. The fact that he was the person I sought out whenever Adam and I had problems was just a telltale sign.

My heart still very much belonged to him while Adam's belonged to his best friend.

"So what are you trying to say?" he muttered, a little broken.

I reached out and took his hands, bring them to my lips to softly kiss his knuckles, "Adam Nicholas, you've been the best thing to happen to me here and I will forever be thankful."

And so I willed myself to finally look him the eyes, to face that sorrow in them, and say one hard apology, "I'm sorry."

Because that was our goodbye.

To be honest, we were silent after I said my last line and while I knew it was a lot to take in, I was mentally begging him to say something because I couldn't take it. If he was going to argue with me, then go ahead. If he wanted to express that he's okay, then say it.

But don't make sit there in agony, trying to read your mind.

In the end, all the words he thought I deserved was, "You can go now."

And he was right, that was all that I deserved.

Chapter 34

When I got into class, I never expected Vance to still take the seat next to mine. Obviously, Adam would have already told him about what happened so I imagined that he would prefer some distance between us.

But when he sat down and silently slid a heart-shaped chocolate on top of my notebook, my emotional self just wanted to bawl right there and then, "A little birdy told me something and I think you need a little bit of cheering up just as he does as well."

"How is he?" I dared to ask quietly.

"Hating life and everything about love," he chuckled, too lighthearted for my liking. Hold on, I thought that he wanted to cheer me up – couldn't he sugarcoat just a little bit?

"Well, he has all the right people there to comfort him," I scoffed, half dejected and half bitter, "You and Heart included."

He then paused for a moment when I practically spat that out. And if my eyes dared to deceive me, I swore that I could see ghost of a smile gracing his lips.

"He hasn't told her, you know," he informed in a concealed smug tone, "Seems like you're wrong about one thing."

I huffed and turned away from him, instead focusing on rewriting my notes because whatever mind games he was thinking of, I was not in the mood to play with him.

Yet I still cared that he told me that Adam had yet to tell Heart about how I somewhat took his heart, threw it to the ground, and stomped on it like a bitch. I could almost imagine the fury that would shoot my way once he does.

She was fiercely protective of him so might as well say my prayers now and hope that she doesn't kill me on sight.

Meanwhile, I couldn't even tell my best friend because I was afraid she might actually do what she had promised – to fly here. I have to remember that Gracie was as spontaneous as I was so if she said that she would travel across the Atlantic Ocean for me then I had no doubt in mind that she would.

I want to go home.

A full week later and it was still like that. I've yet to remember the last time I had a full meal, aside from the small snacks Meg and Julia forced me to eat because they were worried about me. Not only that, I was losing sleep over this.

There were times when I would just stare at the closed curtains of the windows, imagining what it would be like to run out again like that morning when I've finally decided. Of course, I was tempted to but I don't think my body would hold up a random jog at dusk, no matter how much the weather reports kept telling that warmth would finally squeeze itself soon into this horrible, cold, bleak, weather.

On a particular day when I was just busy attempting to finish my report, I almost screamed when a video request popped up.

Justin.

Instead of answering immediately, I scrambled around for my phone to turn on the front camera to at least see if I was decent.

Spoiler alert, I wasn't.

My hair was a bird's nest on top of my head, my eyes were bloodshot with dark circles under them, and my skin was incredibly sallow.

I pulled out my hair tie and attempted to comb my hair using my fingers, trying to fluff up some life into it, but sadly, it fell limp.

Well, this was as good as it was going to get.

I accepted the call and while it loaded, I slapped my cheeks to bring back some color to my face. Of course, he caught me while I was doing it but that was the least of my worries.

I just knew that there would be questions that I had to answer.

He saw just how down in the dumps I was. To my surprise, instead of asking, he simply stood up and got back with a mug in his hands and he instructed me to go down and get myself a hot beverage as well.

"Seriously?" I gaped and he nodded, shooing me away.

So I went down to the kitchen and fixed myself a mug of tea. I flashed a smile to our dorm mother and walked right back to my room where my laptop was still wide open.

And he just talked about anything and everything – how his day went, what the boys were up to, even the damn weather.

"A little sun every now and then but it's still freezing most of the time," he chuckled, "How about there?"

"Absolutely miserable," I replied and it was obvious that it had a double meaning.

"Nothing a little hot chocolate and a fuzzy sweater can't fix," he shrugged, trying to be lighthearted, "And if that doesn't work, you know I'm all ears."

I felt the corners of my lips tugging upwards, "You always have been."

"And always will," he stated, his tone gentle and soft, "Are you tired?"

While I haven't told him anything yet, I guessed he figured it out on his own.

It was already two in the afternoon but because of what happened, I still haven't found the motivation to do anything productive. Meg and Julia constantly have to check on me and I only went out to go to my classes or to use the bath-room.

It was incredibly pathetic.

"Yes," I said quietly.

Oh how I wished you could just come over and gently run your fingers through my hair. That was the surefire way to get me to sleep.

"Then I'll tell you a bedtime story," he laughed, the mischie-vous glint back in his eyes, "Now get comfy."

I blinked at him and shrugged before I placed my mug on my bedside table. I shifted my phone to my other hand so I could get myself underneath the covers, "Okay, I'm ready."

He reached for something beyond my view and he whipped out a familiar book. When I looked more closely, I almost screeched at my story.

Well, our story.

"How is this going to make me relax?" I huffed.

He placed a finger up to shut down my protests and flashed me that goofy smile, flipping through the pages and scanning the text. He already knew what he was looking for so once he saw it, he instantly perked up and dramatically cleared his throat.

I swear, this boy. He was really an open book. His expression were so upfront, you just knew what he was thinking. There was no wondering, he shows the world what he feels and takes no shit from it.

"When I had to take do huge presentation in front of the class, I was on my wits end. It was three in the morning and I was still wide awake, staring at my ceiling as if it was the most fascinating thing in world," he read out loud and I had to blush because I knew exactly what happened next, "Out of desperation, I texted him. To be honest, I didn't expect a reply because I was sure that he was already fast asleep."

Another little spoiler for you – he wasn't.

"He called me and asked me out for ice cream. Yes, you heard it right, ice cream."

I remember that but it wasn't actually ice cream. He just asked me if I wanted to go out and walk around with him. The ice cream was just added for comedic purposes. Still, there was still disbelief when he suggested that and I, being the lovesick fool that I was, said yes.

So I tiptoed out after he told me our meeting place. He did say to bring my school stuff so that he could help me just in case I needed to double check some things. He also specifically told me to wear something appropriate for outside. I slapped on a fresh new outfit – which was literally just a pair of jeans and a plain top – and sneaked out.

"He tricked me though because instead of actually buying me ice cream, he just brought me back to his place," he said and I hummed, reminiscing those days, "He threw towards me one of his shirts and shorts, telling me to wear them and neatly fold the clothes I was wearing."

Now ladies and gentlemen, get ready for the part that made me squeal, that could make butterflies erupt in my stomach, and just remember how wonderful it was to be with him.

"He instructed me to lay down on his bed and of course, my heart was about to beat right out of my chest because we all knew where this was heading," yes, I had a dirty little mind. To be fair, at that point in our relationship, we had already done it so it wasn't like our first time together, "But when I did what he told me, he simply placed the covers on me and went to the other side of bed, laying down and pulling me right to his side. His lifted his hand and ran soft strokes through my hair, bathing us in silence."

And let me tell you, that worked. I was knocked out within seconds and the next thing I knew, he was shaking me awake. The reason why he made me wear those specific clothes and bring my stuff with me was because he already knew that we wouldn't make it in time for school if I had to sneak back. Plus, he wanted me to get as much sleep as possible.

"You're not here to play with my hair though," I muttered softly, though he was right, I was slowly getting relaxed.

"But I will stay here until you fall asleep," he whispered, promising the same thing that night.

To the sound of him breathing, my eyes closed and I finally went to sleep after what felt like so long.

While I did finally catch up on some needed rest, what woke me up wasn't any of my friends calling me down to dinner, but it was the loud blaring of my phone. I squinted with one eye open and tried to feel around for the device, finally finding it under one of my pillows.

I peeked at the name on the screen and my heart dropped down to my stomach when I saw Adam's name.

"H-hello?" I stammered, my voice still croaky.

"Is this a bad time?" he questioned.

Darling, I gave you a bad time, which consequently ended with moping around here, so you could go on and bother me anytime.

I cleared my throat, "No."

"I know you don't want to talk to me but can I ask you for one more favor?"

"Yeah, sure," I nodded as if he could see me.

Though what he did say next caught me off-guard and to be honest, if I wasn't so cautious of what I was saying, I would have cursed out loud.

"Can you pretend that we're still together when Soph comes to visit next weekend."

Excuse me?

Chapter 35

"So let me get this straight," Meg waved her hands in the air to silence me, "She doesn't know that you broke things off with him and she suddenly asks Adam to bring you for a night out so you both have no choice but to pretend that everything is still alright?"

I glanced away from the mirror, holding my curling iron in my hand, "Pretty much. It's her last day before she goes back to America and she asked me to go with them."

"Why didn't you say no?" Julia frowned.

Because this crazy amount of guilt was just radiating.

"I think I at least owe him this," I murmured with a sad smile, gazing at my reflection.

But I really do wonder why he hasn't told her yet. I would have assumed that they constantly share everything to each other, so something as big as this would have surely been talked about. Yet it was already approaching a month since that day in his apartment and still, he hasn't uttered a single thing.

Then again, I wasn't so innocent as well. Aside from Meg and Julia, no one else knew this. I told them not by choice, they initially observed my very noticeable change in attitude so they knew that there was something going on. In end, I caved in and told them.

At least it relieved me of the stress of pretending that everything was fine in front of them.

"So you're going to walk there?" she gasped, looking down on my high heels that was settled near my feet.

Adam didn't have the obligation to pick me up here anymore.

"No, I'll carry those and wear flats. I'll just change when I get there."

And maybe I'll take my sweet time while doing so to clear my head.

How will I face him? I don't even know how to act when I knock on his door. On top of that, we had to act as if nothing was wrong in front of Heart, to pretend that we were still happy sappy.

When in fact, I've been nothing but a sad slump and from what I've heard from Vance, he wasn't in the best state as well.

If you're going to play the game, play it well.

Sadly, we both gave up.

Was I half expecting that he would at least chase me? Yes. Did he? No.

The bigger question: Would I have stayed if he did?

With a last sigh, I ran a comb through my hair to loosen my curls then I finally finished with my look. If I was going to sit next to Heart Valentine all evening, then of course I would care about my appearance. Besides, Adam told me to dress fancy.

"Here we go," I announced with most deflated enthusiasm ever. I bent down to pick up my heels and slipped my feet into a pair of flats, "Wish me luck."

"Just call us if you need an escape route," Meg said, standing up with Julia to walk with me towards the door.

"Don't worry, my finger will be hovering on my phone all night," I joked halfheartedly, going down the steps of the dorm building.

The entrance was still wide open, which was typical since we only close it right after dinner. But because of that, I could see a clear view of what laid outside. Just before the front steps was Adam, staring down on his phone and I could see him repeatedly tapping on the screen, placing it against his ear, then tapping it once again within seconds.

I stopped midway through the steps because it was my first proper look of him in what felt like the longest time. I just stood there, taking in his troubled features but all I could think about was how much I missed him. If we were just like we were a few months ago, I would have ran up to him and give him a huge embrace.

But here I was, glued to the floor because I could only admire him from afar.

Julia saw him immediately then her gaze switched to my forlorn expression and so, she snatched my heels from my hands and went down a couple of steps to drop them near my feet, "Do your best, Sienna."

"Ignore what I said about playing or whatever," Meg told me, giving me a hand in order to balance myself to put my shoes on, "Just be happy."

Her words entered one ear and went out the other. I couldn't even imagine myself smiling tonight.

I watched as Adam did the phone thing once again and this time, he didn't turn off whatever call he was doing immediately. To my surprise, my phone started blaring inside my clutch and I shared a look with the two other girls.

I didn't bother with picking it up. I simply inhaled sharply and walked down the remaining steps, knowing that Julia would take care of my flats for me. Walking out, I kept my head focused with my steps slow and precise.

As I finally came into view, he didn't bother with turning off the phone. His eyes locked onto mine and he didn't move a single muscle as I made my way towards him.

It was only when I was inches from him did I stop and he put down his phone.

"You look beautiful," he muttered, causing me to become more bashful than I was cautious. I murmured a small thank you under my breath and watched as he stretched out his arm, "Shall we?"

I nodded slowly, taking his offered arm and allowed him to escort me to the car waiting for us. He opened the door for me and slid in right after, "We're just going to go back to the flat to pick up Soph, she was the one who planned everything."

Of course she did.

Who knew we could make a five minute drive an awkward one?

When the car did stop in front of the complex, Adam whipped out his phone and shot her a text. Within minutes,

I once again saw Hollywood's Princess in the flesh. The only thing was, we were both expecting her to be dressed up to the nines as well, but she waltzed right out wearing nothing but a shirt and a pair of pink sweats.

I glanced back towards Adam and quirked a brow – he was dress as formally as I was so what gives?

"What are you wearing?" he shot.

She laughed and lifted up the picnic basket resting on the crook of her arm, "Here you go."

"What?" he fired once again.

"He knows where to go," she said, gesturing to the driver, "Here's your food, I got everything prepared already."

"Soph..." he trailed off, looking nervously towards me, "I thought this was a dinner between the three of us."

She opened his door and dropped the basket on his lap, "I think a little date between you two is well-deserved."

Oh god, please don't tell me this was happening.

"N-no, you really don't have to," I stammered because just the thought of sitting with Adam alone was definitely not on my agenda. Not now and not ever, "I know you're going back to the States soon so I insist you eat with Adam, I can just go and leave you two alone."

I didn't dare to look at Adam for fears of what his reaction was. Just by the my tone and my words, he would realize how much this situation stung.

But to my surprise, Heart's fierce expression turned soft and she gently shook her head, "Trust me when I say that this is what I want to happen."

Here was the thing – Adam and I were not comfortable with each other anymore. She meant well, but if only she knew how much suffering she was submitting us to.

"Do this one favor for me," she smiled, stepping away from the car and closing the door, "Have fun!"

With that, she gestured for the driver to drive away and I could only clamp my mouth shut because I felt like everything was happening faster than my brain could process it.

"Just bring us back to the university please," Adam spoke to the man behind the wheel, "We're just going to call it a night."

For once, I was in full agreement.

But to our surprise, he shook his head and kept on driving, "I'm under strict orders from Miss Valentine."

Of course he was.

So there we were, sitting in compromising silence with the picnic basket sitting between us. I wished that the driver at least turned on the radio so something could mask the tension but nope, there was no sound aside from the leather squeaking with our movements.

We managed to reach the main city and that was when I finally pulled my attention away from the man beside me towards the outside world. We drove past the different houses and stores, easily maneuvering through the familiar roads.

The vehicle finally came to a stop in front of fairly large building and right at the front was a man standing with his eyes on his wristwatch. When he glanced up to see our car, he plastered a polite smile and walked ahead to open Adam's side, "Welcome, Mister Nicholas and Miss Clark."

Adam stepped out and the man reached inside to get the picnic basket. Instead of also getting out, I was too busy trying to calm myself down.

What the hell was happening?

Adam's outstretched hand came into view, his expression apologetic, but it was still urging me to take it and get out of the car.

With my hand shaking, I gently placed it on top of his and he helped me get out. Once I did, we let go and I even flinched at how fast it happened.

Well, it was understandable since he probably thought that I didn't like him.

No, Adam, I really do like you but if I stayed, both of us would get hurt.

"Follow me," the man said, closing the car door behind us and started to walk in front. He opened those double doors and continued inside while we obediently trailed after him.

I gasped when I realized where we were. This was like the heart of the city because of what it was known for. Like I said before, a university highly associated with the arts demanded a city that mimicked the talents of the students. Hence, the buildings, the establishments, and almost every corner you looked at, reflected the visions that the university boasted.

And the one place that could be the consider the epitome of art preservation? The museum.

Which was exactly this building.

We weaved through different rooms, some showing sculptures, other paintings, another filled with photographs, and those of mixed arts.

He stopped in an empty one, a picnic blanket on the floor. He settled the basket on the corner and he turned to us, that practiced smile once again on his face, "Please enjoy. If you're in need of any assistance, the office is located near the entrance."

The museum, the picnic, the driver, this date, and even this guy... I wanted to scream.

"I'm really sorry for this, but can you please explain what the heck is going on?!" I almost screeched, turning to the poor man that was about to catch all of emotions, "We've been given a basket then suddenly we're taken to this museum and I still have no idea what's happening!"

"Sienna..." Adam trailed off, his head starting to panic, "Calm down, I'm a bit lost as well, but..."

But nothing!

"You!" I pointed towards him, "You told me that this was going to be nothing but an innocent dinner with Heart. I get it, you haven't told her yet and I'm a hundred percent on board with pretending, but you can't expect me to stay composed when I've been on my wits end for weeks just for all of it to explode on this incredibly unexpected turn of events."

Darling, I've lost it. Just completely poof!

The man cleared his throat, trying to diffuse the situation by remaining undisturbed, "Pardon that I don't know the full circumstances but Miss Valentine had rented the whole museum for the night and has asked to accommodate the two of you. You can walk around and look at all of our displays, there would be no one else here except for our staff. She has also requested an empty room for us to lay this blanket, with the intention that you two are going to hold a picnic here."

We didn't have any reply to that so when we didn't say anything in response, he bowed his head and turned on his heel, walking out of the room and leaving us alone.

So let's see, I just threw a very irrational outburst. Just great.

"Might as well eat," Adam said with an exasperated sigh. My shoulders slumped because after all that's been said and done, we had no other choice but to make do with what was presented to us. He bent down in front of the basket while I stood next to his figure, watching as he did so.

The second that the lid was off, my breath hitched because instead of being greeted by actual food, what was on top was an assortment of pictures. And not just any ordinary photos, but images of Adam and I.

Most of which I have never even seen before.

There were candid shots of me, some a few pictures wherein Adam was holding the camera and I was turned away, others were both of us smiling happily towards the lens.

Adam froze and this time, I threw away any bashfulness and kneeled next to him, reaching out to take the pictures, "When were these taken?"

He didn't reply, he even refused to meet my eyes.

One by one, I took them out and when I flipped over one particular picture, one that I was fast asleep on the couch and Adam was right at the corner, flashing a peace sign, I noticed her writing on it.

Sienna,

I know you're clever enough to find this. If you're curious, these are just few of the many pictures of you that Adam sent to me, all with words of praise and adoration. This was the solid proof that I needed in order to be completely sure that you had Adam's affection. I hope the two of you enjoy this surprise I prepared, because I wish you both nothing but happiness.

Sincerely, Heart.

He sent all of these to her?

I glanced towards his face and reveled at his blushing features. I almost dropped the pictures because I just felt the urgency to touch him, to feel his skin underneath mine to prove to me that this wasn't all a dream.

"Adam..." I trailed of, unsure of how to approach this sudden piece of information.

"I'm sorry," was the only thing he managed to say.

If he was apologizing for the fact that he took all of these without my permission, then he should just take it back. These photographs were like precious treasure to me, a testament that during the time that we were together, he thought that these mundane moments were important enough to capture.

I peeked back inside the basket and saw the tupperwares of food in there. Reaching in, there was a sticky note on it, 'I heard this was your favorite.'

Taking off the cover, my heart dropped at the lasagna. From when I first entered his flat, to that first real date, to when I came back from home.

Who knew one dish could hold so much importance?

I reached inside for a fork and tapping Adam on the shoulder, I hesitatingly offered the container and cutlery to him.

"She means well," I assured, though I feel like those words should be from directed towards me and not the other way around, "But I'm surprised she knows so much."

And yet you didn't tell her that I broke everything off.

But for tonight, can I be with you without worrying every little second?

Chapter 36

I couldn't bare how thick the tension was inside the room so instead of sitting on the blanket, both of us opted to stand up and be as far apart as possible. This was so sad, we were literally thrown into a situation wherein it could be a perfect opportunity to talk everything out, but instead, we were scared to utter a single word.

Hey Adam, can I tell you a secret?

I miss you.

"I know you're curious why I never said anything to Soph," he finally spoke out and I could literally play the fanfare at that instant because hallelujah, we were finally talking.

I pushed back my excitement and nodded slowly. He exhaled loudly and ran a hand through his dark hair, "Because I feel like if I told her, everything's actually true."

I lifted a brow because of that explanation. Did he think that this was all a hallucination? Sorry, but while I do want to turn back time and do things differently, I didn't want to be the one to burst this bubble for him. Though to be honest, I was the queen of in denial so I wasn't the one to talk.

The only thing I wanted to turn out another way was how I was suddenly banished from his apartment before we could have an actual conversation. However, if you were to ask me if I regretted breaking things off, then it was an automatic no.

While he did hold a piece of my heart, things weren't meant to be.

He saw my inquisitive look and he finally dared to turn towards my direction, finally giving me glimpse of his handsome face, "I didn't want to believe that you walked away from me and I kept hoping that you would come back."

Why were those words so reminiscent of what I told Justin?

And why was my heart breaking all the same way?

"Adam, if you only knew how much I wanted to see you," I muttered softly, "I couldn't sleep, I couldn't eat, and as much as I wanted to call you, it wouldn't be fair."

He started to walk towards me, his steps heavy and calculated. Just when he was near, he reached out his arm and even though he was good at showing composure, the slight shakiness of his hand and the sheen of sweat on his palm said otherwise, "Then let's not throw Soph's gift to waste."

It's just one night, right?

"Okay," I murmured in agreement, placing my hand on top of his and I watched as his fingers gently enclosed it. His hold was loose, signifying that he was allowing me to pull away at any second.

Just one night.

I, for one, did the complete opposite and clasped his hand tightly. I caught his gaze and tried to convey to him that just for the hours that we were here, it was like we were back to his apartment when everything was still so right.

He led me out of the room where the picnic was left. Our meals were half-eaten and the bottle of champagne was still unopened.

"You know the fascinating part about this museum?" he said, walking right next to me, "All, except for one room if I remember correctly, are filled with local artists. Many of those were once students of the university."

He then tugged me towards another room, one in particular that reminded me of something Emma made. At the entrance, there was brief explanation that this was project done by a couple that wanted to tell their story in a different way.

The walls were painted in the image of a beautiful sky on the brink of sunset. The floor was one that reflected a river stream and in the very middle of the room, the centerpiece of a room filled with different sculptures and mixed arts, was a bridge.

That, along with the beautiful lighting, this room was like a whole other world.

River Future, I remember Emma say, And these two, they don't know each other yet and they're unaware of each other's existence but this river shows that at some point, they're going to fall in love.

Although her painting was slightly different because she painted a dull sky and an explosive river, it portrayed the same thing – how strangers, so unaware of their future, met each other and nothing was ever the same.

When I boarded that plane, I was a hundred percent ready to give up. I've prepared myself beforehand for the disappointment that I was sure would come to me.

But then, a man, who had this sincerity in his eyes, proved me wrong. I thought that small encounter on the ride to England was all it was going to be, but once again, he arrived into my life and nothing really was the same since.

While I craved for that floating feeling once again, he showed me that having my feet planted on the ground was where I should be at the time.

And sadly, I wanted to soar again. The book was done and I felt like little old Sienna was back again.

Yet, little old Sienna was also suffering because she broke off a relationship... for the second time, if I may add.

He pulled me along until we were on the foot of the bridge. He urged me to go up with him but I shook my head, "We might break it."

"I've seen pictures of people on this thing all the time," he chuckled, tugging on my hand, "It's perfectly safe."

"If you say so," I said, my voice filled with uncertainty. When I did step on the bridge, it didn't even creak or made a single sound, it held up without any strain. I was honestly impressed because I thought it was just for display.

But with the little elevation, I was given the full view of the whole room. It showed the meeting of two people, the falling in love phase, the turmoil, and finally, the reconciliation.

When I turned to the wall behind me, I paused to see our silhouette. The spotlight that was shining on the bridge hit it at the right angle and there we were, just two people hand in hand on top of the bridge. Our shadows hid the sculpture that portrayed the 'falling in love' part of the room.

Oh how poetic.

But I tried to ignore it and only looked at our figures. What I saw wasn't two people who were so scared of doing something wrong. They weren't overthinking everything, they weren't in love with different people, they weren't in an awkward date.

They were just a couple enjoying their time with each other.

"Now that's beautiful," I sighed and it wasn't the room or the artworks that I was talking about, but that image that we somehow portrayed.

I was just staring at it, admiring how our shadows were touching even though the only thing connected between us were our joined hands.

"I like you, Sienna Clark," he suddenly spoke out of the blue.

I gasped and tore my gaze away from the shadows and looked at him with eyes wide in surprise. I felt as if he threw a knife right through me and scarily enough, I didn't flinch or took my hand away.

What shocked me more was how stunned I was with that simple confession. It shouldn't catch me off-guard, but it did.

"And I regret that I've never said that out loud to you," he added and I watched with the dim lighting how his ears started to turn red but he kept his expression serious, "But I really do like you and it was pure torture being away from you when I had you in my grasp before."

If his hold of me was so loose before, this time he was gripping on my hand like his life depended on it. I, on the other hand, was attempting to process those three simple words.

I think we've established that fact during the beginning stages of our relationship but he was right, he had never told me those words.

Just like I never said that to him.

"Please give us another chance," he pleaded, taking a step closer, "And no more of that ambiguous relationship, I want you to be my girlfriend."

My heart dropped and it felt like somebody punched me in the stomach at how quick my breath was taken away. Even though he was avoiding me for the better half of our time here, his eyes were right on me.

Wouldn't be more romantic if I said yes? If I jumped into his arms like a tearful reunion?

Only for me to feel insecure throughout the following days. That high wouldn't last forever, this was just a moment for the both of us.

So I let go of his hand, my fingers finally straightened and the hurt was very much evident in his features. Still, he didn't let go.

"Adam, this date was planned by Heart and the only time I slept was when I talked to Justin," I pointed out to him, "There's never going to be 'just us' and it's going to be a very crowded relationship."

"You shouldn't always care what other people think."

"I know I don't," I quipped back, "But we both do anyways."

If he really didn't, then he wouldn't have dragged me in this entire situation. He wouldn't go through this trouble just to please his best friend's request. And I get it, because I was like that too.

With those words, he finally released me. I took a step back and flashed a small apologetic smile, "After all that's been said and done, I still want you in my life, even if it's just as a friend."

"Friends," he said again the word and the fact that his voice had no emotions made me internally shudder. His tone was flat so it meant that I couldn't read or even take a guess of what he was feeling. But from my experience, being 'just friends' was never an easy transition to glide through.

He went down the bridge from the other side and hastily exited the room while I was left standing there alone. I blinked at the spot he once occupied then ever so slowly, I turned to the wall behind me once again. There was some melancholy attached to seeing my lone figure without him by my side.

Somebody please tell me that I was doing the right thing.

When I glanced towards the door, it was that exact moment that Adam passed through with the picnic basket on one hand and the blanket on the other. Realizing that he planned on leaving, I recollected my thoughts and rushed to follow him.

Just saying, these heels were not the best for chasing.

I tried calling out his name, but my words died in my throat. Not because I couldn't even say it out loud, but because the view I had of him was something that should have been exclusively for the good times. He had his back turned to me and I reminded me so much of how he pulled me along after our first fight.

His excited chuckles and my confused laughter.

And look where we were now.

"I like you," I declared before I could even hold my tongue. While it wasn't my plan to suddenly blurt that fact out, it did effectively stop him.

Sienna Clark, you're digging yourself a bigger hole and I recommend you stop this instance.

But when was I ever obedient?

He whipped around to face me, his face probably mimicking the one I had when it was him who confessed. My hands balled up into fists to the point that my nails were digging into my palm and I could almost hear my heartbeat in my ears.

"I like you," I repeated, gathering up every single drop of courage I had in my body, "I like you so much and that's why I don't want to hurt you. I know it feels terrible right now and trust me, I'm suffering as well, but in the long run, there will be no happily ever after if we continue whatever we had. At the end, we would still go our separate ways and even right now, we're not on the same page."

I will leave to go back home and you will stay here. I'm in love with Justin and he loves Heart. I was looking towards the future while he wanted to live in the present. I wasn't ready for a relationship with him, even during the start, and he wanted to jump into one just minutes ago.

We wouldn't work out, it was simple as that.

I've always been reckless, but my heart was the only thing I wanted to be cautious about.

"You never gave us a chance," he pointed out.

"I did," I corrected him because I truly did, I was open to the prospect of falling for him. However, it only took us just a few moments before I realized it wasn't meant to be, "And whenever you weren't being possessive or those little gestures, I felt like second fiddle all the time."

"You think I'm comfortable with you talking so casually about and with your ex?" he shot back, "I don't, but I trust you."

"And I trust you too, I know you will never ever do something wrong, but I cannot control who your heart chooses to love," I spoke, "Just as I cannot control my own."

He loves Heart and I can't change that. No matter what, no matter when, no matter where, he will always choose her. And I wasn't the one to talk because I've tried to change the way I loved Justine, but that was out of my control as well.

I unclenched my fist and slightly flinched at the pain of my nails peeling away from my skin. Still, I kept a straight face and walked forwards, removing the distance between us.

With my shaky hands, I reached forwards and placed them gently on his cheeks, cupping his face with the lightest touch. I looked at him right in the eyes while he remained unmoving. While every second spent in this museum was like a stab through my heart, I persisted through, "One day, you're going to meet a girl so wonderful that you might even forget about me."

Actually, he already had a girl like that. Only problem, she wasn't his.

I didn't want to be that girl that he will expect to mend his heart, to make him forget the girl he loved for so many years. I didn't want to be that girl who he got into a relationship just because he accepted that his best friend loved somebody else. Was he really happy with me? Or did he think he was because he felt something other than the pain of unreciprocated love?

"Then you're going to fall for her, you're going to treat her well, and she'll be everything that you've been looking for," I continued, taking one last step so our chests were almost touching, "And like I said, I'll just be a distant memory but please, don't ever regret meeting me."

"You know that's impossible," he whispered and I heard the picnic basket and blanket fall to the floor with a thud. He placed his hand on top of mine, shaking his head, "How could you say that I would forget about you?"

Because I'm one of those people who was replaceable.

"Just promise me," I practically begged.

He leaned forward and pressed his forehead against mine, his gaze still locked with mine, "Sienna, I will never regret meeting you."

"And I will never regret meeting you," I repeated, "Adam Nicholas, the boy who saved my spirit and held my affections."

His hands mirrored what I did to him by also cupping my face and what I thought would stop there, escalated more.

He angled his head so that our lips were barely touching, just centimeters apart.

My heart was beating in my chest and I truly wanted to kiss him. But we both know that that wasn't fair.

I shut my eyes and refused to move, however the sharp inhales gave me away immediately. But he was a gentleman and instead of actually closing the distance between us in the way we wanted, he moved his hands and settled them around my waist. If it was possible, he pulled me closer towards him.

A single tear escaped my eye as I tried to identify all that he wanted to convey. From the heartbreak to the appreciation, it was all there in the embrace.

And I embraced him back, my arms around his shoulders. I also attempted to say everything that I couldn't even find the words to describe. As a writer, it was a shame, but as a simple girl who fell for a guy, it was the reality.

He pulled away but still kept our forehead touching. My eyes remained closed because whatever scene that was waiting for me when I opened them was something I surely didn't want to see.

So I wrapped my arms around his neck and for what felt like forever, we just held each other.

Chapter 37

T he drive back was weird to say the least. If before it was heavy with tension because we weren't on speaking terms, now it was because we had no idea where we were at.

That embrace felt so different from the ones before.

Adam told the driver to let me down first so we passed by the apartment complex and went straight towards the university. It was rather late already but knowing those two, Meg and Julia were probably still awake and waiting for me.

Not once did I reach for my phone to ask for a bail out and that was telling.

The vehicle came to a stop right in front of the building and I knew it was time to say goodbye. Now I could approach this situation in several ways. One, I could ask him if we were good friends, but that was too heartbreaking for the both of us. Two, I could just make do with an awkward side hug and a thank you for the evening, yet that still didn't sound good to me. Or third, I could open the door and make a run for it.

Last one was definitely not an option.

Second one it is!

"I had a good time," I turned to face him, "Say thank you to Heart for me."

Now I just needed to commence the side hug and I could go. Of course, even this was something I had to overthink. I tried to look for least compromising position but I honestly looked like freak staring at him with this wondering expression on my face.

My eyebrows were scrunched up and my mouth was jutted into a small pout while I continuously swayed from side to side to see if there was an opening I could swoop into.

Then, out of nowhere, he let out a small laugh, "What are you doing?"

To be frank with you, I had no idea anymore.

Although this master plan was already formulating in my head, all thoughts flew right out when he leaned towards me and robbed me the pleasure of the one initiating the side hug.

My mouth tugged into a small smile, appreciating the small gesture because I honestly thought this would be more awkward than it was, "Good night."

At the very least, I didn't need to jump to the third option. With that, I opened the door and walked right out. I was actually impressed that after everything that had been said and done, I was rather calm.

When I got inside my room, Meg and Julia were both sitting on the floor with a laptop on top of a stack of pillows, playing a move they decided to watch. They heard the door opening and like a couple of dogs hearing the word squirrel, they turned their heads to me at the exact same time.

Meg reached forward to pause the movie while Julia stood up to guide me towards my bed, "What happened?"

"Well, everything was a surprise," I stated, falling onto my mattress, "Though I'm scarily calm about this whole thing."

"The last part is pretty obvious," Meg laughed, "So give us the details."

"First of all, it wasn't a dinner with Heart and Adam, but it was her ploy to get the two of us alone," I started off with the first tragedy of the evening, "Then she rented out the city's museum for our date."

Julia gasped in amazement, "Having a rich best friend must be nice."

Well, if I looked at things from Adam's perspective, not everything has been sunshine and rainbows.

"It was ridiculously uncomfortable because we couldn't even talk to each other and we barely touched the food," the part about the dozen pictures that Adam had secretly sent to Heart was exclusive for my memory, thank you very much, so I was skipping that part, "But we soon made an agreement to put whatever we went through behind us and enjoy the night."

We lasted a successful hour before all that stuff happened.

There was a long pause after that because even I had to think about it for a while. How even though I liked him, I had to reject him, "He asked me to be his girlfriend."

"And?!" they managed to both ask in unison.

And? And then I turned him down. That decision wasn't easy because all the events happened in such a short amount of time. People might be angry at me when I tell my reasons, but have they ever been in love? Do they know what it feels like to try your best and look at other people yet end up realizing that you just loved this one other person this whole time?

"I said no," I finally replied, my voice quiet and almost breathless. I didn't address that answer to them, but it felt like an apology that I hoped the wind would carry to Adam.

"Wait, but why?" Meg questioned, her eyebrows knitting together in confusion.

I stood up and sighed, "Because of what you said."

"Me?" she gaped.

"The thing about being moving on and being able to love again," I clarified, looking down on them, "He wasn't ready to love again and let's be honest, I haven't truly moved on yet."

I thought I did. But as the days go by and my head had only been occupied by thoughts of Justin, I've slowly come to the conclusion that I haven't. What I've moved on from was not being in a relationship with him, but I haven't moved on from loving him.

And Adam? While I did adore him to bits and pieces, I wasn't his golden ticket to forgetting that he had feelings for his best friend. While I knew he had no intentions of doing so, he made me feel like I always ranked second, that I was an afterthought.

I didn't want to be in a relationship like that. He'd find another girl that will be so right for him, but that girl isn't me.

"You're so right when you said our first impression of you was wrong," Julia piped in with a held back chuckle.

While I do appreciate the jab, I was not in the laughing mood.

"Julia, not now," I frowned, kicking her slightly so she would get off of my bed, "To be honest, I just want to sleep, this had been a long night."

Forget about my outfit or my makeup and hair, let me get out of this mental space. This day was so weird that I didn't want to believe that it was real.

And let me tell you a little lesson I learned the morning after – no matter how much you want the day to be over, wash your damn makeup off and wash your hair to get rid of all the products in. When I woke up, there was a variety of stains on my pillow and no matter how hard I tried to comb my hair, it wouldn't budge.

I spent more than an hour in the bathroom to get myself together. Needless to say, both Julia and Meg found my predicament hilarious.

"Now I'm really curious to know what your plan is now," Meg chuckled, taking a bite of the bread in her hand. I released another groan, taking my seat next to Julia and set my own plate of breakfast on the table, "Your story is far more interesting than the movie we watched last night."

Really, I've had enough of this.

"Well, I'm just thankful that last night was over. After I cool off, I'll call Adam and try to talk to him," I nodded with determination. Though the moment I picked up my fork, my phone that was next to the plate lit up. I peered over and I slumped against my seat, "And looks like the universe is not yet finished messing with me."

Heart Valentine: Come on out, I'm waiting in the car.

Just one day! Can't I have one day?

"You guys can have this," I sighed, pushing my plate away and standing up, "The princess is right outside and wants to see me."

Before either of them could voice out their excitement, I shut them down quickly, "Alone."

I quickly ran a hand through my hair to make it look like I didn't just tortured it and walked outside, there was the same vehicle that drove us around last night. I started to approach it but when I was at a good distance, the door opened and out came one sneaker-clad foot then followed by the other.

This certainly made me wonder because except for the times she was in the comfort of her own home, she was usually in heels. As if she ever needed them, she was already tall on her own, but I guess it did make her more intimidating and imposing.

She removed the sunglasses from hiding her blue eyes and she grinned towards me, "Sienna."

How much does she know?

"My best friend is studying here and I share a flat so close to it, yet I haven't been around the university yet," she told me, that sweet plastic smile on her face once again, "How about we walk around?"

Right now I was sincerely regretting my decision not to have Meg or Julia tag along. She wouldn't be able to kill me if there were witnesses.

"Sure," I replied an if it was possible, my voice cracked halfway. It was one damn word with one damn syllable.

We were quiet for the first few minutes because for one thing, I was hell sure that I wasn't going to be the one that started the conversation. Heart took her sweet time observing our surroundings and impressively ignoring all the obvious stares she was getting.

We did get stopped multiple times by others asking for a picture or an autograph. While she did say yes to the signing, she refused the photographs. She even goes as far as telling her fans not to post anywhere on social media where she was currently at.

"I don't want them to know where I am then suddenly hound me," she explained after a group of people waved her goodbye after thanking her for the autograph.

It was hard to believe at times that we were the same age. Then again, she was forced to grow up while I enjoyed my youth to the fullest.

"So how was your date with Adam last night?" she finally started the talk I was dreading.

At least she didn't beat around the bush so I was thankful for that.

"It went..." I paused for a moment to find the right word, "Interesting."

She raised a brow but continued walking nonetheless, "Just like how Adam described it."

Again, the lingering question: Does she know already?

"When I left back in January, I asked you to take care of Adam," she reminded and oh gosh, I should've prepared my will. At least let me publish the book that I wrote, "And almost every day, I got a play by play. I'm sure he left out the intimate parts but I could just see how quick and hard he was falling."

This was the one that made me stop my tracks. Adam, you were so open about me to Heart and sadly, you haven't been like that to me.

Why couldn't you have said anything?

"Then somehow, a week after my birthday, everything changed," she said, turning to me, "Do you know why?"

Oh because I shattered his heart?

Though with her tone I guessed all this time, she had it figured out.

"He would talk about his classes, his friends, and yet, not a word about you," she told me, "And I know Adam, enough to realize when he's not happy."

You know, I was expecting her to be angry at me or shout at me for the audacity of hurting her precious best friend. Instead, all I got was a sad frown, "I knew something was wrong but he wouldn't tell me. When I said I was coming back to the flat before I leave for America, I insisted that I wanted to see you, just an assurance that everything was still alright between you two."

And instead, she got a lie.

"But the moment I arrived, his body language was plain obvious so I thought of a plan," she explained, "Rent that museum, create the perfect romantic setting, and give you both that extra push. I printed out those pictures as a reminder to you that Adam deeply cares for you. I think I wasn't that successful in the end."

If it was any consolation, her idea with the pictures did work. It gave me a huge reminder that Adam thought about me that way. His pictures was my book. It was sweet when we were experiencing it in the moment, but rather bitter now that you look at it.

Now I just want it to turn into a beautiful memory.

"He wouldn't tell me anything so I thought about going to you for an explanation."

Alright, that at least answered my unspoken question.

But Adam didn't want to tell her anything so it wasn't my place to be the one to spout everything to her. Of course, now I knew the reason why he hid the whole story and while I didn't agree with him, I shouldn't be the one to blab.

So instead, I'd take this time to stop being so afraid of her and come clean. Essentially, I wasn't saying anything bad about him, but I was expressing my own side, "I like Adam, but I'm not in love with him."

"I don't expect you to be," she shook her head, "Especially since you just started dating and..."

I cut her off, "I'm not in love with him."

The special emphasis on the last word was enough for her to understand what I meant. I cared deeply for Adam, I adored him even, but I cannot force myself to love him, no matter how much I wanted to.

And I was sure that he felt the same way about me. He likes me, I'm not insecure about that part, but how much space did I occupy in his heart relative to his best friend?

Now, this was the time I really was expecting her to explode. But once again, she surprised me by flashing me an empathetic look, "I know what that feels like."

"Axel?" I dared to ask and she nodded.

"I admit it, I loved Adam more than as a friend back then, but Axel started to like me. I thought he was a good choice, but I couldn't give my all to him because I still loved someone else," when she came to me and expected that I was going to say my side to the story, I never expected her to say hers. While I did know a little bit because Adam told me the whole gist of things, this was the first for me to hear the history of the celebrity couple, "But you know what? Axel had this special way of making me turn to him and slowly but surely, I came to like him. To just put a final stamp to everything, I confessed to Adam and the only reason I did was because I wanted to be Axel's."

Hold on, wait a minute, stop for a second! This girl went on her way to tell her best friend, the love of her life for several years, her true feelings just so she could give her heart away to someone else?

And from what Adam had told me before, all of this occurred in one summer?

Geeze, if New York was fast, then what was California?

"He rejected me and he revealed that he helped Axel this whole time," ah, now that was the part that I knew, "Of course I was upset for a while but in the end, all the pieces went into place. I love Axel, he's my boyfriend, and yet that didn't remove the fact that there was a point that I loved somebody else while I liked him."

Although I had a huge doubt that things would smoothen themselves out like hers did, I found a bit of comfort that she experienced what I was currently experiencing.

"I don't fault you for being in that situation, but I hope you won't hurt him."

Your highness, it was too late for that.

"I'm leaving tonight so I won't be here to breathe down on your necks anymore," she sighed, "So do whatever you think is right."

The thing was, I had no idea what was right anymore.

Chapter 38

Have I talked to Adam yet? No. Have I avoided him like the plague? Oh you bet.

As I was going down the steps of the faculty building, I nearly jumped up when my phone started vibrating in my pocket. With my brows furrowed, I stared in confusion at the unknown number.

I've been so jittery since that museum trip. Then again, I've been back to consuming copious amount of caffeine just to keep me going because I've been losing so much sleep. I was always going to feel guilty, wasn't I? That talk with Heart barely helped at all.

Damned if I do, damned if I don't.

Looking back down on my phone screen, I just thought screw it and answered it. If they were kidnappers then go ahead, at least they would knock me out, "Hello?"

"Go to the university entrance," a familiar voice said and my eyes widened at the realization.

A voice that I've purposely missed every single call of. A voice that would instantly know that something was wrong the second I open my mouth. A voice that belonged to my best friend.

With every ounce of energy I had left, I broke into a sprint, my phone still pressed against my ear.

I needed this.

I looked absolutely ridiculous but I didn't care. My last ounce of happiness was waiting for me so I just ran for it.

As the gates got nearer, my legs went faster. When I got a better view, I slowed down at what I saw. My heart, that has been so tired and weak lately, suddenly brightened up.

"Gracie!" I screamed, lunging for my best friend, causing her to release the phone she was holding and enthusiastically hugged me back. When she did so, her laughter chiming in my ears, the tears welled up in my eyes, "I missed you guys so much."

It wasn't all her, but our whole group of friends was there. Once I was in someone's arms, they all gathered up for a huge group hug.

For being such a self-proclaimed cry baby, I haven't shed a single tear since that museum date. And yet when I saw all of my friends from back home, here in this foreign land right in front of me, the emotions I was holding back suddenly came out.

Gracie shushed me immediately and started rubbing soothing circles down my back, "You missed us that much?"

Girl, you have no idea. While I did miss you all, the lack of comfort that you guys usually provided didn't give me a crutch that I desperately needed. And I couldn't even tell you that everything was going south because the last thing I wanted was to worry you.

So I kept it a secret to all of my friends in America.

Well, except for one person.

I felt Justin's hand on top of my head and I had to look up, which was quite a difficult process because of my current position. He offered me a small smile, one I couldn't even return because just when I tried to move my mouth, a sob escaped my lips.

"Come on now," Gracie tried to stop my cries, gently wiping away my tears.

"What are you guys doing here?"

"Spring break," she reminded with a laugh, "We decided back in January to visit our wonderful best friend who we were all sure has been missing home more than ever."

Oh gosh, she had no idea.

When you've been friends with somebody before you could even crawl, there was always this urge to tell them anything and everything. That was Gracie to me, but one aspect of my life that I always held back from speaking of was my love life.

And what I've been through with Adam was no exception.

She looped her arm with mine and smiled brightly, "So when are we going to meet your man in person?"

Suddenly I knew what Adam felt like when Heart asked to see me.

"Why don't you invite him for dinner tonight?" another one piped in, clapping her hands with enthusiasm, "We're staying in the city until Monday since we plan to go on a road trip so we're yours for the whole weekend."

I stopped and Gracie groaned loudly, elbowing her harshly. While I happy, elated even, that they were here, I still couldn't help but feel a little down. They were on a break, they were out there going on road trips, they were traveling to another country, they were doing the things we all talked about doing before.

While I was holed up in here.

"Well, I have one more class to attend and then I'll chat you guys," I plastered an energetic smile. Thank god I decided to put on makeup today, even though I felt like absolute shit, at least it covered up how ridiculously worn out I really looked, "Don't worry, I'll call Adam and introduce you guys to him."

"Sienna..." Justin trailed off, obviously sensing I was far from preppy.

I shook my head, still with that grin, "I'll see you guys later."

I gave each of them a quick hug before I more or less sprinted away. In actuality, my last class was still a full hour away so while I did want to spend as much time with them as possible, I couldn't stomach it right now.

I don't want their whole trip to go bleak because of me. I couldn't tell them how sorry I felt for myself.

"Sienna?" I heard a familiar voice call and of course, he was the exact same person I've been trying to avoid so I pretended that I didn't hear him.

He had other plans though.

He grabbed me by the shoulder to stop me from my wonderful run and turned me so I could face his concerned expression, "Are you alright?"

Not now, he was the last person I wanted to see because I didn't want to combine my previous stressor with the new one, "Just peachy."

"I believe you," he shot sarcastically, accompanied by an eye roll, "Come on."

"Where are we going?"

"I heard from Soph that you two took a walk and she told you what happened with us then you shared your own thoughts," he explained and my heart skipped a beat at the thought of him hearing from his best friend that I wasn't in love with him, "She wouldn't say anything aside from that though."

Oh.

"She was pretty upset that you wouldn't say anything to her," I told him. I wasn't so innocent though, I was hiding it from my friends that I've broken up with him.

Wait, was it considered a break up if we never made it official in the first place?

"Walk with me?" he asked, gesturing to the long sidewalk in front of us.

I glanced behind my shoulder as if my friends were still there, as if they were watching my every movement. They've always been there for me, ready to catch my fall.

Except for this one time when I didn't want them to.

"Okay," I murmured in agreement, my legs moving forward.

I walked by his side while he just talked to me about whatever we saw – whether it was the girl sitting under the tree with her sketchbook on her lap, the decaying bench that was covered in all sorts of paint, the group of students doing who knows what kind of dance by a patch of grass, and just the scenes that I overlooked during my whole year in the university.

My freshman year had always been between my dormitory and the apartment complex. I didn't loiter around after class, I already had a set list of restaurants and cafés that I go to, and I didn't really roam around that much.

How ironic that I was searching for the adventure when there was still uncharted land right in front of me the whole time.

"I can't remember if I told you this before, but I finished my book."

He paused on his steps to turn to me, a questioning look on his face, "When?"

"A week before I came to your apartment," I replied, gesturing to the university breathing with its own life through its students, "I finished at a crazy hour in the morning and I just ran right after. I didn't know why, but I felt so strangled so even though it was dark, even though it was freezing, I just went."

It was pitch black when I went for that spontaneous sprint so I didn't get to marvel at the beauty of the university that I have failed to explore before.

It embraced me, encouraging me in a way I never knew it was trying to do before. When Uncle Levi suggested I pack my bags and study here, I was unsure if it would even work. Soon, I realized that I simply had blinkers this whole time, stopping me from looking around. I've been so focused of getting out of this rut that I've failed to see that all I had to do was let life take its course.

And that was what happened with Adam. Everybody around us encouraged us to be together, to push us into dating. They expected us to go out, heck even I somewhat thought of that as well before I actually grew feelings for him. We rushed into everything, not even thinking that having a genuine friendship between us might have been the best possible thing.

"Adam, I wrote you a love letter," I said, genuinely smiling at him. There was no hidden pain or forced happiness, but just sincere appreciation towards the man in front of me, "A love letter that had forty chapters."

"Me?"

I nodded, "You. From the moment you sat next to me on that plane, I knew it was you."

He appeared so dumbfounded by this and I had to laugh. He had seen my sketchbook on multiple occasions, hasn't he noticed that I constantly wrote about him? Our highs, our lows, all of them were there.

Don't worry, I promise that the best parts were excluded because those were ours and not the world's to see.

"Can you do me a favor this time?" I spoke, finally addressing what I didn't want, "My friends are visiting and..."

"And you haven't told them that we're no longer together," he finished for me and then there was a small smile gracing his lips. I laughed and nodded because instead of being offended or whatnot, he was amused that I found myself in that same predicament he did, "I'd be happy to."

I blinked at him, first registering his response inside my mind. I've been nothing but selfish, but to my complete surprise, he just said yes. I grinned, stopping on my tracks,

"Thank you and don't worry, I promise there's going to be nobody that will rent a whole museum behind our backs."

He chuckled and offered his arm, as if we were going to venture into a ballroom together, "That's disappointing, I really like art."

We've been doing this dance for almost a complete year now and while it had its ups and downs, I do admit that it was pretty fun, "Then let's go there soon, but on a normal day this time."

"Deal."

And we continued to stroll down. Our arms linked, the smiles on our faces as if the past months never occurred. It was like we were back to our 'getting to know' stage. There were no voices teasing us, we didn't feel pressured to move on, and it's just the two of us enjoying each other's company.

When you stop thinking about it over and over, everything would just fall into place.

That evening, it was my turn to pick him up. Good thing all of us agreed to just go to a casual restaurant so there were no heels involved with the short walk. I rang his doorbell and waited for him to open and thankfully, he was already dressed and ready to go.

"Hold on, I'm just going to get a coat," he said, leaving the door ajar as he walked back inside.

Wait, was I allowed to go in?

I took a cautious step as if alarms would suddenly go off if I did. To be honest, I wouldn't put it past Heart to suddenly ban me from this apartment.

However, it seemed like it was safe so I fully went inside and closed the door behind me. I didn't know what I was expecting when I looked around. Everything was still exactly the same, save for some objects that Heart probably left here.

I walked up to the couch and instead of sitting, I just stared down on it. Right there was where Adam sat right before I spontaneously kissed him for the first time.

That was all we needed and our months of hovering around each other finally ended.

I sighed and turned, plopping down on the soft cushions. From this angle, I noticed the small shelf underneath the coffee table. It used to be filled with his school books, and it still was, but smack on top of one of them is the booklet I made him.

I swore that he would have thrown it out the moment he made me leave.

Reaching for it, I let my hands feel the Dear Adam that I've written on the front page.

"You know, Soph found that just minutes before she had to leave," he suddenly said, coming down the stairs, "She never looked down there because she knew from before that it's just textbooks but while waiting for her car, she laid down on the sofa and saw that there."

"I'm surprised it's so out in the open," I told him, "If I received something like this, I would have probably hidden it away from view."

"I did think of that," he admitted, sitting right next to me, "But I figured that you worked hard on it, you clearly thought it through, and I should be thankful. You simply didn't knock on my door, told me that we were done, and then left."

Well, that's what I did for Justin and it didn't go as well as this did.

At least I didn't have to wait years before we could even go back to speaking terms.

"I thought you were angry with me."

He shrugged, "I guess I was upset, but you know I could never get mad at you."

Just like his touch, his words so warm that it enveloped me with assurance.

"Thank you."

Hey universe? I want to take that genuine friendship route now.

Chapter 39

Whuen we arrived at the restaurant they told me about, I could see them on the long table near the middle. They were talking amongst themselves and while I knew they didn't mean to be rude or annoying, the accumulation of their voices created a noise.

"You mean all of them are here?" Adam questioned once he saw the big group and I nodded. Not one of us turns down an adventure and it was reminiscent to the ones we used to do when we were back home – they just took it to another country.

I gave his hand a small squeeze before plastering a grin on my face and walking up to them, "Hey guys."

They looked up from their conversations and I was greeted with a bunch of smiles and hellos. I held onto Adam's arm and gestured towards him, "I'd like you to meet Adam, he's the guy I've been talking to you about."

Majority stood up to shake his hand or give a friendly hug and this did not bode well with the other diners. We were already obnoxiously loud but pair it up with our various scraping of chairs and moving around, we were just asking to be kicked out.

So I tried to act as the mediator by urging them all to take their seat again, "Calm down, he'll be here the whole time."

While they all shuffled around back to their chairs, I introduced them one by one as we took our own seats, "Then that's Justin and this girl right here is Gracie."

"It's actually Grace but no one ever calls me that," she laughed, "It's so nice to finally meet you in person, Sienna has told me a lot about you."

Just not the latest happenings.

"Good things, I hope," he chuckled playfully and I internally cringed at myself because we all knew the answer to that.

The way they were conversing made it appear as if I wasn't sat smack in the middle of them. While I knew Adam wouldn't expose me, I wasn't so sure about Gracie because we all knew that as my best friend, it was her job to embarrass me.

I quickly glanced around the table to observe my other friends and my eyes suddenly met Justin's, who I failed to notice was sitting right in front of me. I gripped onto the edge of the table when I saw his concerned expression.

I'm okay, I wanted to tell him. I had to convey that I wasn't forcing myself, that I no longer felt like I wanted to crawl my way back to bed at any given moment, that I didn't want to hide from the world anymore.

And that Adam wasn't the cause of worry anymore. In fact, I've been too drowned with what happened so recently that it completely slipped my mind that Adam was first of all my comfort. He had been my escape and while he did admit that I was the one that saved him, both of us discredit how much he helped me.

Now we were back to being like that again. He could have easily denied my request since I basically broke his heart and it was wicked of me to keep on lying to my friends. Instead, he accepted with no hesitation.

"Sienna, your order?" Gracie called my attention and I snapped right out of my trance. I tore my gaze away from Justin and turned to my best friend as she looked at me expectantly. I looked up and the waiter was also waiting for my words.

"Uh," I stammered, frantically looking around for my menu and guess what, it remained untouched on the table.

Can you believe in my frenzy, I almost dropped the damn thing? Why was their menu so offensively large? I almost elbowed Gracie when I practically tore it open.

"She'll have the special burger with the side of sweet potato fries," Adam jumped in and I could have hugged him right there when he rescued me from future embarrassment, "Did you want the dip with that?"

"Sure," I nodded violently, anything to get me out of this situation.

Guess convincing Justin that everything was a-okay was out of the window.

Apparently, I was the last person the waiter was waiting on so after he jotted down my order, he left. I turned to Adam and mouthed, "Thank you."

He squeezed my wrist for a quick second before turning to my friend seated on the other side of him after his name was called. Gracie winked at me with a proud smile, "He's nice."

"Very," I agreed and she laughed.

"And you seem to be doing well, it looks like I've been worried for nothing."

That made me freeze in my chair because all this time, I've just been hiding everything from her. Everything appeared fine and dandy, when in fact, everything was over for a while now. It was easy to lie when there's a barrier of a computer screen between us. But now, seeing those blue eyes eternally trusting my words, I couldn't help it anymore.

"Gracie, can I talk to you..." I trailed off, scanning around the room, "Alone?"

Like a flip of a switch, her smile slipped off of her face. She nodded slowly and carefully stood up, ignoring all the questions fired her way. I also got up on my feet but before I walked out with her, I shot Adam an assuring smile when he reached out and touched my wrist with the tip of his fingers.

"Are you going to be alright?"

Perceptive as always.

"I'll be fine," I said, patting his hand lightly.

We got outside of the restaurant and out into the streets. It was quite busy considering it was the start to the weekend but even though this was a city, busy equates to a number of relaxed people strolling along.

Again, the peaceful opposite to New York.

We stopped right in front of the restaurant since it would be useless to walk farther. I twiddled my fingers first, trying to string across my words into a coherent explanation inside my head.

Though with her, I rarely have to do that, "Is this the part where you tell me that it's over between you and Adam?"

"You knew?"

She then lifted her hands and slapped them on my cheeks. I screeched at how cold her skin was and I tried to pull them away, but she was far stronger than I was, "You're an idiot, you know that?"

"I do but it would be nice if you tell me in what particular way this time," I muttered, still trying to get away from her freezing palms.

"Because I warned you over and over again that you're going to get hurt. News flash, I'm your best friend so I know when you're acting differently and you've refused to talk about Adam to me the same way you never even uttered Justin's name when you two broke up."

When I meant that none of our friends were involved with the development of Justin and I's relationship, I meant it. Yes, they were always there because we did have the same friend group but like I said before, they never knew anything was going on until we made it official.

The same thing was when we broke up.

We mutually decided not to make a big deal out of it because we never wanted it to be the source of tension in our group so we just continued on as if everything was normal. Apparently, we weren't that good at hiding it because Gracie eventually decided to confront me about it.

I was actually surprised that she took this long before she said anything about it.

She released me with a deep sigh, "But I still stand with my judgement earlier – he's nice. If not, he wouldn't put up with this pretense."

"Actually, there's a lot more to this story," I frowned, "But I have no idea where to start."

"Well, I'm going to read about it eventually," she shrugged, already pertaining to my book, "Congrats on finishing it."

"Okay, the thing with Adam I can understand how you could find out, but how the heck do you know about the book?"

She raised a finger and tsked, "As if our moms don't enjoy a weekly lunch out together."

"They sure are close," I commented with an exasperated look. My mother was very cold to strangers, it was one of the reason why she was so respected – everybody was afraid to let her down. All that was different to Gracie's mother and she was an exception to everything. Even some people in her team didn't know about my book yet and somehow, she already managed to blab to her best friend.

Gracie's gaze softened, her corners of her lips turned down slightly, "I wonder when we weren't, Lili."

Being left alone with your own thoughts was scary, but what was more terrifying for me was to see Gracie's disappointed face. Contrary to what many may think, she was the more levelheaded one between us. Not only was she one of the top in class, but she was editor-in-chief for the school's newspaper.

I adored creative writing just as much as she loved journalism, which explains her observant nature.

Don't label her as a serious student though, but did she have skill. She was the type of person to show up to class with a nasty hangover and still manage to deliver a satisfactory report.

But she always took care of me and I've lost count of how many times she rolled her eyes at me after I sheepishly deliver some not-so-good news towards her way.

Now how could I possibly say to her that not only did I break my own heart, but also another guy's, after she had warned me multiple times?

Then again, I've messed up more times than I could count and she never left me before.

"I don't know where to begin," I breathed out, hugging my body tighter, "I've never been so out of myself before and trying to figure my way around is so exhausting."

"Did I at least get it right?" she questioned, her eyebrows knitting together, "About you and Justin."

I groaned, stomping my foot lightly on the sidewalk, "You know I hate it when I have to admit that you were right."

"Does Adam know though?"

About the fact that I somehow broke up with him partly because I was still madly in love with my ex?

"I gave him a small hint," was all that I could reply.

"Actually, I do."

Both of us froze before slowly looking over our shoulders. There stood the said man, his hands stuffed inside his jean pockets, looking intently right at us.

Oh crap.

While I didn't want to be left alone with him right now, I knew that it was the right thing to have this kind of conversation with him. Gracie thought of the same thing, so she gently touched my shoulder and gave me an encouraging nod, "I'll see you in there."

She flashed him a tightlipped smile – one that might have conveyed a some sort of apology because I know she felt like she was partly responsible for this whole falling out – then walked right back inside the restaurant.

I remained on my spot while he walked forward, stopping right where Gracie once stood.

"I'm sorry," the words flew right out of my mouth before I could stop it.

"I know," he assured, his voice as gentle and caring as always, "You said it yourself, we can't choose who our hearts fall for."

My gaze turned to him, how his hair slightly moved to the direction of the wind and how his brown eyes stared straight in front.

"I wonder what would have happened if I did fall for you the way I wanted to," I mused out loud.

He chuckled lightly under his breath, shaking his head, "I don't want to even think about it."

With one step forward, he looked at me expectantly, urging me to follow. I quickly glanced towards the restaurant then to him. He didn't move, not even a tug of my arm or anything, just patiently waiting until I made my own decision.

The corners of my lips tugged into a smile, my feet driving my body to follow him. I wrapped my arms around one of his and settled right by his side, our pace was slow and leisurely.

There was the high, and this was the low.

"You're right, he's nice," he spoke and I hummed in agreement.

"Told you so," I laughed.

When I meant by low, I didn't mean that we were in an argument and everything was crumbling down. That already happened.

What I meant was that we finally slowed down. We fell into this comfortable friendship, knowing fully well that whatever happened was finally behind us.

He was Adam and I was Sienna. We had our own lives to live, our own loves to pursue, and maybe for most, it may be viewed that we were unfortunate that we had to go through all the 'what ifs' before settling into this realization that we weren't right for each other.

But I think I am fortunate that I've met him and went through this journey with him. Yes, I did like him and he liked me in return.

Though sometimes, we just have to accept that those are not enough.

And besides, I have a book that hid his name but yelled our story. From those small moments we shared to the inside jokes we laughed about. It may have not been as heart stopping and tumultuous as the one I shared with Justin, but it was still our little magical story.

Through that, I can relive just how much he made my heart race, just how much he made me smile when I thought everything was going bleak.

We write to taste life twice. Writing allows us that second taste, to once again have that sense of what it was like to live in that specific moment.

And Adam, I'm beyond grateful for that small portion of my life that you weaseled yourself into.

Chapter 40

"Sienna Clark has once again wooed us with the realness of a young adult love," Gracie read out loud from her phone's screen, her voice filled with giddiness, "Her story creates a fresh balance against her uncle's philosophical stories and her cousin's dramatic readings, showing all of us how talent truly runs in their family's veins."

Our other friends gave me a teasing applause and I laughed, snatching the device from her hands, "Alright, that's enough."

With what I thought was a miracle, I managed to survive my first year of university. I spent ample time of my first couple of weeks of vacation in England with Julia and Meg like I promised them before I flew back home.

My book got published a few weeks before my finals and so, I didn't do much publicity or promotion for it because I was too busy monitoring my school work. It was only after did I manage to do the huge amount of interviews for various blogs and also actually reading the reviews left by the readers.

Safe to say, I managed to get a rather good response to it.

"So what did he think?" she asked, obviously talking about Adam.

"I highly discouraged him from reading it," I replied with a grin right on my face. It was quite embarrassing for me if he was going to read my interpretation of our relationship, "But he called me the other day and won't stop laughing at me for what I wrote."

There were no hard feelings, I know that all of this was just playful teasing. I adored Adam and we stayed close friends even after what we've been through. Obviously we didn't go back to the way we were exactly, though we still hung out but rarely just the two of us. It was usually with Vance or with my two roommates.

But we were friends. No awkwardness or anything, just simply friends. We didn't belong with each other and we accepted that.

"I'd say that's a better reaction that what I did," Justin chuckled, sitting down next to me and handing me a drink, "I think I was gaping for five whole minutes."

"And I'm fully disappointed that I wasn't there to see it," I teased, taking a sip from the cup.

It took me until university to even find out that he read it. What we shared was ten time more tumultuous than what I could ever experience. I was just thankful that Adam's was far from that.

While we did have our highs and lows, everything was relatively a simple and calm ride. We met, became friends, tried the dating thing, realized it wasn't meant to be, broke up, then remained friends. We were part of each other's journeys, but we weren't one another's destination. Sure, it was rather fun but it wasn't the real deal. A little bit of funny business when you look at it in retrospect.

And speaking of business, there was one unfinished business. This one, had been unfinished since high school.

The group fell into another conversation and I sighed, pushing myself up and walking towards the window, staring at the view outside. New York, the beauty that I craved for months was finally within my sight. Those busy streets, those people practically pushing each other just to rush to their destination, and the beautiful view of the skyline.

This was home.

"So what now?" I heard Justin ask right before he walked past me and leaned against the window, "You broke up with him and published the book, what's next for our banana?"

"Finish university?" I said, shrugging, "I don't know."

He nodded along, looking around the room first and observing our other friends. They were still deep within their own chatter, drinks were flying by and the night was still fairly young for us.

I expected him to join them again, but to my complete surprise, he caught my eye and held my gaze right there.

"Go back to me?" he sheepishly threw in there.

Safe to say, I felt like somebody punched me in the gut and knocked the air right out of me, "What?"

"I'm kidding," he chuckled, reaching out and placing a hand on the top of my head, "Only when you're ready."

You want to know what really happened when we broke up? How it played out? What were the words spoken?

That would be too time consuming. All you need to know is that both of us promised that we will wait for each other. No matter how long, no matter who we meet along the way.

Yes, it ended in tears, but he was adamant that we would still be together. As much as I wanted to laugh at his face at the somewhat lie, deep inside of me I prayed that he would actually keep his word. And that he did, even to this very day.

That was why I was open to the idea of having a relationship with other people. I doubted him, I doubted us. In the end, I had nothing to be afraid of.

We were still together. While we were not in a relationship, my heart belonged to him and apparently, his belonged to me.

How much longer was I going to make things complicated for us?

I stared into his face – that goofy smile, those crinkles by his eyes behind his glasses, that floppy hair. I saw all the features that made me blush whenever I saw him. But his kind words, that gentle yet playful personality, was what made me fall in love with him.

Fine, I'm done.

I took one big step forward and grabbed the sides of his face, smashing my lips right onto his.

I felt him smile, his arms instantly wrapping around my waist as we heard the collective cheers and wolf whistles coming from our friends behind me.

And a rush of electricity coursed through me, from my fingertips that touched his skin up to my toes that were planted on the carpeted floor. I haven't been this close to him in such a long time, I haven't felt this giddiness, this pure explosion since high school. As corny as it sounded, sparks flew all over the place. And yet, being in his arms once again and kissing him like this felt like home, there were no awkwardness or testing waters.

He was just there, perfectly fitting together with me.

We pulled back and his lips were grinning from ear to ear, one of his arms reaching up to gently caress my cheek, "I missed you."

"I missed you," I repeated, resting my forehead against his, "Thank you for being patient with me."

He laughed heartily, lifting me off the ground and I squealed in both surprise and excitement.

"And they're back!" his best friend yelled, "Everyone get a glass."

"To Sienna and Justin!" Gracie yelled at the top of her lungs as I could barely control my giggles, submitting myself into a tirade of Justin's cheek kisses.

Some people are stopovers, some people are destinations.

And sometimes, you need a stopover to realize where you really and truly belong.

Everybody eventually went on their separate ways and the moment I got home, I quickly went to my room. Tucked underneath my suitcase that even until now was unpacked was Uncle Levi's sketchbook. It just didn't feel right to return yet.

Until right now.

Adam, in the months that we were stuck in a limbo that our relationship, gave me flowers twice and only twice. One single flower during our first sort-of date on the night of the party and a bouquet during the Valentine's Day.

They were the mark of both the beginning and the end.

Before the party, I was completely sure that I only saw Adam as a friend. After that night, the hurt I felt opened my eyes that I did indeed have feelings for him. And on that fateful night back in February? It was when I realized we weren't meant to be. That sinking feeling in my heart when he attempted to tie up a last-minute date idea was all I needed to confirm this uneasiness within me.

I plucked a flower from the bouquet and put it in-between the pages of the sketchbook. The single flower he gave me during the party was also pressed somewhere in there and it remained there through it all, even when I ripped off all the pages related to him when I got angry and felt so sorry for myself.

I had one shelf just dedicated the works I published. There was a complete line of the old one and a line of the new one.

I plucked one copy out, feeling the embossed text on the cover. While it would be very easy for me to ask Emma to design me a book cover, I went through a different route.

I asked Adam for one of the candid shots he got of me. It was nothing special – just me sitting on his couch with my eyes focused on the notepad in my hands. I wasn't even smiling, I wasn't looking at the camera. Heck, I didn't even know that he was taking a picture of me.

But it was those simple moments that defined our story. We didn't have a grand heart wrenching love. Our relation-ship wasn't built on grand gestures. But most of our moments of affections were simply done in the safe confines of his apartment, loving the mundane that everyday life presented.

There were packages on my desk, each one containing a book that had a special dedication for the person receiving them. Of course there was one for Meg and another for Julia, I also packed one for Vance because he gave me that right kind of push from time to time. There was another for Axel and Heart each.

Speaking of which, Heart got a hold of a copy and showed it to her social media. Let's just say my sales practically doubled when she did.

Even though they probably already got one, I think it was a nice gesture to give them one with a personal note.

There was only one person that I haven't packed yet.

The one who captivated me for forty chapters, that made my head spin for months, the guy that gave me a new start and an inspiration.

He knew I was a writer from the start and he willingly became the subject of my imagination. I made a vow that I will only write stories that were mine to tell and I think my side of whatever we shared made itself known onto print. Whatever his side or his perspective may be, that was his own to tell as well and I have no right to do for him.

I grabbed a sharpie from my desk and flipped it open to the first page.

Adam,

Thank you for making me taste life different from the way I was accustomed to. You gave me everything I never imagined was missing from my life and I will always be thankful for that. While our story may not have been the way we both imagined when we met each other on the plane, I wrote it down because this was something I would want to go over and over again. Whether it was bittersweet for you or not, let this book be a second taste of all the affections I have for you. I adore you, always have and always will.

Sincerely, Sienna.

I plucked two petals from each of the pressed flowers and taped it securely right beside my handwriting. I smiled softly and closed the book, grabbing the mailer that already had his address.

Before I slid it in, I took one more long look at the text printed on the bottom – the title that was decided by whatever brain juice I had left during the editing phase of this book and let me tell you, I was still studying full time so there wasn't much to work with.

"We write to taste life twice," I said softly, opening the mailer and slowly putting it in, "In moment and in retrospect."

The last thing I saw before it completely went inside were the words Writing's Second Taste.

Chapter 41

P OV of Adam's future wife.

"Alright, so I need somebody to do the write up of interview we got for the sixth avenue story," the man in front all of us said, looking around the room. His permanent frown on his face did nothing to soothe the high tension from every single person.

So I internally sighed and raised my hand, "I'll do it, sir."

He slammed his hand on the table then pointed to me, "Good, send it to my e-mail by four."

Before I could even ask for the file of the said interview, he had already turned around and exited the room. I groaned, sinking down onto my chair and scratching the side of my head in frustration. I turned to my side and saw my co-interns, all turning their attention back to their computer screens.

I clicked my tongue loudly with my arms crossed, "Are you guys ever going to volunteer and do some work or are you just here for the sake of saying that you got intern at one of the biggest newspapers in New York."

"Hey!" one protested, glaring at me through his square hipster glasses, "That's really unfair for you to say."

"Is it really?" I huffed, pushing myself up from my seat, "Because from my end, this is already the third time he entered here to give us a task and somehow, all three of those ended up falling onto my shoulders."

And this guy just had the nerve to fight back, "Nobody asked you to volunteer all three times."

"Well, from my perspective, not one was going to do it anyways. Might as well get him out of this room as fast possible," I replied, walking over to his desk and peeking at his computer screen, "Seriously? You wrote a five page story on Heart Valentine's twenty-first birthday? That's the reason why you can't even volunteer for at least one of the things he wanted us to write?"

"Her birthday happened on February and she only held the party this month," he explained as if it would actually excuse him, "Isn't that a little sus?"

I rolled my eyes and took a step back, using every willpower in me not to yell at him for being such a slacker on the job, "Everybody was most probably busy during her actual birthday so she waited until summer to celebrate so more people could come. Twenty-one is a pretty big one so the more, the merrier."

As much as I know that celebrity gossip is part of the news business, I would hardly think somebody simply wanting to celebrate her birthday could warrant that long of an article. Even I would be admittedly bored with it.

"Just do something more productive and don't dump the whole internship work on me," I said firmly, turning on my heel and walking towards the man who gave me the assignment. He, on the other, just won't let it go and kept on following me.

"You think you're the boss of us when you're just another intern," he practically spat out but at this point, I decided that listening to him was just pointless.

The man was hunched over his desk, his eyes going over a piece of paper with so many red marks and post-its stuck to it. I cleared my throat to get his attention, "Sorry to bother you sir, but can I please have the file of the interview?"

He didn't bother to glance up and only clicked his tongue, opening up his computer to give me what I asked for, "Name?"

"Grace Lelyveld, sir," I replied quickly and he simply started typing. However, I watched as his eyes widened and he rotated his chair so he could face me.

Oh gosh, here we go.

"Don't tell me, you're..." he said almost breathlessly, "Are you related to him?"

I simply flashed him a smile, opting not to verbally agree or deny his question.

"Why didn't you say so?" his frown slowly lifted into a grin, surprising both me and the annoying person buzzing behind me like a bumble bee who wouldn't get lose, "You have a bright future! I'll send those files to your e-mail quickly."

"Thank you, sir," I told him and while I do appreciate my connections, I didn't like parading them around. After giving him a respectful nod, I went back to the other room.

"Lelyveld?" Mister Annoying questioned out loud, wracking his brain up for the probably familiar name. I managed to get back to my desk when he finally figured it out, "Wait, Pulitzer winning Lelyveld?"

His voice was so loud that the interns turned their attention to us. They connected the dots immediately and another one piped in, "Former executive editor Lelyveld?"

I truly wanted to scream.

I ignored them because at this point, I might strangle somebody if they utter another word towards my direction. I plopped down onto my office chair and grabbed my phone, calling my best friend because I've honestly had enough of these people.

"Hey Gracie," she chimed happily.

I placed my hand over the mouse and started going back to work, "Are you free for lunch? I really need a pick me up."

I thank the heavens that she was home for the summer. Even though I wasn't much to talk because I could be just as busy, knowing that she was in another continent did make me miss her more.

"Oh, well I was supposed to meet a friend but you're more than welcome to join us."

I lifted a brow, pausing from my scrolling, "Friend? A friend that isn't my friend too?"

Sienna and I have been best friends before I could even sit up as a baby. Meaning, throughout our lives, we share our friends. We were always in the same group.

"You remember Adam, right?" she told me and it instantly click.

"Yeah, how can I forget the guy who takes care of you at uni?" I joked, "Is Justin tagging along too?"

"No, he said that his mom made him her personal butler for the day," she laughed.

I smirked because there was one thing I loved to do and that was to tease her, "So you're meeting with your former love interest when your boyfriend's not there? So scandalous."

"Gracie!" she yelled and I continued to chuckle at her expense, "I already told Justin and he's completely fine about it."

While I did like to joke around like this, I was quite envious. Sienna found her person, the one she was completely sure of. Even if they did hit a rough patch somewhere down the road, that didn't hinder them from realizing that they truly belonged together.

Sure, I've been dating and I've had multiple ex-boyfriends in the past, but it was different when you managed to finally meet the person you were meant to be with.

I wanted something like that.

"Either way, I still want to have lunch so if you don't mind, I'd like to join you guys."

"I already said you can," I could practically hear her smile, "I'll text you the restaurant. See you later."

I placed my phone on the desk and picked up the mouse once again, ready to go back to doing my work. Before I could even click on the sent files, I heard a loud angry yell from the other room, "Who the fuck submitted five pages just for a celebrity's birthday?"

I tried to hide my snickers as I watched all color from mister annoying's face disappear.

Oh sweet karma.

I stepped inside the restaurant and immediately spotted that head of brown hair. She was laughing along to something that her companion said, creating a laxed feeling around them. It was exactly what I needed after all that tension in the office.

"Hey, sorry I took so long," I apologized once I got to their table.

"No problem, it was a good thing I decided to ask you if I should order for you," Sienna said, gesturing to the plate of salad that she got for me, "Adam, you remember Gracie, right?"

"Met her over a year ago when they all visited you," he nodded, "It's so nice to see you again."

Adam Nicholas, he was Sienna's friend at university in England. I first met him when we all visited her for our spring break back during my sophomore year. He was nice, almost too nice if I have to say so, but he takes care of my best friend and I was extremely thankful for that.

But, even if they have such an adorable and genuine friendship, it still did not erase the fact that they did try dating. Of course, I knew her better than herself at times and guessed from the start that they wouldn't last long. She came to her senses eventually and got together with Justin, something I was extremely glad of.

Because it was painful to watch her mope for over a year because of him. Neither of them wanted the break up to happen and it was so obvious that they still loved one another.

I was just thankful that Adam learned to accept that and move on... hopefully he did.

"So what brings you all the way to New York?" I asked, sitting down on the chair next to Sienna.

"My best friend, who moved to America, had her birthday so she flew a bunch of us from England to celebrate with her here," he explained and I attempted to hide my surprise. Sienna already mentioned back then that his best friend was extremely wealthy, even for our standards.

I stabbed the green on my plate rather harder than I intended and flashed him a smile, "How wonderful of her."

"So got rid of that guy who's in charge of internships yet?" Sienna asked, effectively steering away the conversation.

"He figured out my last name, so it was a weird day," I sighed, once again assaulting the poor vegetable because there was nowhere else I could take out my frustration.

I love journalism, that was something I completely fell in love with back when I joined the school newspaper back in high school. From there, I knew that this was the career I wanted to pursue. So that was how I quickly took it up as my major and now I found myself interning for one of the biggest newspapers this summer.

It was like the opposite end of the writing spectrum from Sienna's love. She found her passion in creative writing and I remember dragging her along to write for the school newspaper against her will. While she won't admit it, I knew she enjoyed her time there.

"Well, I think it's amazing you're doing something productive with your summer," Sienna laughed, "I've just been laying around in bed all day."

"Wait, we asked you if you wanted to go out last Saturday and you said no because you had other plans," I remembered, "Where did you go?"

And if they think for a second that I missed that quick glance they shared, boy they were wrong.

My heart dropped in my chest. Sienna told me everything, except for one aspect of her life – her love life. Oh god, what was happening?

Somebody please tell me they didn't what I think they did. No, Sienna loves Justin, she wouldn't do that to him.

I transferred my attention to Adam for any hints. He pretended not to hear my little question, finding his food all to fascinating. I observed his brown hair flopping about with his movements, those matching brown eyes that stared at his plate, his long fingers that held his fork.

He was attractive, that was for sure. He also brings in this innate charm that just makes you want to know him more, to somewhat be closer to him. That was something I immediately observed when I first met him.

I know why Sienna liked him. While I do think he was the perfect balance of handsome and cute, his history with my best friend alarmed that he was definitely off limits.

Which I admit, is a complete bummer for me.

So that was why I went back to my harassment of the poor lettuce with my fork and tried to let these thoughts go.

Chapter 42

I put on my denim jacket and grabbed my bag that settled on the floor underneath my desk. This day was more exhausting than usual because my precious co-interns just love this job so much that they kept dumping all the work on me.

I didn't even bother with saying goodbye to any of them. They were just going to make my head hurt.

You know that an elevator is supposed to stay open for twenty seconds before it closes again? And in that twenty seconds, Mister Annoying and his little posse managed to get inside the same elevator as me, much to my dismay.

"Grace!" he grinned, as if we weren't in the middle of an insult match this morning, "Why didn't you tell us you were a Lelyveld?"

Please take that fake pleasantries far away from me.

"I don't see you parading your last name, so why should I?" I replied with a raised brow, my eyes focused on the screen showing the descending floor numbers.

At this point, I didn't care if they thought that I was rude.

Still, for this little buzzing bumblebee that won't shut up, it wasn't enough to deter him, "So we were planning to go drinking tonight, want to come?"

And by the grace of god, the elevator doors opened to the sight of the ground floor. I marched out with a huff, but still not forgetting to send a friendly smile to the receptionist and security guard.

These people were seriously thinking of drinking? When we have another day of work tomorrow? Unbelievable!

"Grace? What do you say?" he kept of probing and I was a hair's width away from snapping on him once again. When we all managed to get out of the building, I felt like the universe decided to bless me with one thing to make it up for the shitty day that I just got.

I saw Adam walking along the sidewalk, looking around with a to-go cup in his hand. We might not be close, heck I don't even consider us more than acquaintances, but it was enough for me to get these people off of my back.

"Adam!" I yelled out, faking enthusiasm, "It's so nice of you to pick me up."

He was so confused, it was written all over his face. Still, I continued on with my act and turned to the other interns, "Sorry guys, but I already have plans."

I shot them a tightlipped smile and stood next to Adam, silently urging him to walk away with me. Even though he had no idea what was happening, he followed me until we rounded up the corner and I was sure they couldn't see us anymore.

"I'm so sorry but I really had to make up an excuse to get them away from me," I explained hastily, constantly looking over my shoulder as if they were going to appear at any moment, "Thank you so much for playing along."

He blinked for a second to let my words register before his lips turned into an amused smile, "It's alright, I was just on my way back to the hotel. I tried to go around but it's rather boring when you're alone."

"Where's Sienna?" I asked because if he had only asked her, I was sure that she would say yes, "Didn't you ask her to go with you?"

"Well, she went me for a while but her boyfriend called and I told her to go ahead," he said, "I didn't want to go home just yet so I thought I would stroll around for a bit."

Wait, didn't he say that the main reason he was here was because he came for his best friend's birthday, "And your best friend?"

"Uh, she and her fiancé had to go to California for work reasons," he told me, scratching the back of his head, "I was supposed to go with them, but I already promised Sienna that I'd meet her in New York so I told them to go ahead without me. She booked me a flight for tomorrow morning instead."

California for work reasons? Extremely wealthy? Recent birthday? I'm just ticking the boxes until I come to a wonderful conclusion.

Instead of going all detective mode, I observed his features. His face was a little pink because even if it was summer, the nights could get really cold here. When I saw him earlier, he looked just little bit like a lost boy.

And there was something inside me that was screaming to accompany him. Maybe, just maybe, I wanted to spend more time with him.

What I was thinking of was wrong. I had no right to like him, if he wasn't for his momentary fling with Sienna, we wouldn't even know each other.

Strolling around together wouldn't hurt, right? It wasn't like I was going to jump on his bones or anything like that.

"Adam," I called out softly, doing an impulsive decision once again, "Want to take a walk with me?"

Even for a little while, I think he didn't want to be alone and I desperately needed to cool my head.

"Okay," he replied in a quiet voice, but that smile was still pulling up the corners of his lips.

"Come on, there's a guy who sells pretzels just by the other corner," I said, my legs starting to drive forward while he went to my side, "He's been there since we were young so he knows us pretty well."

The stroll there was rather quiet. Mostly because I didn't know how to keep the conversation. Trust me, I was a very talkative girl but there were just some cases where I wasn't.

And this was one of them.

We managed to get to the pretzel cart, the man busy with entertaining another costumer. I tapped Adam on his shoulder, tearing his attention away from the very fascinating stoplight he was looking at, and pointed towards the cart.

"Gracie!" the man greeted me joyously, "I haven't seen you in a while, I thought you forgot about me."

"Never," I gasped dramatically, followed by a lighthearted laugh, "Two pretzels please."

"Coming right up," he said, already going to work on preparing our orders, "And who's this fella over here?"

Adam waved rather awkwardly and I still kept that friendly grin, "This is Adam, he's visiting from England."

"Pleasure to meet you, sir," Adam nodded just as the vendor gave us the pretzels we ordered. I handed him the exact money.

"Well, you two take care."

We started to walk away again and when Adam took a bite, I watched as his eyes widened in delight at the taste, "This is amazing."

I laughed and also took a bite. Seriously, this and a huge ice cream were my ultimate comforts whenever I experience heartbreak – whether it was from a failed exam or a horrible break up.

Or when I had to sit there while my best friend obviously suffered from writer's block while still mending a broken heart she caused herself. And I couldn't do anything, because all tactics of even getting her out of her home was useless. I was busy with college also so while I did want to give her my undivided attention, I couldn't. I knew that I had no choice but let her sit out, wait until she was ready herself to move on.

Then she did. She moved to England and eventually, I heard about this man walking beside me right now.

"Sienna, met any handsome British men yet?"

I watched as there was a flicker of sadness in her eyes but she did her best to hide it. We were just talking about our experiences these past months and I knew Sienna felt like hers was less significant than ours.

But then, something managed to regain her peppiness and she smirked at the camera, "Yes, and he asked me out."

This was the very first time I heard about a guy. Though, that wasn't so surprising since Sienna did have a history of hiding her relationships from us. I wouldn't be shocked if she suddenly texted us that she finally got another boyfriend.

Yet I knew, even with her false cockiness, she hasn't completely moved on from Justin.

"Show us a picture!" I demanded enthusiastically, playing along.

In our group chat, she did. It was a picture of him smiling brightly at the camera, his eyes squinting a little bit due to the sun. His brown hair was styled, just casually and nothing too much, and he was posing right in front of the Hollywood sign.

She would soon tell us that his name was Adam Nicholas, a student in the same university she went to. They met at the plane and as if fate dictated it, they saw each other once again.

And from the get go, I knew she was going to get hurt. Or worse, she was going to hurt him.

But after I did meet him, I could see nothing but kindness and patience in him. From there, I figured out why Sienna wanted to fall in love with him. And if I could ever be so brave,

I admit that I wanted to go out with him if my mind wasn't stuck with the fact that he used to date her.

Handsome? Very. Good personality? Check to that.

"Want to take a break over that bench?" he asked, snapping me right out of my thoughts. I nodded numbly and followed him, sitting beside him as he settled down and threw away the piece of paper that held the pretzel into the trashcan nearby.

"You know, there's something oddly therapeutic about just walking around in this city," I spoke out loud, watching as the people passed by us. They didn't care about their surroundings, they all had places to be, "I mean, the smell is horrible, the traffic will get you nowhere, and there is a possibility that you might bump into somebody every five steps or so, but this is where I belong. You know what I mean?"

I turned to face him and I had to stop myself from flinching back when I saw him staring intently at me. He was looking for cracks, a way to decipher who I was without actually having to ask. But after a full second, he replied, "Yes. I do understand."

You can't out-observe a journalist. If he was looking for my cracks, I can clearly see his. I remember that expression when I saw him as I got out of the building – he was lost. Perhaps not literally, but there was clearly something wrong.

"So, what's up with you?" I fired, taking a bite of the now cold pretzel, "What's in the mind of the Adam Nicholas sitting next to me?"

"What?"

Alright, tone down a little bit. You're not here to interview somebody for an article, "Just tell me a story. Something about you? How has your stay in New York been?"

Simple questions, like the customary getting to know inquiries.

Hey Adam, do you see me as anything more than Sienna's best friend?

He was quiet once again, looking down on his hands with his elbows resting on his thighs. I sincerely thought I had to wrack my brain up for another way to lead this conversation elsewhere but fortunately, he spoke, "Can I be honest?"

"We're on a bench in NYC sitting next to a trash can with absolutely no idea of where to go," I laughed, "Go, be honest with me."

"I feel like shit," he blurted out bluntly and I had to retrack inside my mind.

Alright, this was something I didn't expect.

"I just feel like everybody around me has been moving on, going other places in life. My best friend just got engaged for Christ's sakes!" he exclaimed, releasing a frustrated grunt at the end, "And me? I feel like I'm stuck. I'm not improving, but I'm not regressing."

There it was – the feelings he had been bottling up. It must have been so difficult, and probably even seeing Sienna was another reminder of how everybody around him has been moving. She was happily in a relationship again and from what I've gathered, he was stuck to being single.

And honestly, I felt this guilt that I even had the audacity to like him. Right now he didn't need a girlfriend, but just one friend to bring him back down to the ground.

"Everybody moves at their pace," I said, finally giving up on this pretzel and just letting it sit on my other side, the one that wasn't next to Adam, "Just because you see somebody sprinting in front of you while you're taking a slow stroll doesn't mean you have to run as well. He's going to a different direction, somewhere where you aren't supposed to be."

I gestured to the sidewalk filled with people, pointing to one person talking loudly into his phone as he attempted to weave through the crowds of people as fast as he possibly could, "That guy is obviously in a rush, but you don't see us getting up on our feet and feeling nervous because we also think that we have to hurry."

"We're just sitting on this bench because we have no place to be right now," he finished my whole speech for me, "But that doesn't mean we'll just sit here forever."

"Precisely," I smiled, taking one his hands and clasping it between mine, using the other hand to pat his reassuringly, "We'll get where we're supposed to be at some point, but for now, relax."

Be a friend, Gracie, be a friend.

He chuckled under his breath, covering my hand that was holding him with his free hand. He enclosed that one hand, gracing me with that gentle smile as he stared straight into my eyes, "Thank you, Gracie."

And needless to say, I was captivated. For the words that I managed to spit out to encourage him, all of it died down in my throat. Because that stare, it held me down. The way he held my hand, it wasn't forceful or any of that sort but I still felt his warmth radiating through it.

From that lost expression, it morphed into one that was filled with gratitude. He made me know that it was all for me.

"Adam," I didn't know how my voice could crack with just saying his name, but it did, "Shall we go?"

"Okay," he replied breathlessly, but neither of us moved. We still sat there, our hands together and just looking into each other's eyes.

I didn't know who started it. In fact, it all happened so fast. However, the next thing I knew, we were both leaning closer and our lips were mere centimeters apart.

"We should really go," I spoke so softly that if we weren't this close, he wouldn't have been able to hear it.

"Yeah," he voiced out his agreement, but instead of moving back, he finally closed the distance between us and pressed his lips against mine.

My eyes closed and I gladly reciprocated the kiss, feeling as he intertwined the fingers of our joined hands. I felt my hair whipping towards his direction and I could still smell the horrible smell of New York trash. Yet, none of those mattered in that very moment.

Forgive me, but I like him.

He pulled away, moving back just a few inches, "I feel like I will sincerely regret it if I let you go right now."

"And I feel like I will regret it if I go home now."

Spoiler alert, I didn't go home that night.

Epilogue

I woke up to the sun literally blaring on my face. Alright, next time, I should really close the windows. I turned to my side in order to get that brightness out of my face and felt around for a nice comfy pillow to hug.

When my hand felt something, it started to move. I may be tired, but I knew for sure that pillows weren't sentient.

My eyes cracked open and I had to stop myself from gaping when Adam's sleeping face was literally inches away from me.

Oh right, I didn't go home last night. I stayed in his hotel.

I pushed myself up into a sitting position, running a hand through the scraggly blonde mess that was known as my hair. I sighed and got out of the bed, but I made sure to pull the covers over his body so he wouldn't get cold. Releasing a deep yawn, I walked into the bathroom and observed myself in the mirror, hoping that I wasn't in too much of a mess.

You could say I was gravely disappointed.

I didn't take off my makeup so it was smudge city, my hair was a tumbleweed on top of my head, and I simply looked exhausted. From where I was standing, I could still see my clothes neatly folded inside the closet through the open door.

Adam graciously lent me his shirt and a pair of boxer shorts to change into so I wouldn't be stuck in jeans. I attempted to redo my makeup with whatever was in my bag and I pulled my hair into a bun just to mask how much of a wreck it was. I used one of the spare disposable toothbrushes that the hotel provided because there was no way in hell was I leaving with morning breath.

I fished around the room for my phone and I finally found it on one of the couches. When I lit up the screen to check for any notifications, my eyes bulged out at the time displayed, "I'm late!"

Right, work.

I grabbed a pillow and hit poor Adam with it in attempts to wake him up, "Adam, get up! I'm late for work!"

Looks like I was going to wear the exact same thing as last night. Gosh, the walk of shame.

Well, technically we didn't have sex so was it still the walk of shame?

"Adam!" I yelled, finally stirring him up. I had already gotten out of the boxer shorts and into my pants.

He opened one eye to look at me and I paused in my movement when he shot me a tired and lazy smile, "Good morning."

How can he look so fantastic just after waking up? His hair was disheveled, his eyes half open, his smile was leaning onto one side so it made it look like he was flashing me a smirk.

Everything in me was trying to calm me down because if I lose control, I would definitely jump on his bones.

Focus, Gracie, you have work.

"I really need to go," I told him, snapping right out of my train of thoughts before I fully swooned at his features.

When I made the move to grab the blouse I wore yesterday, he shocked me by speaking in such a low and husky tone, "You can borrow one of my white button ups. Just tuck it in or tie the bottom."

"God, do you have any idea how much you saved me with that idea," I said, opening the closet and snatching one that was on a hanger. I changed into inside the bathroom and when I got out, he was already out of bed, bent over to grab a water bottle from the minifridge.

"I'll return this when I get off work," I told him, putting on my jacket. He stood straight with his eyebrows knitted together, causing me to stop my hasty movements.

"I have to be at the airport in an hour," he reminded me about one topic of our conversation last night, his voice now low and quiet, as if he didn't want to bring it up, "I'm going to California, Gracie."

You know during those moments when you have absolutely no idea how to respond? Yeah, this was one of those moments. Look, I wasn't the type to be awkward, even when it comes to these situations. I've slept with someone on the first date and even then, it was never compromising.

But this was different.

This was a very unique situation I was in. Last night was not a date, we didn't even have sex, and the creepiest fact that

I have almost forgotten, I met him because my best friend used to go out with him.

Very weird.

"So how will I return this?" I asked quietly, tugging on the rolled up sleeves.

He was silent for a while and I knew that with every second ticked by, doubt creeped itself inside his mind. I wouldn't blame him if he was full of regret right now. He wasn't in the best position emotionally – he even admitted to it me last night.

You know, the logical thing to do was to comfort him after that speech, not kiss him that will end up with me spending the night with him.

While he may regret it, I didn't. I wanted to because that was the right thing to feel, but I just couldn't. Because I liked him and even if last night was the only time we would be together then so be it.

"I'll just give it to Sienna so she can hand it to you when she flies back to England," I told him, coming to my own conclusion. Remember? My best friend? The girl you liked about a year ago?

Shame, that was it. Shame was the only thing clouding my whole system.

And what broke my heart more was that he didn't even say a single word. He just stood there, his eyes wide as if I suddenly reminded him how wrong this was supposed to be.

"Until next time, Adam," I muttered softly, the defeat pouring itself out, "Goodbye."

When I got out of his hotel room, I waited. I simply stood there with my back turned to the door in hopes that he will open it and ask me not to leave. But the numbers on my phone screen kept on changing, telling me just how long I waited for nothing.

So I left and tried to think that he was just another of those one night stands. He wasn't the first guy to do this to me, I have been ghosted many times before.

Then why did it hurt so much?

I wasn't like Sienna who found her Justin and decided that he was it. I shuffled through relationships, dating then breaking up wasn't out of the norm. I was still looking for my one and only. Yes, even if I didn't look like it, I could be a hopeless romantic when I want to.

"Somebody's later," Mister Annoying drawled out in a sing-song voice. I rolled my eyes and immediately went to my desk, trying to drown whatever thoughts of Adam with work.

My eyes kept switching to my phone as if he would call or at least message me. Weirdly, I didn't have his number. Most of our interaction were through Sienna – scratch that, all of our interactions except last night was through Sienna.

Whenever she was one of those moods, the person I usually talked to was her roommate, Julia. But Adam? We had no means of communication.

My phone started buzzing and I hastily tore my gaze away from my computer screen and to my phone. I grunted in disappointment when I saw Sienna's name.

No, this is not good.

I shook off any negative emotion and accepted the call, "Hey!"

"Gracie..." she trailed off, her tone far from chirpy. I felt my stomach drop because I had a huge hunch that she knew, "Do you have anything to tell me?"

I audibly gulped, my eyes switching around the room as if my dirty laundry was just hanging for everybody to see. I was fidgeting so much, almost like they knew what happened last night. Of course, that was just in my head. They were all focused on work, for once.

"Lili," I started off, hoping that her nickname would soften the blow, "Did he tell you?"

I heard her sigh, "He didn't say it directly, but he called me to ask for your number. I managed to connect the dots on my own."

"This is something I don't want to talk about on the phone," I said, "Can we just meet after I get off work?"

"I'm not mad and I'm not against it," she assured, "And to be honest, I'm not the one to complain about you hiding it from me. You and I both know that I haven't been the most open when it comes to relationships and the people that I like."

And once again, I was reminded of that awkward goodbye, "Don't worry, there will be no relationship. I'm a hundred percent positive that he doesn't like me."

Actually saying it out loud made it more painful than I originally thought. But it wasn't a lie though, the way he acted just made it clear to me that last night should have never happened. That everything was just because of the heat of the moment.

She clicked her tongue in disappointment, "You need major cheering up. I'll come over to your place later."

"Thank you," I voiced out my appreciation. There was also some kind of relief knowing that she wasn't upset at me for what I did.

Because I cannot fathom what would happen if she was. She and I have fought a thousand times, but those were all about petty things. It was never about a guy, we had this silent agreement that we will never like the same boy. If one tells the other who she likes first, then that person was off-limits.

That was why I have such a hard time wrapping my head around this situation. Even if she was dating somebody else already, she somewhat already called dibs on Adam on the virtue that she liked him first. Not only that, our friendship group never goes out with the ex of another friend.

I hung up the call and returned to the article I had to write. I didn't even bother with eating lunch, I just ate the protein bar I stuffed inside my bag the other day. Thankfully, Mister Annoying finally got the hint that I was in no mood to interact with anybody. Either he noticed the glares I gave when he as much as glance towards my way or it was when I sent him a massive middle finger when he tried to call my name.

No matter, at least the bumblebee was no longer buzzing around me.

The day ended with much less drama than yesterday. The whole Brady Bunch didn't bother with inviting me again to their little drink sessions and I peacefully got out of the building.

I decided to walk home, whether that was a good decision or not was debatable. I was sure that Sienna would call me if she arrived at our building before I could.

But I didn't have to worry about that in the end. Because standing right there in front of the glass doors of our apartment building was Adam, looking like another lost boy just looking around. The same way I saw him last night.

Was this the part where I turn back around and wait until he gets too cold and leaves?

Or was this the part where I actually face him?

I got nearer and when he finally caught sight of me, his wandering eyes stared into mine and gave me his undivided attention. Goosebumps erupted from body at the way he was obviously keeping his focus on me and away from the bustling surroundings known as New York City.

"What are you doing here?" I managed to ask when I stopped just a couple steps away from him, "I thought you were going to California."

If his eyes were filled with nervousness when I left him this morning, now there was nothing but absolute certainty in them.

"I said that I will regret it if I let you go," he stated, his voice not even wavering for a single second, "So I'm not going to."

He was so confident with his decision, he made sure that I knew that.

"And Sienna?" I dared to ask. Our history wasn't the smoothest it could be.

"Why do you think I'm here?" he pointed out, his feet closing the rest of the distance between us and we were now chest to chest, "I asked her and she gave me her blessing to chase you."

My heart felt like it wanted to beat right out of my chest. Our faces were so close that I could actually feel his breath. I prayed that this wasn't some dream, that this man was actually standing right in front of me.

I raised a brow, "Chase me?"

I had to stop myself from screaming, from letting myself drown in this undeniable happiness I was feeling. I was afraid that if I didn't, I would only get hurt.

"I like you, Gracie. As I said, I'm not going to let you go."

Oh fuck the uncertainties, I wanted him.

I grabbed the sides of his face and brought him down to me, capturing his lips with mine. The electricity was different from yesterday. If that one had this tension with it, this just had the feeling that everything was so right. That this was meant to be, that there were no need for overdramatics.

He wrapped his arms around my waist to bring me closer to him, as that was even possible. And I smiled into the kiss, because it was like he was keeping his word – he wasn't letting me go.

And Adam? I promise you too, that I will not let you go as well.

www.ingramcontent.com/pod-product-compliance
Lightning Source LLC
Chambersburg PA
CBHW071425190726
48292CB00001B/121